Suzy Spitfire and the Snake Eyes of Venus

SUZY SPITFIRE AND THE SNAKE EYES OF VENUS Copyright © 2019 by Joe Canzano. All rights reserved. Printed in the United States of America. No part of this book may be used or reproduced in any manner whatsoever without written permission except in the case of brief quotations embodied in critical articles and reviews. For contact information visit Happy Joe Control at www.happyjoe.net.

Happy Joe Control books may be purchased for educational, business, or promotional use. For contact information visit www.happyjoe.net.

Cover design by J Caleb Clark at jcalebdesign.com

Library of Congress Control Number: 2019917624
ISBN: 978-0-9906365-8-8

For Jill (again)

Suzy Spitfire and the Snake Eyes of Venus

Joe Canzano

Happy Joe Control
www.happyjoe.net

Chapter 1

Suzy Spitfire ran a slender finger through her coppery hair and tried to smile. With a little luck, she looked like all the other peaceful pedestrians strolling through downtown Atlanta. It was a hot summer night, and the hover-cars roared by, and it would be nice to blend in with the waves of smiley people on the busy sidewalks—but no, they all seemed so distant. They're all part of a big pretty picture, she thought, *and I'm part of something else.* Of course, none of them were wanted fugitives throughout the Nine Nations of Earth, not to mention the rest of the solar system. None of them were being followed by an ugly guy with bad intentions.

Suzy squinted at the carnival scene on the street but kept smiling. She sauntered past a few touristy bars, and a pounding dance club, and a writhing three-dimensional advertisement for cosmetic body sculpting. The light from every window was blasting her in the face like a firing squad. Her skin felt fried and her eyeballs ached.

I've got no regrets, she thought—*but it would be nice to have fewer people chasing me, or at least someone more attractive.*

She glanced at a reflection in a flashing window. Yeah, the ugly dude was still back there.

Then she saw the slick showroom of an air taxi service offering fast rides to Daytona Beach. For one second, her smile became real as she recalled her sister, walking on a different beach so long ago. She used to follow me, too, Suzy thought. But her intentions had been sweet.

Her mind filled with a picture of two little girls. Trish was four years younger, giggling as she followed Suzy around in the surf with a pail and shovel. She was looking for seashells and building a sand castle, and crying as it collapsed beneath a diabolical wave. Suzy was laughing as usual, telling Trish it was no big deal, they could build another one tomorrow so don't worry about it. But Trish was always worried. It was just her nature. Even in old photos, at the age of three, she had a worried look on her face—like she knew what was coming.

But I didn't know, Suzy thought. And now Trish was gone, and she was on the run—and she was going to shoot this fucker who was following her. *Because that's my nature.*

She dropped her hand down near the Series 7 pulse pistol strapped to her thigh, right under her jet-black skirt. Was she proud of her nature? Not always. And was this guy a cop or something worse? And did it matter? A cop would be part of a team, harder to evade. A cop would also have to follow certain procedures, at least out here on an open street. A bounty hunter, on the other hand, would be more inclined to do something desperate and stupid.

And this guy looked stupid, based on the conspicuous trench coat he was wearing in the sultry summer heat. But an opponent with a small brain isn't always a good thing. A dumb guy will often take a big risk, something crazy and unpredictable. Sometimes the dumb ones are the most dangerous.

She had a quick vision where she just whirled and shot him in the face. She paused and gave a grim sigh. I'm not that dumb anymore, she thought. *And sometimes it's a shame. Being smart is no fun at all.*

It was too bad this had to happen now; she had somewhere to go. It was a hopeful place, too—maybe. A place where someone like her might get a new start. But this guy was screwing everything up. She swore softly to herself and took a deep breath, cooling her rage a bit. The last thing she needed was to end up surrounded by bloody body parts—again.

She stopped in front of a Mexican restaurant called El Sol and glanced sideways down the expanse of Peachtree Street. The smell of spicy rice and burritos wafted into her nostrils, just like it had back in her hometown of Diego Tijuana, where *other* people sometimes tried to kill her. Meanwhile, the guy had also stopped. He was looking at his allcom, maybe just staring at a blank screen, or maybe actually communicating with somebody. All right, it was time to make her move.

Then her own allcom rang. Damn! Only two people on the planet had this number, so it was either Danielle calling to cancel their meeting—or it was Ricardo, probably telling her to not go in the first place.

She silenced the ringer. It had been Ricardo. Well, maybe he'd been right. Maybe she should've stayed back at the house. But there was nothing there for her, only him and his criminal friends—and she was tired of that scene. Was she tired of him, too? No, not really. He was a good guy, exactly her type, and she loved the way he sexed up her space ship. But sometimes a girl has to cut her losses, even if she's cutting away something wild and sexy and thrilling and—hey, where was she going with this? And was that potential assassin still back there?

She resumed walking down the sidewalk, quicker this time, but not too quick. Yeah, the guy was still following her. The pedestrians were thinning out as she kept heading south, past the grassy plot of Patriot Park and the three monolith-sized black buildings looming behind them. There were no storefronts or shops down here, just noisy hover-cars racing by, and shiny office buildings that looked like they were made from ice, and a few spurting fountains—but wait. Here was an outdoor lounge between two office towers, complete with benches and a few trees and a statue of a guy on a horse. And it looked deserted.

She made a quick turn into the shadowy lounge. Then she took ten more steps and spun around, pulling her pistol and aiming it back toward the street—and then a shot rang out.

What the hell? An energy blast exploded against the nearby building, sending a cloud of dust against her cheek. Then two more shots boomed out as Suzy dove to the ground and returned fire.

She cursed and pumped three rounds into the darkness. So her tail had a partner. Where was he? Luckily, he was a lousy shot, and he kept splattering energy bullets across the wall above Suzy's head. She saw the flashes from the gun—the sneaky bastard was behind the statue. She snarled and ramped up the power on her pistol, well beyond the stun setting. She leaped to her feet and started blasting.

The monument was a horse standing on its haunches, and the shots echoed like thunder, and with a splintering sound the statue came crashing down. She heard a scream as it hit the ground. She crouched down and darted forward.

There he was, sprawled on the pavement with his lower body crushed under the fallen stone horse. His gun was a few centimeters from his hand, and he was reaching for it—just as the other guy stormed into the lounge with his rifle up and ready.

Suzy gave a shout and kicked the fallen guy's gun into the darkness. She whirled and fired at the other guy, hitting him in the face. His head exploded. Right, damn, the gun had still been set for maximum power. *Well, that's what you get for rushing me.* A siren started to sound.

Suzy got down low and shoved her weapon against the trapped guy's ear.

"Hey," she said. "It looks like somebody's getting put out to pasture. But first, let me ask you a question: Who the hell are you?"

He was a white guy with pockmarked skin, shaggy brown hair, and small, frightened eyes. She noticed a tattoo on the back of his hand—the head of an angry-looking snake.

"Don't kill me!" he said. "I was firing stun shots! I'm a bounty hunter, and we wanted you alive."

"How did you find me?"

The whooping sirens were getting closer.

"Lenny had a tip from one of your amigos. He was supposed to get a piece."

"Is Lenny the guy I just killed?"

"Yeah."

Then he gasped, and he died.

Suzy shook her head and ran off into the night. She didn't have time for this stuff. She was busy searching for something better.

Chapter 2

Suzy stopped running and started walking. With a touch of her allcom, the fabric of her skirt flashed through a range of colors. She settled on burnt copper before adjusting her shirt, changing it to pale yellow. To change her hair, she used another screen to select a shade of dark blonde. She stared at her reflection in a window and watched as the bio-engineered transparent dye she'd recently installed caused her natural coppery locks to turn gold.

I look nice, but do I look innocent? She sighed, because she'd crossed that bridge long ago. Yeah, she'd blown it to smithereens. Still, she felt her actions had been justified. She liked to think she wasn't stuck, and maybe she still had a chance at—what? Something better.

Stay calm. She shuddered and then tried to smile. Maybe she'd find it tonight.

Luckily, she wasn't going far. Electric eyes were everywhere but it was useless to worry. She'd had her picture taken more times than a movie star.

A storm of thoughts whirled through her head. The bounty hunter had claimed one of her "amigos" had ratted her out. This was a direct reference to someone in Los Pocos, a vast criminal organization based in the United Mexican Union that she was connected to—or was she? Did having a boyfriend involved with organized crime automatically make her connected? And would one of those people really rat her out?

Hell, yes. No honor among thieves, and even less among drug dealers and murderers.

Her allcom started ringing, and once again it was Ricardo. She once again declined the call.

She turned down Decatur Street, hurrying past the stylish shops, with their rounded archways, wide windows, and pinkish stone facades. She kept scanning the shadows near the streetlamps as they poured out fountains of blazing yellow sparks. Finally, she reached her destination, a chic little restaurant called The Storm Shelter. The sign on the wooden door was discreetly sized and glowed in a serene shade of aqua. Suzy slipped inside.

The room was small and the crowd was sparse. The décor was blue, like the bottom of an ocean, and there was a polished mahogany bar, and burning gold orbs that radiated low, blurry light. So it was dark, and that was fine. Now, where was the back door—okay, there was a lighted exit sign across the room, and a woman at the far end of the bar was raising a glass her way.

Suzy kept her hand close to her pistol as she moved forward. The woman was beautiful, statuesque with dark brown skin and ropes of braided hair that fell to her shoulders. She wore a flowing dress, blood red with some black, and a striking smile.

"Hello, Suzy. I'm Danielle. It's good to finally meet you."

She stuck out her hand and Suzy shook it.

"Hi," Suzy said. "I guess it's been good so far."

So this was Danielle Banks, husband of Federal Strike Force Major Andre Banks, a law enforcement officer Suzy was acquainted with. Like her husband, Danielle radiated a sense of confidence and dignity.

"Won't you sit down?" Danielle said.

"Sure, but how about over there?" Suzy motioned to a table in the corner of the room, facing the main door and near the backdoor exit.

"Is someone after you?"

"Is this a trick question?"

"I mean tonight. I just saw a message on my allcom about a shootout a couple of blocks away."

"Oh, yeah? Do they have any suspects?"

"Nothing yet."

"Too bad," Suzy said in an even voice. The bartender poured her a Jack and Coke, and she and Danielle moved to the table in the back where Suzy sipped her bourbon and waited for Danielle to speak.

Danielle drank red wine from a pinot noir glass. "I've heard a lot about you, Suzy 'Spitfire' Castillo. I know your father was Mexican and you're fluent in Spanish, and your mother was an Irish girl from New York. I've also heard you handle yourself quite well."

"Sometimes. I sure don't like letting others do it."

Danielle smiled again. "So how's your mother? And your grandmother? I heard the operation was a success."

"It was," Suzy said. "My grandmother has to take it easy for a while, but hey, I told her she's been lying around for years. I can't go see them, of course…" Her voice trailed off, but then she said, "I'm glad I'm getting to meet you. I want to thank you for your help."

Danielle shrugged. "I was glad to do it. I try to help when I can. I don't know if you keep up with these things, Suzy, but I recently opened a clinic to help victims of sexual abuse."

"I know," Suzy said. "I saw it on the grid." Then she added, with her voice almost cracking, "I think what you're doing is great."

"Thanks," Danielle said. "It's tragic what happened to your sister, but unfortunately, it's all too common. And most of the time the guys get away with it."

At the mention of her sister, Suzy caught her breath. He didn't get away with it, she thought. *But I'll feel the pain forever.* Danielle must have seen the flicker of hurt and rage in Suzy's eyes, so she quickly went on. "We have three full-time people," she said. "We're mainly dealing with the traumatic effects. We also have an attorney working with us and I have plans to expand the place, if we can get the funding. We're just starting out, but I *know* we'll make a difference."

"I'm glad to hear it," Suzy said. And she *was* glad. Obviously, Danielle was passionate about what she was doing, and this was inspiring. It was hopeful.

Danielle put down her wine. The glass made a hard clicking sound on the tabletop.

"I know you're busy so I'll get to the point. Suzy, have you heard of a guy named Shogun Hunter?" Before Suzy could answer, Danielle spat, "He's a piece of shit! An attorney who raped and murdered over a dozen teenage girls. One managed to escape before he could kill her, and he was finally arrested. At his house, authorities found the belongings of people who were missing, but no bodies. The detectives guessed he disintegrated them in a disposal unit. He was involved in other crimes, too, including drug distribution, and he was convicted of that, plus the one rape. And then he escaped and ran to Venus." She scowled. "It's been over three years, and he's still there, and I'm tired of waiting. I want the bastard brought to justice—but I don't want him killed. I want him brought back alive to face the reprogrammer. Can you do it?"

For a second, Suzy's mind whirled, trying to think, to decipher her feelings. So this was what Danielle wanted, but was Suzy really the best person for the job? Hearing about the reprogrammer brought a chill to her bones. It could be her own fate someday—if she were ever caught.

"Why me?" Suzy said. "What about the cops?"

"Hunter is on Venus, in Baadal Shahar. Our law enforcement has no jurisdiction there, but the local cops have been alerted—and done nothing. Of course, the situation there is unstable. The government is having lots of problems."

"Danielle, *I* have lots of problems. One of the problems is that I'm not a bounty hunter."

"Maybe you should be." Danielle reached out and took her hand; she had warm hands. "I know you've been through a lot, Suzy, and you're young, and maybe you need to sort a few things out. But while you're thinking about it, this is something you can do that will help. I'd love to offer you something safer, or better, but… "

"I understand," Suzy blurted. "I've got a lot of baggage. Listen, I'm glad you contacted me. I appreciate it."

"I appreciate you considering it. Anyway, there's a big bounty on Hunter's head. You can collect it through me, as a consultant with fake info. Plus there's more I can pay you."

Suzy nodded, feeling better every second. "So other people are looking for him?"

"Probably. But other bounty hunters are inept. Haven't you met a few?"

"Yeah. Mostly dumb guys who watch a lot of bad martial arts movies. How do you know Hunter is in Baadal Shahar?"

"I know someone there, a good friend I've worked with for years. Her name is Anika Anand, and she's given me good reason to believe Hunter is there. I can give you her contact info and you can talk to her. Plus, I have access to police records, from my husband. Trust me, he's there. He probably changed his identity, too, with a complete package—we're talking facial reconstruction, eyeball alteration, fingerprint replacement, whatever."

Suzy gulped down her drink. "Does your husband know what you're up to?"

Danielle's eyes got wide. "Of course not! If he found out he'd be furious. And I don't want him to know because it would endanger his position and career. I'm doing this on my own because I have to. Do you understand?"

"Yeah, I do."

"Take a few days and think it over. I'll understand if you don't want to do it."

Suzy stood up. "I told your husband I'd try to do something better with myself." She looked across the room and spoke softly. "I'm not really sure I can do that, but I'm happy to help. I don't want any extra money from you. Just the bounty."

Danielle also rose to her feet. "You'll do fine, Suzy, I know you will. Thank you. I'd really like him brought back alive, too—that's important. I want the families of the victims to see his mind erased."

Suzy hesitated, once again feeling a chill. Finally, she said, "I know I've done some serious things, Danielle, but I'm not an assassin for hire."

"I never said you were," Danielle said in a rush. "I'm just telling you my feelings…about him."

"Okay. I'll do my best."

For an instant Danielle was quiet, and Suzy sensed she was giving careful thought to her next words. Finally, she said, "Suzy, you might find other things to do on Venus. A lot is happening there—talk to my friend Anika. She's one of the best people I know. I'll tell her you're coming."

Suzy's pulse quickened a bit. "That sounds good," she said, but didn't quite smile. "I'll be leaving in a few hours."

Chapter 3

The hover-car roared down a snaky highway, heading through a dark tunnel of trees. Suzy changed the color of her clothing to black and gray, a good combination for a coming storm. Then she shifted restlessly in her seat and checked the *energy clip* in her Series 7 pistol. It was just a habit. A fight was coming but it wouldn't involve any shooting. Unfortunately, this was often the worst kind of battle. Either way, she'd be back in her ship soon.

The *Correcaminos Rojo* was docked at a private landing field behind a house thirty minutes from the glow of the city. The ship was sleek, red, and shaped like a glorious bird in flight. It was registered with a variety of false names and numbers courtesy of her connections in Los Pocos—and someone from that criminal organization would be waiting for her. It was someone she wanted to see, and it was someone she didn't want to leave. But her mind was made up.

The sprawling house was owned by one of Ricardo's criminal friends. It had been built in the style of an old Southern mansion, like something from a few hundred years ago, with a wide wrap-around porch and a lamp that seemed to flicker with an ancient gas flame.

Ricardo was standing on the porch, looking sexy as always. He was lean and muscular with skin so smooth and bronze—except for his teeth, bright like the moonlight. He liked to write poetry in his spare time, and she recalled a few ridiculous verses. She laughed out loud.

He grinned as she stepped out of the car, watching as a summer breeze blew through her hair.

"Suzy, you changed your hair."

"Yeah, for now."

"It looks good. Why did you ignore my calls?"

"It was a bad time to talk, Ricardo—I was tired. Plus, a couple of guys were shooting at me."

She stepped onto the porch and he wrapped his arms around her.

"There's never a bad time to talk. I'm glad you're safe."

"I'm serious about the shooting."

His eyes opened wide, and she told him about the two bounty hunters, especially about the claim that one of his Los Pocos friends had tipped them off about her location.

"He was lying," Ricardo said, waving his hand in the air. "Why would you believe him?"

"I don't know. Maybe because your friends are a bunch of greedy crooks who'd do anything for some easy cash."

"Suzy, no one I know would sell you out."

"Ricardo, I'm going to Venus."

"What?" He pulled back from her a bit. "You can't go to Venus. We're supposed to go to Uhuru Wa Jiji tomorrow. I've got something lined up."

"I'm not going. I've got something else to do."

"What are you talking about?"

She stepped away from his embrace.

"I'm talking about Los Pocos," she said. "And the way you're not getting out. And I'm not getting in."

He looked around and lowered his voice. "What do you mean I'm 'not getting out'? You know I want out."

She rolled her eyes. "Your sister just married Pablo Juarez, and he's the boss of the organization, right? So she's not getting out and neither are you."

"Suzy, Maria is going to *change* Pablo. She's going to get him to go legit."

"Sure. And I'm going to start drinking milk and knitting sweaters."

He gave a fierce scowl now. She'd rarely seen him angry, but his normally pleasant personality was frayed.

"What did that woman say to you, Suzy? You don't owe her anything."

"I don't? I think I do—and so do you. But I'm not doing it because of that. I'm doing it because I want to. And I *don't* want to do the things you're doing."

"I'm not doing anything terrible."

"You're shipping illegal guns around the solar system."

"It's only temporary. Besides, what's the difference whether you're getting paid to run a few guns or do other things? Hey, by the way, we need to talk about the guns."

She started to shout—but then stopped.

She sighed. "Ricardo, I don't want to do the 'other things,' either. I'm going to Venus."

"You're really serious? Without me?"

She stared into his eyes. She would miss him. But she wasn't going to keep standing here and talking about it. She wasn't going to start crying, either. Maybe she'd do that later, when no one was around.

"Yeah," she said. "I need to go. And I'm going alone."

She walked away from him.

He followed her around the perimeter of the house. What was he saying? It was a blur. She stormed across the blacktop of the landing field, heading toward her ship. To his credit, he never once called it *his* ship—because he'd given it to her, after Pablo had given it to him.

Now he was yelling after her.

"Suzy, wait! Suzy, you can't go. Can't you at least turn around?"

Yeah, she could do that—but she didn't want to, because she was afraid that she'd change her mind. But at the bottom of the gangway she whirled to face him.

"Ricardo, I told you—"

He kissed her hard. She started to yank herself away—but then she didn't.

I'm such a fool, she thought. But she was too busy melting in his arms to think much more. For one brief second, every bad thing in the world disappeared.

He stopped kissing her but kept his lips close.

"I love you, Suzy."

She blinked a few times. "That's nice, Ricardo. But I'm still leaving."

He pulled her close again and whispered, "My mind will be blown if you leave me alone, like a minstrel who's lost his best song." Then he smiled. "I just wrote that. Can't you wait until morning? Please?"

She frowned. Waiting was a bad idea. In fact, it was almost as bad as his poetry. But then she heard herself say, "Maybe."

She followed him back into the house. She changed her hair back to coppery red and then went upstairs with him, to a bedroom with a king-size bed near a window with a view of the inky night sky, and the winking stars, and the prickly woods all around. She didn't wait until morning.

She waited a few hours. She waited until their bodies were done moving together. She waited until she was finished moaning and sweating and squeezing him close between her thighs. She waited until there was one long, last kiss.

She waited until he was asleep.

She scooped up her silver dragonfly earrings. Then she tiptoed out of the house and walked fast through the summer night. She looked up at the moon and for the first time that evening, she noticed it was full. Dawn was still a few hours away—but it would come. She walked up the ramp and into her ship. In a few minutes the engines roared to life, and in a ball of fire and light she was gone.

Chapter 4

Andre Banks stood on the balcony of his high-rise home in downtown Atlanta and rubbed his aching head. Then he put down his allcom and watched the reddish sun rise above the hazy city. The fiery view would be so much more beautiful if people weren't calling him already, but what else was new? Every title comes with a territory, and as a major in the Federal Strike Force of the Free Northern States, the territory was always a jungle.

At least he had Danielle to make him feel better. She always managed to do that. He heard her moving around in the kitchen, and he moved toward the smell of morning coffee.

She was up early, as always, making something with avocados. She loved smashed avocados spread on toast, but she put her knife down and embraced him. It felt good like it always did, like electricity crackling through his body.

"Good morning," she said. "You look so handsome today."

"I look like I always do."

"And I always like it," she said with a laugh.

He almost laughed, but didn't. He knew she liked his height, his shaved head, his smooth skin even darker than her own. And he was glad about it.

"What's wrong?" she said. "Are they calling you already?"

He sighed. "It's the whole Suzy Castillo thing. I won't bore you with the details."

She raised her eyebrows. "You're not boring me," she blurted. And he noticed her genuine interest. "What's going on?"

He poured himself a cup of coffee. "You know I could've put her away. And I let her go."

"Yeah, I know. I like to think I convinced you to do that because her only crime was killing the uncle who molested her sister."

"That wasn't her *only* crime. She also killed a federal agent."

"Who murdered her father."

"Right. But we've been through this. Unfortunately, now the top brass is upset. They think she escaped because of my incompetence."

"But they gave you a promotion."

"Yeah, because of all the other stuff. But due to politics and bullshit, they now want me to make Suzy's capture a top priority. And guess what? Apparently, she's here on Earth. Can you believe it? She killed a couple of bounty hunters last night, right here in downtown Atlanta. She was identified on a surveillance camera—right under my nose."

Danielle was quiet. "They couldn't track her after it happened?"

"No. She went into an area with minimal surveillance and disappeared. We're trying to find her, but right now it looks like she got away. A few ships without flight plans took off from the area and we're checking that out. That's not the point; I'm pretty sure we won't catch her. But they want me to assign a special task force to do that—can you believe it? They want me to track her down no matter where she is, and I just—I don't know." His voice trailed off.

Danielle was quiet once again, and he noticed her fidgeting with her knife.

"I know you think Suzy is some kind of hero," he said. "But she can't just go around shooting people—even bounty hunters. She's making things difficult for me."

She was looking at him now with those soft eyes. Finally, she said, "Andre, do you really want to get her? You don't, right?"

"Is that what you want me to say?"

"Yes."

He shrugged. "There are bigger things to worry about. But it's my job, so what can I do?"

She reached out and touched his hand. "Maybe don't try so hard."

"What?"

"They want you to assign a special task force. So assign an idiot."

He crinkled his forehead and stared at her. "Interesting idea. And I might have no choice, really. After all, we've only got so many people who aren't idiots. But assigning an idiot might make things worse."

"True, but didn't you tell me the other day that Commissioner Stone had a nephew looking to redeem himself after a major screw-up?"

"Yeah, I did, but he's a real moron—huh."

Danielle nodded, obviously pleased. "I'll bet the commissioner would like it if you gave his nephew a shot, even if he fails. Plus it might take him a while to totally fail, and by then maybe you'll be promoted again. Either way, you'll get in good with the commissioner."

Banks cocked his head and studied his wife. "When did you get so devious?"

"I'm not devious," she said with a smile. "I'm just helping you play the game."

He didn't smile. But he did feel better, at least for now.

Chapter 5

Suzy rubbed her bleary eyes as she sat in the glowing cockpit, watching through the broad windows as Earth disappeared like water down a drain. She was trying to concentrate as she set a course for Baadal Shahar, the largest city-state in the Cloud City Consolidation of Venus. She should've been smiling, with Earth and Venus so close together right now. But she didn't smile. She kept thinking about Ricardo, and all the burning hoops of fire they'd passed through together—and all the steamy nights, and now this cold, cold ending.

It's not over, she thought. *But here I am, all alone. Again.* Then she heard a noise and spun around fast in her chair.

Maybe not so alone. Was someone in the crew lounge?

The lounge was down a short passageway from the cockpit. The main entry to the ship was also at the end of this passageway, adjacent to the lounge—but she hadn't seen anybody in there when she'd come aboard. Then again, she'd been busy at the time destroying her love life.

Her allcom started ringing. It was Ricardo.

And she swore she heard a voice coming from the lounge. She killed the buzz of the device and yanked out her pistol.

Her mind started racing. Who could be in there? No one could've known she was going to take off; she hadn't been sure herself until two minutes before she'd done it. But someone could've known the ship was supposed to take off in the morning.

A few lights flashed on a nearby console. There were three ships closing fast. *Damn!*

Her allcom rang again. She once again silenced it.

She spun back toward the console and checked the readouts in front of her. She'd rather not get shot in the back of the head but sometimes a girl has to pick her poison, and the interceptors were the bigger pill to swallow right now. They were coming in at an angle. She checked her ship's deflector shields and started to take evasive action—and watched as they sailed overhead. Then the radio crackled.

"Hey, hey!" said a young guy's voice. "That's a fast ship you've got there. Any nice-looking girls on board? Want to give me a visual?"

Suzy breathed a sigh of relief; they were not interceptors. They sounded like a bunch of guys in scooter ships, just fooling around the same way she'd done it, back when she'd been a student at Force Four Vocational.

Suzy hit the radio button. "Sorry, guys, there's no visual available, and you'll just have to use your imagination. But imagine someone hot."

She stared sideways as she spoke, keeping an eye on that passageway. Still empty.

Meanwhile, a few more male voices chimed in on the radio. They whooped a couple of times and said, "Tienes novio?"

Someone over there spoke Spanish, asking if she had a boyfriend.

The allcom rang again. Ricardo again.

She declined the call. Then she said, "No tengo novio." They were cheering and hollering as she shut off the radio and headed down the passageway.

It wasn't the best time to be leaving the cockpit because real law enforcement could show up any second. But the course was plotted, her ship was speedy, and she had to know who else was on board.

She squatted down low and kept her gun up as she crept along, trying her best to be quiet. She reached the end of the passage, staying very still—listening.

No sound. Just the engines. And then her allcom rang *again.*

God dammit! Why didn't I turn the damn thing off?

It only buzzed—but to her, the sound exploded like an alarm bell.

She made a quick decision and leaped forward, her eyes searching the sparsely furnished lounge. No one behind the bar, no one near the medical station in the corner—no targets. She sighed and answered the call.

"*What?*" she whispered fiercely. "I'm kind of busy right now."

"There might be someone on your ship," Ricardo said. "Two people."

Damn! His voice was garbled, and she knew she'd soon be out of range for a conversation.

She dropped down low, between a cherry-red table and a cushy black sofa. She could see the entire lounge from here, including the opening to a dim passageway that lead to the ship's cabins.

"Who?"

"…helper… cook named Kiara…one of Lance's people… Listen, come back! I need to tell you something…"

The call descended into fuzz and static.

For a second, she thought about how nice it would be to have Ricardo here with her. He was good in a fight, and he was good afterwards, too. Then she shut off the phone, gripped her pistol, and started creeping toward the passage that led deeper into the ship.

As she moved, her mind reeled, trying to decipher Ricardo's static-filled message. Who the hell was Lance? Okay, wait—Lance Odee was a Los Pocos associate who owned that house she'd just left. But that was all she knew. She'd only been there a short time and hadn't really met anyone else.

She slipped into the passageway. No one was there now—just the three cabin doors, all closed. She tip-toed up to the first cabin and put her ear against the cool metal.

The sound of urgent voices filled her ears. She strained to make out the words, but she couldn't. Judging from the tone, it sounded like an argument. She pressed a button and the door flew open.

Two wide-eyed people were standing there, a guy and a girl. They seemed vaguely familiar from the house in Atlanta. The guy was maybe seventeen, but the girl looked a few years younger, and she was pretty, despite a face filled with desperation. She was lean like a rail with brownish skin and frazzled black hair tumbling down her back. She also had a light scar on her jawline, and wore only a pink

T-shirt and black panties. The guy was pasty white and wore no shirt. He was slim and muscular with a crisscross of scars across his chest and shoulders. He had chiseled facial features and short red hair that matched a ragged beard.

Suzy didn't like his eyes. They were ice blue, cruel, and jittery—and they glanced down at the bed in front of him where there was a Series 7 pulse pistol.

But Suzy was pointing her own gun. "Don't move," she said. "Go for it and I'll shoot you."

He smirked and put up his hands.

"We're not dangerous!" the girl blurted. "We're just looking for a ride."

"Really?" Suzy said. "Why didn't you ask me? It's usually easier than getting shot."

"We thought you might say no," the girl said in a shaky voice. "I'm Kiara… I mean that's me—my name! I was a cook for Mr. Odee. We're just looking to get away."

"And he remembered to bring a gun," Suzy said. "But you somehow forgot your pants."

"No!" Kiara said, stammering now. "It's not like that. We came in here last night, and we were asleep. We woke up when you took off, and my pants are right there." She pointed to a chair, where a pair of black cargo-style pants had been tossed, along with a beat-up black bag and a faded green army-style jacket. The bag was open and looked like it was stuffed with a few more shirts and undergarments.

Suzy made the guy step back a couple of meters. Then she snatched the gun from the bed. It was an illegal pistol, the kind powered by a *variable energy clip,* meaning it could fire both stun shots and the more powerful "fully-maxed bullets" reserved for military and law enforcement personal. The shots were actually blasts of pure energy, and there were no bullets in the old-style sense of the word. She carried the same kind of outlawed weapon.

An alarm sounded, splintering the air. *Damn!* It meant another ship was approaching. Maybe nothing, but maybe something, and she couldn't take a chance.

"She's telling the truth," the guy said, and he flashed a quick grin at the girl. "We're just looking for a little adventure. I carry the gun because I was part of the security team for Mr. Odee. Just ask him about Jack Ray. You can tell him I quit, too."

Suzy just nodded her head. "Do you know anyone in Atlanta, Jack? Any bounty hunters?"

She studied his eyes.

"What?" Kiara said. "Jack wouldn't do anything to hurt you, Suzy."

"You know my name?"

"Yes," Kiara said, stammering again. "I—I mean we—didn't mean any harm."

Suzy stayed frosty cold, still pointing the gun at Jack's chest. "Someone told a couple of guys I was going into Atlanta last night, and there weren't many people in that house who knew. But *you* probably knew."

He gave a big shrug. "I don't know what you're talking about. Did something happen?"

"Yeah, but not to me," Suzy snapped. "And you were in on it."

"No," he said, shaking his head. "You've got the wrong guy."

"Do I? You two are going into the hold."

Meanwhile, the alarm sounded again. Crap, she had to get back to the cockpit.

"I can't go into the hold," Kiara said. "I'm claustrophobic."

"Okay," Suzy said. "How about if I put you in the Grand Ballroom?"

"Really?"

"No, not really. Start moving."

Jack just shrugged again. Why did he seem so smug? Suzy gripped her pistol harder.

The only access to the hold from the interior of the ship was a brass-colored hatch built into the floor near the engine room. Suzy unsealed the circular hatch with an eye scanner on the wall. Kiara peered with huge eyes at the ladder heading down into the darkness. Then some lights below flickered on.

"Get moving," Suzy said. "You first, Jack."

She didn't want to shoot him, even with a stun shot, because then she'd have to drag his body somewhere and lock him up anyway. It was easier to stick him in the hold and maybe shoot him later, depending on any new info she got from Ricardo.

He gave her a wise-ass kind of stare. She stared right back and smiled—*because the one with the gun gets to smile the most.*

Then he descended down the ladder, moving fast.

"Go," Suzy said to Kiara.

"I really don't want to go down there," Kiara sputtered.

"And I really don't want to shoot you."

"I can't! Please don't make me!"

Kiara's chest started heaving, almost like she was hyperventilating.

Suzy hesitated. She had a sudden feeling, an instinctive vibe, that maybe Kiara was just a nice girl with a bad boyfriend. Nothing uncommon there. But unfortunately, nice girls sometimes help their loser boyfriends, so Kiara still had to go into the hold.

"Kiara, it's a big hold," Suzy said. "It's bigger than the cabin you were in, right? So you'll be fine." Then she softened her voice and said, "I'll let you out pretty soon, okay?"

Kiara stared with frozen eyes, but Suzy was done talking. She pointed the gun at Kiara's head.

Kiara winced and turned her face way from the weapon. "Okay, I'll go!" she shrieked. "Don't hurt me. Please!"

Kiara took a deep breath and started muttering to herself. It sounded like she was giving herself a pep talk. Then she fumbled a bit and headed down the ladder. Suzy leaned over the hole and watched her descend. But what was this? Suzy's face scrunched up into a question mark—why was the hold filled with crates? It had been empty when she'd taken that hover-car into Atlanta.

Jack appeared at the bottom of the ladder.

Her brain barely had time to notice the rifle. Then she heard a shot and everything went black.

Chapter 6

Guns. Ricardo must have filled the hold with guns.

Damn that sort-of-ex-boyfriend! He'd been running guns, and he'd apparently been all set to try and talk her into running some, too. He'd also taken the liberty of filling the cargo hold of her ship with illegal firearms—thanks. Right on the day when she needed to stick a dangerous dirt-bag in there.

Had Jack known those guns were in the hold? Hell, he was probably the guy who'd loaded them. No wonder he'd looked so smug.

So, how long have I been out?

It was hard to guess, but the more she revived the worse she felt. She'd been shot with stun blasts before—and it had felt terrible before, and this was no better.

Wait, that wasn't true. Her head was throbbing, her body ached, and she felt dizzy and nauseous, but she didn't feel as bad as last time. She vaguely recalled Ricardo telling her to wear body armor more often. She also recalled he never did it himself. It was a dumb macho thing on his part, while in her case it was just damned uncomfortable.

The blurry room came into focus, with scattered socks and shirts, a pair of grimy boots, and an opened box of cheese crackers. This was the same disheveled cabin where she'd found Kiara and Jack. But now the view through the porthole showed only a starry sky, and Suzy was on the rumpled bed, flat on her stomach, with her feet tied together and her hands bound behind her back—and additional straps across her shoulder blades and lower thighs that kept her secured to the mattress. The bonds were so tight they were cutting into her skin. Her fingers were tingling from lack of blood.

Her stomach was aching because that's where she'd been hit. In a way that had been lucky. Getting shot in the face would've involved a lot more pain and trouble. Also, she could've fallen down into the hold—over three meters down, a long way to fall in an unconscious state, and an easy way to get a broken neck.

So things could've been much worse. Then again, the lack of mobility was inconvenient. It was going to be hard to use the restroom from this position. It was going to be hard to shoot Jack dead.

The door opened and Jack strutted in. Kiara followed behind him, looking jittery.

Jack had a shirt on now, a tight pullover with short sleeves that showed his muscular arms. Kiara had put on her black cargo pants and the frayed, olive-colored army jacket over a pink T-shirt. Jack was grinning and holding a bottle of Jose Cuervo.

"Look who's awake," he said.

"Are you all right?" Kiara blurted.

"What did you shoot me with?" Suzy said, needing a truckload of restraint to keep from cursing at the motherfucker.

Jack grinned again and took a big slug from the bottle of tequila, splashing some onto his shirt and scraggy red beard. "An M-52 combat rifle," he said. "You've got 5,000 on board, plus lots of other interesting stuff—and all I can say is I'm glad Ricardo wasn't smuggling dried fruit."

"Ricardo's more of a steak and potatoes guy," Suzy said. "Where are we going? There was another ship out there."

"Don't worry about it," Jack said. "Just a freighter, and the ship is fine."

"We're going to Venus," Kiara said. "And we have no idea how to change course."

Jack flashed Kiara a vicious look. "Why are you saying that? I could figure it out if I had to."

"Jack, you could *not* figure it out." She nervously twisted strands of her long hair. "We need to untie her. You have no fucking idea how to fly a spaceship."

Jack's left hand shot out, scrunching up the front of Kiara's T-shirt and shoving her toward the wall. She hit it with a thud that made her grimace while Suzy watched with disgust.

About what I expected, Suzy thought.

Jack sneered. "I'm tired of you telling me what to do, Kiara. You hear me?"

"All right, all right," she squealed, putting up her hands. "I hear you. I just don't think—"

"That's right! You don't think," he said, letting her go after one final push. Then he put the bottle of Jose Cuervo on top of a dresser and pulled out a Series 7 pulse pistol. He pressed the barrel against the back of Suzy's skull. "I should put one in her head right now and save myself the trouble later."

"No! Don't hurt her," Kiara said. Then she quickly added, "Ricardo won't like that."

"Fuck Ricardo!" he bellowed. "Those greasy Mexicans haven't done shit for me, and I don't need them now, anyway."

Now Kiara's eyes lit up. "Kill his girlfriend and we're both dead," she snapped. *"And I'm a Mexican!"*

She stormed out of the room, her long hair flying, and her head held high.

Jack watched her go and gave a snotty laugh. "Yeah, I get that," he said. "I get a lot of other stuff from you too, Kiara, whenever I want it—wait a second! Come back here."

He leaped up, ran to the open door, and shouted, "Kiara, come back! I didn't mean it. You hear me? I was just kidding! Damn."

He swore again and turned his attention back to Suzy. "She'll calm down," he said. "Sometimes she's a couple cards short of a full deck, but she's real sweet. In ten minutes she'll be naked and bent over a chair, and her skinny little ass will be loving every minute."

"I'm sure," Suzy said. "And if she's really good you'll give her that second centimeter, right?"

Jack stopped laughing. Some guys have no sense of humor, she thought. *Especially when you hit the tiny nail on the tiny head.*

He put the gun away and stood next to her helpless body. He ran his hand over her lower back and then down a bit farther.

"Speaking of ass, you got a nice one, Suzy, you know that? In fact, you got a nice everything—except for your mouth. I'm thinking I might show you what I got before this is all over. But not yet. Kiara wouldn't like it, and I want to keep her happy."

Suzy bit her tongue hard and cleared the boiling mushroom cloud out of her brain. *What does this guy want to hear?*

She tried to sound smooth. "Jack, I think you got yourself into a situation, and you're not sure how to get out, right? So how about this—you let me go and I'll forget about everything. Hey, I put a gun on you, and you put one on me, and it's all fair. Besides, we're on the same side, right?"

Jack picked up the bottle of Cuervo and took another sloppy gulp.

He gave a snort. "You think I'm in a tight spot because of Los Pocos, don't you? Well, I'm not afraid of them, and I'm not afraid of Ricardo, either. You're still alive because I got *other* friends who want you alive, at least for now. See, you're a hostage Suzy. So get used to it."

"What other friends?" Suzy said.

"You'll know pretty soon," he barked. "But I'll tell you this, you killed two of my friends. That's right, I was in on that thing in Atlanta. I figured they'd take you alive and I'd get a piece of the reward. I figured Ricardo would feel bad for about ten minutes and then take off with the ship full of guns just like he planned, and I'd hijack it and make him take me to Venus. But then look what happened—you ditched his dumb ass and set a course for Venus anyway. Good for me and bad for the tough girl tied to the bed."

He reached out and gave her an upward smack on the butt, right above her lower thighs. "You jiggle nice," he said.

He laughed and walked out.

Chapter 7

Maj. Banks frowned as he sat in his office high above downtown Atlanta. While hover-ships drifted through the sky outside, he eyed the burly man in front of him. Then he turned his attention to the screen on his desktop.

Banks rubbed his chin and continued to scan the dismal information. No doubt about it, Burt Stone was not the best guy for the job. His record was a monument to overenthusiasm and stupidity. But he was also Commissioner Edward Stone's nephew, and when Banks had suggested the nephew take the assignment, Uncle Eddie had loved the idea. Danielle had loved the idea, too.

Ideally, it would be best for someone lazy to chase after Suzy, rather than a fanatical dimwit—but unfortunately, the laziest people were all busy working on more important cases. Pulling them off those assignments would mean all the non-work they'd accomplished would be re-evaluated by someone new, and that might cause trouble. So Burt Stone would have to do.

"At ease," Banks said. "Do you understand the mission, Lieutenant?"

Lt. Stone's eyes lit up. He was a white guy with a square head, blue eyes, and closely cropped hair, like a peach.

"Yes sir," he said. "I'm going to form a task force to capture Suzy 'Spitfire' Castillo. And I'm going to *take her out.*"

Banks narrowed his eyes. Not what he wanted to hear.

"Lieutenant, you've had a problem in the past 'taking people out.' We need you to use good judgment and not generate any bad publicity, is that understood?"

Stone stiffened. "I understand, sir," he blurted. "No bad publicity."

"The last thing we want is something like the situation you had in New York with the mayor's wife."

Stone winced while Banks remembered.

Stone had tracked a dangerous fugitive to New York City. The local cops surrounded the guy in a fancy spa downtown; apparently, the villain had a girlfriend and he was buying her a gift card. Then Stone showed up, cowboy style, and by the time the smoke cleared the place was a pile of cinders, with burned out foot baths and massacred massage tables scattered across the streets of Manhattan. And the mayor's wife was in the hospital.

"I understand, sir," Stone said. "But in my defense, I didn't know it was her day for a body scrub."

Inside his head, Banks groaned. In every way, this guy was a terrible match for Suzy. It was like throwing fire at a pile of dynamite. But it was too late to change the plan, so he flashed a grim smile and tried to reassure himself. After all, Stone would have to find Suzy first, and he'd need to get close to her to do any real damage, and those things probably wouldn't happen because she was pretty smart and he was too damned stupid.

Then Stone started stammering. "I know what people think about me, sir," he said. "But it's not true. I went through the satellite reports of *every* ship that took off from the Atlanta area during that time span—over a hundred. There was a no-plan ship that went up from west of the city, from a private field owned by a guy with Los Pocos connections. I went over there this morning and a housekeeper told me she was definitely there. And then I interviewed people from the flight logs. The *Correcaminos Rojo* was spotted by some guys in scooters right after that no-plan took off. They even talked to her! And then later the ship was spotted by a freighter. I compared the two points and her course was dead set for Venus—right for Baadal Shahar."

Banks raised his eyebrows a bit. Okay, maybe this guy was more reckless than stupid.

"I can do this job, sir," Stone said. "I'm not a bad cop." Then he added, "I want to do a good job," and his voice trailed off.

Banks was quiet. For a second, his mind filled with an image of his wife, and she was smiling. He knew she was busy right now, doing something she loved.

Well, so was he. He took a deep breath and rose from the chair.

"Good work, Stone. Suzy Castillo isn't the worst person in the solar system, but she *is* dangerous. Then he paused and added, "She's had her chances, but if she's working with Los Pocos and shooting people in downtown Atlanta, her chances have run out. Baadal Shahar is a touchy place right now with a lot of instability. So be careful. Now go get her."

"Yes, sir," Stone said. His face was bright.

Chapter 8

Suzy was in that delicate dream state, not quite awake yet barely asleep. Was she dreaming or just remembering? It was a little of both.

She was at a wedding, the recent union of Ricardo's sister Maria and Los Pocos crime lord Pablo Juarez. It was on a tree-covered hill, piney green and summery gold, just outside the city of San Miguel de Allende in Mexico, and she was speaking with Maria right before the ceremony.

Maria smiled and said, "I'm sure I want to do this, but I'm not sure I won't regret it."

Maria always reminded Suzy of a fierce little bird. She was small and fast, with her black hair flying and her dark eyes darting around. Suzy didn't have many real friends, but she had a bond with Maria. They'd both made extreme choices in life, and they'd done what they had to do. And now Maria was making another choice, and Suzy was embracing her.

Maria looked beautiful, as all women do on their wedding day. She wore white, very traditional, and went to stand beside Pablo's beaming fireplug-of-a-mom who was happy her son was marrying a smart girl and not "one of the stupid ones always looking for a party." Suzy looked at Ricardo and wondered about his thoughts.

While growing up, Suzy rarely talked about being married. The idea scared her, and more than anything she hated to admit she was scared. But now on the day of Maria's wedding, she saw two people taking a chance. As they exchanged their vows on a flower-festooned dais with an orange sun hanging behind them in an endless purple sky, Suzy realized they were no braver than her.

Suddenly her eyes snapped open and she was back in reality.

Damn! She was also gulping deep breaths of air. The room was spinning and her stomach was heaving. She was overwhelmed by nausea, and it made her feel powerless. Being strapped to a bed while her stomach churned only made things worse. The last thing she wanted was to end up with her face floating in a pool of puke. She sucked in more air and exhaled as hard as she could.

She was barely holding on. This did not look promising. Then the door opened, and there was Kiara.

Kiara stared at Suzy. "You're so pale," she said.

Suzy gasped a few times. "Yeah, I haven't been getting much sun lately. Also, I feel like I'm going to be sick. Maybe if I could get to my knees I'd be okay."

In her hand, Kiara held a pair of scissors, and then she was cutting the straps that kept Suzy tied to the bed. She didn't cut the other bonds, the ones wrapped around her wrists and ankles, but she helped Suzy get to a kneeling position. Suzy put her head down on the rumpled sheets and kept breathing. A cold sweat drenched her skin, and the nausea seemed to wash away.

Kiara reached out and rubbed Suzy's back. "Are you okay?" she said.

Suzy fell back on her side. "Yeah, thanks. So why are you in here with a pair of scissors? I'm guessing you don't want to style my hair."

"No," Kiara said while shutting the door and lowering her voice. "I don't want anyone getting hurt. I'm having some trouble with Jack, and I came to cut you loose."

Suzy squinted up at her. Kiara looked as frazzled as her faded green jacket. Her eyes were bloodshot, and her long black hair was in tangles, and her face was streaked like she'd been crying. Obviously, Kiara was having a rough time, and Suzy felt her heart going out to her a bit. But then she decided not to talk. *Stay quiet until she cuts the straps.*

Kiara said, "First, you have to promise you won't hurt Jack."

Jack—right. That stupid bastard who was destined to be a girl-friend/wife-beating piece of shit.

Suzy didn't answer too fast. She needed to make her lie sound as convincing as possible.

"Okay, I promise."

"Are you telling the truth? I've heard stories about you, Suzy, and—"

"Stories? What stories?"

Kiara hesitated. "They were good stories," she said. "But I don't want you to hurt Jack."

Good stories? "I won't hurt him if he doesn't try to hurt me. How's that?"

Kiara eyed her for a long second. Finally, she said, "Okay, that's fair. But also, don't tell Ricardo he tied you up. That's important."

"I won't tell him. It was all just a misunderstanding, okay? It was no big deal."

Kiara studied her a few more seconds. "All right," she said.

The bonds were made from a type of plastic used to tie cargo. They weren't too hard to cut, but it took at least a few seconds for the scissors to get through them. She freed Suzy's feet and then started toward Suzy's hands, still bound behind her back. And then Jack walked into the room.

Suzy swore to herself. *So close!*

Jack stared at Kiara and narrowed his eyes. "What the hell are you doing?" he said.

Kiara froze. Then she spoke in a shaky voice. "We need to let her go, Jack."

He stormed into the room and snatched at the scissors. "Gimme those!"

But Kiara whipped the scissors behind her back. "No!" she said. "We can't keep her tied up like this. It's wrong, and it's stupid."

Jack sneered and backhanded her hard across the cheek.

"Gimme the fucking scissors!"

She gasped but stayed on her feet. Jack grabbed her around the throat and shoved her against a dresser. It rattled from the impact.

"Jack, stop!" she squealed.

But he seemed drunk and furious, and he punched her in the face.

Kiara yelped as blood spurted from her nose, and Suzy suddenly felt more angry than sick. She leaped from the bed and lunged forward, kicking him hard in the ribs.

"Fuck!" he shouted and whirled to face her—right as she kicked him in the balls. It was a nice solid shot with the top of her toe. "Fuck!" he said again and doubled over.

Perfect. Now his head was at the optimum height for a knee strike—*bam!* But unfortunately, she didn't have a free hand to really drive his face into the bone, so it did minimal damage.

Kiara screamed, "Stop! Stop!"

Jack was on the floor, rolling toward the door. Suzy went after him, but Kiara grabbed her around the waist.

"Suzy, stop! You promised!"

Jack was pulling out a gun. Suzy gave him a swift kick in the face, snapping his head back.

"Uh!" he said. Then Suzy stomped on his hand with her heel—twice—and the gun was loose.

He screamed again and tried to snatch it, but she used a quick move with her foot to sweep it underneath the bed. Jack cursed and grabbed at his injured hand. She wanted to kick him again—but now Kiara was pulling her backwards. Suzy tried to shake her off, but she wasn't at full strength and Kiara was surprisingly strong.

Damn this girl!

And then Jack was back on his feet. He swung at Suzy, but she ducked under his fist and kicked him again yet only hit him on the thigh. Then he grabbed her around the neck and slammed his forearm into her face. He punched her in the stomach and grimaced in pain like his hand was broken.

"You bitch," he said with a snarl. "I'm gonna kill you."

Now Kiara reached out and shoved at Jack. "Stop it, Jack! Leave her alone."

Kiara poked him in the eye. Maybe it was unintentional, but a good poke is a good poke. Jack swore and squinted through his other eye just as Suzy twisted out of his grip. Jack and Kiara were tangled up now, pawing and scratching at each other. Jack threw her to the ground but she pulled him down on top of her. Suzy watched them grapple for an instant and then bolted from the cabin.

She ran a few steps down the passage, past the second cabin and into the third one. She ducked inside quick and used the eye scanner to seal the door shut. She paused to catch her breath and think.

Jack wasn't going to kill Kiara. He was going to hit her a few more times, but she'd be okay. Suzy felt a pang of guilt about running, because it wasn't her nature to run—but dammit, if she'd stayed and continued to fight, Kiara was just as likely to ruin things as she was to help.

Besides, she was tired of fighting with her hands tied behind her back. She scanned the room fast. This was her cabin, and it looked like someone had rummaged through it. Hopefully, no one had moved the thing she needed.

She ran to a desk and opened a drawer. Yes! The knife was still there. It wasn't easy to hold the knife behind her back and cut the straps, but it was doable. She fumbled with the blade, sawing against the bonds. She also kept listening, waiting for Jack to start pounding on the door. It didn't take long.

"Are you in there, Suzy? Open this door or I'll blow it down."

So he'd gotten the gun from under the bed. But Suzy knew the doors on this ship were highly reinforced. Were they blast proof? No. But it would take a lot of blasting.

Predictably, Jack fired a shot. Then he screamed, "Damn!" as the energy shot failed to open the door and no doubt ricocheted off the metal and hit the bulkhead behind him and probably almost killed him. Then Kiara shrieked again.

"Jack, no!" Kiara said. "Forget about it! Just leave her alone. *You're going to get yourself killed!*"

Meanwhile, Suzy kept cutting, wiggling the blade, back and forth, up and down.

Jack pounded on the door again. "You're trapped, Suzy," he said. "And I've got a gun. Open the door—*will you get off me?*"

Kiara screeched and something hit the door hard—probably Kiara. Then it sounded like he threw her to the deck and said, "Am I gonna have to shoot you, too?"

Meanwhile, Suzy was still cutting, cutting—that's it, Kiara, she thought. *Keep the asshole busy for another few seconds—yeah!* She was free. And Jack was in more trouble than he knew.

She turned toward the desk and her fingers flew over a small console. The *Correcaminos Rojo* had been custom-built for a crime lord and it was loaded with little perks—things Jack couldn't know about, like the perfectly disguised wall safe near the bed that was now sliding open.

In a flash, she was reaching inside and grabbing a Series 7 pulse pistol. Outside, Jack was still talking.

"Suzy, I don't want to start shooting again, so why don't you just—"

The door flew open, and she shot him in the chest.

She loved the look on his face. It was the astonished look of an imbecile getting what he deserved. Then again, it was less than he deserved because the gun was set to fire a stun shot. But it didn't completely knock him out. Stun shots were unpredictable that way.

He dropped his gun and hit the wall hard before falling to the floor—and then he had some kind of seizure. Kiara was screaming as his body started jerking and writhing around.

Suzy kicked his weapon down the passageway. She knelt beside him and pointed her gun at his twitching face. The dirtbag wasn't going anywhere. Finally, his body stopped convulsing, and he stared at her in a state of wide-eyed paralysis.

Suzy smiled and leaned close to his ear. "You jiggle nice," she said.

His eyes closed and he went to sleep.

Chapter 9

Ricardo came charging onto the stone patio at Pablo's sprawling ranch high in the hills just outside Migeul de Allende. He was in a sweat, even though the day was mild and a gentle breeze was blowing through the bushy purple flowers of the jacaranda trees planted all around. He took a few deep breaths, trying to hide any scent of desperation—but then again maybe that was a bad plan. Maybe a look of desperation would generate some sympathy. Yeah, he needed sympathy because he'd just lost five thousand of Pablo's guns.

Also, Suzy had been kidnapped! Maybe Pablo would have some sympathy for that. After all, it was definitely the bigger thing on Ricardo's mind. As soon as Ricardo had gotten the message, he'd left Atlanta and taken a quick shuttle to Mexico.

If those things didn't get him much of a break, Pablo had just married his sister, and Ricardo breathed a sigh of relief at the sight of her. Pablo didn't take orders from anyone, but he listened to Maria. Everyone did. And here the newlyweds sat, together like two young love birds at a table topped by a wide, cherry-colored umbrella. On the corner of the patio was a wiry man with a wide-brimmed hat on his head and a gun across his back.

As Ricardo approached, Pablo put down his glass of beer and laughed. "So here comes my brother-in-law," he said. "Coming to plead your case, Ricardo?"

Pablo and Maria both rose to embrace him before they all sat down. Maria gave him an encouraging glance and he felt a few more jitters drain away.

Maybe it was best to start with the Suzy situation. "Pablo, they hi-jacked the ship and took Suzy hostage."

Pablo nodded his head, seemingly unconcerned. "I know."

"You do? Okay, well, they also grabbed the guns that were supposed to go to Uhuru Wa Jiji."

"I know that, too."

Ricardo glanced at Maria, who just shook her head. Then she activated a screen sitting on the tabletop and three messages popped up.

First, there was the video message Ricardo had sent to Suzy, the one with his heartfelt apology about putting the guns on her ship— and then he was begging her to forgive him and *please, please don't go to Venus.*

Second, there was a text-only message from Jack Ray that he'd already seen: *We got Suzy and your guns. If you want to see her alive again, stay away from this ship and wait to hear from us.*

Last of all was a visual message from Suzy. He caught his breath; this was a message he hadn't seen, and there was poor Suzy, no doubt being held at gunpoint. His pulse started pounding—but wait, she was not being held! A sense of relief washed over him. *She's alive. She got free!* But then he was in a sweat once again. *She's probably mad at me—damn.*

At least she was smiling, but Ricardo knew that simmering smile. She said, "Hi, Ricardo. So, do you know anyone who wants a ship full of guns? It looks like maybe 5,000 combat rifles, a few hundred pulse pistols, six or seven crates of grenades, and lots of ammo. Maybe I'll dump them off at the first pawnshop I find. Anyway, I'm not being held hostage anymore. I've got the guy here, and I'm not sure what to do with him—but I'm not much of an interrogator. It brings back bad memories, you know? Anyway, if I were you, I'd find out who Jack Ray is working with while you're busy *never talking to me again!*"

She gave another quick smile, all filled with sweetness and rage, and then she was gone.

Ricardo was speechless while his mind whirled. Why had he put those guns on her ship? How would he feel if she'd been hurt? And was any girl sexier than Suzy when she was angry?

"That's it?" he said. "That's all?"

Maria gave a soft laugh. "She transmitted those messages and asked us to give them to you. And it sounds like 'that's all' to me."

"No," Ricardo said. "She's a little annoyed right now, but I'm still the love of her life. It's not my fault that guy snuck onto her ship. If she'd left with me in the morning none of this would've happened. I'll see her again! You'll see."

"You'll see her sooner than you think," Pablo said. "I want you to go to Venus."

"What?" He felt his heart leap. "Yeah, great idea! I'll go and find her." Then he quickly added, "I can get the guns back, too… Sure, I can do that."

"It's more complicated than that. Maria has a plan."

Ricardo paused. As far as he knew, Maria's plan was to get Pablo to retire from a life of crime and live happily with her and their future children. At least, that's what she'd said. But now she was leaning forward and talking about a different plan.

"Taking those guns to Uhuru Wa Jiji was never a great idea," she said. "What's there? A couple of thugs fighting over another pile of shit. But Venus is a much better situation. Baadal Shahar has a new product called *veluva*; it's super addictive, people love it, and it's almost impossible to overdose from it. Right now the government is heavily involved in the distribution—but luckily, Venus is on the verge of a political revolution. If we're smart and play our cards right, we could take it all."

Ricardo smiled. He was thinking about Suzy. *What a woman!* Then he said, "Count me in. So, do we have any friends in Baadal Shahar?"

Pablo grinned. "We'll have you, once you get there. We'll also have Suzy, when you recruit her. And yeah, we have a few people there. There's also a local guy named Marcos who wants to work with us, and he might just become the next president—so you'll need to arrange a meeting. I'm sure you'll get it done. Keep in mind, we'll also have a small arsenal if we can get Suzy to convince this punk to get the guns through security."

"What?"

Maria said, "I did some checking. Jack Ray is part of a group called the Snake Eyes. They're more than a business organization—they're a cult, and they're based on Venus. They're fanatical and secretive, and they're fighting the government for control of the veluva. They also have contacts in the city security department, good ones. Jack might know who they are... Suzy just needs to get the guns through. Then we send an army to Venus and support the revolution."

Ricardo forced himself to smile. "I don't think Suzy is going to do that."

"What do you mean?" Pablo said. "Doesn't she want to help the 'love of her life'? You can reason with her."

"Sure, I can do that. I mean I can try. But how will I convince her to get the guns into the city? She's not here, so I'd have to send her a message, and I don't know if I can convince her with just a message."

"So you're powerless without your physical charms?" Pablo said. "Is she too much for you?"

"No!" Ricardo said. "I can handle her." Then he paused and added, "But you know how she is."

Pablo laughed. "Yeah, I do, and sometimes I don't like it." He glanced at Maria, who gave him a dirty look. Then he laughed again and said, "But don't worry about it, lover boy. We have a plan to get her help. Maria will send her a message, too."

"What?" Ricardo said. "You think she'll listen to you and not to me? What are you going to do?"

Maria sighed and tossed back her hair. "I'll be honest with her, Ricardo. It's usually the best way." Then she said, "Pablo has a few other details to go over with you, but come inside when you're done. We're having chilaquiles."

She gave Pablo another sharp look but said nothing else. Ricardo watched as she got up and sashayed into the house. So now he was alone with Pablo, and Pablo was grinning.

"Ricardo, you're lucky I like you. And you're lucky you have such a smart sister."

"Right," Ricardo blurted. "She's the smartest person I know."

For an instant, Pablo's grin faded. But then he flashed a thin smile. "She's smart," he said. "That's why I married her. Anyway, you're going to take a few people with you to Baadal Shahar, to help out. There's a woman there with lots of influence, especially with the people who are against the government. Maybe you can meet with her and give her a dose of your famous charm. And while you're doing that, I want you to find somebody. He's a piece of shit distributor who ripped us off and then got arrested and broke jail. I know he's there. He probably changed his identity, too—but see if you can find him and take care of it."

Ricardo gave a blank look. "Me?"

Pablo waved his hand. "I know you're not an enforcer, but you're going to be right there."

"Hey, I've done stuff."

"Like what?"

Ricardo shrugged. "Stuff I had to do."

"This is something *someone* has to do." Pablo put his hand on Ricardo's shoulder. "I know you've helped Maria a lot over the years, but she's right, you don't like to hurt people—don't give me that look, those are her words, not mine, and it's okay. So I don't care who does it, but it needs to happen." Then he gave another thin smile. "If you don't want to do it, give it to Suzy. I'm sure she'll take care of it."

"I can do it! Who is he?"

Pablo laughed. He reached into his pocket and handed Ricardo a scrap of paper. On the scrap was the name "Shogun Hunter."

Chapter 10

"You killed him!" Kiara wailed. Jack was flat on his back, knocked out cold. Kiara came rushing over and knelt by his side. She was sobbing hard.

Suzy stood up and Kiara lunged at her.

"You said you wouldn't hurt him!" she screamed. Kiara was shouting and flailing her arms, throwing flurries of punches. She had wiry strength.

"Cut it out!" Suzy said. She batted away Kiara's hands, and they grappled a bit, and then Suzy finally managed to grab Kiara's wrists and pin her against the bulkhead—and then Kiara collapsed into her arms, and Suzy was embracing her and holding her close.

"Don't worry about it," Suzy said. "It'll be fine." She stroked Kiara's hair.

Kiara was talking fast now, a stream of words and sobs. "I made so many mistakes, I did everything wrong… But Jack helped me a lot—he did, and I only got on the ship because I wanted to meet you."

Suzy blinked. "What?"

"It's true," Kiara squealed, still sobbing. "I heard stories about you while I was at the house, and I wanted to meet you, that's all."

Suzy was speechless. Finally, she said, "I'm sorry things didn't turn out better."

"It's not your fault! You've been great. I wish I could be more like you."

"No—you don't," Suzy said. "You're fine the way you are. You've got your whole life ahead of you." Then she paused for a second and studied the girl's teary face. "Hey, how old are you?"

Kiara hesitated. "Fourteen," she said.

It could be true, Suzy thought. But she looked younger.

Meanwhile, she was still talking and crying. "I left Miami, my mom married this guy, an asshole, a pervert, so I left, I just left, and everything got so fucked up. I met a guy in Atlanta, and he said he'd help me, but that's not what he did—and it was horrible—and Jack saved me. He did—he *really did.* He got me out of there, and he got me the job at Odee's place, and he was great, except when he was drunk, and I didn't know he was going to do all that stuff. We were arguing, and you came into the room, and I didn't know he loaded any guns onto your ship. When he pulled out that gun I just...I didn't know what to do. Do you believe me? You believe me, right?"

"Yeah, I do," Suzy said. "Now listen—"

"What?"

"I need some help here. Can you help me?"

Kiara stopped crying. Suddenly, her eyes were brighter. "Me? What can I do?" She sniffled a bit and wiped away her tears. Then she said, "Sure. Can we help Jack?"

"Yeah," Suzy drawled as she studied Kiara's bruises. "But you first."

"Suzy, I'm fine. This is nothing."

"It'll only take a minute. Come on."

Suzy pulled Kiara to the auto-doc located in an alcove of the crew lounge. The doc was an examination table surrounded by silvery sensors and snaky mechanical tentacles that held a spiky assortment of tools. Kiara protested, and mentioned Jack again, but Suzy made her sit on the table as the tentacles swooped in and surrounded her. There was a moment of blinking and whirring, and then the machine's pleasant female voice said her eye would be fine, and her swollen, bloody nose was not broken. Suzy smiled and gave her a pain killer.

Kiara gulped it down. "Thanks. Now what about Jack?"

"We'll take care of him," Suzy said. *We'll get him checked out and chained up.*

Suzy and Kiara lugged his unconscious body to the auto-doc. The table lowered to the floor, making it easy to get him into position, and then the machinery once again performed an examination. The voice informed them that the stun shot hadn't done any internal damage, though he did have two slight metacarpal fractures in his hand that nicely matched the heel of Suzy's boot. He didn't need surgery, but since his hand was swollen like a raging balloon she bandaged him up and gave him an anti-inflammatory patch.

Then Suzy locked his legs in a pair of old-style leg irons and moved him into the first cabin, where she connected the irons to another chain that looped around the toilet in the lavatory. She liked the old-fashioned hardware; it was cheap and reliable and had a certain pirate-flavored jangle to it. She also stuck a camera chip in the corner of the room, out of reach.

Kiara shook her head. "He's chained like an animal."

"Yeah," Suzy said. "And you've got a black eye and a bloody nose."

Kiara frowned. "He's not Prince Charming, I know that. But you'd be surprised. He was nice to me when I had nobody."

"Nice? When a guy starts punching you in the face, you're better off with nobody. It's three days until we get to Venus. I know you feel bad about this guy, but I think you have some mixed feelings, right? I think you should let me handle him."

"What? Why? Are you afraid I might let him out? I won't, Suzy—*I promise.*"

"All right. But I still don't want you to visit him without me."

"You don't trust me?"

"I don't trust *him.*"

"I just don't want him to die, that's all. You're not going to kill him, are you?"

"It's not part of the plan."

"What's the plan? You're going to let him go when we get to Venus, right?"

Suzy cocked her head. "I'm working on it, Kiara. I'm trying."

Kiara's lower lip was trembling, and her whole body looked tense like a bowstring—and no, Suzy didn't trust her, not one bit. But it wasn't because she thought Kiara had bad intentions. It was because she seemed too damn vulnerable.

Luckily, Jack didn't start to wake up until Kiara was asleep. Kiara had gone into one of the cabins—her cabin, for now—and finally fallen asleep. Suzy stayed in the cockpit, watching Jack on the camera. She saw him groping around, pawing at the tile floor.

She walked into his prison lavatory just as he rolled onto his back and rubbed his face.

"Hey, where am I?"

"You're dead," Suzy said. "This is the afterlife, and I'm the judge of your soul. And things are looking pretty grim, motherfucker."

"Oh," he said, and his bleary eyes opened wide. "Well, shit. Listen, I know I made a few mistakes, but it wasn't my fault! I stole stuff, and I tangled with a few people, and some of them got hurt—and then my luck went bad! And—hey, wait. Damn, it's *you!* And I'm chained up."

Suzy laughed. "Yeah, it's me. Here, I brought you some food." She pushed a plate of spaghetti forward. "Do you feel as bad as you look?"

He started thrashing around, trying to break the chains—and then he stopped, overcome with nausea. Suzy could relate to his situation, having been stunned a few times herself.

"Keep it up and I'll shoot you again," she said.

"You can't keep me here forever. Let me go… Hey, where's Kiara?"

"She's resting. Some dirtbag punched her in the face."

Jack frowned. "Ah, I didn't mean to hurt her. Is she okay?"

"She'll heal just fine—on the outside."

"Right," he said, shaking his head. "Can I see her?"

"Hell, no. And by the way, isn't she a little young for you?"

"She's not!" he snapped. Then he gave a sardonic laugh. "I guess you don't know what she was doing when I met her."

"Yeah, and I don't care. I know what she's *not* doing now—talking to you. Get used to it."

Jack snorted. "I heard you were a real bitch, and I guess it's true. You tell her I'm asking about her, okay? She's a sweet girl, the sweetest girl in the world. I never wanted to hurt her. She's been through a lot. I just lost my temper, that's all. Hell, I've been beat way worse than that."

"It wasn't enough. And if you do anything else to hurt that girl, this bitch will kill you—*just try me.*"

"Won't you kill me, anyway?"

"Probably not. And you can thank Kiara for that. But I'm watching you, Jack."

She pointed to the camera chip stuck to a corner of the ceiling, well out of his reach. Then she walked out. He started pulling on the chain again and then shouted a few times. And then he ate the spaghetti.

Suzy watched from a monitor in the cockpit. Did she feel guilty about putting a sedative in his tomato sauce? No. Some people are nicer when they're unconscious.

So Jack slept a lot over the next few days, and when he wasn't asleep he was groggy. Apparently, he made no connection between the food and his tendency to keep dozing. And every time Kiara went to see him, he was sleeping like a cinder block. While they were sitting on the black sofa in the crew lounge, Suzy explained that Jack was fine, and a stun blast affects some people more than others.

"Like I said, he's not all bad," Kiara said. "But don't worry, I'm done with him." Then she slid a little closer to Suzy. She pointed at the ring that hung from a chain around Suzy's neck, always.

"That's nice. Where did you get it?"

Suzy hesitated. "It belonged to my sister."

"Oh. I heard about her. I'm sorry about…all that."

"Thanks."

There was silence, but Suzy could tell Kiara wanted to say something else. So in a soft voice, Suzy said, "What?"

"Nothing," Kiara said, not meeting Suzy's eyes. "I just wanted to say…I think it was great, the thing you did for her."

"I did it for me, Kiara. I was too late to help her."

"Oh. Well, I'm sorry about that, too… You probably think I'm a loser for being involved with Jack, don't you?"

"No."

"But you're so sure of yourself, Suzy, and I always feel like I'm falling apart. I feel like everything is crushing me."

Suzy wasn't sure what to say—because yeah, she actually knew the feeling. But she said, "Kiara, you're doing fine."

A tear ran down Kiara's cheek. "I shouldn't be bothering you with this stuff. I'm not always such a crybaby. Just lately, that's all."

For a second, Suzy thought about her sister Trish. She'd been about Kiara's age when she'd died. How many times had she cried alone—before her suicide? *I want to help but what kind of help am I?*

"You're not a crybaby," Suzy said. "You've been through a lot, and you're still here."

Kiara wiped her eyes. "Thanks," she said. "I'll go away now." And she tossed back her hair and stood up straight—and for an instant Suzy saw Trish standing there, with the same dark hair and skin tone as their dad. A chill went down her spine.

"You don't have to go," Suzy blurted. Then she said, "I'll be around, Kiara. I'll be right here, okay?"

Kiara smiled, and then Suzy stood up, too, and once again they embraced.

"Thanks, Suzy," Kiara said. "I'm just tired, really tired. I never sleep."

"I have a pill you can take."

For the next few days, Kiara spent a lot of time in her cabin. With some effort Suzy left her alone, guessing she was staring at a bulkhead, not sleeping much, and thinking about the storms raging around her life. And I'm doing the same thing, Suzy thought. *Except I'm drinking whiskey and staring at empty outer space.*

She did most of her staring—and drinking—in the darkened cockpit, while sitting in the wide pilot chair with her feet on the blinking console and a bottle of bourbon in her hand. She didn't get too drunk, but why not? There was a time when she would've gulped the bottle down and barely lived to tell about it. Maybe she wanted to have some booze left for the ride home. Or maybe, just maybe, she didn't want Kiara to see her pie-eyed and stupid.

Kiara's recent words about "being sure" echoed in her head as she gave a sarcastic laugh. Then her eyes wandered to the communications log that showed a list of messages from Ricardo—all ignored. This trip to Venus had started out as a hopeful quest to do something better with her life, but would it end that way? Her eyebrows shot up as she saw a new message coming in—from Ricardo's sister. She put the bottle of booze down and directed the computer to play it.

Maria's pretty face appeared on the screen. She was sitting outdoors, on a sunny patio somewhere in Mexico, with a breeze rifling through her dark hair. Maria's hair was much like Kiara's, only neater. But that's where the similarities between the two ended.

Maria wasn't outwardly emotional; however, this was one of those uncommon moments. She was smiling, she was actually gushing, and were there tears in her eyes?

She said, "Suzy, when we got the ransom message, I thought you were dead. I'm so glad you're alive. I don't know what I'd do if anything happened to you. You were right to go, to get out, and I hope we can all do it soon. So why am I going to ask you to do something crazy? It's part of a plan, Suzy, a plan I have to help you and everyone here. If you can deliver the packages my brother left, we might be able to work with some locals there who want to take over the city, and you'll never have to be a fugitive again. None of us will." Then she paused and leaned forward a bit. She said, "You don't owe me anything, Suzy, and I'm only asking you to consider this, but I think it can work. Your kidnapper is with a group called the Snake Eyes—look them up on the grid. He also has connections with the city security unit, and maybe you can use him to get you into the city. I'll send you the contact code for one of our people on Baadal Shahar—a guy named Farouk—and he'll take care of the arrangements on the ground. If anything seems too dangerous, don't do it." Then she smiled one more time. "Whatever you decide, just know that I love you, and I hope to see you soon."

The message faded to black. Suzy saw it was set to self-delete after playing, so now it was gone forever. She picked up the bottle of whiskey and leaned back in her chair.

She felt better. Maria seemed so obviously overjoyed that Suzy hadn't been hurt or kidnapped—and it made Suzy feel uplifted. Everyone wants to be loved, she thought, *and I guess I'm no different.* On another note, Maria also had a plan. Baadal Shahar was a boiling cauldron of unrest, and the direction of Maria's strategy was interesting. At the very least, it might become a wild adventure and a welcome distraction from other things—like Ricardo.

But Ricardo was Maria's brother, so maybe not. And Maria hadn't even mentioned him, almost like she knew their break-up was temporary. Was she wrong? Maybe it was time to answer his messages. Suzy had said they were done talking, but it wasn't true, so why play games? Well, because he'd brought all those guns on board, and those guns symbolized how he wouldn't leave Los Pocos behind, at least not for her. And she would have left *everything* behind for him, and she'd never been one to get so wrapped up in someone else—and now that she'd done it, now that she'd admitted it was something she could do, he'd rejected her. He probably didn't see it that way, but that's what he'd done, and it made her feel—what? Regretful? Embarrassed? Angry?

It made her feel hurt. And that's why his messages weren't being returned—not yet. Maybe after the job was done. Maybe after she'd captured Shogun Hunter.

***

At the end of three days, Suzy leaped out of bed wide awake and peppy. Hey, maybe getting buzzed instead of shit-faced drunk was the way to go. Their destination was up ahead, and it was almost party time—and there was Jack's prostrate body on a nearby monitor, about to cooperate more than he knew. His dinner of rice and beans had been spiked with a low dose of sleep stuff, and he'd be waking up soon.

Suzy ate a quick breakfast of peanut butter on rye toast and an avocado, and then she went to see her prisoner. She stood over him with a shiny object in her hand. It was square, about the size and thickness of a cracker, and made of coppery metal. It was unlikely Jack would recognize the thing because he seemed like a generally ignorant guy. That's okay, he'd be getting the explosive news soon.

In her other hand was a tube of adhesive. She squeezed a drop onto the object. Then she pulled up Jack Ray's shirt and pressed it onto his bare skin, a bit below a scar on his shoulder blade. It stuck instantly. She tested the bond and found it to be strong. She put another one on his lower back, at the base of his spine, because it was good to have options.

Right on cue, Jack opened his eyes.

He seemed lost for a second but then gave a grunt of awareness and sat up. "Why are you here?" he said. "What's the fucking story?"

"Nice to see you too, Jack. So here's the fucking story: It looks like you sent a message from this ship to someone in Baadal Shahar, telling them you had the guns and you'd be arriving in three days, so stand by. And then a little while ago you sent another message telling them you'd be arriving in three hours." She paused to let her words sink in.

"What are you talking about?" he said. "I didn't say that."

"Oh, that's right," Suzy said with a smile. "I guess I sent that second one, pretending to be you. Don't worry, I sent it text-only and spelled a bunch of words wrong. And guess what? Your friends are going to have 'their guys' at city security come out to the ship for the inspection. So all you have to do is play along and everything will be great."

"Now why would I do that?" he snapped. "I'm going to tell them to help me out, and I'm going to kill you first chance I get."

"Jack, are you trying to sweet-talk me? Even after I glued such beautiful bombs to your body?"

He started to say something and stopped. "Bombs?"

"Yeah, bombs. Like this one." She held up one of the smooth objects and noted his quizzical expression.

"You can check for yourself but be careful," she said. "If you try to rip them off, they'll explode. If you try to cut them off, they'll explode. They're not that strong as bombs go—just strong enough to destroy a major organ or two, or maybe your spine. They're also *extremely* sensitive to vibration. So if you start throwing punches, they might go off. If you frown a little too hard, they might go off. So try not to act like an animal—and smile."

She pulled out her pistol and tossed him a key. "The remote control is in my hand," she said. Then she showed a tiny black square, paper thin, stuck to her palm. "It's a lot less obvious than sticking a gun in my pocket, right? And if you do *one* wrong thing during the inspection, I blow you to pieces. If you try to run, or if you get away from me, I hit the button and you blow up wherever you are—and then I shoot your security friends, turn the ship around and leave. They'll never catch me. Now let's go."

She kept the gun pointed at him as he unlocked his chains and cuffs. Then she forced him into the passageway, through the lounge, and into the cockpit where she tossed him the handcuffs and made him chain himself to the copilot chair. She knew there was nothing nearby he could use as a weapon. She planned to free him just before the inspectors boarded.

Through the cockpit windows, blinking ships and satellites were scattered across the darkness like glowing dice. In the distance beyond was the fiery yellow ball of Venus, and about 50 kilometers above the searing surface was the city of Baadal Shahar. But before they could get to the city they had to deal with the city security unit. The city supposedly had strict laws regarding weapons, and with the recent unrest things would probably be even tighter. A nearby screen showed a scooter ship approaching. It reminded Suzy of a big glass running shoe.

A message crackled over the radio. "City security here. Calling Jack Ray. Is there a Jack Ray on board?"

Suzy started to respond—and stopped. Did they know Jack personally? Maybe not. She pressed the button and said, "Yeah, there's a Jack Ray on board. Come on over." Then she turned to Jack and said, "What's the name of your contact?"

"Fuck you, Suzy. Go ahead and hit the button. Blow me up and you won't get shit."

"Not true, Jack. I'll get to pick up your spine with a sponge."

"Who's getting blown up?" Kiara said.

She was standing in the doorway, looking at Suzy with wide eyes.

"Kiara!" Jack blurted. "She glued bombs to me!"

"No, Kiara," Suzy said. "No one's getting blown up."

"She's lying," Jack said in a shaky voice. Then he pointed at Suzy. "She glued bombs to me, and she's going to kill me when we land. It's true, Kiara—and remember, I could've killed her and I didn't! And she tried to lock you in the hold, remember? Even though you were cluster phobic."

The scooter ship was close now. They'd be boarding in a minute.

"Are there bombs glued to him, Suzy?"

Suzy frowned. She didn't need any complications right now.

"Kiara, go to your cabin and let me handle this. It'll be fine."

"Kiara, I love you," Jack said. "And I'm sorry I hit you. I was drunk! I promise I'll never do it again—*I swear!*"

"Are you going to kill Jack?" Kiara said.

"No!"

"Of course she is! Why would she leave me alive?"

"Are there bombs glued to him, Suzy?"

"Kiara, you don't know the whole story."

"Neither do you! Are there bombs glued to him?"

"Kiara, forget about the bombs and trust me."

Jack waved his one free arm, the one with the bandaged and fractured hand. "Why would you trust her, Kiara? Has she done anything for you? Compared to what I did? Go meet the security guys at the airlock. Tell them to sound an alarm—otherwise, she'll kill them and blow me up! That's her plan. And she'll probably kill you, too. *Do it!*"

There was a clanging noise. The scooter ship had attached a passageway, and then a message came over the radio, requesting the airlock be opened.

"Kiara, you asked me to trust you," Suzy said. "Now you need to trust me."

"But you didn't trust me," Kiara said, and her voice was trembling. "You didn't tell me you were going to glue bombs to Jack. And you didn't tell me you were putting drugs in his food."

Crap! How did she know about the drugs?

"I saw you do it," Kiara said. "But I didn't say anything."

The radio whistled again and a voice said, "Security. Open the airlock."

"The drug was just a sedative," Suzy said. "It was harmless."

"And what about the bombs?"

Suzy narrowed her eyes. "The bombs are there because Jack is an asshole."

There was a long moment of silence as Kiara stared at Suzy. Then the voice on the radio said, "Security—open the airlock." Suzy had one hand in the pocket of her flight jacket and the other on her pistol.

Jack said, "Kiara, don't listen to her!"

Kiara glanced down the passageway with jumpy eyes. Then she looked back at Suzy. She stared at Jack and spoke in a shaky voice.

"Jack, I'm sorry. I can't do it."

Suzy smiled and tossed Jack the key to the cuffs. "Play along, Jack. And don't be stupid."

Suzy took a few steps back, standing farther away from Jack, and told Kiara to do the same. Then she hit the button to pressurize the airlock while Jack scowled and un-cuffed himself. But Kiara didn't move back far enough—and Jack lunged forward and grabbed her.

Kiara shrieked. Jack said, "Don't move!" He glared at Suzy and gave a giddy laugh. "Who's stupid now, huh?" He had one arm across Kiara's throat and one wrapped around her waist. "We're walking to the airlock, and if you try to touch me we'll both blow up."

Kiara screamed as Jack started inching them both out of the cockpit. Suzy aimed her gun at Jack's head, but he kept moving and bobbing, hiding behind Kiara.

"Watch it!" Jack said. "Vibrations, remember? You gonna risk it?"

Kiara squealed. "Let go of me! How can you do this?"

The airlock was pressurizing.

Jack screamed down the passageway. "In here!"

Suzy said, "Jack, you dumbass, those aren't bombs. They're chips from the Last Chance casino on Neptune."

Jack's face went blank—and Kiara twisted around and clawed at his eyes, and he swore and tried to hit her, and she shouted, *"I hate you!"* and bit down hard on his un-bandaged hand.

He let out a howl as blood spurted. Then Kiara pushed him away.

"You ungrateful twat!" he roared.

Suzy shot him in the face. Kiara screamed again as he smashed against the bulkhead and dropped to the floor. She clapped her hands to her head.

"Oh my god!" Kiara said, gasping. "Is he dead?"

"I don't know," Suzy said. "But keep an eye on him."

She shoved the gun into the pocket of her jacket and ran down the passageway, into the lounge, and over to the airlock that was sliding open. Two people dressed like cops were inside, a man and a woman. Suzy kept one hand on her concealed weapon.

"Hi," the man said. "We're here for the inspection." He grinned. "Is Jack here?"

Suzy held out her free hand. "Yeah… Jacqueline Ray," she said. "But my friends call me Jack."

She studied their faces.

They seemed happy enough. "Oh. Nice to meet you. We thought you were a man."

"No. I'm a woman."

"Well, that's fine."

"I like to think so. Do you need to look around?"

They both grinned. "No. We just need to stay long enough to make it look like we did."

"Do you want a drink?"

"No, thanks."

"Okay, fine. But I'm going to have one."

Chapter 11

Danielle sighed and shook her head. It was a warm summer night, and she was sitting on her breezy balcony surrounded by the winking towers of downtown Atlanta, rereading the message from her long-time friend Anika Anand. The news could've been better.

Anika was in Baadal Shahar, where she'd lived for fifteen years. Anika was familiar with Shogun Hunter, from the days when she'd worked in New York City. He'd been a crooked attorney helping drug dealers go free, and she'd been an assistant prosecutor trying to beat back the ocean with a spoon. She was sure he'd come to Baadal Shahar a few years ago, right after he'd escaped from prison. He'd been spotted downtown checking out the surgery swaps, those shadowy places where someone could find a new face, a new body, and a fresh beginning for a rotten past. Unfortunately, there was no sign of him now. So he'd either left town or turned into someone new or both.

I hope Suzy's not out there wasting her time.

The door to the apartment slid open, and her husband came striding onto the balcony. He glanced at her and put his big hands on the rail. He stared at the sweeping view as he spoke.

"Something wrong?" he said.

"No, I'm fine. I'm just looking at a few messages."

"You're not a good liar."

"Is that so? Maybe you'd be surprised."

"Maybe. So what's the problem?"

He turned to face her, half smiling yet looking stern. She called it his "cordial cop look."

She shrugged. "I got a message from Anika. Things are getting crazy over there."

"So I've heard. And still no sign of Hunter, right?"

She felt a jolt of alarm. "Hunter?" she said, trying her best to look surprised.

Damn, I guess it's hard to lie to one of the country's top cops.

He shook his head. "You need to let it go. It's been three years, and ever since the trial—and Hunter's escape—you've been obsessed. He's long gone, Danielle. And that city is out of our jurisdiction."

Now she felt her blood pressure rising. "His crimes don't have boundaries," she said, managing to keep her voice even.

"Interesting choice of words," he replied. "Danielle, I think I know what you're doing."

She caught her breath. "You do?"

"Yes. You're getting Anika involved in a search for this guy, and it's a mistake."

"Oh," she said. And she sighed. "No. I just asked her if the local people have heard anything, that's all. She's got her ear to the street. She knows everyone." Time to change the subject—sort of. "So how's your man Stone doing?"

Andre raised his eyebrows. "Stone? Funny you should mention him. He's going to Baadal Shahar, and he might be smarter than I thought. He figured out that Suzy was heading there. Can you believe it? In fact, I should contact him and tell him to talk to Anika. Like you said, she knows a lot of people. She might hear something."

"Oh. Sure, that's a good plan."

He started to say something else and stopped. Then he opened the door to the apartment and said, "Are you coming to bed?"

"I'll be right in," she said with a smile. He smiled back at her and went inside.

Her smile vanished as she cursed her own big mouth. Yeah, going to bed sounded good—*but first I need to send a message to Venus.*

Chapter 12

Jack was still alive.

Suzy swore. Okay, he was one tough hombre, but really—*god dammit!*

A stun shot had been a smart move at the time, since he'd been entwined with Kiara. But she'd shot him in the face at close range, and it was the second time his nervous system had been blasted in three days, and he could've easily been killed.

"We can't let him die," Kiara said. She knelt down and gripped his hand.

Suzy held her tongue. Jack was sprawled on the deck of the cockpit like a bag of dirt. Kiara started crying, but Suzy noted there'd been more tears at Jack's last shooting. *Maybe when I finally kill this guy she'll be down to a sniffle.*

Kiara wiped her eyes. "I know what you're thinking, Suzy. But I'm glad you didn't kill him. It's just the way I am."

For a second, Suzy felt her heart melt a little. What was it like to be so forgiving? Then she shook her head while her brain whirled; there were some big problems with Jack being alive. Mainly, that he would wake up and become a complete piece of shit—again.

"Suzy, you're thinking that when he wakes up he'll be a problem, right?"

"I was thinking different words, but yeah."

"You're not going to shoot him again, are you?"

"No," Suzy said, surprised by how quickly she answered. But she wasn't going to kill Jack execution style, and a surprising ripple of satisfaction went through her.

"We have to get him to a hospital," Kiara said.

Suzy gave a grunt and slid into the pilot chair. She snapped a few switches, initiating the docking sequence that would land the *Correcaminos Rojo* on Baadal Shahar. She didn't have the heart to explain Jack's future to Kiara. The fuckwit had hijacked Pablo Juarez's shipment of guns and had then taken Suzy hostage—Suzy, who was the girlfriend (maybe) of Pablo's brother-in-law, and who was also a close friend of Pablo's wife.

Jack's future was rock-solid like a tombstone.

"They're going to come after him, aren't they?" Kiara said.

Suzy glanced at the girl. *Should I tell her the truth?*

"Yeah, they will," Suzy said. "You need to stay away from him."

"I will," Kiara said, blinking back new tears. Then she raised her eyebrows. "What about me? Will they come after me? I suppose I deserve it."

"No!" Suzy said. "They'll leave you alone—I promise. Now let's get this deal done."

She turned on the communications console and sent a text message from the ship to a contact code Maria had sent her in a separate transmission.

Coming in now. Docking bay 867. ETA 30 minutes.

She immediately received a response.

All ready here.

Then she sent another message to the text address that Jack had been using to communicate with the Snake Eyes.

There's a delay. They're switching us to a different docking bay. Will give the number soon. ETA three hours.

So hopefully the Snake Eyes would be standing around like a bunch of sawed-off stumps, waiting to unload the guns that Maria's friends had unloaded a few hours before. Unless, of course, something went wrong. She received another quick response.

No problem. We're all set.

Suzy frowned. They hadn't questioned the delay at all. Was this an agreeable bunch, or was she just being paranoid? She gave a grim laugh because paranoia was sometimes a good friend. Then she noticed Kiara staring at her.

"Is something wrong, Suzy?"

"Always, Kiara. Hey, we need to cuff Jack to something. And you need to stay in your cabin when we land. Keep out of sight, okay?"

"But I can help."

"You can, by not getting yourself involved, okay?" She gave Kiara a sharp look. *"Okay?"*

Kiara shrugged and tossed back her black hair. "It depends. I want to help, and I want to get Jack to a hospital."

"First we have to get him out of here."

Kiara said nothing as they dragged Jack into the lounge and cuffed him to the leg of the sofa that was bolted to the floor. He was limp and had two black eyes, but he was definitely breathing. Kiara wanted to give him some medication, but Suzy explained there was nothing on board that would help until he was awake. Suzy knew he might have an internal injury, maybe to the brain, but since they couldn't help with that situation there was no point in telling Kiara and upsetting her. Suzy didn't try to force Kiara to leave Jack's side; she just told Kiara he'd probably be all right, and it was time to land the ship. Then Suzy went back to the cockpit to watch the approach. She was hoping Kiara would follow. A minute later Kiara came in and stood behind her.

"Do you mind if I sit in this chair?" Kiara said, pointing to the co-pilot seat.

"No," Suzy said with a smile. "I'll show you how to land a spaceship."

Kiara's face was still streaked from tears, but now she gave a little laugh. "I'm a cook, Suzy. The only thing I ever fly is a stove. If you want to show me something, show me how to call for help."

"I can do that. It's always good to know how to send an SOS."

"A what?"

"It's an old expression, from back when ships sailed on oceans—Save Our Ship. They used to do it by sending electronic beeps, some long and some short." She looked around for something that beeped and found a particular button on the console. "Every letter had a combination," she said. " 'S' was three short beeps and 'O' was three longer ones." She reached out and demonstrated the pattern.

Kiara watched and listened. "Why didn't they just call on a phone?" she said. "Or a radio?"

Suzy paused and cocked her head. "Hey, I never asked. But now you know how to do it this way."

"Thanks. I guess I'll try and remember it. As for landing the ship, well…I make good tomales, Suzy—with refried beans, guacamole—whatever you want. I make good lasagna, too."

Suzy laughed. "That sounds like more work than landing this thing. It's all done by computer. You only need to initiate the correct docking sequence and you're all set."

Kiara was staring intently at the view.

They were on the side of Venus that faced the sun, with the sun behind the ship, lighting up the planet like a globe of molten gold. As they started to descend, a wall of apricot-colored clouds filled their view, billowing in all directions like a dense, rolling blanket. Suzy knew the clouds were made of sulfuric acid, and as the *Correcaminos Rojo* skimmed above the raging vapor, they looked across the horizon and saw the silhouette of their destination—Baadal Shahar. Roughly translated from Hindi it meant "Cloud City."

Baadal Shahar was a city of five million people, a massive collection of golden domes and spires that floated about 50 kilometers above the burning surface of the planet on a platform that resembled a gigantic pie plate. Beneath the plate were a series of massive anti-gravity thrusters that kept the city aloft in the relatively temperate zone that existed there. The city was powered by a combination of fusion and solar energy. Suzy didn't understand all the details, but she definitely understood why no one lived on the surface—too freaking hot.

For a second, she thought about Ricardo, and the view they'd shared as they'd approached a different city-state not so long ago. But now it seemed like a hundred years had passed.

Maybe we'll come here together sometime, if I don't get killed unloading the guns he left me.

The docking bays looked like honeycombs, and there were thousands of them surrounding the main dome. Suzy didn't trust the computer guidance system the way most pilots did, and she was always ready to take over and fly. But in this case, the computer guided the ship perfectly, hovering above a honeycomb before descending straight down.

The ship landed with a soft bump. Almost immediately, a readout showed the energy barrier above had closed, and the bay was filling with atmosphere. On a series of monitors, Suzy scanned the area outside the ship. Now came the tricky part—getting rid of the guns without actually having a gunfight.

Inside, the bay looked like a crater made of metal with a shimmering reddish roof. Suzy couldn't help feeling trapped, and it was one of the things she hated about city-states. On Earth, she could always fire up the engines and head for open sky.

Kiara was still wide-eyed, staring out the windows at the landscape of grey steel.

"So, what happens now?" Kiara said.

Suzy adjusted a few controls, mainly the ones that operated some small guns that were mounted on the outside of the ship. She said, "We wait for the welcoming committee and maybe a red carpet. No sign of them yet."

"What does that mean?"

"It means there's no one to shoot right now."

"But you sent a message to someone, right? Why aren't they here?"

"They're probably behind that big metal door. When you get assigned a bay, Kiara, they give you and your ship access to the doors. But don't kid yourself—that doesn't mean we're safe in here. Bad people find a way. Hey, I've done it myself a few times."

She pulled out her allcom. Up until recently, she'd been using old-style phones that couldn't be traced—but this new device was much better, and supposedly it was equally discreet. She punched the code that Maria had given her.

"Farouk here," a deep voice said. "We're outside the docking bay."

"How many are with you?"

"Just three."

"What about the Snake Eyes?"

"We took care of those people. If any more show up, we'll handle them, too."

Suzy hesitated. Then she said, "Stand by."

She disconnected the call and turned to Kiara. "Do me a favor and wait in your cabin."

Kiara's eyes flashed. "I'm not a little girl, Suzy. Believe me."

"I know. But it might be good if they don't know someone else is on board."

Kiara hesitated, like she was trying to figure out whether Suzy had some special plan or was just trying to get rid of her.

"What about Jack?" Kiara said. "I'm serious, Suzy. I don't want them taking him anywhere. We have to do that ourselves."

"I'm not negotiating here, Kiara."

"I don't want them taking him because they'll kill him! And I couldn't live with that."

Suzy started to raise her voice—and then stopped. She sighed instead. "Kiara, if I promise they won't take him, will you go to your cabin?"

Kiara paused. "Yeah."

"Okay. I promise we'll take care of Jack. Now get out of here. Please."

"All right," Kiara said. She started to go but then turned back around. "But I'll be close by, Suzy. I'll be ready."

"Good."

"I mean it. I can help."

"I *know* you can, Kiara. But don't do anything unless I tell you, okay? Please."

Suzy shook her head and watched her go. Then she checked her pistol and pressed a button on the ship's console that caused the wide steel doors of the bay to slide open. Just behind the doors were four guys, a beat-up hover-truck, a hover-car, and a gleaming black hover-bike dripping in chrome. Were they armed? No weapons were visible but they probably had them.

The biggest guy had dark skin, a beard, and dreadlocks that tumbled past his shoulders. He wore a sleeveless shirt that showed off his bulging arms. The other three guys were shorter with lighter skin.

Suzy knew Baadal Shahar was an ethnically diverse place with a complicated history. The city had been built 150 years ago by a consortium of Earth investors, eventually becoming the largest of seven independently governed city-states belonging to a trade organization called the Cloud City Consolidation of Venus. Several political upheavals later, it was now a splashy conglomeration of casinos and nightclubs filled with people from across the Earth. The result was an ever-evolving social fabric with a confusing crime structure. On most planets and city-states, any one criminal organization was often dominated by a single ethnic group—but it wasn't the case here, and especially not with the Snake Eyes. The Snake Eyes were a cult that welcomed all people with equal enthusiasm. Sure, this was a victory for equality and cooperation, but it also made it harder to figure out who wanted you dead.

Luckily, Maria had sent Suzy more than Farouk's contact code. She'd sent him an image, and when she used a camera to focus on the face outside, the computer made a positive match. So these were the right guys—or at least the guys she was supposed to meet.

Of course, sometimes the right guys can go wrong.

Suzy picked up her allcom and called Farouk again. Outside, she saw him put his allcom to his ear and smile. He was looking up at her face through the cockpit window.

"Nice ship," he said. "And hey, nobody told me you were so pretty."

"That's because you're just here to pick up a bunch of guns."

He laughed. "I could stay a bit. Do you need your windows cleaned?"

"You sure know how to win a girl's heart."

He laughed again. "It was the first thing that popped into my mind."

"Well, I do kind of like to see where I'm going."

She touched the console in front of her, opening the outside entrance to the cargo bay. Farouk barked a few orders to the other guys and they started loading the guns into the hover truck. They had a few mobile platforms with sensors and arms that made the work easy. It wouldn't take long.

She didn't open the main airlock, and she didn't unseal the hatch leading from the cargo bay into the interior of the ship. Okay, everything seemed fine—fine enough to let them have the guns. But there was no real reason to let them into the ship.

After a bit, Farouk called again.

"Aren't you going to come out and say hello?" he said. "We're all friends here."

"Maybe later. I need to take a shower first."

"Don't worry about it. I like a dirty girl."

Suzy laughed. "People tend to think I'm dirtier than I am."

She didn't open the door. Then there was a scream from outside, and Farouk was on the allcom again. But now his voice was filled with urgency.

"Hey, we've had an accident! One of our guys needs help."

Suzy looked at her monitor screen—*damn!* One of the guys was seriously bleeding from his hand. For an instant, she wondered if the injury was real—but then she saw two of his fingers lying on the deck.

"Get him to a hospital!" Suzy said. "We don't have a doctor here."

"He can't go! He's wanted and they'll arrest him. Please, Suzy, help us out."

That's when Kiara came into the cockpit. Obviously, she'd been monitoring things.

"Suzy, we have to help him," Kiara said. Her voice was loud, yet trembling. "We can't just let him bleed to death. Besides, aren't these people our friends?"

Yeah, supposedly. Suzy looked at the image of the guy clutching his hand, and she looked at Kiara. Then she swore and yanked a gun out of a compartment. It was Jack's gun.

Suzy ran into the lounge, where there was a granite bar, and a red table, and a dirtbag named Jack cuffed to the leg of a sofa. On top of the bar was a hat with a wide brim, a red band, and a purple feather sticking up; it was a prop once used in a Shakespearean play and a souvenir from a past adventure. Kiara watched as Suzy put the gun under the hat. Of course, Suzy still had her own gun strapped to her thigh.

"All right," she told Kiara. "Open the airlock."

A few seconds later Farouk was inside with the injured man. The guy was grimacing and trying to stop the bleeding with his good hand. But the blood was flowing fast, pouring onto the deck. Meanwhile, Farouk was holding the guy's severed fingers. He seemed surprised to see Kiara. He also noted Jack's unconscious body.

"Thank you, Suzy," Farouk said. "So I guess we meet after all."

"Yeah, but I didn't get too far in medical school," Suzy said. "Trust me, the robot had better grades." Then she pointed toward the auto-doc station in the corner of the crew lounge. "Get him over there."

Kiara helped get him onto the table. She was breathing hard but working fast. Thanks to Jack's injury, she now knew how to initiate the examination and diagnosis procedures. She was a quick learner, very impressive.

"Hold your hand up to the scanner," Kiara said. When he appeared to be confused, she took his injured hand and gently placed it in the proper position.

The machine hummed a bit and then spoke in a smooth female voice: *The patient has two severed fingers. These fingers can't be reattached here—more sophisticated surgery is required; however, I can stop the bleeding and administer a pain medication.*

The guy grimaced again while Kiara held his hand. Then the silvery tentacles of the auto-doc applied two metal caps to the stumps of the severed fingers while another tentacle injected him with a pain killer. Finally, Kiara wrapped the two severed fingers in some special perma-freeze material.

The guy said his name was Michael. He was young and rough looking, with barely the beginning of a beard showing on his face, but he smiled at Kiara and said, "Thanks." Then he reached into his shirt pocket and pulled out a pink pill. He crushed it between two fingers and snorted the resulting powder. In an instant, his head rolled back and he grinned.

"Want some V?" he said, and he pulled out another pill. "It's the thing to do on Venus."

Kiara just shook her head. "No, thanks." Then she looked at his injury again and said, "How did it happen?"

Michael just shrugged while Farouk grinned and picked up the two wrapped fingers. "It was all about dedication," Farouk said. Then with another grin he tossed them at Suzy.

What? Suzy jerked herself away from the grisly missile. When she looked back at Farouk, he was pointing a gun at her head.

He smiled. "A small price to pay for the capture of Suzy Spitfire."

Suzy narrowed her eyes. "You motherfucker," she said.

Farouk laughed. "I've been called worse, and you better be nice to me." He raised his eyebrows up and down. "I can be friendly, or maybe not. And I'll have a good time either way. But if you move the tiniest bit I'll shoot you dead."

He motioned toward Michael. "Good job. You're a loyal Brother of the Snake. Get in the car. You can go to the hospital with Jack."

Michael gave Kiara a narcotic grin and scurried off the table. He picked up his fingers like they were a pack of matches and then left the ship.

Kiara's eyes were jumping around. "What are you doing?" she said in a shaky voice. "What is this?"

"Shut up," Farouk said. Then he looked at Suzy. "Who is she?"

"She's not involved, Farouk. Let her go."

"I can't do that. Hm, maybe I should kill her."

"She's not involved!"

He grinned again. "Oh, so you like her? We'll take her, too. Maybe you'll behave better if you know we *might* kill her—or do something worse. Now toss your gun on the floor, Suzy—slow, very slow. And then give my guys the keys to those ancient handcuffs."

Suzy felt her fingers itching to make a quick move and shoot Farouk, but experience had taught her it was a bad plan. Besides, she still had that gun under the hat. So she showed no expression and followed his instructions. I'll wait for my chance, she thought. *But I can only wait so long.*

Two other guys came into the ship. "All done," one of them said. They looked at the situation and grinned.

Farouk nodded. "Good." Then he handed one of them the keys to Jack's handcuffs and said, "Put him in the car."

"Where are you taking him?" Kiara said.

"He's one of us," Farouk said. "We'll take him to a doctor and he'll be fine."

"I'm his girlfriend!" Kiara blurted.

"Really?" Farouk said. "You haven't been treating him too well. My girlfriend usually cuffs me to the bed."

The two guys laughed and unchained Jack. They started carrying him out of the ship. Kiara's jaw dropped, like she was in shock, and like she might do something stupid. Suzy stared at her and gave a tiny shake of her head while mouthing the word "No."

Kiara stayed frozen, and Suzy turned her attention back to Farouk.

"So, you guys switched sides," she said.

Farouk smirked. "We were always on this side; your dumb Earth friends just didn't know it. Jack's messages and your messages went to different people, but both of them were *us*. We are all brothers and sisters of the Snake. He cocked his head. "But do we kill you and send a message to your friends, or do we keep you alive and make a deal? I don't know. We're famous for our use of the blade—maybe I'll carve up that pretty face of yours. At the very least, I should cut off an ear." Then he pointed the gun and said, "Come on, let's go—both of you. Move!"

"Fine," Suzy said. "But I need a drink first. Do you want anything?"

She started to turn toward the bar.

"No!" Farouk said. "Out of the ship now or you die."

As he barked his orders Kiara burst into tears. "I'll go, I'll go!" she said. "Please don't hurt me. Jack is my friend, and I just met Suzy. I'm just a cook! *I only wanted to cook!*"

Farouk stared at the wailing girl, and his eyes seemed to soften. "Don't worry, honey, you won't get hurt if you do what you're told. Now come on, let's go."

"Can I take a few things with me?"

"Like what? Hostages travel light."

"How about my hat?" she said, pointing at the bar. She was still sobbing. "It's my lucky hat."

Farouk eyed the hat while Suzy held her breath. Then he rolled his eyes. "Sure, go ahead."

Good girl!

Kiara walked to the bar. She wiped away a few tears, picked up the hat, and put it on her head. Then she grabbed the pistol—and the tears vanished as she started screaming.

"Drop the gun!" she said. *"Drop it or I'll shoot! I'll do it! I will!"*

Her eyes were bleary and wild, and she was practically jumping up and down.

Farouk froze as a look of surprise crept across his face—and then annoyance. But he still kept his pistol pointed at Suzy. He looked at Kiara and laughed.

"Nice trick. Did Suzy put you up to that? Put down the gun. Put it down before someone gets hurt."

Suzy was ready to spring—but she didn't, because she was too far away, and in the back of her mind she recalled how she'd seen this scenario before. When a girl is holding a gun, a guy usually takes the situation less seriously than when a guy is holding a gun. And in her experience, this was a big mistake. Of course, in her experience, she was usually the girl holding the gun. But today she was not holding the gun, and it still turned out to be a big mistake.

Kiara shot Farouk in the chest—twice.

Suzy leaped aside as Farouk gave a grunt and hit the deck. Kiara froze and dropped the gun, clapping her hands to her head.

"Oh, my god! Is he dead? Is he dead? Did I kill him?"

She crumpled to the deck and started gasping for air. Suzy knelt down and put her hand on Farouk's neck. He'd been hit with fairly high-powered shots, and he was dead.

Kiara was still trying hard to breathe, and then she was sobbing once again.

"I murdered him. I murdered him!"

Suzy felt a sinking feeling in her heart. She had an urge to wrap Kiara in her arms but there was no time. She made a quick decision.

"No," Suzy said. "You didn't."

"What?"

Kiara stopped crying and looked at Suzy.

"He's still alive," Suzy said.

"He is?"

"Yeah."

Suzy grabbed her weapon from the floor. Then she stood up, pointed it at Farouk's chest, and pulled the trigger—*bang!*

"Now he's dead."

Kiara's jaw dropped. She stared at Suzy, then at Farouk, then back at Suzy. Then she gasped for air a few more times.

"I'm sorry, Kiara. We can't let him come after us, and we can't let them have the guns, either—damn! Wait here."

She started to race out of the lounge—but then she stopped. She turned and grabbed Kiara's shoulders and said, "By the way, you're doing great."

Kiara stared through red-rimmed eyes. "No," she said. "I'm sorry I'm such a wreck."

"You're not a wreck—you did real good. But wait here."

Suzy raced out of the cockpit and dashed down the ramp into the bay. Crap, the car carrying Jack was gone. The other two guys obviously heard the shots and had guns in their hands, but they looked jittery. At the sight of Suzy, they both gave a shout and fired—and Suzy felt one energy blast blow right past her ear. But they seemed hurried and most of their shots missed by a wide distance. She fired back with fully-maxed bullets as they scrambled for cover behind the truck.

She knelt behind the landing gear and fired another salvo, shattering the rear window of the truck and blowing up a taillight. She heard the guys cursing and fumbling around.

Then the small guns mounted on the ship started to fire. Did Kiara know how to work those? No, of course not, and they sprayed a bombardment of energy blasts throughout the bay and hit nothing. But the firestorm panicked the two guys outside. The one guy swore and the truck pulled away fast, into the passage outside the bay, while the other guy jumped onto the hover bike close by.

Suzy shot the biker in the head. He was dead for sure, but what the hell, she was now more or less committed. She ran toward the sleek black bike and jumped on. No problem—it was just a souped-up version of the one her parents had hated, the one she'd had as a kid growing up in Diego Tijuana. She let the engine rumble to life as she screamed at Kiara.

"Kiara, stay in the ship and lock the bay. I'll be back!"

She roared into the passage and headed after the truck.

Chapter 13

Burt Stone squirmed in his chair and prepared to dock the cruiser in Baadal Shahar.

He took a few deep breaths. It's perfectly normal to be nervous, he thought. *Especially with the way things are going.*

Maj. Banks had told him he would get a task force, and that he'd be able to pick his own people. And what did he have? One person—a girl right out of the academy—and for a mission this important. For the mission that would redeem him!

He hadn't picked her, either; she'd been assigned to him. He never would've picked her—although she seemed smart, capable, and attractive, at least in a skinny kind of way.

He glanced over at her. Her name was Tala, and she was from San Francisco. She had the large brown eyes and straight dark hair common to her ancestors, who had come from the Republic of the Philippines—and right there he didn't trust her. Earth had nine great nations loosely joined together under one semi-great government, but there were a few independent places, and that island republic was one of them. Why were they a bunch of renegades? He forgot exactly how it had occurred but history had never been his strongpoint. Of course, math and science hadn't been too much fun, either. Luckily, he was a cop and he didn't need any of that crap.

No doubt she was good at all that stuff. In fact her profile was very detailed. She had a degree in chemical engineering, but then for some reason she'd enrolled in the police academy. Yeah, she was good at everything.

He sighed and considered how he should've studied harder in

school. He tapped his fingers on the armrest and then told himself to stop fidgeting.

"What are you thinking about, sir?" Tala said.

He almost jumped. She had a light, musical voice. She was smiling too; she smiled a lot.

Burt tried to think. "Nothing," he blurted. Then he grimaced, because that was a stupid thing for a commanding officer to say, and he said, "Almost nothing." Then he swore to himself and finally said, "I was just wondering about the city security inspection. I can't believe they won't respect us as police officers and let us carry guns."

"Yeah, that's too bad. Especially since Suzy Castillo is known to always carry a firearm."

"Exactly," he said. And he said it with maximum authority.

Should he tell Tala about the weapons he planned to smuggle into the city? No, probably not. Her profile showed she was a real stickler for the rules. In fact, she'd been disliked by other cadets because of her strict adherence to academy rules and regulations, including the ones governing alcohol and extracurricular fun. Really, that stuff had been the best part of the academy. It had been the only part he'd liked.

"We'll catch her quick," Burt said. "No problem."

"Maybe," Tala said. "At least we have a starting point—this woman, Anika Anand, who the major mentioned. But if she doesn't work out I'm sure we can improvise."

In a flash, he felt the blood rushing to his face. "Are you talking about my disaster in New York?" he snapped.

"Sir?"

"My competency hearing," he sputtered. "I told the panel I'd been 'improvising.' "

"Oh," she said with a quizzical look. "I'm sorry, sir. I didn't realize that was something you said. What hearing are you talking about?"

Now his head almost exploded.

"Nothing!" he said. "I'm a good cop. There's nothing you need to look up."

Tala narrowed her eyes a bit. Then she turned them back to the windshield.

"I'm not looking up anything, sir," she said with another smile. "I'm just watching the stars."

She thinks I'm a moron, he thought. A complete and total moron. *And she's two hundred percent right!*

He straightened up in his chair and told himself there was no harm done. A sharp girl like Tala probably had better things to do than worry about the incompetence of her commanding officer.

God dammit!

Maybe he should eat a chocolate bar. Yeah, maybe it would have a calming effect. He pulled one out of his shirt pocket and fumbled a bit to unwrap it, dropping the wrapper on the floor. As he leaned over the chair to retrieve it, the candy bar rubbed against his uniform, smearing a tasty-looking skid mark across the fabric. He cursed softly and decided to leave the wrapper where it had fallen. After all, there were other wrappers down there. And there were other things smeared on his uniform.

Of course, Tala's uniform was spotless and perfectly pressed, and her side of the deck was free from garbage. He sighed. Okay, he was a slob, and no one would ever confuse him with Albert Einstein. But he could get things done—that's right, dammit, *he was a cop who could get things done.* He cleared his throat and reached toward the console with one of his big hands.

"I've initiated the docking sequence," he said in his deepest voice.

Then he looked at Tala and felt a stab of alarm. Why was her face screwed up like that?

"I think you activated the wrong sequence, sir."

"I did?" he said, and his head started to swim. "No, that's right… Isn't it?"

"No, sir, I don't think so. We'll crash into the city. But you'll get a warning first."

Right on cue, a bunch of red lights blazed across the console and a warning message erupted inside the cockpit.

Incorrect docking sequence activated. Please adjust immediately or sequence will be aborted.

Burt rolled his eyes. Even the ship's computer was against him. He reached over and started to select a different sequence, but which one was correct? The console was a blur, and everything was whirling— and then Tala reached out and hit a few switches.

"Don't worry, sir. I've got it."

For a moment, he felt a spark of rage—*my father was right, my family was right, my teachers were right*—but then it stopped. As he sat there, with sweat dripping down his back, he saw Tala staring out the window, looking perfectly pleasant and not even noticing. He let out a sigh of relief.

He gave her a tired look. "Thanks," he said. Then he heard himself add, "I had no clue."

She smiled yet again. "Everyone forgets sometimes, sir."

Burt looked down at his hands and saw they were shaking. He clamped them onto the armrests. He almost smiled back at her, but he didn't.

He hadn't picked her, but she'd been a good choice.

Chapter 14

What the hell am I doing? Suzy thought. Attracting attention was a bad idea, but was there a quiet way to hi-jack a truck full of guns in the middle of a metropolis?

The truck was hurtling through a tunnel-like passageway. The wind blew through Suzy's hair as she watched the taillights of the truck and guessed it was a hundred meters away. Did the driver know he was being followed? Maybe not. He might think it was the other guy, the one who was lying dead in the docking bay. So it was probably best to stay back a bit. Her mind was racing, trying to think of a plan.

She had no real contacts in Baadal Shahar. When the truck reached its destination, she'd probably be outnumbered with no help. Right now was her best chance, when it was just her and the driver, *mano y mano.*

Suzy revved the engine of the bike while making sure her pistol was still strapped to her thigh. A couple of cars zoomed by in the opposite lane, heading toward the docking bays—damn, what about Kiara? The girl had seemed totally crazed when she'd shot Farouk. Hopefully she'd calm down, lock the docking bay, and wait inside the ship. *But I can't worry about it now. Besides, she seems smarter than I was at her age.*

Up ahead, there was a flickering ring of light, and then the truck disappeared through it. Suzy gritted her teeth as she twisted the throttle and sailed under the blazing archway. Her eyes and ears were instantly filled by an explosion of color and sound. She was in downtown Baadal Shahar, where it looked like someone had merged a city with a circus.

The streets were jammed with hover-cars, and the sidewalks

were overflowing with people, and a canyon of glitzy hotel casinos stretched upward toward the artificial sky. The sky was set to display late evening, complete with a field of winking stars, but was it ever daylight here? This rowdy world looked like it was built for eternal night, and it was a night filled with light. Every sign, every billboard, every marquis was like an explosion of suns blasting Suzy's eyes.

As she squinted at the fiery display and zipped past the soaring buildings, she recalled that they were made from biodegradable plastic, lightweight yet strong—and they were colorful, too, molded in semi-translucent hues of amber, emerald, and gold. Then she darted under a shimmering silver walkway spanning the main street, connecting two of the towering hotels. Floating beneath the walkway was a bloated holographic image of a man's face, and he was screaming about something, but Suzy was too busy to care.

She came to an intersection that was a maze of signs and stoplights. The truck was heading under an overhead sign that said "UPTOWN" in six different languages. She zigged and zagged around a few vehicles but overall it was easy. If the driver was trying to avoid her, he wasn't showing it. He was driving through a storm of cars, but he was doing it in a normal fashion.

She kept him in sight, mainly by using a blend of determination, driving skill, and selective obedience to traffic laws. She recalled her days growing up, when she'd used a similar style bike to get in and out of trouble. Then the traffic came to a stop. Up ahead was a surging crowd of people and a dense wall of cops.

It was some kind of screaming protest and the main street was closed. The cops, dressed in black riot gear, looked grim and held hefty batons. There were thousands of people shouting and carrying signs, and they looked like a human dam about to burst. Then the truck swerved down a side street and Suzy followed.

She guessed the side streets usually had less traffic, but due to the protest they were packed. She hung back a bit and watched the truck crawl along. Hopefully, the crowds would start to dissipate. Something had to happen soon but it couldn't happen here—too many people, and no way to escape quickly.

Finally, the crowd started to thin, and the traffic started to dwindle, and the truck entered a quieter neighborhood. It wasn't exactly a desert, but the taller buildings were blinking in the distance now, and the sidewalks were empty, and the area was populated by colorful apartment buildings topped with mimosa trees and vegetable gardens. The apartments were pale pink, sky blue, and tangerine; there were scores of plants lining the sidewalks and growing all around the buildings. In some places, the buildings almost seemed incidental, tucked behind a chaotic jungle of foliage. Suzy noticed several pineapple palms, standing like leafy fountains, and for one sweet instant she recalled her home in sunny Diego Tijuana—but that was far away.

Her heart was pounding. With one twist of the throttle, she could zoom up beside the truck and shoot the driver through the window. Then she could ditch the bike, toss the guy onto the road and snatch the vehicle. She narrowed her eyes and took a deep breath. The truck was slowing down at a cross street, so it was now or never.

She gunned the engine. The bike lurched forward—and slammed to a halt.

What? Suzy stared at her hand, the one gripping the brake, and she shook her head like she was in a fog. Meanwhile, the truck drove past a few palm trees and went through the intersection.

Dammit! What's wrong with me?

But maybe she knew. Maybe she was remembering why she'd come here in the first place—to get away from this lifestyle. Of course, she'd killed the owner of this hover bike, and she'd promised Maria she'd deliver an arsenal of illegal weapons—and so the lifestyle was being a bit clingy, and it was possible she deserved no better kind of life. So maybe the problem was something else.

Maybe it just wasn't the right time. She'd always had good instincts about when to start shooting. She swore to herself and nudged the bike forward. Then the truck turned into a garage.

It was a plum-colored two-story building surrounded by coconut trees, with an open garage door on the lower level and a roof deck filled with more blooming trees and shrubs. The place was sandwiched between a grungy apartment complex and a tacky-looking orange storefront that advertised chiropractic services. Suzy saw a couple of people standing in front of the building, and as soon as the truck drove into the garage the door slammed shut.

Suzy cursed again and glided past, parking around the corner.

Now what? Before she could think about it, she checked her allcom and saw that Kiara had called. A tightness gripped her chest. As she returned the call, she ran across the street to a corner opposite the hideout, where there was a delicatessen crammed among some pink shrubbery. The place was called Slices of Life, and it had a dented silvery facade and wide, smudged windows. There were a few outdoor tables near the front door and two scraggy-looking people slumped against the nearby building, apparently asleep. She noticed more tables inside but saw no one eating the sandwiches and potato salad—and why was the allcom still ringing? Why wasn't Kiara picking up? She pressed the thing against her ear while keeping her eyes on the shadowy street. She breathed a sigh of relief as Kiara's voice came on the line.

"Suzy?"

"Kiara, are you okay?"

"Yeah, I'm fine," she said, sounding surprisingly calm. "Where are you?"

"I took a little ride downtown. Where are *you?*"

"I'm inside the ship. I locked the bay. A hover-bike came right after you left; I saw it on the cameras. There was a guy with a pistol, and he stopped for a second, and then he left. But he looked interested in what was going on."

"What about the dead guys?"

"They're still here."

"Right. I guess that makes sense. I'll be back soon. Keep the doors locked!"

Suzy disconnected the call, and then watched as a hover-bike came riding past. It stopped a bit down the street from the Snake hideout, and a guy slipped off. He had a pistol in his hand, and she watched as he hid behind some thorny-looking bushes. Had this guy followed her here? She hadn't noticed anyone, but she'd been very focused on what was in front of her. Then a long black hover-car came driving slowly past the deli.

There were several people inside, along with the silhouettes of a few hi-powered rifles. Suzy grimaced. These people weren't coming to get any coleslaw. This would probably be a good time for an innocent bystander to disappear, but of course that didn't include her.

The car parked right in front of the garage—and then they poured out fast, like commandos. There were four of them, dressed in black and holding assault rifles. They seemed to know exactly where they were going, two of them heading to the side door, and the other two racing through the shrubs and around the back of the building. There was a noise, like a door being blown down, and then the shooting started.

Suzy moved into the deli and ducked down just inside the doorway.

A thundering storm of shots rang out, followed by a couple of shouts and a scream. There was a brief silence and another loud salvo sounded, and another scream, and Suzy saw the blazing light of gunfire in an upstairs window. Then one of the guys in black came running across the sidewalk in front of the building. He was limping, and bleeding from a head wound, and yelling for help. He fell to the ground just as another guy came running around the corner. He took steady aim and shot the downed man in the back, splattering blood and body parts. And then the door to the garage swung open.

One of the commando guys was in the hover-truck—but now the guy on the sidewalk whirled and fired a shot through the driver's side window. With a splash of blood the guy in the truck yelped and slumped over. Then a shot came from somewhere else and the guy on the sidewalk went down, just as the truck lifted off the ground and moved partly out of the garage. But then the wounded guy inside the truck opened the door and his bloody body tumbled out.

The guy who'd fired was the guy hiding behind the bush. Suzy squinted her eyes; yeah, he must have tailed her here. He called out a few names and got no response.

Suzy gritted her teeth, aimed her pistol, and told that stupid voice in her head to shut up. Maybe this is all I deserve, she thought. *And maybe it's all I'm good at.* She fired once and he gasped, and his dead body hit the ground. Then she ran across the street, staying low.

How long until the cops showed up? And would they even bother? Crooked cops in city-states were even more common than crooked cops on Earth—and besides, even the good ones were busy downtown with the protest. She didn't know what they were protesting, but she hoped it wasn't violent crime.

She gave a quick look at the guy on the ground. He was dead now and no one else seemed to be alive. She jumped into the vehicle and grabbed the steering wheel. In a second, she roared around the corner and disappeared into the darkness.

Chapter 15

Danielle Banks liked her man on top. She knew Andre liked it, too.

Certainly, variety was a beautiful thing, but in the movies it seemed like a woman was often bouncing around on top. Maybe that position was more photogenic, but so what? No one was taking her picture.

They moved together perfectly, and it had always been that way. She remembered that first summer night when he'd hugged her, and then kissed her, and then watched as she'd stripped off her clothes and pulled him close; she recalled how they'd moved together like a beautiful machine. And after all these years it was still so sweet.

By the orange light of a candle, the king-size bed continued to rock gently. It was serene and rhythmic, like a calm, rolling ocean, before finally turning into a thundering deluge that washed over her like a pounding surf. Now there was one final moan from each of them, and then he stared into her eyes, and they kissed long and hard, and then he rolled off her. He made a joke about something, and she wasn't sure what it was, but she laughed anyway. Then she put her arm across his chest and they lay together in the shadows of their sprawling bedroom and listened to the breeze outside.

"So," he said, "did it feel any better, doing it with a Lieutenant Colonel in charge of all criminal investigations for the Northern Free States?"

"Oh, it was much better. I could feel all that new power."

He laughed. "I was never in it for the power."

"I know. It's something I always admired. Even when I thought you were crazy for not caring."

"I won't say I *never* cared. I won't say I didn't notice the times I was passed over for something I probably deserved. But right now, I can't complain."

"You never complained much, either."

"You're full of compliments tonight. We should do this more often—not that I'm complaining."

She laughed. "You better not be. I know how often my friends do it, and we're way ahead—not that I'm keeping score."

"You like to keep score."

"You know I do," she said.

"Fine, I've been scoring well lately."

"You sure scored tonight."

She laughed and kissed him again. "So, Lieutenant Colonel, what does this job really mean? Are you going to be working on some big, secret project?" Then she added, in a light tone, "Or are you still going to be chasing after Suzy Spitfire?"

Damn, why did I say that? Well, I'd like to know, and it's a good time to ask.

Andre gave a grunt. "It's funny you should mention her. I have to admit that sneaky idea you had to assign the commissioner's nephew to her case worked out real well. I'm sure it helped me get the promotion. But now I'm going to be involved with a big initiative to stop the flow of a new drug from Venus, and guess what? Supposedly, Los Pocos wants to get involved with distributing it—and by coincidence, Suzy went to Venus."

Danielle was quiet for a few seconds. Then she said, "Suzy's not a drug dealer."

"As far as I know. But she's involved with that organization, and on a high level. She was at the wedding of Pablo Juarez. She's a good friend of the bride, and she's been romantically linked to his brother-in-law. So I tend to think Suzy might be getting in deeper and deeper."

"That doesn't mean she's involved with drugs," Danielle said, trying not to sound agitated now. "Maybe she went to Venus for another reason."

"Like what? To work on her tan? No, she's part of that group, and narcotics are their main business, and she's a great pilot with a fast spaceship." He gave a soft laugh. "Would you like me to enroll you in detective school?"

"No," Danielle said with a frown. "But I thought she was likeable—I mean, you said she was, when you met her."

"Sure, I liked her. She's very likable when she's not shooting at you, or maybe transporting a few thousand kilos of veluva. But I'm a crime fighter, and she's a criminal. I know you like her idea of vigilante justice, but I think you should forget about Suzy. She's headed down a bad road, and you can't save a man from himself—or a woman, either."

In the darkness, Danielle felt her heart beating faster. *Maybe I should just come clean.*

But she didn't. Instead, she said, "So are you going to send a whole team to Venus?"

Andre laughed again. "Now you want to join the Strike Force? I can't talk about secret operations."

"I was just wondering," she said, trying to sound nonchalant.

"If you're really so concerned, I can tell you we have no authorization to send a team. Stone and his partner are going to have to do more than we intended." He got back on top of her and kissed her neck. "But really, stop wondering. We've got better things to do right now."

She forced herself to smile.

Chapter 16

Suzy only had one name to try in Baadal Shahar and that was Anika Anand. Danielle had given Anika strong words of praise, and Anika was supposedly expecting a visit from Suzy. Unfortunately, Anika wasn't expecting a pile of illegal weapons and a trail of dead bodies—but Suzy needed to hide these guns fast. Maybe next time she'd bring a box of chocolates.

Suzy always carried a couple of anti-tracking devices with her, and now she placed one on the dashboard of the truck. The thingamajig was about the size of a cracker, wafer thin, and totally against the law to own, but at this point in her life the legal status of any electronic doodad was trivial.

She put the truck on auto-drive and gave the voice-activated navigation system the address Danielle had supplied. She sat back as the vehicle headed to an area west of downtown, not far from the strip of glittery casinos, where the buildings weren't so tall and the sidewalks weren't so clean. The buildings here weren't made from plastic; they were made from locally grown bamboo and were surrounded by plants, just as she'd seen in the last neighborhood. She knew the plants provided oxygen to the city, and there was wild, bushy vegetation everywhere, lining the streets, growing in the yards, and sprouting from the rooftops. They were the plants of a temperate climate, and they had a certain appeal. Unfortunately, there were also raggedy people sleeping under palm trees and desperate-looking souls scrounging for scraps among the poppies. The truck stopped in front of a pock-marked bamboo building that looked like a warehouse with wide dirty windows.

The vehicle parked and Suzy exited, and then dropped her hand close to her pistol. A rowdy swarm of people was coming down the sidewalk, marching from the direction of the downtown. Many of them were carrying signs, chanting, and singing. Most of them were also drinking happily from cans and paper cups, and Suzy relaxed a bit. They looked like part of the group that had been at the street protest.

The signs were in different languages—Hindi, Spanish, Turkish, English, and a few others. All of them seemed to be talking about justice concerning some sort of atrocity. One of them said, "JUSTICE TODAY OR BUSO WILL PAY!" Buso was the current President of Venus, and these people were obviously not his fans. There were other signs that seemed to offer support for another pair of names, Marcos Reddy and Mert Kaya.

At the front of the group was a dignified-looking brown-skinned woman with a youthful face and waves of dark hair. She was average height, slender, and wore a blazing red dress, and people were buzzing around her, obviously wanting to be in her orbit. As the group came closer, one of them pointed to the truck and said, "Look, you've got a delivery. I hope it's something to eat."

A young girl with slightly lighter skin but equally dark hair said, "I hope it's a truck full of guns," and a few people laughed. The woman shook her head and said, "I hope it never comes to that, Sara. I think we've got food inside. Nuru ordered rice and samosas."

The girl smiled, and there was a collective cheer as people streamed into the battered building. The ancestral roots of the group seemed to span many of Earth's nations, from India, African Alliance, Euro, United Mexican Union, China, and the Northern Free States. They were still chanting and shouting. The woman in red broke from the group and approached Suzy, while a hulking bearded guy in a pinkish turban stayed by her side. He stared at Suzy with alert brown eyes but kept the rest of his face blank.

Meanwhile, the woman scanned Suzy from head to toe. "I'm guessing you're Suzy Spitfire," she said.

Suzy cocked an eyebrow. "Is it that obvious? I'm trying to be discreet."

"You don't look discreet."

Good point. Was it the light skin, coppery colored hair, and the black skirt and flight jacket? Everyone here wore bright colors and loose clothing.

"You're right," Suzy said. "But nothing my size was on sale. Are you Anika Anand?"

"Yes. Danielle told me you were coming, and I did some research."

"About Hunter?"

"No—about you." Anika smiled and then lowered her voice. "The Federal Strike Force on Earth is sending two special agents here to find you."

"What? How do you know?"

"Danielle told me. They're from her husband's group. But supposedly the agents are stupid."

"Thanks," Suzy said. "But stupid people can still fire guns."

Anika nodded. "Yeah, I've noticed that over the years. I'm glad you're here, Suzy, but this isn't the best place to talk. So, what's in the truck? Danielle didn't say you'd be making any deliveries."

Suzy paused. Why was Anika glad she was here? *Sure, I'm hilarious, but she hasn't even heard my best material.* She didn't want to lie to this woman about the truck, but sometimes the truth was a lousy option. Then again, she had a feeling this woman would smell a lie, especially since Suzy was a horrible liar.

Suzy leaned a bit closer to Anika. "The truck is filled with guns and grenades. Are you still glad to see me?"

For a moment, they locked eyes. Then Anika flashed a sly smile and said, "Maybe," and she waved to someone nearby, a handsome guy with dark skin and a short afro. He wasn't tall but seemed powerful, with broad shoulders and a neck like a fireplug.

"This is my husband, Nuru," Anika said. He gave Suzy a friendly nod. "Nuru, Suzy has a truck that needs hiding."

"And you think we should hide it?" he said. His voice was deep, like the bottom of a canyon. He had an accent Suzy couldn't identify.

"Yeah, I do. So please take care of her."

Nuru grunted. "What's in the truck? Some kind of trouble?"

Anika whispered into his ear. He raised his eyebrows as she spoke and then eyed Suzy with more interest. "All right, that might be good," he said. "But she still looks like trouble. Maybe it's the way she's dressed."

"No," Suzy said. "I was born this way. The clothes came later."

She smiled and changed the skirt to a shade of crimson—but the jacket was old-school and not adjustable, and she didn't change her hair. Nuru gave a wary glance and then motioned for Suzy to follow him as he headed toward the vehicle. As Suzy settled into the shotgun seat, he gunned the engine.

"I didn't mean to seem unfriendly," he said. "But we need to be careful. There are people who support our cause, and there are others who just want to profit from it. So when I meet someone new, I ask myself, 'Is this person good or bad?' "

"I've had some bad moments," Suzy said. "But I've done good things with them." Then she stared out the window and was quiet.

He glanced at her, like he was expecting her to say more. But she didn't. He hesitated, and then said, "Well, it might be good that you're here. So, how do you like our city?"

"Nice," she said, deciding not to mention all the fuckheads trying to kill her.

"Do you speak any languages besides English?"

"Spanish."

"Do you always talk so much?"

"Too much. Ask anyone."

Now Nuru laughed. "Spanish will be useful. A lot of recent immigrants here speak Spanish, and they're now about twenty percent of the population. Over fifty percent speak Hindi, and almost all of those people speak English; those were the predominant two languages when the city was built. We also have people who speak Mandarin, Swahili, Arabic, Turkish, and other languages. Anyway, Danielle gave you strong words of praise."

"Ha. Don't believe everything you hear, in any language."

"I don't," he said with a smirk.

Suzy shrugged. "I'm just here to find a certain scumbag."

"That's easy. Start with the president. We have problems here, but we're fixing them."

"Yeah, I see. But I'm not too interested in politics."

"This isn't about politics, it's about justice. Are you interested in that?"

"Depends who you ask."

"I'm asking you."

She paused. Maybe this wasn't the best time for a joke.

"Yeah," she said. "Sometimes I am."

"Okay. That's why my wife is glad to see you. And maybe I will be, too."

Suzy didn't respond. What the hell, she was happy they were helping her, assuming that's what they were doing. But what did Anika want in return? Suzy was here to catch a murdering rapist, not wave signs in the street. In fact, right now she was just looking to ditch this truck, get a sandwich, and call Kiara.

Their destination was a white building located just off the main drag, a compact collection of ornate pillars and lofty towers topped by bright turquoise domes. The structure looked like it was made of stone but Suzy guessed it was actually something synthetic and light-weight, like most things in a floating city. They circled around to a shadowy rear area where there was a high steel gate with pointy spikes on top. Nuru touched his allcom and the gate slid open, leading to a walled compound behind the main building, and a flat, paved drive-way surrounded by a few garages and smaller buildings. There were no plants in here. No bushes to hide behind, Suzy thought. Nuru touched another button and one of the garages opened like a yawning mouth. When he looked at her and smiled, his teeth seemed to glow.

Her hand stayed close to her weapon. She didn't know him, and she didn't know who could be waiting inside the garage. But there was nothing in the darkness, and no one else was around, and after they parked the vehicle Nuru handed her a key. Apparently, the key could be used as well as the allcom to open the garage door.

Perfect. She didn't like thumbprints or eye scans because that kind of information could be traced. Maybe this was why they didn't use a modern lock. These people were up to something more than shouting slogans. She opened the rear door of the truck and leaped inside.

"What are you doing?" Nuru said.

"I just want to grab a few souvenirs," she said. But that wasn't what she wanted to do.

One of the containers was cracked open. She pried off the lid and examined one of the pulse rifles—serious firepower here. Then she reached into her jacket and removed a miniscule tracking device; it easily attached to the underside of the gun barrel. Had Nuru seen her? It was dark in the truck and her back was turned. She grabbed a few grenades and jumped down to the ground.

Nuru nodded his head, seemingly oblivious. "I hope you don't have to use those," he said. "And don't worry about the truck. This place is well-guarded by good people. You won't see them but they're here, and your things will be safe. What you've got here will be in great demand."

"Why? I've been here a few hours and everybody has a gun. And it doesn't seem like a great thing in a city with a dome."

"Don't worry about it. The dome is self-healing; small arms fire isn't a threat. And only a small number of people have guns—the kind you tend to deal with, I suspect. Most people here are unarmed."

"I can see you've got a real high opinion of my social circle."

"I didn't mean it as an insult. I didn't say your friends were bad."

"Oh. Well, they're not good. I flew all the way from Earth to get away from them."

He laughed. "Do you need somewhere to stay? Your ship might not be the best place."

This was true. The *Correcaminos Rojo* had a sophisticated security system, but it was a vulnerable location because the Snake Eyes knew about it. They could be waiting to ambush her whenever she arrived or left. It might be best to lock it up and stay somewhere else.

Nuru motioned toward one of the other nearby buildings. "You can stay here. We have a nice apartment that we keep available for special visitors. Do you need to get anything from your ship? We can help you, Suzy."

Sure, Suzy thought, *but at what price?* "No thanks, Nuru. I appreciate your help but I can handle it." She paused and then said, "Do you have a car I can borrow?"

"A car? I might... I'll go with you."

"I want to go alone."

He cocked his head. "You don't trust me, do you?"

Actually, she *was* trusting him, but there could be more trouble and she didn't want him getting killed. Also, there were a couple of dead bodies she didn't want him to see. Dead people are terrible at making good first impressions.

"No, it's not like that," she said with a smile. "I just need a little time before I let a guy see my spaceship."

"I see." He was quiet for a second and then touched his allcom. Another one of the garages opened to reveal a sleek and silvery hover-car. "Here's your car, Suzy Spitfire. Call me if you want the apartment and I'll meet you there."

They exchanged some information and Suzy was on her way.

She put another anti-tracking device on the dashboard of the car. Then as the car rode through the city, she settled back in her seat. It felt great to sink into the soft cushions and relax for a second. Was her adrenaline finally running dry? Her eyelids started to close—but then she jerked herself awake, slapping her face a few times. Get a grip, she thought. *I can sleep when I'm dead, or maybe when everyone else is.* She took manual control of the car and slowed her approach as she neared the bay. Now she was wide awake again, looking around with fast eyes as the car slipped into the loading zone beside the double steel doors.

Grim ideas flashed in her brain. She'd talked to Kiara not long ago and the girl had seemed fine, but a lot could've happened since then. She saw no other vehicles, but an assassin could still be lurking inside the bay. And what if Jack had regained consciousness and returned? She tried not to go crazy pondering all the negative possibilities.

She pushed the code to open the doors. As they slowly slid open, she crouched down and pulled out her weapon, straining her ears—listening.

No sound. She gave a quick peek around the corner.

Where was the dead body she'd left on the deck? He should've been lying right there with the back of his head blown off, but he was gone and there wasn't even a drop of blood. On a positive note, she also didn't see anyone waiting to ambush her—and the bay was all open space, with the *Correcaminos Rojo* just sitting there and nowhere for anyone to hide.

Her thoughts were shattered by the buzz of her allcom. She frowned and yanked it out—Kiara's number. Her heart pounded as she answered it.

"Hello," she said.

"Suzy, what are you doing?"

Suzy paused. "What do you mean? I'm coming back to the ship."

"Yeah, I know. I'm watching you on the monitors. But why are you trying to sneak up on me?"

"I'm not sneaking up on you. I'm just being careful."

"Oh. Well, there's no one here but us."

"Where's the guy I left on the ground?"

"I took care of him. Farouk, too."

"What?"

"I took care of the dead guys, and I made you an omelet. Come on in."

Suzy eyed the large disposal unit in a corner of the bay. Sure, a couple of bodies could be disintegrated in there, and there was a robot loader in the cargo hold that could've been helpful. But she was shocked Kiara had done it, and a chill went down her spine. She closed the steel doors and watched as the gangway to the ship descended. Then Suzy headed into the ship with the gun still in her hand. But everything was fine.

Kiara had breakfast laid out on the cherry red table in the lounge: omelets, refried beans, and tomatoes on the side. It smelled good.

"Why did you do that?" Suzy said.

"Because I thought you'd be hungry."

"I mean why did you get rid of those bodies?"

"Oh. I wanted to help."

Suzy wasn't sure what to say. Her mind was swirling; she couldn't picture Kiara doing it. She wondered what else Kiara had done over the last few years. Well, there was no point in making her feel bad. But now Suzy was grim.

This is what happens when someone hangs around with me. They learn body disposal.

Suzy sighed and forced herself to smile. "Thanks," she said, and then sat down. Breakfast looked good. Maybe she'd eat something. Maybe.

Chapter 17

The police cruiser was docked and Burt Stone was smiling. Now came the good stuff, the part where he stormed this punk-filled party town and bagged a dangerous desperado, thus redeeming himself in the eyes of Banks, his family, and the police force in general.

Of course, first he had to convince Tala they would need to carry illegal guns. He looked at his reflection in the cockpit window and shuddered. *Why am I sweating?* He stared at the Series 7 pulse pistol in his hand, one of three he'd smuggled past the city security force.

The city had refused their official requests to carry firearms. In fact, they'd refused to even recognize their status as police officers, so technically they were private citizens, or maybe special undercover agents, or possibly just tourists—whatever. He hated reading documents.

Either way, he needed the guns. He had to have a gun and so did she, and he had three of them right here, lying on a table in a glorious display. He touched the linkchip on his collar and said, "Tala, are you ready to disembark? Meet me at the airlock."

"Yes, sir," she said in her typically pleasant voice.

As he marched to the airlock, he debated different ways to convince her to break this local law, because what was the big deal? Every criminal broke this law. Well, maybe not every criminal, because guns were supposedly hard to come by in Baadal Shahar—but certainly Suzy was breaking it, and that was exactly why they needed to break it, too.

That's the ticket, he thought. Tala loved to read boring files and forms, and he knew it was in Suzy's file—he specifically recalled seeing it there—that Suzy Castillo *always* carried a Series 7 pulse pistol. Plus, Tala had already mentioned this herself, so this was a good way to go. Then he frowned and clenched his fists.

What was he thinking? He was the commanding officer! He wasn't going to convince her of anything. He would *order* her to carry a gun. *Be a man, dammit!* Like Dad and Uncle John and all the other cops in the family.

Now she was walking into the room. She smiled—and then she saw the guns.

Her smile vanished. "Why do you have those weapons, sir?"

He swallowed hard and spoke in his deepest voice. "Officer, we need to carry these because—"

"I won't carry a gun, sir. It's against the law here."

"What?"

"It's against the law, and we can't break the local laws. I will not carry a gun. Furthermore, we're now in violation of the laws for smuggling an illegal firearm into the city."

"What?" he sputtered again—and now his voice was sounding feeble. "No, I don't think so."

"We're in the city, sir. The ship is docked. We are now breaking the law and we can be arrested. They can charge us under a general smuggling statute, as well as a law specific to firearms. These guns are jeopardizing our entire mission. At the very least, someone could revoke our visas and send us home."

"Home?" he blurted. "I can't go home." His head started spinning, imagining the humiliation of facing his family after such complete and utter failure. All his plans were slipping away, but what could he do? She was a smart cop who'd scored *so high* on those damned tests—and she was probably right.

She crossed her arms and shook her head. "I'm afraid we need to get rid of these weapons, sir. You can put them in the disposal unit and disintegrate them." Then her almond eyes softened a bit, and she spoke in a soothing voice, like he was a child. "We don't need a gun to catch her, sir. We just need to find her and then call on local law enforcement for assistance. They're aware of her status as a fugitive. I submitted the proper form."

"The proper form?"

"Yes. We might be able to capture her without incident, but if not we'll have help from the locals. That's the procedure, sir, and we have to follow it."

In the back of his mind, he heard a desperate wail. He hesitated, and then finally heard himself say, "I suppose I can work with you on this issue, officer. I suppose…" His voice trailed off.

"That sounds great, sir. The information we got from Lt. Col. Banks looks promising—did you see he was promoted? Anyway, we can start by finding Anika Anand... I'll meet you outside. I'm sure you'll do the right thing." She gave a sharp salute and walked through the airlock.

He hung his head. What had gone wrong? As he considered the situation, a slow rage began to boil in his gut. Suddenly, he was snarling and looking for something to smash—but the main thing he wanted to smash was himself.

He took the guns into the engine room and started the incinerator. He stared at the fiery opening while his hands shook. Then he dropped one of the guns into the chute and pressed a button. There was a fizzing sound as it was destroyed. He did the same with the second gun but looked away as he hit the button, like he couldn't watch.

He picked up the third and final gun and felt his heart pounding. He grimaced and started to drop it into the incinerator, but he stopped. This was his official weapon, the one issued to him by the Strike Force. It was the one he'd shown his father on the day he'd received it. It was a moment that had made Dad proud.

What the hell am I doing? In his mind he saw his uncle and his father. Real cops. Real men.

Tala was a smart officer. She was smarter than he was, no doubt— and she'd probably report him if he used an illegal weapon. *But I gotta be me, dumb as I am.* Besides, he'd rather get into trouble than be shot down like an unarmed fool against a known killer. In his mind, he heard the echo of his father's advice: *"Better to be judged by twelve than carried by six."*

Damn right, Dad. He gritted his teeth and felt like a weight had been lifted from his heart.

He shoved the gun into a waistband holster specially designed to conceal the weapon. Then he smirked with satisfaction at his reflection in the polished metal of the machinery. While wearing a shirt and jacket the gun was virtually invisible. No one would ever see it—except for Suzy Spitfire, when he pulled it out and shot her.

He took a deep breath and hurried out of the airlock. Tala was waiting, and he didn't want to make her mad.

Chapter 18

Once again Suzy had nowhere to go, but she also had no intention of staying in Nuru's sugar shack. It was one thing to trust Danielle's friends with a truck full of Pablo's guns, but it was a whole other bag of boulders to trust them with her life, and Kiara's.

Suzy checked into the Happiness Hotel on the main drag. She would've preferred something smaller and more discreet but there was no such place in this city. Luckily, the hotels of Baadal Shahar didn't cooperate with off-world law enforcement. She wasn't wanted here, and all the AI recognition software wouldn't flag her. Of course, she still changed her hair to black, registered with a phony name, and used a fake retina lens—and she gave no mention of Kiara at all.

Kiara smiled as they walked into the living room of their two-room suite. "Nice," she said. "But how come you don't want to stay with the people you met?"

"I don't know them that well," Suzy said. She was standing over the sink in a small kitchenette, removing the fake lens from her eye. It was sophisticated, expensive, and had been a gift from Ricardo—but what the hell, she'd never been that into diamonds. "If anyone asks where we are, don't tell them."

"So you don't trust them."

"Maybe, maybe not—but either way, I'm thinking these Snake Eyes could have members in Anika's gang. Of course, they could have members here in the hotel. Hopefully, your friend Jack isn't a bellhop."

Instantly, Suzy regretted mentioning Kiara's ex-dirtbag. But Kiara took it well.

"He's grabbed my bags for the last time," Kiara said. Then she shuddered. "Do you think he's going to come looking for me? I hope not."

"I hope not, too." *Because then I'll have to kill him.*

Suzy walked into the large bedroom, a room with a stunning view of the bustling street fifty floors below. Kiara followed and said, "Why were you coming to this city, anyway?"

"I'm looking for a serial killer named Shogun Hunter. I'm going to bring him back to Earth."

"Really? That's so great. Can I help? What can I do?"

Suzy sighed. "Kiara, the best thing you can do is get away from me."

"What?"

Suzy flopped down onto one of the two double beds in the room. "There's something I need to tell you. I'm not that great."

"What are you talking about?" Kiara said, sitting down on the other bed. "You've been great to me. You've helped me a lot. You're a real friend."

Suzy laughed—she didn't mean to, but she did. Then she quickly said, "I'm sorry, honey. I'm not laughing at you. But you hardly know me, and that's a good thing."

"You're the best person I've ever met."

Now Suzy rolled her eyes. "I'm a fugitive, Kiara, and I'm up to my neck in bullshit. I've got the Snake people after me, and probably another gang of thugs, and also a couple of Strike Force agents from Earth, and I've only been here a few hours. I've always been in trouble, my whole life, and you should make some plans to get the hell away from me."

"I'm not going anywhere," Kiara said with a frown. "Don't you like me?"

"Yeah, I like you. I like you a lot."

"Then why do you want me to go?"

"It's hard to explain," Suzy said, and she hesitated. "Maybe because I might not be able to keep you safe."

"Oh. Well, maybe you could teach me to be more like you."

Suzy laughed again. "Did you hear anything I just said?"

"I'm serious."

"And so am I, Kiara. I'm not a good influence. In fact, I've already done you more harm than good. I got you involved in a couple of shootings, and you've even disposed of two bodies, right? I feel bad enough as it is, and I don't want to get you into more trouble."

Kiara narrowed her eyes. "I'm not that innocent, Suzy. I've done some really fucked up stuff, and if I was tough like you I'd be better off. Believe me."

"I'm not that tough, and it didn't help anyway. Not when it really mattered."

Suzy took a deep breath, and then she was quiet. Kiara was quiet, too, for almost a full minute. Finally, Kiara said, "I only know what I've heard, Suzy, but what happened to your sister—it wasn't your fault. People who do those things, they're good at making their victims hide it, and they're good at making other people not believe it. Maybe you couldn't have…kept her safe."

Suzy's mind was spinning. Why was Kiara talking about this? She didn't want to talk about it. She rolled onto her side and jammed a pillow over her head.

"I need to sleep, Kiara. You should try and sleep, too."

She was hoping Kiara would listen. But instead, she sensed the girl standing beside her, just staring. Finally, Kiara spoke.

"I'm sorry, Suzy. I didn't mean to upset you. But you *are* my friend, like it or not."

She heard Kiara drop back down onto the other bed. Just before she fell asleep, Suzy heard Kiara whisper, "I'm staying right here."

Chapter 19

What time was it?

Suzy sat up quick on the bed and squinted at the simulated sunlight bursting through the windows. Her eyes scanned the room and saw Kiara sitting in a chair facing the door. In one hand she held a candy bar, and in the other hand she held a pistol. But there didn't seem to be anything dangerous happening.

"Hi, Kiara," she said. "Was there a gunfight while I was asleep?"

Kiara laughed. "No, but you would've slept right through it. You were *really* sleeping… Hey, someone blew up a casino across town. It looks bad."

Flashing on the wall was a news story about a bomb that had blown up inside the Diaun Casino. Blood and bodies were everywhere and crystal chips were scattered like confetti. It was being blamed on the Snake Eyes.

"Where did you get the gun?"

"This is Jack's gun," Kiara said. "But don't worry. If someone came charging in here, my plan was to scream and hope you woke up."

Suzy wasn't sure how she felt about Kiara and the gun. On the one hand, she didn't like her having it. On the other hand, who was she to disarm the girl? It would be a red-hot kind of hypocrisy. Then she looked at the screen again, filled with raging images of death.

Okay, she can keep the gun.

Kiara took a bite of her candy bar. "I read all about Shogun Hunter," she said. "He's a scary guy. We need to be careful."

"We?"

"Yeah, me and you. Some people think he might've killed thirty girls." Then Kiara paused and said, "They were all street girls. I guess he figured no one would miss them."

Suzy already knew this because she'd studied Hunter's profile. The one girl who'd escaped said he'd chained her to a basement floor and raped her repeatedly over a period of three days. He'd tortured her with a variety of nasty tools and told her repeatedly how he planned to hang her and watch her die. Yeah, he was a real bastard whose capture was worthy of excessive force. But she didn't want Kiara to be there at the time.

"Did you eat anything besides the candy bar?" Suzy said.

"No, I found it in the little refrigerator. I haven't left the room. It's nice in here. Nicer than it is outside."

"Right. I'm going to take a shower and then we'll go get something."

The steaming hot water felt great. As it washed over her skin, Suzy found her mind drifting away from a world of bombs and brutal killers. She was thinking about Ricardo. Yeah, she missed him, and not just because he was good with a bar of soap. She'd gotten used to his touch, and to his jokes and bad poetry—but mainly, she'd gotten used to having him around, even though she didn't need him. Or did she? She'd certainly gotten used to not being alone, and now that no one was shooting at her for a few minutes she realized how much she'd like to see him.

But I might never see him again, she thought. And for a second, her heart filled with a cold emptiness. She blinked back a tear and let the water blast her eyes. She had other things to worry about, at least for today. For instance, why were there never any avocados in the little refrigerator? Why was it always a bunch of fucking candy bars? And why hadn't Ricardo told her she was more important than *anything?*

She switched the shower from "water" to "air" and blew herself dry. Then her allcom rang.

For an instant, her heart leaped—maybe Ricardo had chased her to Baadal Shahar! But the incoming number was unidentified. She let it ring and waited for a message, but there was none, and it was disappointing. Who had called? Almost no one had her number. Maybe it was time to get a new allcom.

"Okay, Kiara, let's get something to eat. Leave the gun here."

"Why?"

"Because you're not going to shoot anyone at breakfast."

Kiara started to protest, but then she saw Suzy's stare and reluctantly put the weapon in a drawer. Down in the hotel restaurant, Kiara said, "There are lots of junkies in this city. I noticed them before, too."

Suzy and Kiara were sitting in a booth by a window, eating vegetable stir fry and looking at the people outside. There were two scruffy-looking people sitting on the ground nearby, and two more slumped against the building, and a few others lying in some purple wisteria bushes. Apparently, the drug made them sleepy, and for a brief second it looked appealing. But it's not my thing, Suzy thought, and she remembered a lecture from her old friend Akio about not doing drugs, and how she'd actually listened to him. Except for all the booze.

A holo screen in the restaurant showed a man talking, and it was the same face she'd seen under the silver walkway when she'd first driven into the city. Apparently, his name was Buso, and he was the President of Baadal Shahar. He was a good-looking guy of mixed ethnicities, and he was raving about enemies, hope, and freedom. Suzy figured this was a good time to go shopping. Sure, some people were talking about the violence downtown, but others still needed to mix and match.

Bright colors and loose clothing ruled in this city, and while Suzy could adjust the color of her outfit accordingly, it still wasn't in style with the street. So she bought herself a loose-fitting skirt and a shirt made from a popular smart fabric, and she turned it into a nice shade of scarlet. Suzy liked skirts and the way they concealed her weaponry in an easy-to-reach style. Her main concern was that the bottom hem was the proper length to grab her pistol but she didn't mention this to the salespeople.

Meanwhile, Suzy bought Kiara a few outfits that were also color changeable. Kiara left the store in a pair of black pants and a cheerful violet top. She also got a couple of skirts similar to Suzy's. Maybe too similar, Suzy thought. Suzy also picked up a new pair of boots because they looked sharp and the price was right. Plus, they were perfect for concealing her boot-knife.

"Do you always carry a knife?" Kiara asked.

"Kiara, you don't need a knife."

"I don't want one. But I guess sometimes you have to use it, right? Have you been in lots of knife fights?"

Suzy sighed. They were standing on the busy sidewalk now, outside the store, and Kiara was staring at her with those big brown eyes. She looks so much like Trish, Suzy thought.

"Kiara, no one has been in lots of knife fights. That's all bullshit."

"Why?"

"Because you pull it out, and you stab someone—and they're dead. That's a knife fight."

Kiara hesitated. "Yeah, okay," she said. "So it's something you don't really think about, right? Is that what you've done?"

"Don't worry about me," Suzy said. "But you do what you have to do." Did Suzy's voice have more swagger than she'd intended? Kiara seemed happy with her answer, and Suzy quickly added, "Now let's go find Anika and Nuru."

Nuru had asked her to call first, but she'd decided to skip the call. Sometimes it was good to surprise people. She parked the silver hover-car down the street from Anika's headquarters and walked with Kiara toward the building. And then she saw Ricardo.

What? Her heart skipped a beat.

He was walking out of Anika's place, along with a guy she didn't recognize. He was about 40 meters away, but she would know that profile anywhere. Her breathing stopped, and so did her feet. In a flash, she grabbed Kiara and pulled her into a doorway.

"Shhh!" she said. Then she peered out, looking down the city street.

He was walking in the opposite direction and hadn't seen them.

"Who's there?" Kiara whispered. "Was that Ricardo?"

Suzy said nothing.

"You don't want to see him?" Kiara said. "Maybe he's looking for you."

"Me or my guns, though I guess they're his guns." But why hadn't Maria mentioned he was coming? Maybe he'd mentioned it himself in one of those messages she hadn't listened to. She watched him get into a lime green hover car and drive off in the direction of downtown. Then there was deafening silence.

Finally, Kiara said, "He likes you."

"Maybe."

"Why did you leave him?"

"Because he likes his gangster friends more."

"No—I don't think so. I saw the way he looked at you back at the house. He's not here because of guns or gangsters. He's here because of you."

Suzy wanted to disagree and say something snotty about Ricardo and *the organization*, but she didn't. She couldn't deny her feelings. She was elated he was here.

"Come on," Suzy said. "Let's see what Anika and her husband have to say."

At first glance, the faded brown exterior of Anika's bamboo building looked worse in the daytime than it had in the evening. But a closer look showed the dilapidation was superficial, and the building was stately and solid, and the double front doors were wide open, so Suzy and Kiara walked inside. Above the door was a large hand-carved sign that said, "The Citizen Collective of Baadal Shahar."

They found themselves standing in a spacious room that reminded Suzy of a high school gymnasium. There was a lectern at the far end and a bunch of red folding tables scattered around. Banners splashed with hand-painted slogans hung from the walls and high ceiling. They were written in different languages, but English and Spanish were two of them and Suzy noticed several references to a "drug free zone," a *zona libre de drogas*. There was also a huge picture of a guy with a shaved head. He had light brown skin and blue eyes, and a caption in English below his name said "REDDY IS READY!" There were other pictures of him, often standing beside another guy named MERT KAYA. Mert also had light brown skin but dark eyes, a black beard, and a full head of matching hair. Both guys looked youthful and photogenic. Apparently, Kaya was Reddy's lieutenant—but he also had his own caption, and it said KAYA CARES.

Suzy almost laughed. They looked like a couple of guys sincerely trying to look sincere. She had a flashback to her days at school, when they'd held pep rallies that she'd always skipped by sneaking out a side door. Then she'd walked to the beach, laughing and looking for a good time. Now she scanned the room, searching for the exits, and she laughed to herself in a grim way. *After all these years I'm still looking for that side door.*

There were a few people sitting around, but not too many. Most of them were either reading or tapping on digital devices. Then Suzy noticed the giant guy in the pink turban, standing there like a stern-looking tree. But he spotted Suzy and smiled.

"Ah, someone Anika actually wants to see," he said.

Suzy cocked her head. "Do you get a lot of people in here she doesn't want to see?"

The guy paused, like he was regretting his words. Then he said, "All good people are welcome here, and she's been expecting you." He smiled again. "This way, both of you."

Suzy wasn't sure what to make of the guy or his comment, but did it involve Ricardo? Suzy and Kiara followed the guy through the big room, down a short hallway with a low ceiling, and then down another hallway toward a closed wooden door. As they approached, Suzy heard two voices arguing.

The arguing stopped as their companion knocked on the door. It swung open, revealing a cramped room mostly filled by a sprawling table covered by a paper map of the city. The map was decorated by pins and multi-colored plastic markers, like some kind of ancient board game. There were also two people standing there, Anika and Nuru.

Anika turned away from Nuru's frowning face and smiled as Suzy and Kiara entered. Anika motioned toward Suzy's new clothes and said, "Hello, Suzy, I'm glad you're here. Very pretty outfit. You'll blend in much better now. And who is this?"

"This is Kiara," Suzy said. "She's travelling with me."

"I'm her assistant," Kiara said. She stood up straight as she said it. Anika studied Kiara a bit and then nodded her head.

"Thanks for hiding my stuff," Suzy said. "I appreciate your help."

"It's no problem. We appreciate you being here."

"That's nice, but I haven't been here long. Anyway, I don't want to wear out my welcome. I was hoping you could point me to Shogun Hunter."

Anika and Nuru looked at each other. Nuru shrugged and said, "That's what she's here for, isn't it?"

Anika just laughed. "You're not wearing out your welcome," she said. "We love having guests—but you get right to the point, don't you? Danielle told me you were like that. But she didn't tell me you'd have a supply of weapons with you."

"That was an accident."

"An accident?"

"Yeah. Kind of like slipping on a banana peel, only with weapons."

"I see. I'll tell you what I know, but it might not help much."

"Danielle said you saw him hanging around Baadal Shahar."

"Long ago. And I know someone who works at one of the surgery swaps downtown, and Hunter was there, too. But he didn't use their services. Apparently, he went somewhere else."

"So you have no idea where he is?"

Anika once again glanced at her husband, who seemed to be deliberately staring at the wall. Then she said, "It was three years ago, and we lost the trail… I'll be happy to help you, but I'd like to talk to you about some other things, too. And I'd love to show you more of what we're doing."

"Sure," Suzy said, putting a lid on her impatience. After all, they'd helped her with the truck and offered her a hideout, so the least she could do was listen. Maybe she'd get some news about Ricardo.

Anika led everyone back into the hallway. She started talking while Nuru was quiet, like his mind was underwater. She was talking about something political. Apparently, the government and the casinos were involved with distributing drugs, especially an addictive one called veluva. Meanwhile, Suzy was busy thinking about the security and surveillance in the building. Was there *any* kind of security in here at all? She was scanning the rooms as they walked and saw mostly small offices and cut-rate furniture. She noted the lack of windows, other than the two big ones in the front. There were two exit doors that probably led to the alley outside.

Most of the offices were draped in banners and slogans. One banner said, "Take A Drug To Stop A Drug" and showed a smiling young woman with a syringe in her hand. Anika saw Kiara staring at that one and said, "It's known that the government puts a low dose of veluva into the air supply, so watch yourselves. The drug promotes a general good mood and causes people to spend more money in the casinos. Do you feel it?"

"A good mood?" Suzy said. "No, not really."

"The government denies it, but we've had people inside the air-handling facility, and we know it's equipped to do this. It's one more thing that needs to be stopped. Luckily, we've got an antidote that will make you instantly immune. You might want to take it." Suzy just grunted at the idea of shooting herself up with some alien potion. *Maybe if I find myself suddenly feeling euphoric.* Then in a tiny room they found a good-looking boy sitting behind a bamboo desk. He had dark hair and eyes.

"This is our son, Nirav," Anika said. "He's fifteen, and he helps here. So does my daughter, but she's in school today. Nirav stayed home to do a good deed."

"It's all done," Nirav said. "The doctor said she'll be fine."

Anika smiled. "He was helping an eight-year-old girl with no parents or family. He's a good kid."

Nirav looked at Kiara and said, "Hi. Do you need some help?"

For an instant, Kiara looked annoyed. But then she seemed to reconsider and said, "No. I'm okay."

"What's your name?"

"Kiara, and I don't need any help. That's not why I'm here. But I guess that's what you do." And she nodded toward a wall filled with photos of women, young girls, and some boys, under a heading that said, WE'RE HERE TO HELP.

"Yeah," Nirav said with a grin. "Let me know if you need anything."

Suzy noticed Kiara studying the pictures. "Who are they?" Kiara said.

"They're volunteers, people who work here," Anika said. "They help victims of sex trafficking, a huge problem in this city. We provide financial help when we can—but mainly mental help, because that's what they need most. Underage sex workers are the reason many 'tourists' come here, and it's one of the things we want to end. For me, it's a major issue."

"Oh," Kiara said, and for a second she seemed lost in a distant place. Then she added, "What kind of mental help?"

"It depends on the individual," Anika said. "Most of them have suffered severe emotional and physical trauma. But in time, and with therapy, they can recover."

Kiara didn't say anything more, and Suzy put her arm around her. Then they left the room and headed into a hallway. Nirav gave Kiara a wave of his hand and a big smile, and she gave a small wave in return.

Anika opened the door to another office and motioned for them to enter. This room was also cramped and filled with pictures and signs bearing slogans. Suzy noticed a small desktop photo of Anika's family.

"Who's doing the trafficking?" Suzy said.

"The Casino Cartel," Anika said. "Buso is in power, but he's propped up by the casinos. And the casinos make a lot of money from the drugs and prostitution. You might think that in our enlightened times of virtual reality and sex-robots, prostitution would disappear. But it hasn't, not at all. The victims are mostly young girls, although twenty percent are boys, and almost all of them are brought here from other worlds. Many are strays and runaways with nowhere to go, lured with lies, then enslaved—physically, emotionally, and now chemically. It's one of the things we've been organizing protests against, and there's been some violence—and there will be more, I'm sure. But mainly, it's this drug veluva that's been attracting attention from the media. There are people who want to help us, but they're the wrong people. They're people like the Snake Eyes, people dedicated to a bad cause."

"Yeah," Suzy said. "I've met them. We had a few…conversations."

"Right," Anika said. "They're a criminal cult that's fighting the cartel for control of the veluva. That's probably why that casino was blown up last night; a bunch of Snake Eyes were killed a few hours earlier at one of their hangouts, so now they've retaliated, and on and on. The Snake Eyes are good at keeping the identity of their members secret, but we see the damage they do every day."

Suzy had no comment concerning the attack on the Snake Eyes the other night because she'd been there, but now she knew it had been carried out by this cartel. She also knew that the cartel people had all been killed. In fact, she recalled killing the last one herself. But she didn't mention this.

Instead, she said, "Why would the Snake Eyes approach you?"

"Because we have all the people," Anika said with some pride. "All the people who work at the casinos, all the people who run the shops and businesses, all the people who just live here and who have no real power are with us. We're trying to bring about peaceful change, but it keeps getting harder."

Now Nuru spoke up. "We have the numbers, but we don't have the muscle. And that's why we need some help. Like that guy who was just here."

"That guy is just another drug dealer," Anika snapped. "And his poetry was terrible."

"He seemed smart, and he has lots of friends. We should take him to meet Marcos."

"No, Nuru. There are some things we can't compromise. Besides, it would make Marcos look bad to be associated with someone like that."

"Who are we talking about?" Suzy said. But she had a pretty good idea.

Anika frowned. "A guy from Earth, part of a big organization based in the United Mexican Union. They're into all kinds of crime, including drugs. This guy was friendly, but I don't trust him. He says they can help us get rid of the government and put our person in charge, but it will come with a price—mainly, all the same stuff will continue, only a different group will be calling the shots. Well, we can do better than that… We need the help of someone a little more pure." Anika paused and stared into Suzy's eyes. "I was hoping you might be interested."

"What?" Suzy said. And she laughed out loud.

"Danielle says great things about you."

"She said I was 'pure'?"

Anika smiled. "No—but she said you were a good person, and strong. Besides, we don't want someone who is *completely* pure."

"That's good, because my angel wings are a little beat-up."

"We'll do it!" Kiara said.

Suzy looked at Kiara and laughed again. "No, we won't. It's not why we're here."

"Suzy, they need our help."

"Kiara, what they need is complicated."

"But I want to help. I want to do this."

"What they want is going to involve lots of violence. Do you want that?"

Kiara hesitated. "No," she said. "But that doesn't mean I can't help."

Anika said, "We're peaceful people but we want to protect ourselves from the cartel's thugs. They've attacked some of our people and you could help us. You could train us, right? You have all those weapons, and you know how to use them."

"I'm just one person," Suzy said.

"Exactly," Nuru said, looking at Anika. "What can one person do?"

"She can help, Nuru. One person can make a big difference."

Suzy shrugged. "One person can get killed pretty fast. I've always been lucky."

"We could use a little more luck," Anika said. "Our last protest got lots of attention. We're afraid they're going to do something serious, and it's going to happen soon."

Suzy was about to ask, "How soon?" when she heard the shots and the screams.

A barrage of gunfire was ripping through the building.

"Get down!" Suzy said, pushing Kiara to the ground. Nuru said, "Nirav! Nirav!" and Nirav came running into the room with a confused look on his face.

"Get down!" Suzy said again.

She whipped out her pistol, sliding the power selector into a solid kill range. Then she crouched down low, peering into the hall as more shots and screams rang out. *Damn!*

The sounds were coming from two adjacent hallways, one to the right and one to the left. There's more than one shooter, Suzy thought, and in her mind she imagined the attackers—like the group she'd seen that had killed the Snake Eyes. She pictured them storming into the main room, blasting away and then splitting up—and in a few seconds they'd be charging down these hallways. But at the end of the hallway to the right was a heavy exit door.

"Let's go!" Suzy said, stepping into the hallway just as a guy rounded the corner. His weapon was up and ready—but she was an instant quicker and shot him in the chest. Then she spun around and looked back down the hall just as Kiara came racing out of the room. Another guy appeared, rounding the far corner, and he fired right at the girl—but she stumbled and fell, and the shot whooshed past Suzy's neck and exploded against a doorframe. Suzy returned fire and hit him in the head; his brains splattered against the wall.

Suzy lunged forward and pulled Kiara to her feet. "Are you all right?" she said. Kiara looked dazed, but she nodded, and Suzy yanked her toward the exit. "Come on!" she shouted, just as Anika, Nuru, and Nirav stumbled out into the hall. Suzy crashed through the door and into an alley outside. Crap, not a great place to fight. She moved fast down the alley toward the street in front of the building, motioning for Kiara and the others to stay behind her.

Suzy stopped and listened. There was lots of shouting but no more shots. Suzy peeked around the corner where people stood screaming and crying. There were five or six dead people lying on the sidewalk, including the big guy in the pink turban. There was also a car out front with someone inside, shouting into an allcom. Then a guy with a gun came running out of the building, heading for the vehicle. He dove for the open door just as Suzy stepped onto the sidewalk.

She shot him in the back, and he gasped as he collided with the car and fell to the ground. Then the vehicle lurched forward and Suzy unleashed a salvo. The shots shattered the car windows as it started to move. She kept firing, hitting it with every shot. The vehicle burst into flames, screeching and swerving as it plowed into a fruit stand and then crashed to a stop.

A pile of oranges rolled across the sidewalk. Suzy walked through the scattered fruit toward the broken vehicle. The door opened, and a burnt-looking guy staggered out. He was holding a pistol but it slipped from his hand and clattered to the ground.

In the back of her head, Suzy heard a voice telling her she didn't need to kill this guy. But she was furious. He was part of a crew that had just killed a bunch of people, and they'd wanted to kill a bunch more. So she pointed her weapon at his ear and pulled the trigger. His head burst into pieces, but not before she'd gotten a look at him. He was dressed like the people from the death squad the other night, probably part of the Casino Cartel.

Kiara was standing next to Suzy now. She looked shocked, but she seemed okay.

Suzy grimaced, remembering a time not so long ago when Kiara had been more shocked. *That was before she got to know me*, Suzy thought. She felt a pang of guilt in her hollow stomach.

"Who are they?" Kiara said.

Suzy was about to answer when she heard a buzzing sound and saw that her allcom was ringing again. It was that same number.

"A bunch of guys who ran out of luck," Suzy said. She noticed the caller was leaving a message. "Come on, Kiara, let's get out of here."

Chapter 20

Burt Stone hated this rental car. *We should be in a real police car,* he thought. *And I should be driving it manually.* These self-driving hover-cars were like well-behaved turtles.

He was fidgeting in the passenger side while Tala stared at data on her allcom. Meanwhile, the car was creeping through the traffic in downtown Baadal Shahar, obeying every moronic traffic law it could find.

"Can't this thing go any faster?" he snapped.

His anger was real, but he tinged it with a little extra testosterone. She shook her head. "We have to stay at the posted speed limit, sir."

"We can't override it?"

"Of course not. That would be illegal."

"But there's a shootout going on!"

"The shootout is over, sir, and we have no authority on this world. And the last thing we want to do is violate the terms of our visas."

Visas? They had visas? Whatever. They were almost there and that was good. But why had the neighborhood changed from glittery plastic to bamboo? And what was with all the plants? They'd barely gotten themselves situated in this sham of a city when Tala had seen the news stream about a shootout at the exact address they wanted to visit. So now there was big-time buzz about a death squad that had attacked the headquarters of a popular rabble rouser, and a mysterious woman in red who'd shot and killed them all.

But she's not mysterious to me, Burt thought. *A redhead with great shooting skills, and a definite gift for violence—that's my girl.* But of course, Tala said they'd have to get the facts and not jump to conclusions, and she was probably right. He had to not be a dumb-ass and blow it! And he had to get ready for a fight.

The street was closed off so they had to park down the block and run. *Crap!* Burt loved weight-lifting, but cardio wasn't his thing. So he struggled a bit to keep up with Tala, who looked sleek, fast, and pretty as she ran right past him—*ugh!*

He was huffing and puffing by the time they got there but he tried hard to hide it. He doubled over for a second and turned away. *Maybe she won't notice my face is redder than a forest fire—crap!* Meanwhile, the crime scene was a chaotic collection of ambulances, flashing lights, gawkers, police, and general hysteria. No one seemed to be in charge. This annoyed Tala but didn't really bother Burt. He did his best work when no one was watching.

Tala was talking to a couple of cops, telling them something about her special status, and how she and Burt were searching for a dangerous fugitive. The cops looked disinterested and spoke to each other in Hindi before answering her in English. Now Tala was trying to show them some kind of document on her allcom—good, while they were busy looking at that bullshit he was slipping past the yellow tape and walking into the building.

Well, well, a big room and a bunch of dead people. There were also some live people standing around, staring and sobbing. The banners high on the walls were written in a few different languages, and they were burned and destroyed. Whoever had shot the people in here had deliberately blasted the slogans, along with a lot of other incidental stuff in the room. Someone was sending a message.

And what the hell? The ambulance crews were still outside and there were no cops in here at all. Come to think of it, there weren't that many cops out there, considering the magnitude of the massacre. Either the local police force was terrible, or they were being paid to not give a shit. Burt laughed to himself, guessing it was a little of both.

A solid-looking black guy with a neck like a fireplug entered from a hallway, and a couple of nearby people rushed toward him. Obviously, he was someone important. Burt pretended to be looking at his allcom as he slid a little closer, trying to listen.

An old woman collapsed into the black guy's arms, and he tried to comfort her. A casual-looking white guy who was with her said, "Where's Anika, Nuru?"

The black guy said, "She's not here. She's safe."

Burt recognized Nuru's accent as Earth-African, probably from Mandela City.

"Good!" the lady said. "You should get out of here, too."

"I'll be fine."

"What happened? It was a hit squad, right? Who shot them?"

Nuru glanced in Burt's direction. "We don't know," he said. "A stranger."

Bullshit, Burt thought, and someone was bound to have a surveillance clip. He decided it was time to make a move. He walked toward the group and whipped out his badge.

"Burt Stone, Special Investigations," he said.

It wasn't a Baadal Shahar badge, but he figured no one would look at it too closely. It was all about the attitude.

"That's not a Baadal Shahar badge," Nuru said. "And you're not a police officer."

Burt hesitated. "What are you talking about? I'm a special investigator."

"You don't look like a law officer, and I don't know anything."

Now Burt was offended. Of course he looked like a law officer! He totally looked like a cop. It's one of the reasons he'd always been so lousy at undercover work.

He flashed a sardonic smile. "Hey, I'm from Earth, okay? I'm not interested in your piss-pot local politics. I'm just looking for this person—have you seen her?"

He showed a picture of Suzy Spitfire. All three of them flashed a sour look and shook their heads.

"But the description on the news feed exactly matches her!"

No one said a word. Then Nuru said, "There are dead people in this room. Why don't you take your pompous attitude and your piss-pot badge and get out of here?"

What? Burt was furious. He clenched his teeth and lunged at the guy—but the guy was quick, and he knew a few things, and then Burt was flying through the air head over heels. Whoah! He let out a shout as he hit the ground.

He shook his head and laughed. *Big mistake, pal!* He snarled and started to get up—but then the guy was on top of him, and fists were flying, and they were making loud splatting noises as they hit Burt in the face. *What the fuck?* Burt tried to roll the guy off but he couldn't, and blood was streaming from his nose, and then he couldn't breath—some kind of choke hold—ugh! He kicked his legs and flailed his arms but it was useless. He was suffocating! It was over! Fuck! He heard some shouts and screams as everything faded to black.

He opened his eyes. Where was he? He was in the same place, coughing and gagging on his stomach. There were more people around now, including some new cops who hadn't been outside earlier. And Tala was standing there too, staring at his humiliation.

His head spun, and he felt a warm flush of shame, and for an instant he wished the guy had killed him. But where was the guy? He was no longer in the room. Then one of the new cops kicked him in the stomach. Two more pulled him to his to his feet, and that's when his gun fell to the floor.

Oh, shit.

The cops stared at the weapon for an instant, and then they started pounding him hard. People in the room were shouting again. Tala was screaming and trying to show them another document on her allcom. Then another cop came in and yelled something and the beating stopped.

The cop picked up the gun and stared at Burt, who was still being held in place by the two huge cops. He was bruised and bloody.

The cop was big and angry. He leaned close to Burt's swollen face and said, "Who do you think you are, coming in here and pretending to be one of us? And you're carrying a *gun?* You brought an illegal gun onto our world? I could throw you in prison right now and you wouldn't see daylight for ten years."

Burt was quiet. His dad, his uncle, what would they say? He'd totally blown it. *And Tala thinks I'm the world's biggest loser.* Outwardly, he just stared, trying to look tough—but inside, he almost felt like crying.

Then the cop grinned. "Lucky for you that your friend has some real information about the shooter, including her name and DNA profile. Don't worry, we'll track her down. And in exchange for that cooperation, I'm going to give you a break. Now get the fuck out of here. And if I catch you again with a gun you'll be shot."

He motioned with his head to the two big cops and they dragged Burt outside and tossed him into the street.

Chapter 21

Suzy was driving slowly, trying not to attract attention. Of course, it was a little late for that—as usual. Was anyone following them? No one obvious. Not yet.

Meanwhile, Kiara was staring out the window. She seemed fairly calm. She said, "Do you think Anika and Nuru are okay?"

"Yeah, I think they're fine."

"I hope so. Their son seemed like a nice guy."

"Yeah, he did. I think he liked you."

"He doesn't know me, and he wouldn't want to. The stuff I've done."

"He doesn't need to know everything you've done, and don't talk like that. He might not care, and you should meet some new people. Especially since I might be leaving soon."

Kiara's calm vanished. "What?" she screeched. "You mean leave Venus? We just got here!"

"Yeah, and I just killed a bunch of people. That's usually a good time to leave a floating city. But you might be able to stay, and that might be good. It depends on whether or not anyone's connected us."

Suzy's voice trailed off, and she swore to herself, thinking how she'd poisoned this girl's life.

"I'm not staying here without you," Kiara said. "And you can't leave, Suzy. You're panicking."

"What? No, I'm thinking."

"They haven't identified you. Besides, you were just defending the place. You're a hero."

Suzy gave a grim laugh. "I'm pretty sure lots of people won't see it that way."

"The best people will."

"The best people are never in charge." And she had a flashback to another time, not so long ago, when an act of justice had been seen as nothing but a murder.

"But you have friends here—Anika, Nuru. They can help."

"I don't think so, Kiara. They seem likeable enough, but they've got enough trouble just keeping themselves alive."

"What about the guy you're looking for? Shogun Hunter?"

Suzy frowned. Yeah, that's true, she thought. Then Kiara shouted, "Look out! A cop!"

The car was coming toward them in the opposite lane. Suzy ducked down low, almost under the dash. This would've been fine if the car was on auto-drive, but it wasn't. Kiara yelped as her hand shot out and grabbed the wheel. Meanwhile, Suzy kept the vehicle's speed steady with her foot. Somehow they kept the car on track.

"They're gone," Kiara said.

Suzy sighed and sat up. "That one is, but what about unmarked cars? What about surveillance cameras? I'm sure the whole city has eyes… I'm surprised they haven't spotted us. Sure, I want to get Shogun but it's going to be hard. We need some help."

"How about Ricardo?"

Suzy hesitated. Yeah, how about him? She stared at her allcom where someone had left a message. Keeping one eye on the street, she hit the play button—and her heart jumped as Ricardo's voice filled the car. He sounded jovial, but of course he probably didn't know what was going on yet. She couldn't deny how good it felt to hear his voice.

"Hey, guess what Suzy? It's me, and I might be just around the corner. I know you're still mad at me, and I don't blame you, and that's why I want to buy you something. How about a pony? I think you better call and talk me out of it, unless you really want to feed a horse every day. Call me—*please.*"

She was tempted to play it again, but didn't. Then her allcom buzzed. It was him, and she picked it right up.

"Ricardo, I'm in trouble."

"Where are you?" he said, all business now.

"I'm driving around, but I'm a little low on friends."

"Don't worry, honey—you've got one. Is anyone following you?"

"Not yet, but they're combing the city. I need a hideout. I'm not sure I can get back to the ship."

"No! Don't go there. Set the car on auto-drive. Set the address for 447 K Street, and come around to the back." Then he paused and said, "Try not to shoot anyone on the way."

"Don't worry about it. I'm saving my best shot for you."

"That's what I like to hear."

She disconnected the call and set the address. Kiara said, "Suzy, get in the back seat and stay down."

"But they're looking for you, too, Kiara." It hurt to say it but she needed to know.

"Yeah, I know. But there are lots of girls who look like me in this city—but not a lot of Suzy Spitfires."

Well, this was true. The population was diverse but not in a light-skinned, redheaded kind of way. Suzy briefly cursed her mother's genetic makeup and climbed into the back, and then she started calculating. She'd read that fifteen percent of the population was light-skinned, so .15 multiplied by 5,000,000 would be 750,000, and roughly half of those would be women, so 375,000, and maybe two percent of those would be natural redheads, so about 7,500. As she figured out the numbers, she thought about her father, that crazy scientist who'd always been too busy calculating to bother with his family—and she smiled. She'd had some issues with the man, but now after a few years and millions of miles, she missed him.

Suzy pulled out her allcom and changed her hair to black. Kiara watched and said, "I have the replacements." Now Suzy watched as Kiara turned into a redhead with a bob, and then a blonde with a crew-cut, and then a long-haired brunette again—all in under a minute.

That's wild, Suzy thought. Kiara had surgical replacements for the individual follicles that allowed the length of every hair to be altered instantly. By using a Thought Chip implanted in her head, she could easily change her hairstyle to a variety of presets, as well as change the color. The fake follicles were exactly like real hair, too—right down to split ends and tangles.

"I just have the dye," Suzy said. "If they shoot me, I'll go down with my real hair. Also, I didn't want the chip. But hey, aren't you a little young for total replacement?"

Kiara shrugged. "It was a gift, and I used it a lot. I can never get my real hair back, so I mostly leave it like this—how I looked when it was real. I don't care about offering *variety* anymore."

Suzy hesitated, and then decided it wasn't the best time for more questions. "Your hair looks good the way it is," she said.

"Thanks," Kiara said, and then changed the subject. "So…how did you learn to shoot like that? You never miss. You're amazing."

"I miss," Suzy said. "But not too often. I had a game when I was little, and I played it all the time. Plus, I shot all the neighbors—just kidding. I still have a target game, full 3-D holo action, in the lounge on the ship. It's great for stress."

"Really? Can I try it? I think…something like that might help me."

Suzy was slow to answer. "We'll see," she said. Then she decided to focus on the immediate situation.

The address Ricardo had given them was a laundromat just outside of the gaudy downtown. Suzy really noticed the veluva epidemic here—the empty grins, the comatose stares, and people sleeping in bushes and doorways. Kiara kept the car on auto-drive as it slid down a narrow street that was more like an alley before it opened up into a grungy courtyard surrounded by palm trees and a high wall. There was room to park a few vehicles, and there was a back door to the building. Suzy kept her pistol ready as she exited the car and yanked the door open.

She peered into an office that held a desk, a sofa, and lots of junk. There were empty bottles, cartons of take-out food, and heaps of clothing strewn around. There was another door that apparently led into the rest of the building, and then it opened—and there was Ricardo.

He stopped and grinned. Suzy stared at him for a second and

then lowered her weapon. For an instant, none of their arguments mattered. He'd filled her ship with guns, he'd decided to stay with his gang of criminals, and he'd hurt her feelings—and it all washed away like a tidal wave blasting sand from a beach. Nothing could change what she felt, an electric surge of happiness that he was here.

Did he feel the same way? In a flash he was hugging her hard, wrapping her in his arms like an octopus.

He whispered into her ear. "Suzy, I'm so glad to see you. I'm so glad."

"I'm glad to see you, too, Ricardo. What took you so long?"

"It wasn't that long—it just seemed that way. Also, you didn't answer my messages."

"Yeah, that's true. I was mad about something."

"Really?" He was kissing her neck while his hands slipped down her body. "What was it?"

She laughed. "You were acting like an asshole."

"That's right, I was—and I'm sorry. Can you forgive me?"

She pulled back from him and looked into his eyes. "I'm getting there."

Ricardo smiled and then noticed Kiara for the first time. "Hey, what's up?" he said.

"Nothing," Kiara said. "Maybe I'll go do some laundry." Then she gave Suzy a little smile and slipped through the door that led into the main building. It clicked shut behind her.

Ricardo didn't say a word. He kissed Suzy again and they tumbled down onto the sofa. Ricardo stripped off his shirt and pants while she slipped off her skirt. Then she pulled him close and everything faded into a blur. Somewhere nearby, there was the muffled sound of washing machines pounding away.

Chapter 22

Mert Kaya took a sip of beer and studied the two people sitting with him in the dingy booth. They were in the "Eye Cave," a secret pub in a basement level of the city. Only a handful of people knew about the place, accessed through the back room of a warehouse owned by Mert. Were these two guys worthy?

To his left was Elijah, with dark skin, a short afro, and sharp eyes. He was dressed casually in a loose-fitting tan shirt, but he was still stylish, and he was always useful—a police captain who was working against the police. He was a man of few words and even fewer mistakes, and he was definitely worthy.

Sitting across from them both was Jack Ray. Mert vaguely wondered if his own beard made him look anything like this scruffy-looking young sociopath. No, of course not, because his beard was short and well-groomed, just like his coiffed head of dark hair. Meanwhile, Jack looked drunk and disheveled. Well, he was really just a kid, which was good and bad. But his worthiness was questionable.

Kaya spoke in his typically calm voice, though his words were meant to instigate. It was a technique he enjoyed. "So, Jack, are you ready to redeem yourself?"

Jack gave a sarcastic laugh. Even in the dim lighting of the bodega, Jack's face looked swollen from the effect of a recent stun shot. He'd also just had a bone repair done on a hand fracture, but neither of these things had dulled his nasty attitude. His bruised lips contorted into an ugly purple smirk.

"What are you talking about?" Jack said, banging his beer bottle down on the table of the rancid booth. "You're the guys who fucked everything up."

"Are we? You were coming in with a ship full of guns and two hostages—a couple of girls. And you let them take control."

"Is that so?" Jack snapped. "Listen, one of those girls was a real nasty bitch, okay? And famous for it, too. I'll admit, she tricked me—but when she got here, what happened? She killed Farouk, so that was the number one fuck up, right? Plus, one of the city security guys that *you* paid off was playing for the cartel, too, and he tipped them off, and they tailed the truck and raided our place and *killed everybody*—and then they took the guns. All that was your fault, too, so quit busting my balls." Then he puffed out his chest a bit and said, "But don't worry about Suzy. She'll turn up, and I'll take care of her."

He pulled out a dagger and placed it on the table.

Elijah glanced at Kaya, then addressed Jack. "Not necessary, friend."

"Right," Kaya said. "Don't worry about her. We'll deal with her eventually. Right now we've got other things for you to do."

"Oh, yeah? Like what?"

"Like help with the bigger plan. And the bigger plan involves keeping Suzy alive."

"What?"

"We're guessing Suzy Spitfire is here with Los Pocos to protect Anika and Nuru from the government. The Mexicans want to get a foothold in Baadal Shahar… In fact, it's possible Suzy just saved Anika from an assassination attempt. And that's good, because Marcos and I want to take control of the city, right? And Anika's group is helping us do that. They trust me. Obviously, Marcos and Anika don't *know* I'm a brother of the Snake. Do you see?"

Jack hesitated, like a man trying to think, while Kaya studied his eyes. Was this beer-soaked simpleton smart enough to understand?

Jack nodded his head slowly. "All right, I guess. But what about the guns? And when do we deal with her?"

"Elijah is looking for the guns. The cartel has them for now, but we'll find them, and we'll pay them back for what they did, and I'm not just talking about blowing up a casino."

"Right," Elijah said. "We'll find those guns and exterminate every one of those bastards."

Mert nodded. "As for Suzy, we'll deal with her when the revolution is over, after Anika's crew helps us come to power. But first, watch this video of the cartel's assassination attempt. We've been doing a great job destroying the government's surveillance devices—over half the city is blind to them now—but Elijah was nice enough to obtain this from a local business. So, is this her?"

He held up a small screen and Jack watched the explosive ending sequence of the shootout in front of the Citizen Collective. He gave a grunt of admiration as a woman dressed in red slaughtered the final assassin.

"Yeah, that's her," he said. "Can't really see her face but that's her hair, and definitely her ass—good-looking woman, I can't deny. Besides, I know the girl standing next to her."

"Do you? Who is she? Someone else to worry about?"

"Hell, no!" Jack's eyes opened wide and then flashed a fiery glare. "We don't do nothing to Kiara, you hear me? You touch that girl and I'll cut your fucking heart out."

Kaya's eyebrows went up, surprised by the passion in Jack's voice. He waved his hand and said, "I'm sorry, I didn't realize you had a connection. So, who is she? Can she help us?"

"No, she can't help us!" Jack spat. "She's just a girl who had some bad luck. I helped her out some, and she helped me, too, and then things kind of fell apart—my fault, okay? But either way, she's not getting involved. No one touches her."

Elijah laughed. "Jack's in love. Same girl as last year?"

"Same one," Jack said, and he seemed proud of it.

"Fine," Kaya said. "It doesn't matter to me." And it didn't. But Jack still wasn't satisfied.

"It better fucking matter!" he said. "Do you hear me? I said *nobody* touches her."

Now Kaya just stared. "All right," he finally said. "No one touches her."

Elijah grinned and Jack said, "Good. Glad we got that settled."

Then he froze the image on the small screen so it showed the girl, and he put it on the table where he could see it. He smirked and said, "You want to keep Suzy alive, but what happens if she won't go for your revolution? She didn't seem too interested in revolutionizing anything I could see."

"Then we'll change the plan," Kaya said with a shrug. "But either way, she knows you, and it's important she never sees us together. So we need to be discreet." Then he leaned forward a bit and said, "Farouk and his crew were important to our operation. He was our point person for serious business and now he's gone. I'm talking about the V factory, over in The Bowl. And I was hoping you could step up and fill his shoes."

Jack paused, and he glanced back and forth at Mert and Elijah. Then a big smile uncurled across his battered face. "Hey, why didn't you say so straight out? Be happy to help with the V."

"Good," Mert said with a nod. Then he gave a little smile and reached into his jacket, pulling out an injector. "Take this shot."

"What?"

Mert nodded at the device. "It's loaded with the veluva antidote. I know most of the brothers and sisters are using, and in time it's going to stop. But right now we don't want a new point person who's a junkie—like Farouk was. Maybe if he hadn't been high all the time he'd be alive right now."

"I ain't no junkie," Jack said. "I'm a natural guy." Then he scowled and took another gulp of his beer.

"I know. But take the shot, Jack." Mert leaned toward him a bit. "Do it."

Jack hesitated. Then he flashed an indignant smile before picking up the injector and pressing it against his arm. There was a low beeping sound and it was done.

"Happy now?" Jack said. "I'm a loyal brother."

"I know," Mert said with a satisfied smile. Then he motioned toward Elijah. "I wanted Elijah to be here because you'll be working with him a lot. I understand you two know each other pretty well."

"Hell, yeah," Elijah said. "We go back. We knew each other in Atlanta."

"That's right," Jack said with a nod. "He got me in, what—five years ago? Hell, I was about twelve." Then he gave Mert a sideways glance and added, "We've put in our time."

"True," Mert said, and he decided not to acknowledge the subtle inference that maybe he hadn't. Instead, he said, "Elijah has done a wonderful job of infiltrating the police and helping us get more recruits. So he can supply you with good information. But you've got to keep all this stuff secret. Wait for my instructions and keep your mouth shut."

"I can do that."

Could he? Kaya had some doubts, but the curse of being a leader was always needing help from some idiot. Hopefully, Jack could do what was necessary; hopefully, his youth and lack of intelligence were balanced by his obvious mean streak. Of course, Kaya didn't tell them everything. There were some things no one would ever know—like his real identity.

The surgery swaps in downtown Baadal Shahar were famous for being able to give someone any face they wanted. But sometimes it wasn't enough to disappear and then reappear as someone new with a phony past that wouldn't hold up to scrutiny. No, he'd wanted to be more clever than that; he'd wanted to become another person who already existed, complete with a traceable history.

He'd chosen his target carefully. The real Mert Kaya had been a quiet man, a person with no family, a guy who'd come to Baadal Shahar as a teenager over fifteen years ago. He'd come with his mother, but no father. She'd had a little money, and she'd opened a souvenir shop and then died a few years later. Over the next fifteen years or so, the kid had become a man who'd made a decent living while keeping mostly to himself. And so the real Kaya had been carefully vetted and killed, his body disintegrated in an industrial disposal unit.

With the help of facial surgery, hair transplants, skin tone adjustment, vocal cord matching, and other more subtle details, Shogun Hunter had become Mert Kaya—a man who was not wanted by the Federal Strike Force on Earth for multiple murders, and a man who was not wanted by Los Pocos for swindling them in a phony drug deal. He'd gotten involved with the Snake Eyes and within three years had become the leader of the group following the assassination of a few members at the hands of the Casino Cartel.

His eyes fell on Jack's dagger, still lying on the table, and his mind became dizzy with scenes from his brutal crimes. It had been too long, way too long since he'd let the monster inside of him loose. Just thinking about it, he could barely contain his excitement. *I have to be careful. I can't get caught again!*

He glanced at the picture of Suzy and the skinny girl standing next to her. His heart started pounding. Suzy was sexy, but the girl was just his type. He fantasized about meeting her. He thought about what he'd do to her. He shuddered and once again tried to stay calm.

Chapter 23

How long had they been going at it? Time had slipped away during all the thrashing and moaning. For the first time, Suzy noticed a screen on the wall, broadcasting the news with the sound off. Everything seemed quiet and relaxed, and she felt like a drifting cloud after a hurricane. But now came the part she didn't want—the discussion. On the upside, she was sure Ricardo didn't want that part, either.

Well, he was going to get it, but it would be short. So where the hell was he? He'd disappeared, leaving her alone in the back room of this sleazy laundromat, sprawled naked on a creaky old sofa. Supposedly, the place was owned by a friend. Typical.

The door opened and Ricardo walked in. He was wearing khaki pants, no shirt, and his normal grin. Why was he grinning? He knew he looked good, rippling with muscle—but no pretty boy pectorals here. It was a harder look splashed with a few scars. Hey, it was what she liked.

She stood up and started collecting her clothes, knowing he was watching her. She couldn't deny another twinge of excitement. There was a crooked mirror on the wall, and she caught the image of her one and only tattoo, spanning her shoulder blades like a pair of wings. It said NO REMORSE. Yeah, it was still there.

She slipped on her clothes and said, "Where's Kiara?"

"She's upstairs. She's fine, don't worry about her."

"Okay, well, let's forget all the bullshit, Ricardo, and get to the point. I don't care about the guns you put on my ship. It was an asshole thing to do, but I can get past it. But I can't get past the way you won't leave the organization for me, because you said you would, and I want out of the life. I want to do something better, and if you can't go along with me then I'm gone." She paused to collect her emotions a bit. Finally, she said, "That's all I've got to say."

He hesitated. What was he thinking? It was hard to guess. He sat down on the couch and sighed.

"I hear you, Suzy. But do you want to do something better *with me?* Because I'm going to get out—I just need more time. I keep telling you this, but you're so impatient."

Impatient? Really? Okay, maybe a little. Suzy plopped down beside him, and he put his arm around her, and she knew what was coming—a piece of bad poetry. He was going to try and make her laugh, but it wasn't going to happen.

He smiled. "Without you in my day I would wither away, like a pumpkin without any bread."

She laughed—it had been much worse than expected. "A pumpkin without any bread? What the hell are you talking about?"

"Hey, I just go with whatever pops into my mind. It's the muse, honey."

"We were just rolling around naked for half an hour and your mind is in a pumpkin patch? Why do I stay with you?"

"Because I'm a red-hot lover. And it was 40 minutes."

"Sorry. I guess that extra ten minutes gets you a trophy, huh?"

"Every time."

She laughed again. "Well, you *are* good." Then she frowned. "But it's not enough, Ricardo."

"I'll get out, okay? I'll do it after we do this thing for Maria. Her plan is good."

"Maria's smart, but her plan is crazy, and I don't want to live here, anyway."

"Suzy, you can't have everything. You have a past, honey. In fact, some of it happened this morning."

She started to respond and stopped. What was he trying to say? That her plan to escape the lifestyle of a murderous fugitive wasn't supposed to involve multiple shootouts and a pile of dead bodies? Yeah, that was probably it.

"Okay," she said, speaking slowly. "I'll admit my own plan hasn't been going too well."

"Suzy, you've been shooting up the place since you got here."

"Well, yeah. I've had a few setbacks."

"You killed half the population."

"Why do I stay with you?"

"We just covered that, honey. And by the way, how come you never wear the body armor I gave you?"

"I didn't know I was going to be in a gunfight, Ricardo. How come *you* never wear it?"

"I'm too quick for them," he said with a smile. "I'll be fine."

"You won't feel that way when I shoot you."

"Maybe not," he said with a laugh. "But don't do it today. I want you to introduce me to Anika and Nuru."

"What? Why? Didn't you already meet them?"

"Yeah, but I need a new introduction. What did they say about me?"

"They said you were working for a bunch of thugs who want to take over the city so they can sell drugs."

"What, that's it? Nothing about my poetry?"

"Ricardo, how wrong are they?"

He shifted around a bit on the sofa. "Suzy, that's *Pablo's* plan. Maria has a different idea, and she's just telling Pablo what he wants to hear so he'll go along." He took her hand and looked into her eyes. "We could live here together and no one could touch us. We could be safe here, me and you."

She stared back at him for a long moment. She wanted to believe it but then shook her head. "Do you really think that's going to happen?"

"Yeah, I do. If we help make it happen. I'm sure they're grateful you saved them from those assassins. You're totally badass." He paused and gave a shrug. "More than I'll ever be... So I'm thinking if you vouch for me, I'll be in—hey, look!"

He pointed to the wall screen that was displaying images of Suzy shooting the assassins in the street. Suzy winced at the sight. The sound was off, but captions across the bottom referred to her as "a mysterious hero who saved many."

Suzy turned away from the screen. "I'm not a hero, Ricardo. And I'm thinking if I vouch for you they'll stop trusting me."

"No way. You saved them, and they owe you. And hey, why were you even there?"

"They supposedly had some information I needed. I'm doing this bounty hunter thing for Danielle, remember?"

"No. You never told me why she wanted you to come here. You just slept with me and then snuck off on your flying saucer."

"I'm looking for a predator who rapes and kills teenage girls. His name is Shogun Hunter."

"What?" His eyes got wide. He hesitated for an instant, and then said, "I'll help you find him!"

"Oh, yeah? That's nice of you. But why do I need your help?"

"Because every cop in the city is looking for you, and no one is looking for me."

She paused. Well, that was a good point. And he was holding her hand again.

"Suzy, how about this? I'll help you find this guy, and you tell Anika and Nuru that I'm not so bad. You don't have to sell them on the organization because I'll do that. Hey, they probably know you're involved with us anyway, right? If they don't, someone is bound to tell them sooner or later, and the surprise won't look good, will it? Just vouch for me and I'll do the rest. We'll be an unbeatable team!"

Suzy rubbed her temples. That great relaxed feeling in her mind had morphed into a sledgehammer. I'm going to regret this, she thought. Meanwhile, the wall screen was now showing Buso, and he was talking about enemies, freedom, and families. In fact, he was shouting about it.

"All right," Suzy said. "I'll tell them a few good things about you— maybe *one* thing—and that's it. And I'll give you a little time to help them out. But I'm only going to wait so long, Ricardo. I mean it."

He laughed and gave her a kiss.

"You're the best, Suzy."

She kissed him back, but lightly. Then she stood up and said, "I better go check on Kiara."

Ricardo rolled his eyes. "Kiara is fine, Suzy. I told you, she's upstairs. And I'm right here."

Suzy paused. Then she said, "I want to check on her, okay?" She reached down and pinched his cheek. "I'll be back. Hang in there, little man."

"I didn't mean it like that!" he blurted. "And I'm not little."

Suzy smiled and shook her head. Then her allcom rang; it was Nuru calling. She stared at Ricardo and picked it up.

Chapter 24

Maria watched the morning sky above San Migeul de Allende and shouted into a link chip on her collar. "Hurry up! We don't have much time!" Then she swore and headed toward the landing field.

This is the life I chose.

The Federal Strike Force hover-ships were coming in low, firing their guns at anything that moved. It'll be hard to evade them, she thought, *assuming we even get off the ground.*

Suddenly a roar filled her ears as a salvo of shots came blasting up from the dusty ground, joined by more flashes of light from the nearby pine-covered mountain. One of the hover ships burst into flames. But the others were landing, and within seconds of touching down, troops in black battle gear were rushing out like an army of ants.

She was sprinting now, with her long hair flying as she headed for the camouflaged hanger. She never should've been out here, really—but how could she have known the warning would come with so little time? Well, she'd been in tight spots before, and everyone has to die sometime.

Her mind flashed with images of death she'd seen as a child—dead friends, her murdered parents—and people killed in revenge. No regrets, she thought. She gritted her teeth and kept running across the dusty soil, trying not to trip. She wasn't going to die today. No, today was not going to be her day.

Pablo was coming through the door to meet her. He embraced her in a hug, but it was quick, and then they were running up the gangway and into the ship. There was a lot of shouting and a frantic fumbling of seat belts, and then an explosion shook the deck, and she was pressed down into her seat as the ship was hurtling toward the sky.

It was a fast ship, faster than those SF hovercraft. But were interceptors waiting for them? Maybe. Would they be blown to bits? It was possible.

She heard Pablo yelling from the cockpit. For a second, she thought of her brother—where was Ricardo now? Had he found Suzy, her dear friend? Too bad she wasn't here, flying this ship. But it was good that they were both far away, hopefully someplace safe.

The ship shuddered a few times, and her fingers dug into the armrests of her chair. She heard the crackling of talk on a radio, and some shouts, and heard another explosion somewhere outside. The acceleration was squashing her now, pressing her deeper into the seat. She closed her eyes and waited. It was all she could do. And then the ride got smoother.

It was quiet, and Pablo appeared in the doorway with a grin on his face.

"We're safe," he said. "We're too fast for them."

Maria felt a ripple of relief, and then she was angry. "Safe for now, but where are we going? Somewhere far away, I hope."

Pablo shook his head and sat down in the seat beside her. "We're not going anywhere," he said. "This is all part of the new Federal plan, some kind of joint effort between the Northern Free States and the UMU. But it won't work. We went into orbit and now we're coming back down. We're going to land in Lagos."

"Lagos? So we're going to Africa? You don't think they can find us there?"

"We'll be safe there. We've got friends in the right places."

"We had friends in Mexico, a lot more than we've got in Lagos."

"Yeah, but things have changed. They've got a new commander we can't buy off, your friend Andre Banks. So we'll have to deal with him another way."

"He's not my friend. I've never met him."

"When he let Suzy and Ricardo go free, you were there, too. So he's your friend."

"He's not my friend," Maria insisted. "But what are you going to do? Kill a Federal Strike Force officer? Suzy likes him, and she'll be furious."

"She'll get over it. We need to send a message."

"She won't get over it, Pablo. She might even blame me, and I don't want that. This is a terrible idea."

"Terrible for him, but great for us. Listen, don't worry about it."

"Don't tell me what to worry about! We need to go to Venus. We should be helping Ricardo and Suzy to make that city ours."

He laughed. "Maria, I'm sorry for all this trouble but we're not going to Venus. And we'll make Baadal Shahar ours, like you said, but we're not going to live there because that city is shit."

She looked into his smiling eyes and felt only rage—and regret. But she swallowed it all and said nothing. It was the best way to deal with him, at least for now. She rolled her head back in the seat and took a deep breath.

"All right, Pablo, we'll go to Africa."

He nodded with approval. "Good. When we get there I'll buy you something nice."

He patted her hand and walked away, and her heart was filled with fury—and sadness. She wanted to scream but didn't. How could I have been so stupid? she thought. *Men like him never change.*

Chapter 25

"Did you always want to be a pilot?" Kiara said.

Suzy didn't answer right away. She was busy scanning the bushes and trees that lined the shadowy street. She was also looking at addresses, and looking for Ricardo, who'd left them temporarily to go organize things with his crew from Earth.

"No," Suzy said. "When I was thirteen I was racing hover bikes, and getting into trouble, and that's all I wanted to do—and my mom wasn't too happy about it. My dad wasn't, either, when he bothered to check in. But my grandmother was a pilot, and she had a ship, and she showed me a few things. So I went to flight school, and I had a great time. Of course, Mom and Dad hated that, too. They wanted me to learn something more scholarly, but I mainly learned I didn't want to be a scholar. Look, here's Ricardo."

He was standing on the street in front of their destination, right near a couple of tall, jagged bushes. "Here I am," he said with his usual grin. "Waiting for girls who are shiny like pearls. I'm talking about you two. Nice jewelry."

Kiara smiled at him. She was wearing a violet dress Suzy had bought her, and a silver bracelet imbedded with a tracking device. Suzy had considered not telling Kiara about the tracker, but then told her anyway and discovered Kiara liked the idea—because Suzy was wearing a similar one. One touch turned it off, completely dead to any scanning device. Another touch turned it back on. Meanwhile, Ricardo had a similar belt buckle because Suzy had insisted. If she was going to be tracked then so was he.

"Do you think Anika's family will be here?" Kiara said.

"I don't know," Suzy said. "But I'm sure they'll turn up sooner or later. Really, Kiara, *you* shouldn't even be here."

Kiara had refused to stay at the laundromat, but Suzy hadn't argued much. It felt safer to keep her in sight.

They were going to a meeting where there would supposedly be an announcement from Anika's group about how they'd be moving forward after the attack. And yeah, Suzy planned to give Ricardo a short intro, but she'd also get whatever information she could about Shogun Hunter. Then she'd find the evil bastard and get the hell out of this blood-soaked shit show.

They were in the oldest part of the city, but this particular house had no special character. It was a big box of bamboo that reminded Suzy of a packing crate. Suzy recognized a couple of rough-looking guys hanging around outside, near a pair of pineapple palms—David and Rafael, part of Ricardo's crew from Earth. This was good. Were they completely trustworthy? No, but it was still nice to see them. They were more capable than the average felons.

Suzy glanced around quick as they walked into a spacious living room that opened into a kitchen. Nothing too dangerous, unless someone wanted to count the ice-cold décor. There were silver ceiling lights that hung down like daggers, and a floor of grey stone, and lots of steel and glass, and a long black bar in the corner. There was very little furniture, and everything looked precisely placed. Then Anika and Nuru arrived.

They both smiled at Suzy. When they saw Ricardo, Nuru seemed happily surprised. Anika's smile turned quizzical, obviously less enthusiastic.

Nuru gave Suzy a hug. "Thank you for coming," he said. "When you told me you were bringing a friend, you didn't tell me it was this man. You know we've met, right? In fact, he recited a poem."

"I'm sure he did," Suzy said. "But I brought him anyway."

Anika had tears in her eyes as she embraced Suzy. "We lost some good people, Suzy, but it would've been much worse if you hadn't been there. And by the way, have you seen the latest news reports?

You're a hero, at least on the stations friendly to us. Thank you so much for your help."

"Don't mention it," Suzy said. After all, she'd mainly been protecting herself and Kiara. Then she added, "I'm sorry about your losses."

"Thank you."

There was a moment of silence, and Anika seemed to be waiting for Suzy to say more, but she didn't. So Anika turned to Ricardo.

"Hello," Anika said. "You told me about your connections, Ricardo, but you didn't tell me Suzy was one of them."

"I'm not really *one of them,*" Suzy interjected. "But Ricardo..." Her voice trailed off. What was she trying to say? "He's been a good friend."

Ricardo grinned. "I've done my best."

"I'm going to get a drink," Suzy said and headed toward the bar.

She felt a pang of guilt for not giving him a better intro, but did she want him getting involved in this place? Not really. She grabbed a bottle of beer and checked out the exits. Then Kiara came over with a small plate of fruit in her hand, mostly blueberries, and poured herself a glass of red wine.

"Don't get drunk, Kiara."

"Why not?"

"Because it can lead to bad decisions."

"Oh, yeah? You told me your best decisions were the worst ones you ever made."

Suzy laughed. "Did I say that? I was probably buzzed at the time. But look, we have to be careful here, so stay clear-headed and alert. Look out for anything that seems like trouble."

Kiara laughed. "Does that include us?" she said. Then she banged her drink down on the bar and pushed the glass away. "I'll keep my eyes open. I'm really not a drinker, anyway."

Suzy paused, and then put down her own drink. "Me neither. Well, not tonight. Or at least right now. Is that a new purse? Hey—are you carrying a gun?"

"Maybe. Are *you* carrying a gun?"

Damn. Suzy took a breath to calm down. How could she explain this once and for all? Suzy leaned forward and whispered in a fierce tone. "Kiara, I don't want you to be like me. I know you think it would be great—but really, being chased by every cop in the solar system is more fucked up than you think."

"I know," Kiara said. "But my life is already fucked up. And if someone comes after you, I want to help."

"That's great, but you don't even know how to use that thing."

"What's to know? Point and shoot. Besides, I asked you to help me, remember? And you said you would."

"I said 'maybe,' and I didn't show you anything yet."

"Well, you better start soon because I'm keeping it." Kiara flashed her big brown eyes. "I want to protect myself, and you're good at that stuff, Suzy. You're the best."

Suzy hesitated. She felt like throttling the girl, but she also felt a bit flattered. She heard herself say, "All right, maybe later I'll show you a few things. Just don't shoot anyone unless I tell you."

"You like me, Suzy, admit it."

"Yeah, I do. But don't push it."

Kiara laughed once again.

More people kept coming into the house, and it was a diverse group. Suzy noticed Ricardo talking to a couple of good-looking guys with light brown skin. One of them had a shaved head, while the other had thick black hair, perfectly cut, along with a well-trimmed beard. Come to think of it, these were the faces she'd seen plastered on the walls of the Citizen Collective. They both looked smaller in person.

Suddenly, Anika was at Suzy's side. "Suzy, can we talk?" She looked at Kiara and said, "Alone, if that's all right."

"But I'm Suzy's assistant," Kiara said.

Suzy was quiet for a second, and then spoke in a smooth voice. "Yeah, that's true, but maybe you can mingle a bit. Maybe you can meet someone useful."

Kiara hesitated. "Okay," she said. "Maybe I'll do that."

"Don't go far," Suzy blurted. "I mean...I might need you later."

Kiara pointed to the nearby kitchen. "I'm going over there. I think I'll survive."

Anika watched Kiara go. "My son asked me about her. He's not bashful."

Suzy gave a little laugh. "Kiara's real sweet. Come to think of it, she asked if your family would be here. Does your kid have a girlfriend?"

"If he does, he hasn't told me. Where did you meet her?"

"Long story. She was hijacking my spaceship."

"Oh. That's…different. You certainly have an interesting life."

"Yeah, it's interesting. Kind of like a robbery in progress." Suzy picked up her beer and took a short swig. "Anika, I appreciate the help you've given me, but I'm looking for this Shogun guy. So if you've got any information, that would be great."

Anika narrowed her eyes. "Suzy, he's the last man I want loose in this city—unfortunately, I don't know where he is, or who he is now. But I'm sure he had a complete identity change, and I can take a good guess where he had the surgery done. There are lots of places that do it, but there are two that are better and more discreet than the others. I asked them for help with this three years ago, and they refused… But we've now got a contact inside one of these places, and we know he didn't do it there, so that only leaves the other one, right?"

"My dad used to say, 'It's all about the math.' "

Anika glanced around and then handed Suzy a slip of paper. "That's the address; it's a surgery boutique of sorts. The owner lives there, upstairs. He's also the surgeon, and his name is Artemis Hatzi. He'll never give you the records, but I suppose you can ask."

"Thanks, I'll do that," Suzy said. "I'm not shy."

"I've also put the word out that we're looking for Hunter again, and if I hear anything I'll let you know. Of course, he already knows people are looking for him, so it's no surprise, but a little more chatter on the street might cause him to slip up and show his head."

"Yeah, maybe. But when this guy shows his head it's ugly." Then Suzy motioned toward the bearded guy she'd seen before, who was now in the kitchen talking to Kiara. "Who's that guy? Is that Mert Kaya? He's too old for her."

"Yes, that's Mert. He's mostly Turkish, and the number two person in the People for Progress party. I'd like you to meet him. He's a good person to know."

"Anika—"

"I know you're not planning to stay. But meet a few people. It might help you while you're here. I didn't realize you were affiliated with Ricardo's group."

"Kind of ruins my mystique, doesn't it?"

"No. I suppose it's complicated. Personal relationships can complicate lots of thing, right?"

Suzy paused. "Yeah," she said.

"I'm sure things will work out for the best," Anika replied in a warm tone. "But excuse me, Suzy. I have to talk to some of these people."

Anika headed across the room, and Suzy once again found herself scanning the crowd. Kiara was still having an animated conversation with the bearded guy, and now they were coming toward her. He had his hand out.

"Hello," he said in a soothing voice. "So you're Suzy. Your friend Kiara was telling me all about you."

Kiara smiled. "Suzy, this is Mert Kaya, and this is his house. He's been living here for fifteen years, and he's in a political party called People for Progress, and they're against Buso and the Casino Cartel. He owns a gift shop downtown that sells souvenirs, and he offered me a job."

Suzy studied him. He was good-looking in a suspicious way, like maybe a charming jewel thief.

"Kiara, you have a job," Suzy said. "You're my assistant, remember?"

"Yeah, I am," Kiara said, glancing at Mert.

"I understand," he said with a laugh. "But if you ever want more work come talk to me."

"She doesn't," Suzy snapped, surprised by her sharp tone. Then she spoke in a gentler voice. "Right now she's busy."

"Yeah, that's true," Kiara said. Then she added, "You two talk... Tell her what you're doing, Mert. I'm going to get more blueberries."

Mert watched her go. "Kiara seems interested in our campaign. We're fighting for good things."

"I appreciate what you're doing, Mert, but we're here on other business."

"Yeah, she told me. You're looking for a dangerous person." Then his eyes twinkled a bit and he said, "Someone more dangerous than you."

Suzy gave a sardonic laugh. "I'm looking for a guy named Shogun Hunter, who raped and murdered a bunch of teenage girls—and by the way, I'm only dangerous to myself. Well, most of the time."

Mert smiled. "I'm sorry," he said. "I didn't mean to offend you. You are what you are, and that's a good thing. We're all born a certain way."

"Right," she said. "Thanks for the biology lesson." *I guess you were born an asshole.*

He cocked his head. "I'm curious. What makes you think this person you're chasing came to Baadal Shahar? Why do you think he's still here?"

"I have information, Mert. I have a feeling."

Glancing across the room, she noticed Ricardo. He was laughing, looking sexy, and still talking with the bald guy. Nuru was also with them now.

Kaya followed her gaze. "In my experience, Suzy, a person should be careful about feelings. Feelings are often wrong."

Suzy took a swig of beer. "Yeah, true. But so are lots of people who give advice."

"You don't like advice, do you?"

"It depends."

"On what?"

"On how much fun I can have by ignoring it."

He looked amused. Then Ricardo, Nuru, and the other guy came toward them. Nuru introduced the shaved-headed person as Marcos, the leader of the People for Progress party. His blue eyes looked striking against his darker skin tone, and his angular face had a rugged appeal. He seemed to be bursting with energy.

He shook Suzy's hand and then lunged forward to give her a hug. "So glad to meet you, Suzy," he said while hugging a little too hard. "I'm hoping you and Ricardo can help us get rid of this rotten government."

"It's nice to meet you, too," Suzy said. "Usually, a guy just asks for my phone number."

Marcos laughed. "I'm sure they do. Ricardo, you better keep your eyes open. Someone will try to steal this girl away from you."

"Oh, I know," Ricardo said. "I know how guys are."

"Don't worry about it," Suzy said. "I'm not a piece of luggage."

"I didn't mean it that way," Marcos said with a grin. "I just meant that you're someone special—and you're in demand, right? It's all about supply and demand. I'm a businessperson. In fact, I'm thinking that Ricardo and I can do some good business."

"And what business would that be?" Suzy said.

Her tone was sweet but dripping with sarcasm. Ricardo squirmed a bit, and she felt another pang of guilt. But then Marcos just laughed and said, "Helping people, of course. That's what we're all about—helping people realize their true potential."

She suddenly felt less guilty and looked away because it was better than throwing up or maybe punching Marcos in the face. Had she originally thought this guy was good-looking? Now he reminded her of a lizard. It was time to get out of here, but now Kiara was eating strawberries and talking to another girl who was about her age, maybe a little older. Suzy recalled seeing this girl before, when she'd first met Anika. Was her name Sara? They hadn't been formally introduced, but yeah, that was her name. Sara had brown skin, and long dark hair, and could've easily passed for Kiara's sister. Well, it was good for Kiara to make a few friends.

Both girls were listening to Anika, who was giving a speech in the living room. She was talking about moving forward, and advancing justice, and cleaning up corruption. She was talking about stuff that had been in the news for thousands of years. She was also talking about a big workers' walkout followed by a rally designed to send a message to the government and the casinos.

Then Anika said, "And let's stop making Baadal Shahar a safe haven for pimps and sex traffickers. Let's have a government that's more concerned with human rights than the rights of the lowest predators."

Kiara seemed interested in this talk, and Suzy's heart filled with rage and sadness when she thought about why. Then Anika introduced Mert Kaya. Everyone cheered as his baritone voice sang with a eulogy for the people who'd recently been killed by assassins. Suzy was definitely ready to leave. She had a feeling he'd be talking for a while.

Chapter 26

"This is it," Stone said. "We go in."

He was sitting in a hover-car with Tala, staring through binoculars at the ugly bamboo house down the street. Unfortunately, it was hard to see what was happening because the place was surrounded by leafy trees and bushes. Damn, why were there so many pain-in-the-ass plants in this city? He was from Chicago, where a city looked like a city and a plant knew its place.

Tala wrinkled her nose and stared at the screen on her lap. "I think that would be a bad plan, sir. It looks like they have a couple of lookouts. We should call the police."

"What?" Stone hissed. "After what those ass-clowns did to me? No way!"

"You had an illegal weapon, sir. We're lucky we didn't get deported."

Stone frowned. "Don't remind me. I feel like shit about that, too."

Tala shrugged. "I told you, sir, I was going to give them that information anyway, since the plan always involved enlisting their help. Besides, all I gave them was the obvious stuff—her name, photo, and DNA info. It was a fair trade, and now they know who to look for."

"I'm a lousy cop," he muttered.

"No, you're not. You're the one who tracked her here, and that was great police work."

He glanced at her now and saw she was smiling, looking at him with obvious respect. He felt his face getting red. But he also felt better.

He sat up a bit in his seat. "Yeah, I guess it was okay," he said.

It had been a combination of tedious work and good luck, but that's the way most crimes get solved. That talkative housekeeper in Atlanta had told him Suzy and Ricardo were *enamorado,* and Suzy had run out on him, and he was probably chasing after her. So he'd bribed someone at the Baadal Shahar spaceport to gain access to the arrival images of everyone who'd come into Baadal Shahar on a commercial flight over the last week—and after hours of scrutinizing images of eager tourists, he'd found his man travelling under a phony name, along with a few of his friends. He'd then called every hotel in the area, pretending to be a delivery guy, until he'd found someone registered under that name, and they'd staked out the hotel just as Ricardo and his gang were leaving to come here.

They'd seen two people approach from the other end of the street, and while it was hard to see in the dark with these crappy binoculars, one of them had possibly been Suzy with black hair. There was an unidentified girl with her.

"Tala, I'm not letting these local clowns arrest her and grab all the credit. That's not going to happen."

"But it's a joint operation, sir, and we know she's armed. I'm sure Ricardo's people are, too. So we need to make that call to the cops."

Burt felt the sweat dripping down his back. "We need a plan!" he blurted.

"We have one," Tala said. "I call the police. There's no other way to get her, sir."

Burt just grimaced, and then he nudged the car forward.

"Keep staring through the binoculars," he said.

"Sir, what are you doing?"

"Just keep staring at the lookout guys."

Tala frowned but she also kept staring.

"I think they've spotted us, sir. One of the guys is making a call."

"Perfect."

"But now she's going to know we're coming."

"Yeah, exactly. And what's she going to do?"

"Get ready for a fight."

"No." After all, he'd read Suzy's profile, too. "She's got a history of being reckless but she's also smart. In fact, she's been more smart than reckless for a while now. And she's probably going to think a whole bunch of cops are on the way, not just two. So what's she going to do? What would you do?"

Tala hesitated. "I don't know."

"You'd sneak out the back way."

"Oh. Do we know where the back way is?"

Stone grimaced. *Crap!* "No. This is a spontaneous plan. So we better find it quick."

"But sir, we don't have real weapons. Even if we spot her and jump out of the car, she'll probably have time to shoot us."

Damn, that was true. But then again, Suzy didn't know they were unarmed. His eyes fell on the long black batons they were both carrying and he pulled a small energy knife from his pocket.

"Don't worry, Tala. Wait a few more seconds to make sure they've spotted us—then make a U-turn. Circle around and get on the next block. I have an idea."

***

Ricardo was talking into his allcom. He hung up and said, "Mert, do you have any surveillance on the street? Rafael's telling me there are a couple of suspicious people out there."

"Of course," Kaya said. He'd finished his speech to loud applause and was now drinking a common beer with the common folk. He pulled out an allcom and brought up some images, zeroing in on one of them.

Suzy peered over his shoulder. Nuru also stared at the small screen and said, "Those are the Strike Force agents from Earth."

Suzy turned to Kiara. "My fan club is here. Come on, honey, it's time to go."

She already had a pretty good idea of an exit strategy; she'd noticed a side door to the house when they'd approached, and she'd scoped out the appropriate door in the kitchen.

"Right," Kiara said. "I'm ready."

Suzy gave her a sharp look. "Ready for what?"

"Whatever happens."

"Kiara, don't do anything until I do it, okay?"

"Okay."

"I mean it, Kiara."

"I said 'okay!' Don't you trust me?"

Suzy didn't respond. She just looked at Ricardo, who was hanging up his call.

"I'm leaving Rafael and David here for now," he said. "Let's go."

Anika, Nuru, and everyone else seemed concerned, but there wasn't any time for good-byes. Suzy went to the kitchen door, intending to peek outside, but then Mert came over and said, "I have a better way." He flashed a tight smile, using just his lips, and then pressed a button under a counter that caused a section of the floor in a nearby corner to slide away. Suzy looked into the space and saw a ladder leading down.

Mert seemed proud. "It's a passage leading to an alley three houses over. I like to have options, and I extend them to my friends."

Suzy knew passages below ground level were common in city-states, where they were often used to transport supplies. But this one looked like it was strictly meant for transferring fugitives. Suzy glanced at Ricardo, who gave a "what-the-hell-let's-do-it" expression. She pulled out her gun and headed into the darkness with Ricardo and Kiara close behind.

They moved fast through a dimly lit tunnel, soon finding another ladder heading upward that ended on a small platform with a door. Suzy unlocked a latch, opened it a crack, and peered out with one eye. Okay, it led to an alley between two houses, just as Mert had described. No one seemed to be around, so she took a quick step through the door, looking and listening—nothing.

"Come on," she whispered. "Hurry."

Kiara slid into the alley, followed by Ricardo. Then instead of going toward the street they walked fast the other way, into a backyard. The yard was covered by high grass and filled with shadows and bulging bushes. Ricardo grinned. "Plants," he whispered. "Just like back home, Suzy. What a great world."

Suzy laughed. "Did you ever see me slobbering over a plant, Ricardo?"

"Okay, fine. But you would like it here."

"It's nice here," Kiara chimed in.

Through the yard was another house, along with another alley that led to a parallel street. Suzy kept her finger on the trigger as they slipped through the dingy alley. She cursed at the minimal amount of lighting. Apparently, no one in this city minded wasting a billion volts of power to illuminate the splashy main drag, but it was okay to leave everyone else in the dark. Finally, they reached the sidewalk.

"Suzy, put the gun away," Ricardo said. "We're trying to look inconspicuous."

She was holding her weapon down by her thigh. "No one can see it," she said. "Your dream world is too dark."

"There are cars coming by."

This was true, and one of them might hold a bunch of cops. They turned a corner and then turned again, crossing the road of tightly packed bamboo buildings before finding themselves walking on the original street, only farther down.

Ricardo's allcom beeped and he checked a message. "That car drove off," he said. "What do you think it means?"

"Not sure. It probably means a hundred cops are going to raid the house in a few seconds."

"But why wouldn't they hang around?"

"I don't know, Ricardo. My application at the police academy keeps getting rejected."

"Wait!" Kiara whispered.

Suzy stopped walking, and then a voice rang out.

"Don't move! Put your hands in the air!"

Suzy froze—it was the Strike Force guy! He'd been hiding behind a fuzzy bush and a parked car, and now he had a weapon pointed right at them.

He was looking into her eyes and shaking his big square head. "Don't do it, Suzy," he said, very calm. "Drop the gun or I'll shoot you dead."

Suzy had a sinking feeling in her chest. She also wondered why he didn't just shoot her with a stun blast, given her status—but then the other SF officer hopped out from behind a different bush. She was down in a low stance, and her eyes were wild. She started inching forward in a jerky way, like she was being electrocuted.

This one is scared, Suzy thought. Then she stared at Suzy's right hand and screamed, "Drop the gun! Drop the gun!"

Suzy didn't do it. Instead she glanced at Kiara and said, "Don't do anything." Then Suzy dropped her gun.

"Raise your hands!" the woman shouted. She was holding her weapon with both hands, which was not unusual—but one hand was on top of the barrel in an odd way. She seemed to be squeezing it to death.

The other cop said, "Tala, wait! Stop!"

Suzy and Ricardo raised their hands. Suzy glanced at Kiara again. "Do what she says," Suzy said.

Kiara raised her hands, and the female cop slid toward Suzy's gun. But as she reached down her own weapon slipped from her grip and clattered to the sidewalk—and it was not a gun! It was a sawed-off club.

The woman said, "Crap!" as it bounced toward Suzy's feet. Then she swooped in and reached for Suzy's weapon—but Suzy was quick and stomped hard on her hand.

The woman howled. Then the other cop growled like a bear and came charging.

Kiara shrieked, and Ricardo rushed toward the oncoming cop, and Ricardo and the cop started cursing and grappling. Then Suzy snatched her weapon from the sidewalk, and the female cop screamed, and Suzy shot her in the chest. As the shot rang out, the other cop screamed and seemed to freeze—and Ricardo threw him to the ground. The guy's own sawed-off club was rolling across the sidewalk, and Suzy lunged forward and shoved her gun into his face. Kiara also had her gun out now.

The cop looked up with wide and desperate eyes. Then he looked over at his fallen companion.

"Did you kill her?" he croaked.

"No," Suzy said. "That was a low-power shot. She'll be fine in about an hour."

The guy looked relieved but still concerned. "Okay," he said in a shaky voice. "Thanks."

Ricardo laughed. "Thanks? You're very polite."

"You can kill me," he said. "But don't hurt her."

Now Suzy laughed. "Who says chivalry is dead? What's your name?"

"Burt Stone."

"Okay, Burt Stone, so the Strike Force on Earth sent you all the way to Venus to catch me. Did they send any others?"

Stone suddenly became indignant. He gave a snort and said nothing.

"Are you working with the local cops?"

"Hell, yes!" he snapped. "And they know it was you who shot those people the other day."

"You mean the assassins?"

He hesitated. "Right," he finally said. "Those people. We gave them all the info on you. You'll never get away, Suzy."

"So why didn't you call them tonight? Why did you come after us alone, with just a little stick in your hand?"

He was quiet and kept looking over at the other officer.

"How did you find me?" Suzy said.

Stone shrugged. "I guess I did something right."

"Yeah," Suzy said. "You're the smartest cop I'm going to shoot tonight." Then Suzy turned to Kiara, careful not to say her name. "Honey, that slider on your gun is too high, and it would probably kill him. Put it down and watch me."

Kiara's mouth dropped open. "Really?"

"Really."

"Okay," she said, and gingerly put it back into her purse.

"Right about here is where you want to be," Suzy said, moving her thumb. "This will knock him out good. Keep in mind that it *can* kill, if you hit him in the head, or if his body has a bad reaction or whatever. Also, since he'll be unconscious right after the shot, he's going to hit the ground hard, like a bag of meat. It's easy to get hurt that way. But chances are he won't die."

Ricardo said, "Yeah, great lesson, but let's go. Quit fooling around with this guy."

Suzy shot Stone in the chest, noting his defiant eyes. Ricardo seemed happy enough but Suzy just shook her head. That guy's too dumb to quit, she thought. *We're going to see him again.*

Chapter 27

Danielle was shaking as she stared at the news on the living room wall. It was tuned to the feed from Baadal Shahar, where murder and violence was the main story. She was so engrossed in the stressful images of a redhead with a pistol that she didn't hear her husband come into the room. When he poured himself a glass of wine in the nearby kitchen, she was jolted like someone waking from a trance.

"Andre, you scared me," she said. "I didn't hear you."

He motioned toward the screen. "Have you talked to your friend, Anika?"

"No. I mean, when? Not today."

"Today? I mean since all the stuff in that news story happened. It's a crazy situation."

"Why?"

He took a sip of his drink. "First of all, we failed to capture Pablo Juarez, though we did pound his forces and make over fifty arrests. But no Pablo. He escaped and we're not sure where he went." Then he nodded at the screen and said, "I'm thinking he might end up there."

"In Baadal Shahar?"

"Why not? His organization seems interested."

"Oh. Have you seen his people there?"

He sighed and sat down. "We've seen Suzy Castillo there—everyone has. That's her in the video you're watching, killing a bunch of assassins from a local cartel. And I just got news from the hospital. She shot the two agents I sent to capture her."

Danielle suddenly felt the room spinning. Then Andre was leaning toward her, looking at her face.

"Are you all right, Danielle?"

"Yeah," she managed to say. "Yeah, I'm fine. Did she kill them?"

"No."

"Oh," and now Danielle felt a wave of relief wash over her. "That's not so bad."

"Yeah, but one of them is in bad shape, and she could've killed them both and probably will next time. Here's the problem: She's there with Ricardo, the brother of Pablo's wife. So she's obviously working with these people to get control of the drug trade. And if the commander's nephew ends up getting killed in a drug war that'll be bad."

"But I don't think she's there to help with drugs, Andre."

"I think that's exactly why she's there. And she's there because of that time I let her escape." He swore and looked away for a second. "For one dumb minute I thought she could be saved, but I should've known better. A killer is a killer, Danielle—and if she murders a cop I'll never be able to live with myself."

"She's not going to kill any cops! She's not there because of drugs." Danielle took a deep breath and reached out, grabbing her husband's hand. "She's there because of me."

"What?"

She saw the shock in his eyes. Then she felt the guilt in her gut like a stabbing pain, but she kept going, speaking fast. "I hired her to capture Shogun Hunter. I know I should've told you. I know it was wrong, and I'm so sorry."

Andre was totally quiet—a bad sign. When he finally spoke, his voice was trembling.

"When did this happen?"

"I met with her that night she had a fight with the bounty hunters in Atlanta."

For another long moment he said nothing. Then he slowly shook his head. "Danielle, are you telling me you communicated with a fugitive who's wanted for murder? Are you telling me you actually *met* with the high priority criminal who I've been assigned to capture?"

"You weren't trying to capture her then, not really. And you're the one who sent an idiot after her, remember?"

"I sent an idiot—sure," he said, and his voice was rising with anger. "But a lot of times we send an idiot! I was still doing my job in a way no one would question. But you *met* with her and never told me? You *found* her and then hired her? Do you have any idea what you did? *Why would you do that? Why?*"

Her eyes filled with tears. "Andre, I didn't want to hurt you, but I wanted to get that bastard Shogun Hunter. And no one was doing it! You said good things about Suzy—you did. You let her go for a good reason, so I thought she might be the right person to contact. I found her through her mother and grandmother. They'd been lying about having no contact with her, and they trusted me because of the way I helped them once, and then I met Suzy, and I liked her—I really did. She was very sincere."

"She sincerely killed two people that night!"

"There were extenuating circumstances," Danielle muttered.

Andre hung his head, obviously disgusted—and even worse, disappointed. He was silent and frozen like a statue.

"Andre…"

He didn't respond.

"I'll make it right!" she blurted. "I can fix it."

Now he cocked his head, looking at her with an angry smirk. "Really? How? You know I have the Global Law Enforcement Conference coming up in Melbourne, right? Do you know what's going to happen if this comes out? There's no way you can fix it, Danielle. No way."

Danielle felt her fingers clutching the cushions of the sofa. "There must be a way," she whispered. Then she said, "I'll contact her! I'll tell her to forget about Hunter and come back to Earth. I'll set her up and you can arrest her."

"You'll set her up?" He gave a soft laugh of disbelief. "Now you want to help *capture* her?"

"Yes, if it will make things better. I'll do it for you—for us."

Once again he was quiet, and then he stood up. He looked taller than usual, staring down at her. "I have to go," he said.

Her heart was beating fast. "Why? Go where?"

"I don't know."

He turned and walked back through the living room to the front door.

She leaped to her feet. "I'm sorry, Andre—I am. But I'll talk to her."

He shook his head and opened the door. As he walked out, he didn't turn around.

She ran to the door, and now she was yelling. "I know what Suzy wants, Andre. I'll let you know when she's coming!"

He walked down the hall and entered the turbo lift. When he finally turned, his eyes were empty, like they were seeing something far away. But he didn't say another word, and then the doors slammed shut and he was gone.

Chapter 28

Suzy was quiet as they drove down the main drag. Her mind whirled as she stared through the windshield of Ricardo's lime green hover car, hardly noticing the splashy lights and fiery billboards blazing all around. How had Stone found them? It was a nagging question because when he woke up he might do it again.

"Someone ratted us out," Ricardo said. "Someone in Anika's group."

"I doubt it," Suzy said. "Maybe if it had been the local cops or the Snake Eyes, but a couple of bumbling SF agents from Earth? Does anyone in Anika's group really know them? And if they knew anyone, wouldn't somebody give them a gun? It's more likely they tracked us somehow and tailed us to the house. And by 'us' I mean you."

"What? Why me?"

"The SF people know you, Ricardo, and they know that I know you. Plus you probably left a trail of burnt burritos from the spaceport to your hotel."

"Hey, that's ridiculous," he said with a laugh. "I might be a crook but I'm not a litterer. Besides, I used phony credentials. Good ones."

"They record an image of everyone who exits a flight, right? Someone might have made a match. Besides, if they'd tracked me they would've made their move sooner. Why wait until I got to the house? They must have been waiting for me when I got there, and that's because they didn't know where I was—but they knew where you were. So they probably tracked you to get to me."

Ricardo shrugged. "Okay, if you want to be logical about it. Sure, that makes perfect sense." He grinned. "Isn't she a smarty, Kiara?"

"She's smart," Kiara said. "And she's tough. No one's tougher than her, right?"

Ricardo hesitated. Then he said, "She's a tough girl."

Suzy gave a short laugh. "This tough girl needs a place to hide."

"You can probably go back to your hotel," Ricardo said. "The only cops on your tail right now are in dreamland."

Suzy said nothing, but no, not the hotel. Then Kiara said, "We could go back to Mert's place. Maybe they won't look there because we just left. He gave me his number and said if we need anything, he could help us."

"No way," Suzy said. "His house is under surveillance. Besides, I don't want his help. He wants us to get involved in his revolution or whatever."

"But that might be a good thing, Suzy."

"Yeah," Ricardo said. "That might be a good thing. And Marcos can help us, too."

"You mean your sleazy new friend?"

"Now why do you say he's sleazy? He was perfectly nice."

"He was perfectly nice because he thinks you'll help him sell drugs."

"Suzy, I told you that's not the plan."

"Are you sure? Let me tell you my plan—turn here."

She was getting a good grip on the downtown. It was a natural byproduct of constantly evading cops and assassins.

"Where are we going?"

"We're right near the surgery swap Anika gave me. Let's swing by and check it out. Maybe we'll get lucky."

"I love getting lucky," Ricardo said. "Luck is so fine, it has no design—it is random just like the wind. What do you think?"

Suzy laughed again. "I'd tell you to keep your day job, but I hate your day job. There's the place."

They were on a street just off the main strip that was lined with blinking restaurants and blazing storefronts—an explosion of parapets, and statues of elephants wrapped in lights, and flashing signs of pink, green, yellow, and orange. Ricardo parked in front of the New U Surgery Center where a wide glass window was dark.

"Looks like they're closed," he said.

"Yeah, but the owner lives upstairs. Let's see if anyone's home."

"Suzy, maybe you should wait until tomorrow."

"The quicker this gets done the quicker we can leave."

She glanced around and got out of the car. There were people scattered across the sidewalks on both sides of the street but no one looked dangerous. Ricardo stood in front of the place, looking left and right while Suzy searched for a way in. There was a narrow alley along one side of the building where she found a door. This might go upstairs, she thought. It was a heavy door, and there was a camera chip above it, and the lock was broken! Someone had used a tool to burn through it—and it was still warm.

She felt her pulse start to pound.

"Ricardo," she hissed. "Someone broke in."

"Well then let's get out of here! They probably set off an alarm."

But Suzy wasn't listening. Her mind was spinning fast as she pulled out her pistol and slipped inside. Was someone trying to keep her from getting the info about Hunter? That person might still be here. And that person might be a key to his new identity.

She set her weapon to fire stun shots, and then moved fast up the stairs, trying to be quiet. At the top of the landing was another door with a broken lock; it swung open into a kitchen. She stepped lightly across a tile floor. The room was dim, and colored lights from the street below were flashing through a window, creating an eerie, strobe-light effect. She saw two hallways, one leading toward the front of the building, the other leading toward the back. She stopped and listened—and heard a sound in the front hallway. There was someone else up here.

She crept into the darkened passage, past a bathroom and toward two other open doors.

Someone was in one of the rooms. She inched forward, slithering like a cat—and then her foot bumped into something soft. She glanced down for a second and sucked in her breath. It was a body. She bent down for a closer look. It was a man, and his throat had been cut, and there was a lot of blood. Then she stood up and someone hit her hard.

Stars exploded in her head, and she fell to the floor. *Dammit!* She fumbled with her gun, and someone kicked her in the ribs and stomped on her wrist. She let out a shout and lost the weapon as another vicious kick smashed into her cheek. The guy was wearing a mask, some kind of black stocking over his head. Ricardo shouted from the stairs, and the attacker leaped over Suzy, ran into the kitchen, and fired a salvo of shots.

Ricardo swore, and there was more gunfire. Suzy staggered to her feet and saw the attacker running down the other hallway and bolting through a door at the end. She heard his feet pounding down a stairway. Ricardo was close behind but when he reached the stairs a shot blasted just over his head, and he fell backwards and hit the floor. "Damn!" he said. Then he jumped to his feet and whirled back around.

"Suzy, are you okay?"

Suzy was in the kitchen now, but before she could answer there was a yelp from outside.

"Kiara!" Suzy said.

Suzy raced for the back stairs, stumbling down two at a time. The door opened to a yard behind the building. Kiara was crumpled on the ground—but she was moving.

Suzy ran and knelt by her side. "Kiara, are you all right? *Kiara?*"

Kiara seemed dazed, but she said, "I'm fine."

"What happened?"

Kiara paused and rubbed her temples. "Jack," she said. "I was coming around the building and he crashed into me."

Suzy's mouth dropped open. "Jack? Are you sure it was him?"

"He said my name—it was him. Then he cursed and ran away."

Suzy was about to say something else but was interrupted by whooping sirens close by.

Ricardo came running out of the house. "We've got to go, ladies. Quick!"

Without another word, everyone started running through the yard, through an alley and onto the sidewalk of the next block.

"Don't look at anyone's face," Ricardo said. "Act natural."

Suzy already knew this, and if Kiara didn't she learned it fast. Then Ricardo nodded at a blue car across the street, driving slowly, and Suzy recognized Rafael behind the wheel.

"I hit my signal to him when we got here," Ricardo said, fingering his belt buckle. "In case we needed some backup."

The car only stopped for an instant. They got in fast and drove away.

Chapter 29

Stone blinked his eyes a few times but failed to recognize anything. "Where am I?"

"You're in a hospital, sir."

Okay, that was Tala's voice, and that was her face. Yeah, it was all coming back to him now, the complete and total humiliation. He grimly considered that it might not be over; maybe he was paralyzed or something. Maybe he was blind!

"Am I blind?" he blurted.

"Can you see me?"

"Yes."

"Then you're not blind, sir."

"Oh. That makes sense."

"The doctors said you'll be fine. Your mind is just a little foggy."

Everything was coming into focus now. He was in a hospital room, lying in a bed surrounded by pleated green curtains and a few blinking machines. Up above were bright lights, hurting his eyes. He was also thirsty but Tala was offering him a glass of water—and wait, Suzy had shot Tala!

He jerked himself upright. *"Hey, are you okay?"*

"I'm fine," she said with a smile. "It was a low-power shot. She hit you with something a lot stronger." He sighed with relief as she looked away from his eyes. Then she spoke in a shaky voice. "I apologize for my performance, sir. I panicked when I saw her standing there with the gun. I really messed up and I've got no excuse."

"What?" Burt said. "No! You were just a little excited, that's all. You're fresh out of the academy, facing a dangerous fugitive. You did great."

"No, I didn't," she said, and now her tone was sharp. "I should resign. My parents were right. I should've stayed an engineer."

Burt banged his fist down on his leg. "What? No! They were wrong! Parents don't always know what's best for their kids. You were really brave. I never should've tried that stunt with the sawed-off nightsticks." He looked into her eyes and spoke softly. "If you'd gotten hurt I never would've forgiven myself."

He found himself staring at her for longer than he'd expected. And she was staring back.

Then she looked at the curtains and said, "I'm glad it worked out. So we can complete the mission."

"Right," he said. "The mission." *What was that mission again?* He forced his brain to focus. "So, who found us, Tala?"

"Someone in a car stopped and called the police. Then they called an ambulance."

"Did the cops question you?"

"Yes."

"And you gave them a full report, I guess."

"Yes—more or less."

"Oh, yeah?" He put down his water. "What did you leave out?"

She hesitated. "I might have said we were walking to dinner and happened to spot the suspect on the sidewalk, and she recognized you somehow—probably from a picture someone sent her—and she shot us before we could do anything. I might have said she was trying to scare us into leaving Baadal Shahar but we don't scare easily."

Stone cocked his head and grinned. "So you lied."

"Yes, sir," Tala said, squirming a bit.

"You didn't tell them we tracked Ricardo? And that we know he's here?"

"No, sir."

"You didn't mention the idiotic stunt with the fake guns?"

"No, sir."

"I see. Why not?"

She shrugged. "I didn't want us to look stupid." Then she gave him a fierce look. "Also, I don't want them interfering. We're going to get Suzy Spitfire—not them. It's going to be us. And I got these."

She held up a bag and Stone peeked inside. His eyes opened wide. She had a pair of stun sticks, not nearly as good as guns since they required the user to actually stick them into the suspect's ribs—but better than nothing.

"We can still find her, sir. We know she's involved with Anika Anand, and we know she's usually around Ricardo and that girl. We'll get her. We will!"

Stone laughed out loud. He reached out and took her hand.

"Great job, Tala. You're okay."

"Thank you, sir. You're doing a great job, too."

"Thanks. And call me Burt. We're partners, and partners should be friends."

She smiled back at him. "Okay, Burt."

"Great. Now let's get the hell out of here."

Chapter 30

"Are you sure it was Jack?" Suzy said. "Why didn't he kill me? He had a knife and a gun."

They were sitting on the ratty couch in the back room of the laundromat, just Suzy and Kiara, while a platoon of cleaning machines hummed through the walls.

"He's really not like that," Kiara said.

"Kiara, he's totally like that. He killed the guy in that apartment."

Kiara was quiet for a second. "Okay, he's like that, but he knows I'll hate him if he hurts you."

"He kicked me in the head—see? And it hurts." Suzy turned her head so Kiara could view the swelling on the side of her cheek and the deep red bruise. "Also, my ribs are a nice shade of purple. And let's not forget the time he used you as a shield, so I wouldn't blow him up."

"He wasn't going to hurt me. Not really."

"Why do you say that?"

"Jack saved my life, Suzy. He did."

"When was this?"

Kiara shifted around on the sofa.

Now Suzy was quiet, because there were things she didn't like to talk about, either. But she hoped Kiara would talk because she wanted to listen.

Kiara took a deep breath, like she was getting ready to run a race. Then she looked down at her lap and said, "After I left Miami, I had nowhere to go. I was wandering around, sleeping in doorways, trying to find a job—but I was too young to get a real job, and then I met this guy, Daniel. He seemed okay, and he said he could help me." She paused and shook her head. "At first he did help. I was confused, but I liked him because he was nice to me. He gave me a place to stay, and took care of me. He was a lot older than me, but he acted like I was his girlfriend, and it was good. But then things changed. There were other girls… I didn't understand—I was so stupid—and I wanted him to keep liking me. And then things happened."

She stopped talking now and just stared, her eyes focused somewhere far away. Suzy waited, and when Kiara spoke again her voice was soft.

"It was a nightmare, Suzy. I didn't really know what was happening at first, but it was like…an initiation. A bunch of guys, all at once." A tear fell from her eye, but she wiped it away and went on, speaking faster now. "I didn't know this happened to everyone, and I still wanted Daniel to like me—it sounds crazy and fucked up, but that's how it was. So I worked for him, and sometimes he was still nice, but if I didn't make enough money he'd beat me up, and that's how things were for almost two years." She touched the scar on her left jaw line. "I had nowhere to go. He kept everything, so I had no money, no friends, just other girls who were trapped like me. And then I met Jack. I know what you're thinking but it wasn't like that. I didn't meet him like that. I met him at the supermarket. I was with another girl, this girl who helped Daniel run things, but she was in the other aisle and Jack was right there with me, buying frozen waffles."

Now she laughed, obviously recalling a happy moment. "He started talking to me, and he wanted to see me sometime. So I told him no, because I couldn't, not like that—but then I told him yes and gave him my number, even though I knew Daniel would beat the crap out of me if he found out. It seemed so weird and impossible, but Jack called me, and I told him about things, and he still wanted to see me. But I was like a prisoner, so Jack paid to see me, you understand? And he did it a few times, and then a few more, and he told me he loved me, and I…felt the same way. Then he got me out of there. He was good to me, Suzy. I know you don't believe it, but he was. And we went to Atlanta."

"Daniel didn't come after you?"

Kiara turned her eyes away. "No. I told Jack about the things

Daniel did, how he smacked me around, and the way he treated the other girls, too. So Jack told Daniel he was taking me. Daniel thought Jack was another guy in the game, and he wanted big money to let me go. But it didn't work out that way."

She stopped talking again and let a few more silent tears fall.

"Kiara, did Jack kill Daniel?"

Kiara sobbed once and said nothing. Finally, she wiped her eyes again and spoke in a hoarse voice. "They were fighting, and it was horrible, and I just couldn't think. Everything got out of control—and I didn't want it to happen that way!" She paused and took a breath. "I was so scared," she said. "But I still went to Atlanta with Jack, and then things got better. He introduced me to his friends, and when he wasn't drunk he was great. He even told me stuff he wasn't supposed to tell anyone, things about the Snake Eyes. They're very secretive. They're into drugs, robbery, and other stuff—but they don't sell girls. They're not in that game, and they look down on it—maybe because there are lots of women in the group, too, and they were friendly. But then Jack said he had to move out of Atlanta, so he got us both a job at Odee's house. Then you showed up and now here I am."

Kiara breathed a sigh and sat back, like the race was over. She said, "You keep telling me not to be like you, Suzy, but being the way I am hasn't always worked out too well."

Suzy picked up a glass on a little end table and took a swig, wishing it were filled with something other than ice water. She needed something to calm the violent thoughts flooding her brain, thoughts about finding and murdering everyone who'd hurt this girl. She ground her teeth and pushed them out of her mind. Then she put her hand on Kiara's leg.

"That's a terrible story, Kiara. I'm glad you got out of there—but being like me hasn't always worked out so well, either. Just so you know. In fact, it's important that you know."

"But you don't let people push you around."

"I get pushed a little. It's a pushy universe."

Suzy rubbed her forehead now, her mind swimming with her

past. "I've been thinking about the kind of person I am, and I'm not happy with what I see. Lots of people have friends and relatives who are victims of bad things, horrible things. My sister was molested by my uncle, and she killed herself, and my father was murdered. But how often does anyone go and do the things I did? Almost never. Sure, they think about it, but they don't do it. And that's because most people aren't like me. They take a different road and try to make peace with it all, and they end up living a better life, I think—because that great feeling you get when you pull the trigger, it doesn't last. All the pain and anger I felt is still there, every bit. And my sister is still gone, and so is my dad, and I'm sitting in this scuzzy laundromat a million miles from home."

Kiara hesitated. "So you're full of regrets?"

"Hell no," Suzy said. "I'd kill those motherfuckers all over again—but that's my point. What does that say about me? What kind of person am I, really? *Why am I like this?*" She paused, and she considered her own words. Then she said, "Maybe I just can't be any other way. This is how I'm built."

Kiara shook her head. "I don't know about any of that. But I think you're a good friend, Suzy. And I know you were a good sister and a good daughter, too—even if you don't think so. Maybe next time you'll do things differently, but right now I'm glad you're here."

Suzy managed to give her a weak smile. "I'm glad you're here, too. But I won't be around forever, Kiara. So we have to get this whole thing with Hunter wrapped up and get out of this place."

"Yeah, but I don't want to leave yet," Kiara said. "And I don't want you to leave, either. I want to be in the rally Anika is planning. I want to help her." She paused, and then whispered, "I don't know if I can ever live a normal life."

Suzy started to say, "Sure you can"—but then didn't. Because she wasn't sure. So instead she said, "Anika said her son was asking about you."

"He doesn't know me, the stuff I've done."

"If he's worth anything, he won't care. Besides, you're not in that world anymore, Kiara."

"That's true, sort of. But I feel stressed all the time, and I remember things. I want to help Anika because she's trying to help people like me." Then she looked at Suzy with watery brown eyes. "I wish you would help, too."

Suzy stared back at her. How could she say no? Maybe she didn't want to say no.

"I'll do it," Suzy said.

Kiara flashed a huge smile. "I knew you would, Suzy. Can you teach me things? How to fight like you?"

"Don't go jumping into any fights, Kiara. That might not be the thing you need most."

"What's that supposed to mean?"

"It means you probably need some kind of therapy, like Anika was saying—you've been through a lot."

"Yeah, I know. I know I'm a mess. You have no idea… But I need to learn how to protect myself better, too. I can't let people push me around. That's what I need right now, and you're the best. So can you please help me? Please."

"I'm not the best," Suzy said. "I'm okay—I'm…" Suzy stopped talking. Once again, how could she refuse, after the story she'd just heard? Also, Kiara was giving her such a pleading stare. This probably wasn't what Kiara needed most, but then again, it was something Suzy knew.

"Well," Suzy said, "the best thing is to have a weapon because that's why they were invented. If you don't, and you're fighting a guy, attack his balls or his eyes, but do it like you mean it because you won't get many chances. No wild flailing or kicking. Stay calm, be deliberate, and take *one* good shot—okay?"

"What if I get scared? Then I lose control. I go crazy."

"It's okay to be scared, just don't let your fear take over. I can show you some moves, but seriously, I only know a few things—I just know them really well. Also, I practice shooting a lot because it's fun. And that's all I've got to say right now."

"Okay, thanks," Kiara said. It seemed like she wanted to say more, but then she just added, "I'll try and remember that."

"Great. Now let's think about finding Hunter." *But you're not going to fight him—I am.*

Kiara nodded her head. "Yeah, I can help with that. Jack is the key, isn't he?"

Suzy nodded. "Yeah. Whoever put Jack up to that murder is trying to hide Hunter's new identity. Who knows, the guy might even be Hunter. Is it a coincidence that Jack was over there killing the surgery guy right after we left that meeting?"

"You think someone at the meeting is behind it?"

"Maybe, but they would've had to call him the second we left, and Jack would've had to run right over there. Anika said she put the word out about Hunter, so a lot of people knew someone was looking for him. It could've been anyone. So we need to find Jack and ask him a few questions."

"Suzy, Jack loves me. He'll tell me what we want to know."

"Jack is a bad guy, Kiara."

"I know. But bad guys still fall in love. He'll tell me."

Not likely, Suzy thought, *because there's no way I'm letting Jack anywhere near you.*

Suzy heard a beep and looked at her allcom. Apparently, an encrypted message had been sent to her ship. It was from Danielle.

Chapter 31

"No one saw you, right?"

Kaya studied Jack's blue eyes. It was dark in the Eye Cave, but not so dark that he couldn't see the killer sitting across from him.

"No one," Jack said, gulping his beer. "I wore the mask, like you said, and it was clean. Did it with a knife, too—the Snake Eyes way."

"A knife? You mean with a blade?"

Jack laughed. "Yeah, that's the way they come, Mert."

"A pistol is easier. Why use a knife?"

"I just told you, it's the Snake Eyes way. You haven't been a brother too long, right? A couple of years?"

"I've been in long enough."

"Yeah, long enough to be in charge, I guess."

Kaya narrowed his eyes. "What are you saying, brother?"

Jack shrugged. "Nothing."

"I see," Mert said with a nod of his head. "Jack, I've been living here for over fifteen years, and I'm the Head because the brothers and sisters wanted it that way. You've been on Earth a while—everyone is behind me." Then he leaned forward a bit. "And I know how to use a knife."

"I know, I know," Jack said quickly. "I didn't mean no insult. Hey, I just killed a guy for you, right? I ran right over there and took care of things."

"Yeah, that's true—good job."

"Okay. So everything's fine, right?"

Mert sat back and considered how just one dumb remark can get a guy killed—like dumb Jack here. But not yet. His nasty nature made him too useful.

"Right," Mert said. "Here's the plan: Anika Anand is planning a big rally, and we're going to attack that rally. But we need to be secretive; we want the blame to go to Buso and the Casino Cartel. It's important we do some serious damage. We need to kill some innocent people and spark the revolution. Of course, we don't need to kill *everybody*—just enough. Do you understand?"

"Okay," Jack said. "But what if the cartel really does attack? They just tried to kill her, right?"

"Yeah, it's always a possibility, but the rally will be on the main street, in front of the casinos. The casinos and the government don't like to discourage people from coming here to gamble, so we're betting they'll save their efforts for another day and a better location." Then he made his voice as hard as possible and said, "We're sending a team, but only one shooter. Keep in mind, I'll be at the rally, so we need to make sure the attack doesn't hit me. Also, we don't want to kill Anika, or anyone who might be helping her fight the government, like Suzy Spitfire. And our shooter needs to escape. Elijah is helping us with that."

"I get it," Jack said. "It's a good plan."

"I'm glad you approve."

Chapter 32

"Kiara, don't go wandering away, okay?"

The crowd was building on the downtown streets, and Suzy and Kiara were crouched in the darkened doorway of a shop that sold sports memorabilia. Suzy was back in the shadows, watching the scene, and Kiara was on the doorstep, her face highlighted by flashing amber lights advertising the Anti-Gravity Games.

"I'm not a little girl, Suzy. Stop smothering me."

"I'm not smothering you. I'm just looking out for you with great enthusiasm."

"That's good. I'm looking out for you, too—but I want to be out there, waving my sign." She held up her sign that said "STOLEN PEOPLE, STOLEN LIVES." She'd spent most of the day making it over at Anika's place while Suzy had spent most of the day worrying about her being there. Apparently, Kiara had also run into Nirav, and they'd had a friendly conversation.

More stuff for me to worry about, Suzy thought. But it was a happier kind of worry than thinking about Jack and where to find him. How many scummy bars were in this town, anyway?

Then there was that strange message from Danielle:

Hi, Suzy. I hope you're doing well. Things have changed. I have new information, and I now believe Hunter has left Baadal Shahar. I have something better for you to do, and I think you'll like it. Please contact me. I'm looking forward to seeing you again.

What information did Danielle have? Maybe she was getting jittery about being involved in the operation. I tend to make people jittery, Suzy thought. The idea of doing something better sounded sweet, but she'd come here to find a certain scumbag, and she was pretty sure he was here—and besides, she also wanted to help Kiara, who wanted to help Anika. *I'll talk to Danielle when I've got Hunter on ice. It'll be a happy surprise for her.* He could be here tonight, right in this crowd—and what a crowd it was.

The rally was supposed to begin in Mother of Fortune Square, at the far end of the splashy main strip. They were going to march peacefully down the street, through the blazing canyon of towering casino hotels, disrupting traffic and maybe even distracting a few gamblers. Now Anika was coming their way. It was impressive the way she weaved through the crowd with no pomp and pretention. But she also had no visible regard for her safety, not even a bodyguard.

Anika had a big smile for both of them. "I'm glad you two are here."

"Kiara dragged me into it," Suzy said. "A moment of weakness." She stayed in the dark doorway as she spoke, with her hair set to a shade of raven-black.

"She's a good influence on you."

"Yeah, she is," Suzy said with a laugh. "But what am I doing for her? And by the way, Anika, what are you doing about security?"

Suzy frowned as Kiara walked away to talk to someone, a friend she'd met at Anika's place.

"We've taken measures, Suzy, but we're not going to be intimidated or scared into submission. Change requires courage."

"Courage is crap if you're dead the next day."

"I have every intention of being alive tomorrow."

"Your enemies might have a different plan."

"The cartel thugs and the government police aren't going to want an incident on the main strip. It's bad for business."

Suzy paused. "What about the Snake Eyes? Didn't they blow up a casino the other night?"

"The Snake Eyes are a bad bunch, Suzy, but we have no direct fight with them. Their fight is with the cartel." Then she gave a sly smile and said, "We have no direct fight with anyone, except the government."

"I guess that makes it easy to keep track of your enemies."

"Yes. For now."

"Who's the girl?"

"What?"

"The girl Kiara is talking to. I've seen her a couple of times."

"That's Sara," Anika said. "She's one of my best assistants." Then she added, "Sara and Kiara have a lot in common. Are you worried about something?"

"No—no. I was just never introduced to her, that's all."

"I can do that now if you'd like—"

"No, it's okay," Suzy said, and she forced herself to smile. "I don't want to interrupt."

Anika returned to her mingling, and Suzy noticed Sara was gone now, and Kiara was talking to a waifish woman in a turquoise dress. Suzy felt an urge to run over and see what this new person wanted, but she stopped herself from "smothering." Then the woman slid away, leaving Kiara to stare with an open mouth at something in her hand. Right away Suzy knew there was a problem. She moved fast through the crowd.

"Kiara, what is it?"

"It's a message—from Jack."

An alarm shot through Suzy's head.

"What?" She snatched a restaurant menu from Kiara's hand. "Did that woman just give it to you?"

"Yeah. I was standing here, and she came up to me and said, 'Here are some good things to eat—especially the stuff on the back.' I thought she was just passing out menus. Then she ran off."

The note was scribbled in crooked letters on the backside of a menu from The Sitara restaurant, and it said: *Kiara, meet me at the Starway casino in fifteen minutes, out front. Please! I have something big to tell you. Please! I love you, Jack. Please be there!*

Suzy felt her blood run cold, because how had Jack known Kiara was here? He must have seen her! Suzy craned her head, scanning the boisterous crowd—no sign of Jack or the woman. She took a quick step in the direction the mysterious woman had taken and stopped.

No! I can't leave Kiara here, she thought. Besides, the woman would be hard to find; the crowd was thick now and there were lots of alleys and stores to hide in.

But the Sitara restaurant was right across the street. Could Jack be in there? He had to be close by, so why meet at the Starway, a place across town? This made no sense. And was someone talking to her?

"What should I do?" Kiara said. Her voice was shaky.

"Something's up, Kiara."

Anika's voice came over a loudspeaker and people started cheering.

"I told you he loves me, Suzy."

"Yeah, maybe. But he's here, and he wants you to go somewhere else."

"Maybe he saw you, and he wants to separate us. Maybe he thinks you'll go to the casino and then he'll come after me."

That was definitely possible. Suzy reread the note. It sounded so *urgent*. Also, he wasn't alone. He had this woman with him, and who else?

Anika's voice boomed out again, talking about justice. People cheered again and suddenly Kiara held up her sign. "I'm not going anywhere," she said. "I'm marching down the street. If Jack wants to talk to me he can come over here."

The crowd started moving, lumbering like a great herd past casinos that were lit up like Roman candles. Police dressed in riot gear, swinging black batons, were standing on the sidewalks. They started circling the perimeter of the crowd, and Suzy instinctively tried to scrunch herself up a bit. Then she whipped out her allcom and called Ricardo.

He was at the other end of the crowded street, where the rally was supposed to finish. He was schmoozing with Mert and Marcos. In fact, he'd spent the day hanging around with Marcos. She told him about the note.

"Okay," he said. "I'll keep my eyes open. Hey, I heard from some friends downtown. Those cops from Earth are back on the street."

"You have friends downtown?"

"Sure, honey. I have friends everywhere, and I'm making more every minute. It comes with the lifestyle."

"So does lots of other stuff, Ricardo. You know what I mean."

She disconnected the call. For a second, she thought about her father, the brilliant scientist who'd often claimed that every situation could be defined by an equation. Then she shook her head because the numbers here did not add up. Meanwhile, the crowd kept moving down the strip. They marched past a towering fountain adorned with the happy image of Lakshmi, a goddess of wealth and fortune. People were cheering and chanting, and then there he was—Jack.

Kiara let out a yelp. He was charging through the crowd like an angry bull. Suzy reached for her pistol but Kiara put a hand on her arm. "No, Suzy! Not here! They'll arrest you."

Damn, it was true—and his hands looked empty. What the hell? This guy does have balls, Suzy thought. He stopped about two meters away, with a crazed look in his eyes, ignoring Suzy and everyone else. He only seemed interested in Kiara.

"Kiara, didn't you read my note? You didn't want to meet me?"

"Jack, what are you talking about? Can't you see I'm busy? Besides, I'm done with you."

Suzy lunged forward, stepping in front of Kiara.

"Who put you up to that murder, Jack? So now you're working for a serial killer?"

Jack started to scoff in denial and step around her—but then he stopped, looking confused. "What serial killer?"

"Shogun Hunter," Kiara said. "The guy we came here to find."

"I don't know any 'Shogun Hunter.' "

"Maybe that's because he changed his identity," Suzy said. "Probably at that little surgery place. So he wanted the surgeon dead, right? So who put you up to it? Because that guy might want *you* dead, too—eventually."

Now her gun was out, close to her thigh.

Jack still looked confused but he eyed the weapon and snarled. "I don't know what you're talking about, and why would I believe a lying bitch like you?" He thrust his shaggy beard in Kiara's direction. "You've got to get out of here, Kiara. Things are gonna get really fucked up."

Suzy suddenly felt her heart pumping fast. Jack wasn't here to complain about his unrequited love—he was here to warn Kiara. She gave a glance upward at the tall buildings and then scanned the crowd.

"What's going to happen, Jack?"

"All kinds of shit. Get out of here now!"

"Dammit!" she said. "Kiara, we have to move!"

Suzy grabbed Kiara's hand and took two steps—and then an explosion of gunfire blasted through the air, followed by a roar of shouts and screams.

"Get down!" Jack shouted. "The motherfuckers! *I told them to wait!*"

Suzy ducked down. Jack leaped toward Kiara, but Suzy grabbed his throat and smashed the barrel of her gun into his testicles. Jack swore and tumbled to the street, and Suzy once again yanked Kiara away from the center of the crowd. Meanwhile, energy blasts lit up the sky, pouring from a rooftop. People were falling on top of each other—pushing, shoving, yelling—and bodies were hitting the pavement. Two people in front of Suzy were struck in the back of the head; one was a young girl, and blood splattered everywhere.

For an instant, Suzy felt sick. Kiara was screaming as they stumbled past the goddess-fountain just as it was struck by another salvo. Lakshmi crashed down with a splash, there were more screams, and then they reached a doorway with an alcove. Kiara ran into the alcove and got down low. Suzy put herself between Kiara and the street as she looked out at the chaos.

Where's Ricardo? she thought. *I hope he's okay.*

The barrage didn't last long, but it didn't need to. The crowd was in tatters. Sirens were roaring, people were crying and wailing, and the cops were running in circles, shouting orders and trying to help the wounded. Suzy had an instinctive feeling the attack was over—just a quick blast of terror and a pile of bloody, broken bodies. And there was Jack! He was standing in the middle of the mayhem, looking like a delirious animal. He stared at Kiara and Suzy. She aimed her gun at him, but he ducked behind a dazed woman. Then he started running.

Suzy hesitated—and now Ricardo was coming through the crowd.

He had Rafael and David with him. She felt a wave of relief as she leaped to her feet and shouted above the noise. He saw her, and she pointed at Kiara. Then she grabbed the girl and held her for an instant. "Stay here!" Suzy said. "I'll be back."

She took off after Jack. She heard Ricardo shouting something but couldn't hear it. She was focused on her target—and he was weaving through the crowd, knocking people over, heading back up the street. As Suzy stared at the death and destruction, she felt a pang of guilt, but she wasn't a paramedic and Jack obviously knew who was behind the attack—and other things. She had to get him.

He was on the sidewalk now, running past the casino hotels and away from the massacre. She saw him look over his shoulder, and then he turned down a side street. She gritted her teeth. You're not getting away, she thought. She was definitely gaining on him.

She was careful at the corner; he might have a weapon, and maybe some friends, and he could be waiting. So she came to a sudden stop, catching her breath and peering around the edge of a building to scan the street. Lots of blinking shops, and a fair number of people standing around yelling and looking at their allcoms. Jack was about thirty meters away.

She planned to shoot him with a stun shot and call Ricardo, and then get him to a place where they could have a conversation. But there were too many people on the street to start shooting from this distance. She had to get closer without getting shot herself. It was the basic problem with gunfights.

People stared at her as she ran by. Wait—he was stopping. He looked tired, and he was whirling around with a gun in his hand—and he was crashing into a woman on the sidewalk. They were both tumbling to the ground. He was grabbing her, trying to use her as a shield as he fired at Suzy.

She stepped aside and saw two people get hit by his stun shots. Why was he not trying to kill her? She fired two shots of her own and accidentally hit Jack's shield-woman in the chest. Crap! Well, it was also a stun shot, and now Jack was briefly trapped underneath her body. So Suzy shot him in the neck.

People nearby were screaming, probably thinking it was all part of the attack around the corner. Damn, it would be tough to get his body out of here—she needed a car quick. And that's when a car screeched to a stop right across the sidewalk.

She aimed her gun at the vehicle but no one exited. Instead, someone grabbed her from behind.

"Got you!" said a deep male voice.

It was Burt Stone. He knocked the gun from her hand and slid his arms under her armpits, locking his hands behind her neck. She kicked at his shins but he just tightened his grip. She swore as he lifted her off the sidewalk. Then the car door opened, and his partner came running. Her eyes looked wild, just like before—but she also looked less scared and more determined. Suzy tried to kick her in the chest, but the woman grabbed her ankle and then jammed a black stick into her thigh and Suzy felt a powerful jolt go through her entire body.

It hurt like hell. Suzy felt numb, like she couldn't move her leg at all. Then the woman grimaced and jammed the stick into her ribs.

Suzy gave one final shout and blacked out.

Chapter 33

What was going on? Suzy blinked her eyes, trying to get her foggy brain into focus. Okay, not much time had passed. She was lying on her stomach, on the cold pavement with her hands and feet bound. Her body ached, and she had a brief flashback to being arrested as a kid, under a boardwalk with a few friends and a stolen hover bike. At least today she wouldn't have to listen to Mom and Dad talk about her dismal future. She gave a grim laugh. *Hey, maybe I should've paid more attention.*

She thought about her father, who was dead, and her mother, who still loved her. But then she stopped thinking about them because this was no time for gooey nostalgia. *After all, I might have to shoot a few more people today.*

She struggled against the plastic binders cutting into her wrists and ankles. Primitive but effective. Nearby, she saw Jack's unconscious body still lying on the ground, along with the woman who'd been on top of him. There was also another car parked, a police car with flashing lights, and somebody was arguing. Apparently, Burt Stone was fighting with the cops over who was going to take her away to be hanged or whatever. She twisted her body a bit to get a better view.

Where's my gun? She didn't see it. Meanwhile, there was a growing crowd of gawkers looking at her. There were also three Baadal Shahar police officers standing there in black armor—and there was Burt Stone, red in the face and shouting.

"She's not your prisoner!" Burt said. "We tracked her from Earth. We're the ones who identified her. You clowns couldn't find your own asses with a map."

His female friend was trying to show one of the Baadal Shahar officers something displayed on an allcom but he turned away with a snort and said, "This woman is wanted for questioning, and you can't have her until we're done. This is our city, fuck face."

Suzy wasn't a legal scholar, but she had a feeling that fuck face was going to lose the argument. While he was huffing and puffing and waving his arms around, Suzy scanned the crowd, hoping to find a friend—and she did.

Ricardo was standing there, looking sleek and sharp in a red jumpsuit. For one quick second he stared at her, and he winked. Then he stepped out of sight behind the spectators.

Suzy almost smiled but kept it to herself. Despite his clownish ways, Ricardo was good in a tight spot. But where was Kiara? Ricardo was supposed to be watching her and she didn't seem to be here.

One of the cops kicked her with his toe and scowled down at her. "Time for a ride," he said. Then two other cops pulled her to a standing position and shoved her into the back of the police car. They were rough but she'd experienced worse; usually someone gave her a quick grope. But then one of them reached into the car and slapped her hard across the face.

Suzy gave him a glare. "Did I say something?"

"No," he said. "But keep it that way."

"Fine, I won't tell you how to pick up girls. But just so you know, slapping the shit out of them doesn't help."

He smirked and leaned into the car. He squeezed her thigh hard with his big hand and slapped her again—several times. She swore and tried to bite his fingers, but he stopped hitting her and spoke in a low voice. He said, "There's a crowd of people here, so you get a break. But when we get back to the station, I'm going to take my time with you."

He leered and closed the door. Then he started talking into the link chip in his collar. Suzy scowled and glanced out the window, trying to ignore the sting from his blows. Dammit, where was Ricardo? When would he make his move? She didn't see him now, but she saw lots of cops. Too many. She shifted around a bit on the seat, inching her skirt up. She usually kept a knife strapped to her left thigh, but it was gone, along with the one in her boot. So maybe one of the thugs *had* groped her a bit while she'd been unconscious. Meanwhile, Burt Stone was still arguing, and one of the cops said, "If you don't get out of here we're arresting you."

"Arresting me? I'm a cop!"

"Not in this city. Around here you're just another asshole. Now go home."

Someone in a white shirt with a few blinking doodads arrived and started examining Jack. Suzy shook her head. It was the third time she'd shot the guy with a stun blast. *He really should just hit the ground as soon as he sees me.* Hopefully, he'd be well enough to answer a few questions when she finally got out of this mess.

Stone was talking to his female friend. She was listening closely and shaking her head, and now they were arguing. The Baadal Shahar cops were communing by one of the other cars. Then Burt came running.

In a flash, she knew what he was going to do. What a crazy fucker! He yanked open the door of the police car and jumped inside. The woman was right behind him, grabbing the opposite door and jumping in, too.

"Get out of here, Tala!" he said. "I don't want you involved in this."

"We're partners," she said. "So I'm involved. Besides, you need my help."

"I don't, and I don't want you getting into trouble. I mean it!"

"No way, Burt. Let's go!"

He swore and revved the engine, and the vehicle lurched backward, and then jumped forward, and then took off down the street. The cops were yelling and screaming as they fumbled for their weapons. A salvo of shots hit the back of the hover-car, destroying a brake light and blowing a hole in the trunk. Suzy dove down low in the back seat. She was tossed against the door and banged her head but she was okay. Stone gave a whoop as he swerved the car around a corner. Then he shouted, "So long, losers!"

Tala looked back and laughed. "I guess we're in trouble now."

"Yeah," Stone said, and now he looked grim. "And I feel guilty already."

"I wanted to."

He shook his head. "You're breaking some serious rules."

"And it feels great," she said with a smile.

"It won't feel so great if we end up in jail." He gave a quick laugh. "But it feels pretty good now." Then he revved the engine again. "We need to get out of the city quick. This is a police car and I'm sure they can track it."

"Plus, they'll have cops at the spaceport they can notify. This might not be the best plan."

"This isn't really a plan, Tala. It's another one of my hotheaded blunders."

"We'll make it," Tala said with another big smile, and she reached out and held Burt's hand.

Despite the circumstances, Suzy found herself amused. "Would you two like to be alone?" she said. "Because you can stop and let me out any time."

Burt's face turned red but it wasn't with anger. "You shut your mouth, Suzy. You can talk when you get to court. In fact, I should shoot you just for the hell of it. How would you like that?"

"It would probably be better than watching you screw up this escape."

"We're not going to screw it up!"

"Really? You seem like the kind of guy who screws up everything."

Now he gave her a look of snarling rage—mixed with a little fear. Tala spoke in a trembling voice, "I think someone's following us."

Stone gave a quick glance at the rearview mirror. "I don't think so. You're just being paranoid."

"No, I'm not. That car is following us."

Suzy looked out the back window. Yeah, someone was closing fast. Maybe Ricardo? No, he wouldn't start shooting with a hi-powered rifle.

The first blast shattered the back window and almost hit Tala in the head. She let out a scream. Burt swore and swerved the car down a side street.

Tala was shouting now. "Someone's trying to kill us!"

Burt swerved the car again, down another street, going the wrong way up a one way. But the other car was still there. "You've got to shoot back!" he said. "I'm driving."

"Shoot back? Right!" Tala was fumbling around with Suzy's gun.

It was the Casino Cartel; Suzy was sure of it, and Tala looked hysterical—a bad sign. But then her trembling lip curled into a sneer and she leaned out the window, firing away. Burt spun the car around another corner and smashed into a street sign. He drove it over a curb and hit a bus stop advertising Coca Cola and then bounced the vehicle back onto the street, facing the way they'd come.

Suzy cursed at her helpless state. She watched as the other car came skidding around the corner—a perfect shot. And Tala hit it, obliterating a side window and causing it to veer off the street. But the guy in the back with the big gun was still blasting away.

Burt let out a scream as the side of the car was raked by energy blasts. The car lurched forward and crashed into a nail salon. Then Tala fired again and once again hit her target, shattering the back windows of the other vehicle and causing it to smash into a bank. Burt muscled the police car back onto the road and they were zooming down a dark street.

Tala looked pale. "I think I killed someone," she said.

Burt winced, obviously in pain. "Don't worry about it," he said, and his voice was strained. There was blood splattered on the steering wheel and console.

Tala yelped. "You got hit!"

"I'll be all right. It isn't too bad."

"Where are you hit? You need to go to a hospital."

"No, they'll arrest me. I'll be fine."

Suzy could tell he was not going to be fine. In fact, he was going to be dead soon because his whole left side was burned and bleeding.

"Tala, untie me," Suzy said. "I can help."

"You keep quiet!" Burt snapped. "You'll get untied when the reprogrammer erases your brain. Crap, there's something wrong with the car."

They had crossed into an industrial part of town. It was darker here, and the buildings were sprawling silhouettes of spiky-looking structures. These were mostly automated factories that processed energy, air, and water. It seemed peaceful enough but Suzy was sure the area was under heavy surveillance. Certainly, the air-processing factory they were driving past had a security force inside. But no one was around as the car came crawling to a stop. Then the anti-grav thrusters cut out, and with a jarring thud the car hit the ground.

"They're going to find us," Suzy said. "The cartel is after me but they're in with the cops, and the cops can probably track this car—and I'm guessing the cops will be fine with the cartel killing me. You too will just be a bonus. We've got to get out of here now."

"Be quiet," Burt hissed. Then he paused for a second and looked at Tala. "I think we better get out of here now," he said.

"Okay," Tala said, and her voice was shaking. "But where will we go? You need a doctor. And what about Suzy?"

"Untie me," Suzy said. "I can help."

"Will you shut up!" Burt said. Then he swore again and gritted his teeth. "Tala, untie her feet. We need her to walk. But if you try anything, Suzy, I'll kill you. Do you hear me?"

"Of course I hear you," Suzy said. "You're spitting your last breath in my face, and that's because you're bleeding to death. You can go to a clinic, Burt. There are lots of them in this city, no questions asked."

"She's right," Tala said. "You need help."

"I'll be fine."

Tala gave a disgusted shake of her head and ran to the back door. She pulled out a familiar-looking knife and cut Suzy's leg binders. So that's where my knife went, Suzy thought. "Hey, do you have my allcom, too? I can call someone."

Tala didn't answer. She was watching as Burt stumbled out of the car and hit the ground. He looks pretty awful, Suzy thought. There was lots of blood and he wasn't going to last much longer. Tala let out a yelp and jumped toward him. She also left the knife sitting on the back seat.

Tala raced around the car and got down on her knees. She was frantic, cradling Burt's unconscious head in her hands, trying to get him to speak. She was sniffling and barely holding herself together.

Suzy had the knife behind her back and was cutting the ties on her wrists. *I'm getting good at this sort of thing—there, done.* Sitting in the space between the two front seats was her allcom, and lying on the seat was her gun. She picked it up and checked the power. Okay, still good for quite a few shots. She walked around the car, keeping her eye on the street, waiting for another car to arrive. She found Tala sobbing on the ground.

"Hang on, Burt," Tala said.

"He needs a doctor fast," Suzy said.

Tala's eyes popped open wide. "You're free!"

"Yeah. But don't worry. I can help."

Tala seemed frozen, trying to think. And that's when another car appeared at the end of the block, gliding toward them like a shark. Suzy ducked down quick.

"Tala, be quiet and don't move."

"What?"

"Stay down and don't move. I don't think they can see you."

Suzy crawled fast toward the front of the car and peered from behind the battered fender. Her pulse was steady as the vehicle came to a stop twenty meters away. Then the driver stepped out, along with another person. They were both carrying hi-powered rifles, and one of the guys was on an allcom.

Just a little closer, Suzy thought. Closer, closer—and then her own allcom started vibrating. Crap! It was Ricardo. *Not a good time!* But then she studied the two shadowy guys a bit more, and realized the car was lime green; it had been hard to see the color in the darkness. She glanced down at the tracking bracelet on her wrist. Maybe that special piece of jewelry had been a good idea after all. She stood up.

"Ricardo," she said.

"Suzy."

He came running. He gave her a hug, and she hugged him back. Then he pulled away and looked at the two cops on the pavement.

"So, I see you have things under control."

"Sort of. But we need to get out of here quick. Did you see the cartel people?"

"Yeah. We found them in bad shape, but now they're worse." He glanced at Rafael, who held up his rifle and grinned.

"Great," Suzy said. "These two need a ride to the hospital."

Ricardo hesitated while Rafael stared at the two cops, shaking his head. "Aren't these the two cops from Earth?" Rafael said. "We should get rid of them."

Ricardo frowned. "No, I don't think so. We don't need to be so drastic."

"Yes, we do," Rafael said. "It's the way we do things. These two could cause trouble. Pablo would want them gone."

Ricardo squirmed a bit and Rafael aimed his weapon at the two cops. Tala looked up at him with big eyes—and then Suzy grabbed the gun barrel, yanking it downward.

"Put the gun down," she said. "We're taking them to a hospital."

Rafael gave a snort. "Are you crazy?" He stared at Suzy for a long second, and she stared right back. But he kept the weapon lowered. "Pablo won't like it," he said.

"He can write me a letter."

Ricardo looked relieved. "She's right, Rafael. Let's get them into the car."

Rafael just sneered and glared at Suzy. "You get away with a lot—with all your jokes and your attitude. But then we have to answer for it."

"You won't have to answer for anything," she shot back.

Ricardo stepped between them. "Forget it, Raffy. Just put them in the car."

Rafael stood there scowling for a long second, but then he finally gave a sardonic laugh and loaded Burt into the back of the vehicle. Suzy kept her eye on him while also standing guard in case more cartel people showed up. Tala watched with a shell-shocked look on her face.

Tala wiped her teary eyes and turned to Suzy. "Thank you," she said. "I guess you're not so bad."

"Oh, I'm bad, Tala. Just not right now."

Tala gave a little smile and got into the back seat. Suzy rode beside her while Burt leaned against the door. As the car pulled away, Suzy said, "Where's Kiara?"

"She was with Kaya when I left," Ricardo said. "They were looking for Anika."

Chapter 34

Suzy jiggled one leg as the car navigated a honking jigsaw puzzle of traffic. She was in the back seat, keeping an eye on Burt and Tala, while Ricardo and Raphael sat up front with their rifles. Sirens were echoing in the distance and screaming all around. People were rioting and burning things, not a smart move in a domed city. But they were enraged, and enraged people don't always think about science and asphyxiation.

She fumbled with her allcom and felt a rush of relief when Kiara picked up. Kiara was at the Baadal Shahar City Hospital, where Kaya and Marcos were talking in front of crowds and cameras about the slaughter in the streets. Anika was supposedly on her way.

"Good," Suzy said. "We're heading there now. I guess it's a popular place tonight."

"It's horrible here, Suzy. Be careful." Then she hesitated. "Jack is here."

"What?" Suzy felt a jolt of alarm. "Is he awake?"

"No, not yet. I'll talk to him when he wakes up."

"No! Keep away from him—at least until I get there."

"But I can help, Suzy."

"Kiara—don't," Suzy said. Then she paused. "Listen, it's important no one knows why we're looking for Jack, okay? So don't trust anyone. And wait until I get there. Please."

There was a moment of silence. Then Kiara said, "Okay, I'll wait."

Suzy shook her head as she hung up. *I'll explain it when I see her.*

Ricardo glanced at Suzy in the rearview mirror. "The black hair looks good," he said.

"Thanks, but don't get used to it. I like my natural color."

"But the cops are looking for a redhead."

"They're busy worrying about a revolution. Besides, there are over 7,000 redheads in this city."

"Really? When did you figure that out?"

She didn't answer him, but she thought about her father again, and then her mother, and then she noticed that Tala was holding Burt's hand, seemingly oblivious to the conversation around her. It was a sweet thing. I hope he makes it, Suzy thought. He was still breathing but he couldn't have much time left. Luckily, they reached the hospital with Burt still alive, and they drove to the emergency room entrance. The whole area was a mishmash of people and chaos, but Suzy was glad they'd come here instead of a clinic. Burt needed maximum attention, and being arrested was a lower priority than being dead.

Ricardo and Rafael ran into the huge building and returned with two paramedics and an anti-grav stretcher. Tala stayed glued to Burt's side as they entered a room filled with turmoil and broken bodies. People were standing and sitting in every corner while doctors and nurses rushed around, trying to determine who was most likely to die next. The air was filled with the din of desperate voices, some of them wailing and crying. Tala immediately began shouting for attention but got nowhere. Ricardo smiled, approached a nurse, and had a quick conversation. Suzy noticed the quick exchange of something—money, no doubt, and then Burt was immediately being examined and moved into surgery.

Tala thanked Ricardo. She was more composed now but in a depressed kind of way. She turned to Suzy and said, "I thought I was tougher than this. Maybe I'm just not meant to be a cop."

"I don't think you'd be breaking any laws if you quit."

Tala paused and then frowned. "I was a chemical engineer for one year, and I didn't like it. I wanted more adventure. Now I wish I could do it all over."

Suzy shrugged. "Tala, I'm not the best person to give out career advice, but I could've killed you a couple of times. I hope Burt lives—I do. And then I hope you two go home. Believe me, I'd go home if I could."

Tala looked into Suzy's eyes. "I hope you go home someday, Suzy."

"Thanks."

As Suzy and Ricardo walked away, Ricardo grinned. "See the things I do for you, honey? That dumbass cop is probably going to wake up and kill us both."

Suzy couldn't deny the possibility, but she also felt good about helping Burt. In fact, she felt downright uplifted. But yeah, it would be bad if the idiot did end up chasing her again, so she leaned close to Ricardo and said, "Call the cops after we leave and give them an anonymous tip that Stone is here, just in case it didn't get flagged by some database."

He gave an approving nod. "I like it. You think they'll arrest a dying man?"

"I think if he lives, they'll both get deported. From what I've seen, we're doing them a favor."

"No problem. I'll do it."

Then Suzy spotted Kiara weaving through the crowd, coming toward her. Suzy gave her a big hug.

"You escaped," Kiara said. "I knew you would."

"I had some help," Suzy said, motioning toward Ricardo.

Ricardo laughed. "Yeah, and I'm still waiting for my hug."

Suzy just glanced at him and then looked at Kiara. "So, where's Jack?"

"He's on the seventh floor," Kiara blurted. "They're giving him medication for his nervous system. A doctor told me he'll be asleep for a while. The drug works better if he stays asleep, so they're keeping him sedated. Mert told me he's seen this kind of thing before, and Jack will be fine."

"Mert knows Jack? What did you tell him?"

"Nothing! It was before you called, right after they brought him in. Mert didn't seem to know Jack. He saw me looking at him, and I was upset. I didn't tell him anything."

Mert Kaya and Marcos were both walking among the wounded.

They'd given their statements outside and now they were inside, posing for photos. But why weren't they standing together? Suzy watched one of Marcos's aides coerce a few people to move away from Kaya and come stand near Marcos just as a photo was taken. Then Kaya mentioned, seemingly as a joke, that Marcos had been a little late arriving because he'd only been living on Baadal Shahar a short time and he'd gotten lost. Finally, a few nurses asked them both to leave, unless they were planning to get shot sometime in the near future. A screen on the wall flashed with images of Buso, yelling about enemies, liars, and justice. Ricardo went and talked to Marcos, and then he motioned for Suzy to join them outside.

"Come on," Suzy said to Kiara. "Let's go see what's going on."

"What about Jack?"

"Don't worry, we're staying here. I actually want to keep that *pendejo* alive."

"You think someone wants to kill him, don't you, Suzy? Jack knows who attacked the crowd, so the Snake Eyes are probably involved—and they don't want him to talk. And he also might be able to lead us to Hunter, so Hunter might want him dead."

"Right. You learn quick. So we're going to go upstairs and wait for Jack to wake up. But first I want to know what everyone else is planning."

Outside on the street, Mert and Marcos were blaming the government for the attack, but as soon as Anika arrived the crowd and the reporters abandoned them. Her car was mobbed, and people from her organization had to plow people away so she could exit the vehicle. She was immediately deluged by questions from reporters.

"Wow," Kiara said. "She's got more fans than Kaya and Marcos. I wonder if they care."

Suzy laughed. "If I had to bet on it—hell, yes. They care."

Marcos and Kaya both looked annoyed in a smiley kind of way. For her part, Anika didn't seem too impressed with her fame. She said, "I'm not here to make a speech. I'm here to support those who were injured and killed."

A guy screamed, "President Buso denies any involvement in the attack. What do you have to say to him?"

Anika shook her head. "I don't know who attacked us. We're a group of people trying to make this city better. All we want is an end to the drugs and the trafficking and the corruption." There was a lot of cheering from the crowd. Then she added, "And we'd like the air to be clean." This produced a low rumble from the mob and some dirty looks from a few of the security personnel. The crowd wanted to hear more but she refused and headed into the hospital with a pack of people surrounding her.

Ricardo came over and pulled Suzy aside. "Suzy, I was talking to Marcos—hey, why do you look so skeptical?"

"Do I look skeptical? I thought I just looked disgusted."

"Suzy, we need to talk about the guns. It's important that you know what's happening."

"Let me guess: Marcos wants to give the guns to a bunch of thugs so he can take over the city."

Ricardo rolled his eyes. "Suzy, they're not thugs. They're *friends* of ours, and I've got more coming, on a flight that's landing soon. Also, we've got people Marcos knows, and people Mert knows. It's time for us to make our move."

Now Marcos came over. "Hello, Suzy," he said with a smile. "I'm glad you're okay." When she barely nodded her head, he continued. "So, Ricardo, I guess you two talked? Did you tell her about our strategy?"

"Yes—no."

"What?" Suzy said.

Ricardo sighed. "Suzy, here's the situation: Anika isn't totally on board with the plan. She thinks of the guns as a defensive thing; she doesn't see the bigger picture. So we were thinking you could explain it to her."

"Me?" Suzy said. "Why me? I just got here. I hardly know Anika."

"Yeah, but you saved her life, and she trusts you—also, she likes you. She thinks you're honest."

"Why would she think that, Ricardo? I'm an outlaw."

"But you're an honest outlaw. So just give her a little nudge, that's all."

She gave a short laugh. "If Anika asks me what I think, I'm telling her that your plan is shit. I might even tell her if she doesn't ask."

"No!" Ricardo hissed. "Suzy, you can't do that. Remember, this is Maria's plan."

"There are more people involved in this than Maria—and *Pablo.*"

She practically spat his name, and then regretted it. But then she didn't.

Marcos just grinned, seemingly unfazed. Suzy half expected to see a pointy tongue come flickering out of his mouth. "You're a feisty one, Suzy," he said. "But I think you have the wrong idea about what we're doing here. We're looking to create positive change."

"If you want to make things better, Marcos, why don't you drop dead? I'm going back inside."

"She's joking!" Ricardo blurted. "She doesn't mean that. She's always fooling around."

Really? Suzy thought. *A few seconds ago I was 'honest.'* Marcos was laughing as she turned and walked away. Would Ricardo follow? No, he was still talking to Marcos, probably telling him not to worry, he'd "get her under control." *Good luck with that, amigo.* By now he should know better.

Kiara had wandered away, but Suzy found her inside the hospital lobby, talking to Mert Kaya. Mert eyed her as she approached, so she eyed him back. But then he smiled and said, "So, how are things going, Suzy?"

Suzy moved close to Kiara. "Fine," Suzy said. "Your friends are outside dividing up the world. Why aren't you there? You like to talk."

He hesitated and then waved his hand. "I have other concerns. I just want to be here with the people."

Kiara tugged on Suzy's arm. "Mert says we can stay with him, Suzy."

"Thanks, Mert," Suzy said. "But we've already got a place."

"Well, if you change your mind, you can come over—or Kiara can. She seems interested in what we're doing."

"I am," Kiara said.

He nodded. "Also, it might be safer, Suzy, seeing as how there are people looking for you."

"Suzy, it sounds nice," Kiara said. "He's got an Octavus Six air bath. The kind where you float."

"Does he?" Suzy said. "Mert, someone already tracked me to your house once, and someone else just shot up the crowd down the street from where you were standing—so being around you isn't all that safe, either."

Now she could see him bristling. "Maybe that's true," he said in an even voice. Then he quickly added, "Are you here to check on Kiara's friend? What's his name? Jack?"

"He's not my friend," Kiara said.

"Then why do you want to find him?"

Kiara started to speak and then stopped. She shrugged and said nothing.

"It's a personal issue," Suzy said. Then she smiled. "That means it's none of your fucking business."

Mert laughed and held up his hands. "All right, I'm sorry! I didn't mean to pry. I'm just curious. I saw him when he arrived, and he looked a little rough, that's all. I don't want you getting hurt."

"We'll be careful. Have a great night."

They left him standing there and headed toward the turbo lifts. As they entered the lift and shut the door, Suzy said, "Kiara, I know you want to stay with Mert, but—"

"I don't want to stay with him."

"What? You don't?"

"No. He's not the first guy who wanted to 'help me out,' Suzy. I'm staying with you."

"Oh. Well, that's good. But you seemed to like the idea."

"Yeah, I was faking, so he wouldn't know what I really thought. I'm not saying he's a bad guy—but I'm not staying with him."

"Okay, fine," Suzy said with a laugh. "You're a good faker. You had me fooled."

"I've had lots of practice," Kiara said. Then she added, "You should try it sometime."

Yeah, I should, Suzy thought. But she said, "Not my style," and watched as Kiara grinned.

The turbo lift opened and they stepped out onto the seventh floor. It was a shiny white room that seemed to sprawl toward infinity, and it was filled with rolling beds, hover-beds, tables, and blinking machines that dangled with tubes and silvery tentacles. Kiara pointed toward an area against the far wall where emerald green curtains hung down, forming a row of cloth-walled cubicles. There were robot nurses whooshing around like floating octopi; there were people in blue scrubs moving fast, but no one bothered Suzy or Kiara as they walked toward one of the cubicles that was completely enclosed. Suzy put her hand close to her pistol and then yanked back the curtain.

The bed was empty.

Kiara gasped. "He can't be gone. A nurse told me he'd be sleeping at least another two hours. They must've moved him."

"I don't think so," Suzy said. "Someone took him."

She pointed to a loose tube that dangled from a hanging bag of fluid. The stuff was dripping on the floor—not much, but in a way that indicated someone hadn't bothered to turn it off.

"But he can't walk," Kiara said. "They couldn't have carried him."

"They probably took him in an anti-grav chair."

"With all these people around?"

Suddenly there was a rustling sound, and the curtain moved, and a dark-haired girl was standing there. She wasn't much older than Kiara. She was dressed in standard blue medical scrubs and when she saw Suzy her eyes opened wide.

Suzy said, "Hi. Do you know what happened to the guy who was in this bed?"

The girl just kept looking at Suzy. Finally, she spoke in a low voice. "You're the one on the news. The one who shot those people."

Suzy once again moved her hand close to her weapon. "What news? No, that wasn't me."

Can't you see I'm a brunette now? Besides, there are 7,000 redheads in this city.

"You're Suzy Spitfire. You came to help Anika, and then you saved her life. You're a hero."

"Oh," Suzy said, relaxing a bit. "Okay, I might've been there. But where's the guy who was lying in this bed?"

The woman poked her head through the curtain, back into the main room, and peered around. Then she stepped back inside and closed it, leaning closer to Suzy. "My name is Reshma," she said. "I'm one of Anika's warriors, in the underground."

Suzy slowly nodded her head. "Right. The underground."

Reshma studied Kiara. "You're Suzy's friend. We've heard you want to help, too. Did Anika rescue you?"

"No," Kiara said. "But I'd like to be…a warrior, underground."

"The more we have, the better," Reshma said. "And we already have a lot. Anika talks to us… She knows what's happening in this city—and we're in the shadows, waiting."

Suzy vaguely wondered how many of them knew how to fire a gun, but decided this wasn't the time to ask. "What about Jack, the guy who was in here?"

"They took him right before you came, two of his friends—a man and a woman. I think the doctor here is also a friend of that group. When those people come, you just go along. That's the way it works in Baadal Shahar."

Suzy's eyes lit up. "Right before we came? Which way did they go?"

"They put him in a chair and took him to the lift. They were probably going down when you were coming up."

"Thanks, Reshma," Suzy said. Then she turned to Kiara and said, "Wait here."

Suzy bolted across the room. She knew Kiara wouldn't listen and of course she was right. The girl caught her at the lift.

"Kiara, I really don't want you getting hurt, okay?"

"I want to come. I can help."

The door to the lift popped open and Suzy stepped inside quick— and then whirled to grab Kiara by the shoulders, keeping her out.

"Not this time, Kiara."

"But I want to help Jack!"

The door wouldn't close with Kiara in the way.

"You can help him by not getting killed—now let me go."

Kiara hesitated. Suzy briefly considered hitting her—but didn't. And then Kiara stepped back.

"Good luck, Suzy."

Suzy waved as the door slammed shut. In an instant, the elevator whooshed to the ground floor.

Sure, they had a head start, but Jack was out cold, and loading a bag of unconscious meat into a hover-car would take a few minutes. She leaped out of the lift and surveyed the scene—a cramped lobby area with people rushing around, a busy front desk manned by robots, and some glass doors that led outside to a parking area. She ran through the doors, to a circular drive meant for patient pick-up. There were a few hover cars gliding in now, and some cops standing around.

There was also an anti-grav chair, hovering by the curb. It was empty.

No car, no Snake Eyes, and no Jack. Suzy stared at the chair and swore. Then Kiara was by her side.

Kiara was also staring at the chair. "Jack's in trouble, isn't he? Probably because of me."

"We don't know that," Suzy said with a grim expression. "Not for sure." She put her arm around Kiara's shoulders.

Kiara didn't look at her. "Were you going to hit me, Suzy? When you were getting into the lift."

"What?" Suzy tried to sound indignant, but then she knew it wouldn't work. "I thought about it," she said with a sigh. "I'm sorry, Kiara."

"It's okay. I know you don't want to hurt me, right?"

"Right! It's just the way I am. I have bad thoughts."

Kiara stared across the parking lot. "I have them, too. I'm not as nice as you think. But you keep treating me like a little girl."

"I know you're not."

"Then stop cutting me out. I thought we were friends. You were showing me things."

"We are! And I am... I won't cut you out again." *Unless I really have to.*

"Okay," Kiara said. Then she smiled. "I exchanged contact

information with Reshma. I thought we might want to talk to her again."

"Good thinking. We might."

"So what do we do now?"

"We go get some sleep, Kiara. And then we think about our next move."

Chapter 35

Danielle eyed the cup of dark coffee in her hand. She always took it black. The caffeine wasn't good for her anxiety level, but she hadn't been sleeping much anyway. The bed seemed too big without Andre in it. As she took another steamy sip, she closed the door to her office. Maybe she could submerge herself in her work.

She sighed. Unfortunately, she didn't work in an amusement park. She looked at her desktop and what it represented: the broken homes, the legal battles, and the mental damage caused by a world of villains. Why had she chosen this path? Well, she knew why, and it was probably normal to occasionally doubt it. Certainly, it would be so much easier to become an interior decorator—but in the end, did it really matter whether a silk lampshade was in perfect harmony with a tank of goldfish?

What mattered were the people she cared about, like her husband, who'd walked out on her and was not returning her messages. But that will change, she thought, and she nodded her head. *I hope so, I hope so.* Then she sat down and studied her monitor screen—and caught her breath. She had a text-only message from Venus. Her heart was pounding as she read the words.

Hi, Danielle. I got your message about abandoning the plan, but Hunter is here, and I'm going to get him. Lots of other stuff going on. I'll talk to you soon. Thanks for being a friend. Suzy.

She crinkled her forehead and then banged her head back against the chair. *What the hell?*

After a few seconds, she read it again. Okay, maybe Suzy's reply wasn't so bad. At least Suzy had responded. But then again, she'd actually said she was staying on Baadal Shahar!

As Danielle reread the message a third time, she couldn't keep a delicious feeling from rippling through her body as she imagined Suzy cornering the bastard and then hauling him back to Earth where he'd have his mind erased by the reprogammer. She also couldn't help feeling queasy, sick to her stomach, thinking about how she'd lied to the girl—and how Suzy could suffer the same fate as Hunter. She put down her hot coffee and tried to clear her head.

There was a knock on the door. It was her assistant, Cherry, who poked her smiling face into the room.

"Sorry to bother you, but your husband is here."

Her heart skipped a beat. *Finally!*

"Send him in," she said. And she quickly adjusted her black ropes of hair.

Commander Banks had rarely visited Danielle at work, but it was obvious everyone was impressed—because he was an impressive guy. But now he strode into the room like a chilly breeze. He shut the door and stood there, giving her a tight smile. He looked handsome, and dignified—and angry, but still she was hopeful. He was here, and they were going to talk.

"Andre, it's good to see you."

"I was in the neighborhood. I thought I'd come by."

She wanted to leap up and run to him, but she didn't. It didn't feel quite right.

"I'm glad you're here," she said. "I've been calling you."

"I know. I'm sorry I didn't answer. I was mad."

"I don't blame you. I hope you can forgive me. Did you listen to my messages?"

"Yes."

"I've been trying to fix things."

He gave a grunt, and then he sat down on the edge of the desk, and his glare softened. "Danielle, you've been there for me so many times." He was speaking fast now. "You've been the best thing in my life for years. I don't want this whole thing with Suzy Spitfire to ruin it."

"Neither do I!" she blurted. "I was so stupid. I don't know what I was thinking." She wiped a tear from her eye. "I wanted to get Hunter so badly, but now I just can't stand the idea that you don't trust me. I can't stand that."

He reached out and touched her shoulder. "It's all right, Danielle. I know you'd never want to hurt me. You made a big mistake, that's all—the same way I did when I let Suzy go." He shook his head. "This was really all *my* fault. I sent mixed messages. I never should've let her off."

She shook her head fast. "No! You did a good thing, Andre. Stop beating yourself up over a moment of humanity."

"It wasn't humanity," he said softly. "It was stupidity. And now I'm going to have to pay for it."

"No, you're not. Will you please stop thinking that way? The perfect cop, always following every stupid rule. Why does it have to be like that? No one else plays by the rules, Andre. No one."

He rose from the desktop and stood at his full lofty height.

"You're right, no one does," he said. "But I wanted to be different. I thought I was the guy, and I caused this whole mess, and I was wrong."

"You're not wrong! You're the most honest person I know. Besides, this might turn out fine by itself. I sent Suzy a message. I told her to come back to Earth—so you could arrest her."

"Really? And you think she'll listen?" Then he hesitated and said, "What did she say?"

"She's not coming. Not yet."

He gave a soft laugh. "She's an outlaw, Danielle. Helping you isn't that high on her list of priorities."

"But she is helping me! She says she's going to get Hunter—and if she does that, she's helping a lot of people."

He gave her a long stare and then looked away, like he was contemplating.

"Danielle, if you're serious about capturing Suzy, it might be possible. But you'll need to let us get involved. You *do* have her contact number, and she trusts you. Those are huge assets. But do you really think she's going to get this guy?"

She shrugged. "It's hard to say. She seems confident, and I think she's capable."

"She's both of those things." He looked back at her and crossed his arms. "So let's say she does it—good for her, and good for you. I can give you a location where she can drop him off. It won't be on Earth; let's keep her away from here." He paused and almost smiled. "I'll tell the department I got an anonymous tip, but we'll be waiting there, and we'll get Hunter—and we'll get her, too. We can even tell her an unknown informant was involved. She has plenty of enemies, and she'll never know you set her up. And we both get what we want. How's that? Are you all right?"

No, she was not all right. The sick feeling was much worse and she was having trouble breathing.

"Yes," she heard herself say. "I'm fine." Then she narrowed her eyes and said, "I'll do it."

"Great!" he said, obviously pleased. "I need to recall my team from Venus anyway, assuming they're not in jail by now. But I'll reassign them to Tycho City, and they can be part of the capture. They'll like that, and so will Stone's uncle."

"Smart. Very smart."

Andre smiled big now. "I try," he said. Then he hesitated. "Do you want to go to lunch?"

She wasn't hungry, but yes, she wanted to go.

Chapter 36

Suzy was dreaming.

She was in a shadowy room, strapped to a chair with heavy restraints on her wrists and ankles. She tried to move her head, but her neck was anchored in place by a tight metal collar. She gasped and squinted into the darkness, shifting her eyes around. There was a console on a nearby wall that glowed with cold blue light, and there was no one else in the room, and then she heard a man's voice. It was smug and gruff, and it seemed to be coming from a speaker near the console.

"Are you ready to be reprogrammed, Suzy?"

There was a whirring sound, and a skullcap was lowered onto her head.

No! Her heart started pounding. She yanked at her restraints and felt them cutting into her wrists—but it was no use. They didn't budge.

No! It can't end like this!

"It's time to pay for your crimes, Suzy. You've lived a violent life, but in a few minutes you'll be docile and eager to please. You'll also be a bit of a vegetable, but that's how it goes."

"Wait—stop! I was protecting my sister!"

"She was already dead. You didn't protect her at all, and now your mind's going to be erased. You'll have a few minutes of horrible pain, and then you'll feel nothing, and everything will be fine for the rest of your life."

He gave a low grunt as the blue light on the console changed to a hot shade of red. Something started beeping, over and over, and she tried to scream—but her throat was paralyzed, and her shout came out like a whisper, and it felt like her skull was being pierced by a thousand hungry needles. Something was sucking at her head and clawing at her brain. Something was devouring her thoughts and memories.

No!

Beep... Beep... Beep...

She jerked herself upright as her eyes snapped open. *Where am I?* She was in a cold sweat, and her chest was heaving—and a wave of relief washed over her. It had only been a nightmare. Again.

"Hey, are you okay?" Ricardo said. He was lying beside her in the back room of the laundromat while artificial sunlight streamed through the windows. On the floor, shoes and socks and a scarlet skirt were scattered around like wreckage from a storm.

Suzy shuddered and forced herself to shrug. "I'm fine," she said.

"Another nightmare? Don't worry, honey, the real world is looking good."

She hesitated, wanting to change the subject. "We should've opened this couch up into a bed a lot sooner. Why didn't we think of it?"

"Too much passion to think," he said. Then he rolled onto his side and let his hand rove over her body, stroking a few places. "Did you consider talking to Anika?"

"No, not really."

"You mean there's no chance?"

"Ricardo, imagine a number that looks like a zero." She gently pushed his hand away.

"What? After that wild night of love you're supposed to be like putty in my hands."

"I'm not that kind of girl, Ricardo. I can have five or six orgasms and still laugh at a guy in the morning."

He cocked his head. "Have you ever had six orgasms?"

"Sure. But I was alone at the time." She stood up and gathered her clothes. As she strapped a gun to her thigh, she said, "Anika has a secret group, some kind of underground fighting force. I'm guessing they're mostly teenagers, but I wouldn't call them kids."

"So what's your point?"

"My point is that there's a lot more going on than we know, and it was probably dumb to tell Marcos about those guns. Mert, Marcos, Anika—they all seem to be on the same side, but are they really? Meanwhile, you're supposed to be helping me find Hunter, but you're spending all your time cozying up to Marcos and his sleazy plans."

He was quiet for a second, and she knew he had something to say, something he probably didn't want to say.

"I'm supposed to kill Shogun Hunter," he said.

Well, I didn't think he was going to say that.

"What?"

He spoke in a low voice. "Shogun Hunter was a distributor who ripped Pablo off on a deal. Pablo figured since I was coming here anyway, I could take care of it. I didn't know about the guy's other crimes." He paused, and his eyes were sad. "I'm no saint, Suzy. I've blown up spaceships, and I've shot people who were shooting at me—but I'm not an enforcer; I'm not an assassin. Sure, this guy deserves it, but if I do it, then what? Does he start wanting me to keep doing it? When I tell you I want out of the life, I do. Anyway, I knew about Hunter all along, and I didn't tell you. I thought you'd like it if I volunteered to help, but I was really just helping myself."

I suppose I should be mad, Suzy thought. But she wasn't.

"Don't worry about it, Ricardo."

"Really? I thought you'd be furious."

"I probably should be, but life is short. Maybe those orgasms were worth something after all."

"Yeah," he said with a grin. "That's great. Besides, you're a way better assassin than me."

Now she was mad.

"What are you saying?" she snapped. "You know my story. I never killed anyone for money, and I never hurt anyone who didn't deserve it. I'm not a contract killer, Ricardo."

"Suzy, that's not what I meant. I was kidding."

"No, you weren't."

"Yes, I was—because everyone thinks you're tougher than me,

okay?" He paused, and then he sighed. "I wasn't trying to insult you. I'm just thinking about the way other people look at me. I'm supposed to be a gangster, but my girlfriend is tougher than me and stronger than me. Pablo knows it, Maria knows it—everyone does… I was being insecure. I'm sorry."

Suzy was quiet. Then she gave a soft laugh and sat down next to him.

She put a hand on his thigh. "Ricardo, that's ridiculous. You're plenty strong, and everyone knows it. Definitely anyone who was here last night. Hey, you wore me out."

He looked at her, and he grinned big. "So maybe I'm wrong."

"Yeah, maybe. Either way, it takes a tough guy to admit he's wrong."

"Not if it means he's a sex god."

"Did I say 'god'? I said I was tired. But yeah, you did a good job."

He grinned again. "Suzy, you are the friend that I will defend—until time has come to an end."

She laughed again, and then her allcom started beeping.

She glanced at the nearby device. Someone was sending a message to her ship.

"Ha, it's from Danielle—again."

"Patch it over."

She grabbed the allcom, and in an instant Danielle's voice filled the room:

"Hello, Suzy. I hate to say this, but someone gave me bad information—it's a long story. If you say Hunter is there, and you can get him, go right ahead! But don't bring him to Earth; bring him to Tycho City. Let me know when you're coming and I'll give you a bay number and someone will meet you there. I apologize for any confusion. Be careful, and I hope to see you soon."

"What?" Ricardo said. "So now she says he's here after all? Something's not right. I don't trust this woman."

"Why not? Maybe she's telling the truth, and someone gave her bad info. Or maybe she just got a little jittery about the whole thing—it happens. When I met her, she was good."

"Yeah, but her husband is the one who sent those cops."

"He doesn't know about her deal with me."

"How do you know? Maybe it's a set-up. Maybe they want to get Hunter, and then get you."

"You weren't there, Ricardo. She was sincere. Besides, why send those cops to grab me before I found him?"

"Ha, yeah. That would be stupid. But sometimes stupid stuff happens—actually, lots of times. Maybe he found out about her deal with you later, okay? They *are* married."

Suzy was about to respond when Ricardo heard a beep and picked up his own allcom. He looked at a message and swore. "Look at this! There was a fight. Someone stole the guns."

Chapter 37

Jack's vision was blurry, and his brain was filled with hazy thoughts. What the hell was going on? *Yeah, that's right, the bitch shot me again.*

He blinked a few times, realizing he was lying in the backseat of a hover-car, mostly naked in a hospital gown. He could see the golden lights of the city flashing by, and he could hear the conversation coming from the two people up front. It sounded like an argument.

Brother Divit said, "It's not our call. Mert needs to ask him a few questions."

"Yeah, sure," Sister Zehra said. "But after the questions, Mert's going to want him dead."

"Maybe, maybe not. But he could've blown the whole plan."

"He was just warning his girlfriend. It was a good thing to do. I thought we came here to save him from Suzy Spitfire."

"We did, but now we're taking him to Mert. He'll decide."

"Decide, decide," she muttered. "Always someone else gets to decide."

Jack took a deep breath, trying to control his nausea. Then he barked, "Take me to Mert, you motherfuckers."

The two people up front whipped their heads around.

"You're awake," Divit said.

"Yeah, and I got nothing to hide. I told Mert right off that no one was going to hurt Kiara."

The two Snakes looked at each other. At first they were quiet, but then Divit said, "Okay, Jack. We'll take you to Mert."

"Good. Why would it be a problem, anyway?"

Divit shrugged. "How much does your girl know? If she knows

you're a brother, then she knows we were behind the attack, right? I mean she's not supposed to know, but if she does, or if she finds out, then you really messed up."

Well, crap—that would be true. That would be a serious violation of the oath of secrecy, the one he'd broken long ago when he'd told Kiara the whole story of the Snake Eyes. But she'd liked hearing about it! She'd cared about what he had to say, more than his family ever had, more than anyone ever had.

Jack sneered. "Do you think I'd tell her that? She doesn't know shit. I just told her the rally wasn't safe, on account of all the shootings going on. I didn't tell her I knew anything. So there's no problem."

"Right, that's true. I'm sure Mert will believe you. You've done lots of stuff for him."

"Damn right I have."

In his mind, he heard Suzy saying something about that guy he'd killed in the surgery place—something crazy. But she was a liar, so why believe her? Then again, why had Mert wanted that guy dead? Like a good soldier, he'd just done the job.

Zehra gave a snotty laugh. "I'm sure Mert will be fair."

"Are you being sarcastic?" Divit said. "He's helped you a lot."

"No," she said quickly. "I'm fine." Then she added, "I appreciate his help."

Divit nodded. "He's a straight-shooter, and Jack's a real brother."

"Damn right I am," Jack said. "I'm the kind of brother who's paid my dues."

Zehra gave another light laugh while Divit said nothing.

Jack felt woozy as the car came to a stop in Divit's neighborhood. It was away from the main drag, where there were dimly lit streets, shadowy trees and bushes, and rows of faceless bamboo apartments crammed together like boxes in a warehouse. They were stopping in front of a rundown bar called The Point that the Snakes sometimes used for meetings.

Divit parked the car on the street and popped open the rear doors. Zehra got out and walked around, helping Jack out of the vehicle. Jack was shaky, and he was stumbling—and then he was shoving a finger into Zehra's eye and punching her hard in the stomach.

"Ooof! What the fuck?"

He slammed Zehra against the car, trying to grab the knife from her belt. Divit rushed around the vehicle while Jack and Zehra grappled, and then Jack had the weapon, and Zehra let out a yelp and slumped against the car.

Jack whirled to face Divit, who was unarmed. Zehra moaned and slid to the ground with blood dripping fast through her fingers.

Divit was frozen, his eyes on the blade.

Jack smirked. "Smart of you to stay put—I'm good with this thing, Div. And I changed my mind about talking to Mert. So what size are you?"

"What?"

"Your clothes, asshole. This stupid dress I'm wearing ain't my style."

"Jack, you're making a big mistake."

They locked eyes, and neither guy moved. Then Jack took a quick step back and grabbed Zehra's long black hair. He yanked on it and shoved the blade under the bleeding woman's throat.

"Get out of the clothes, shit head, or I'll make another one."

Zehra moaned again as Divit ripped off his outfit.

"Good, now toss them into the car."

Divit threw his clothes into the back seat. Jack ran around to the driver's side and opened the door.

Jack said, "You get Zehra to the hospital fast! I hear they got an empty bed over there. And you tell Mert I'll talk to him when I'm good and ready."

Divit just nodded.

"By the way, thanks for the rescue. I think."

Then Jack got into the vehicle and drove off.

Chapter 38

Maria was trying to smile, sitting on a breezy veranda with an endless view of blue sky and the Atlantic Ocean. All around stood the gleaming steel towers of Lagos, a city on the rise, if it didn't end up devoured by greed, corruption, and lawlessness.

And we're here to spread all those things, she thought.

It seemed like a bad dream, and yet she'd built it herself, one delusional block at a time. Why had she married him? Well, she'd been in love, and maybe still was. The wedding had been beautiful, too—and probably everyone watching had been thinking it would never work, everyone except the bride and groom. But that's the way love goes sometimes, a thrill hurtling toward disaster.

Now Pablo was coming over to the table, smiling as usual, to probably discuss another questionable plan to commit more crimes and make more money they didn't need. On a positive note, he looked sexy, just like he had on their wedding day.

"So, why are you unhappy?" he said as he sat down. "This city is beautiful and life is good. You worry too much."

"I'm not unhappy," she said. "But I see bad things coming, Pablo, and we need to build a better future."

He waved his hand. "This new plan to target us is just a lot of political bullshit—but we still have friends in the government. They're going to get this stuff under control and things will be fine again."

For an instant, she felt hopeful. "So we're not going to launch a ridiculous attack on the police?"

"No, of course not. We're going to launch a *great* attack on the police."

"Pablo! How will that help our friends to stop all this?"

He laughed. "It'll help a lot. When we show our enemies it won't be so easy, those government windbags will go running for cover. They'll find other ways to get their names in the headlines, ways that don't include pictures of bloody bodies."

"Bloody bodies on both sides."

"That's true," he said with a shrug. "But we can't look weak, Maria. You should understand—you've always been strong."

Maybe. He'd also been strong, too, and her mind flashed back to the times he'd been so quick to help her, to defend her and her family. When he reached out and took her hand, she felt that same old spark toward him she'd always felt, since they'd both been a couple of scrappy kids scrambling around on the streets of Diego Tijuana, a place that seemed so far away now.

"What about Banks?" she said. "Do you really think you can get to him?"

"He's going to the Global Law Enforcement Conference."

"So we're going to kill him at a convention for law enforcement people."

He shifted around a bit in his chair. "It's a little risky, but that's why it'll be great—a small operation that sends a big message. We have no fear."

"Ricardo needs to know. So does Suzy."

"No," he said. "This is a secret. I shouldn't even be telling you, but of course I tell you everything because you're smarter than me."

He grinned again, but she heard the hint of sarcasm in his voice.

"Then why are you doing something that I think is so stupid?"

"You only think it's stupid because of personal reasons—but from a strategy point of view?"

She hesitated. "It's not the best move. The best move would be to get out of here. Take the money and go. I keep telling you, and I keep being right. Besides, Ricardo might let it go but Suzy won't."

"Yes, she will. She's not that close with Banks. He's just the fool who let her escape."

"She knows his wife, and she's my friend. She deserves to know what you're planning."

He tried to laugh it off now, but he was obviously annoyed. "I know she's your friend, Maria—but Suzy hasn't really embraced us. She can be useful, but she's also a problem. She's too independent, too loud—she doesn't *listen to me.* Do you see how these things are bad for the group?"

"I see how they're bad for you."

He hesitated, and then glared. "She's with Ricardo—maybe—but she's not someone who gets to make decisions for the organization. It doesn't matter what she thinks."

"And what about me? Don't my decisions matter? You're not *listening.*"

"How can you say that?" he snapped. "I listen to you more than anyone else in the world, and I would do anything for you."

"Anything except this."

"True," he said with a tight smile. "Anything but this."

She stared at him in silence. Finally, she said, "Pablo—let's go. Let's get on a ship and leave. We have plenty of money so let's just get out. We don't need this anymore."

The smile faded from his face. He puffed out his chest a bit, like an animal trying to look bigger. Then he said, "Maria, have I ever lied to you? Have I ever been dishonest about the person I am? You know the things I've done—and I know the things you've done. This is who we are."

"No, Pablo! It's who we *had* to be. But we don't have to be that way now. We can change."

"I don't want to change. I like who I am. And I liked who you were." Then he paused and said, "If you want to go, then go. But I'll still be here."

He got up and banged the chair back into place. Then he turned and walked into the house.

Maria watched him go, feeling hollow inside. She couldn't deny there was some truth in his words. But I really have changed, she thought. *And I was an idiot to think he would change, too.*

Chapter 39

What a mess, Suzy thought. She was in the passenger side of the car as it jostled through the downtown traffic, sliding past police barricades, broken glass, and burned out storefronts. Cops were everywhere, sirens were wailing in the distance, and the whole revolution thing seemed awfully noisy. A mammoth hologram of Buso's face floated beneath the silver walkway, talking about justice and the enemies of freedom. It was hard not to laugh.

Ricardo looked at her from the driver's seat. "I know it looks bad," he said. "But this whole mess could be turned into one big party if the right people were running it."

"Yeah," Kiara said from the back seat. "If the right people were in charge it could be good."

Sure, and if I wore a funny robe I could be a monk, Suzy thought. But she didn't say it, and then Ricardo changed the subject—sort of.

"So let me get this straight," he said. "You put a tracking device on the guns?"

"I put a tracker on *one* of the guns. But it doesn't work because I left an anti-tracking device inside the truck."

"So what good is the tracker?"

"Someone might move the guns, Ricardo. Unless they only want to shoot things inside the truck."

"Right. Good thinking! Everybody will be glad to know."

"Maybe, but we're not telling everybody."

He gave her a pointed glance. "You don't trust our friends?"

Suzy didn't respond.

"I like Anika," Kiara said.

"I know," Suzy said, surprised by her sharp tone. Then she quickly added, "I mean, she's good—she's fine. But she's not telling us everything."

Kiara smiled. "You're my best friend, Suzy."

Suzy felt her face getting red. Yeah, maybe for an instant, she'd been jealous. Then Kiara pointed at the tracking information displayed on Ricardo's allcom. "It still doesn't show any movement."

"So it might not be working," Suzy said. "Or maybe the guns are still inside the truck. Keep your eye on it, Kiara."

The car pulled into the compound where Suzy had left the weapons, and she studied the scene. The place looked bigger in the light of day. It was a sprawling egg-colored villa with a vivid red roof and archways all around. The garages sat at the far end, near a larger, roundish building with two tall spires. There was a pattern of burned spots above the garage door where the truck had been, and there were smoldering splotches on the ground. Some of the walls had chunks missing, like a giant monster had taken a bite out of them—but really, none of the damage looked significant. Except for a couple of covered bodies on the ground.

Nuru approached the car as they exited.

"Thanks for coming," Nuru said. "Someone burned through the lock on the gate. A bunch of them came through with assault rifles, and they pinned our people down while they broke into the garage and took the truck. It was well-coordinated and planned."

Ricardo nodded. "Sounds like the cartel."

"How many were hurt?" Suzy said.

"Three dead," Nuru said. "We were lucky; they could've killed more. They were all friends. I wasn't here..." His voice trailed off. Then he said, "We had less people around because of the rally downtown. Maybe in a way that was a good thing."

Suzy felt a heaviness in her heart as her mind flashed back to losses of her own.

"I'm sorry," she said.

"Thank you."

"How did they know the guns were here? Did someone talk too much? Or is someone a traitor?"

Nuru hesitated. "We're working on that. Obviously, it's a problem. Here comes Anika."

Anika was walking through one of the arches. She came toward Suzy and embraced her. Her eyes looked teary, but then she flashed a quick smile. "So once again you escape," she said. "You have a knack for getting out of trouble. We've had a hard couple of days. But I'm glad you're on our side."

"Right," Suzy said. Then she pulled back a bit. "I'm sorry about your losses, Anika, but am I on your side? Let's be honest. There are things you're not telling me."

Anika was quiet. "I'm sorry I've given you that impression," she said. Then she motioned toward a doorway. "Let's talk, Suzy. Alone."

Suzy glanced at Kiara and Ricardo. Kiara looked curious while Ricardo just shrugged, as if to say 'go for it.' So Suzy followed Anika through one of the arches and into a dimly lit room.

The room felt calm, with woven wood shades on the windows, and two candles flickering on a wicker table, and air that smelled like cinnamon. There was also a wicker sofa, some matching chairs, and a tank filled with tropical fish. Lying on the bamboo floor was a weaved mat.

"I use this as a meditation room," Anika said. "Have you ever tried it?"

"Yeah. I got bored."

Anika laughed. "You need to give it a chance. It's very relaxing."

"So is a bottle of whiskey. And when I'm done with it, I'm drunk."

Anika sat on the sofa as Suzy took the nearby chair. When Anika spoke, her voice quavered.

"Suzy, I'm sorry we haven't had more time together. I appreciate your help—I really do. I know this isn't your fight but it's a good cause, and your friend Kiara really understands. She's very smart."

"She has good instincts. She's been through a lot."

Anika's eyes flashed with anger. "She's been brutalized! But as hard as I've worked to educate the public about human trafficking, it isn't the thing they care about most. So I talk about other things, like crime, corruption, and drugs—although the drug issue is related, since most victims of trafficking are addicts; it helps dull the pain, and this is why my group is inoculated against it. It's a way of saying 'I will never be part of that world again.' By the way, you and Kiara should get the inoculation."

"Why? I'm not planning to take any veluva."

"I told you, the drug is in the air. We know the air treatment facility is equipped to do it, and the government likes the way it encourages people to relax and spend more money at the casinos. Plus, they get a cut of the drug sales from the cartel. It's a low-level dose but what if they increase it? I'll admit, almost no one outside my organization is protected. They either don't see the threat, or they're users. But why not protect yourself?"

"I thought an overdose just puts people to sleep."

"It does. You go to sleep and then wake up and want more. But do you want to end up addicted? Do you want someone putting you to sleep?"

Suzy sat back and laughed. "I could use more sleep, Anika—but it's not a problem, because I'm not sticking around. I came here looking for a guy."

"And you'll find him, even though it's not why destiny brought you."

"A spaceship brought me."

Anika smiled. "Maybe. Anyway, don't be insulted by things I haven't shared. It's not that I don't trust you—it's just that sometimes it's better to be ignorant. A person can't tell what they don't know. Besides, Baadal Shahar is a world of secrets, and I don't know them all, anyway."

"Okay," Suzy said with a nod. "But who told the cartel the guns were here? Because that's a secret you need to know."

Anika sighed. "I don't know yet. We're working on it."

"Well, how many people knew the guns were here? Make a list, and start going—"

"Suzy, we're working on it," Anika said. She sat back in her chair and shifted around a bit. "Please understand…we're still recovering from this."

"Please understand, if you have a rat, it's a problem. It's the first thing you should be thinking about."

"I know—I know." She paused and looked at Suzy, like maybe she was going to say more, but then said nothing.

There's something strange going on here, Suzy thought. *I can't wait to leave this place.*

"I need to find Jack," Suzy said. "Where can I find the Snake Eyes? Can you help me?"

"That might be a bad idea."

"Yeah, probably. So where are they?"

"Suzy, Suzy… There's a delicate balance going on right now, and we need to keep it in place."

"Are you saying I'm not delicate?"

"Well, I think you're smart, and you're brave, but you're…not delicate, no," Anika said. Then she laughed. "But we love you for it—we do."

"So you're not going to help me?"

Anika paused once again and then said, "The Snake Eyes aren't just a gang of thugs. They're a secret society, organized in *bands,* and the bands are organized in tiers, like a pyramid. Each band has five to ten members, and the members know who's in their own band, and then maybe one band above or below. I know where some of the bands meet, but I don't know what band Jack is in, and any Snakes you find probably won't know either. I suspect he's on a higher tier, near the top. The top person is simply called the *Head.*"

"From what I've seen, he's probably closer to the ass."

"No. A lower tier person wouldn't have been involved in a plot to go to Earth and smuggle guns—and to kill or kidnap people from Los Pocos. Maybe he's more ignorant than stupid, and he doesn't mind doing the dirty work."

"Well, who's in the top spot? You must know who's in charge."

Now Anika narrowed her eyes a bit. "I told you, they're very secretive. Besides, we don't want a war with the Snakes. As bad as they are…they can be useful. You're an outsider here, but try and understand my position."

Suzy already understood—and she didn't like it. "You don't trust me to not cause trouble, is that it?"

"I know you're not *looking* to cause trouble, but things are coming to a boiling point, and we can't throw an explosive element into the equation."

"I'm not that explosive!" Suzy said, throwing up her hands. Then she sighed and said, "You should've seen me last year."

Anika laughed. "Suzy, I like you. But it's unlikely I can connect you with anyone in Jack's band. You'd need to be very lucky."

There was a knock on the door, and Kiara came in. She looked excited.

"Sorry to interrupt, but I just had a call from Reshma at the hospital. She said one of the people that stole Jack was there again—a woman with a knife wound. She's gone now, but Reshma gave me her address. So we can go over there and check it out."

Suzy smiled. "Great job, Kiara. I'll be with you in a second."

"I'll be ready," Kiara said. She was beaming as she closed the door.

Suzy looked at Anika. "I guess we just got lucky."

Anika was quiet for a long second. "I suppose I can't stop you from going," she said. "Is Kiara going with you? It would be a bad idea. She could stay here and help me."

Suzy didn't love either option, but she made a quick decision.

"Kiara's not coming," Suzy said. "If you have something for her to do…that would be great."

Chapter 40

Burt Stone hated hospitals, even the ones that kept him alive. He wasn't sure what had happened to him, but he knew the metal shackle clamped around his ankle wasn't part of the cure.

My head is killing me, and that's the thing that feels the best.

He was flat on his back in a hospital bed, and even from this position he could see the restraint contained a sensor. It was also chained to the bed, just to be sure—and he was in a private room, which probably meant there was a guard outside. The bandages, tubes, and hoses weren't a great sign, either. He felt like he'd been run over by a train, or maybe just shot with a pulse pistol that had almost killed him.

Okay, so I'm not too popular, he thought. *But what did I do?* It was hard to remember. Maybe the smug-looking cop coming through the door would remind him.

The cop was a big Chinese guy. He looked angry, too—but luckily, he wasn't speaking in any language Burt understood. Then he switched to English and the message was clear.

"You asshole!" the guy barked. "Where's Suzy Spitfire?"

Burt winced in pain. Then he said, "If she's not under the bed I can't help you."

The cop was not amused. "Listen, fuck face, you're in big trouble. You're facing a lot of time—unless you help us. Then maybe you'll only get twenty years before we deport your dumb ass back to Earth."

"Where's Tala?" Burt said.

"You mean your accomplice? She got away, but she can't hide forever."

Burt felt a wave of happiness—*she got away!* Then the cop said, "So who shot you?"

"I don't know."

"Where were you going?"

"Don't remember."

"You're not giving me any answers."

"Maybe you should hire a detective."

The guy stared at him and then shook his head. "I thought you were a cop."

"So did I," Burt mumbled, looking away from the guy's stare.

"So why are you being such a jackass? If someone stole *your* police car with one of your prisoners inside, what would you do?"

Right, now I remember! In a flash it came flooding back.

"She wasn't your prisoner!" Burt snapped. "You guys were hardly looking for her until I found her. She was right there, strutting around like she owned the city. You guys are shit cops."

The guy laughed. "And you're so great? You got shot to pieces and let your prisoner escape—after stealing her away from the local force. Maybe you should think about that. And while you're thinking, you can check your messages—at least the first one." He smirked. "Yeah, we already read it."

He handed Burt his allcom and Burt read the communication from Commander Banks. It was short, but the lack of words spoke volumes.

Abandon mission and report to Tycho City for reassignment. Please note your lack of diplomatic immunity. Proceed with caution. Banks.

The cop grinned. "I guess your friends on Earth heard that you totally screwed up, especially since we told them. You might want to let them know you'll be busy rotting in prison. But they probably know that, too."

Burt was in a fog. His head was whirling with thoughts of his father, and his uncle, and how he wished he'd been killed instead of shot and captured. It would've been so much less humiliating. And then he thought about Tala, and the path he'd led her down. Such a smart girl with a bright future—ruined! By the biggest loser in the world.

Burt sighed. "I want you to know my partner had nothing to do with this. She was following my orders, and if I could help you find Suzy, I would. But I don't know where she is, or what happened out there. All I know is I've made a mess out of everything." Then he looked into the cop's eyes and said, "I'm sorry."

The cop squinted at him a bit, and then his glare softened. "Yeah, you sure did. Look, my name is detective Chen Lin. The doctors say you're going to be okay—you were lucky. You had a lot of blood loss and you'll end up with a few nice scars, but no serious damage. In fact, you'll be good to go pretty soon. But you'll be going to prison."

Burt said nothing. He was remembering the big party his parents had given him when he'd graduated from the academy. They'd been so proud. His dad had hugged him, he'd been glowing, and now? The shame was like a weight crushing him down into the bed. Somewhere in the distance, the cop was still talking. He was asking questions.

"Why did Suzy bring you to the hospital? She could've let you die."

"I don't know," Burt said in a soft voice. "I guess she was just being cruel."

Chapter 41

Suzy found Kiara's fury to be unnerving.

"Are you fucking kidding me?" Kiara screamed. Suzy was walking toward the hover-car with Ricardo. "You're cutting me out *again*. You said you wouldn't!"

"Kiara, I'm sorry. But I have to keep you safe."

Suzy tried to embrace her but Kiara shoved her away.

"I'm safe when I'm with you, Suzy. But you don't want me around, and you lied! And now you're leaving me."

"I'll be back. You can help Anika."

"I hate you!"

"Kiara, I'll be back." Suzy got into the car.

"I don't care if you come back or not."

Suzy couldn't look at her as they drove away. Ricardo was quiet. Finally, he said, "She didn't mean it. She'll be fine."

Suzy banged her fist on the door. "I just want her to be safe, that's all! But I'm not sure about the best way to do it." She swore and shook her head. "She wants to be some kind of warrior, and I understand—but at the same time, I want to keep her away from any trouble. I don't think fighting is what she needs."

"You worry too much. She's going to be all right."

Suzy stared out the window and said nothing. A minute passed. Then Ricardo gave a long sigh and said, "Suzy, sometimes I've acted like I don't want Kiara around, because I like having you all to myself—but I think it's great the way you're looking out for her, and I really admire you for it, okay? You're doing a good thing. I mean it."

Suzy turned her head to look at him. "Thanks," she said. "I

appreciate that… And you haven't been too bad. In fact, you're pretty good."

"Pretty good? I'm the best. *I am your man, I have a plan, and it's true like a bottle of beer.*"

Suzy gave a soft laugh. "Well, I never had a bottle of beer lie to me. Now let's find this woman who might lead us to Jack."

All they had was a name and an address. It was in a rundown part of town, where the buildings were old and the drugs were new. Out on the street, and mixed among the flowers and trees, were people who looked worn out and frazzled. Suzy noticed a woman snoring under a mimosa tree; she wore a brown dress that looked like a torn sack. Ricardo parked the car just past a towering bamboo apartment building.

"Why would this woman help us?" he said. "You killed a couple of Snakes, didn't you?"

"Yeah, that's true. So I guess we need to be extra friendly."

"Hey, you should be wearing body armor."

"Are you wearing it?"

"No. They can't hit me. I'm too fast."

"That's what I thought. Let's go."

Suzy checked her pistol and scanned the scene. Not the busiest street, but there was some foot traffic and a steady stream of hover-cars. No doubt there were surveillance cameras around, so she tossed back her hair and smiled. They would be quick.

The front door was open and led to a dark foyer with a door to the right and a staircase to the left. Directly in front was an elevator but Suzy headed for the stairs with Ricardo close behind. She moved fast and stepped lightly. On the third floor, they stopped in front of a gray wooden door and rang the bell. Suzy stood near the edge of the door, listening—and then heard someone coming. She got close to the wall and slid a few steps back. As the door opened, she reached for her pistol and then saw the face of a little girl.

She was about five years old, with brown eyes, tangled hair, and a cheery round face. "Hello," she said. "Can you help my mommy? She's sick."

Suzy lowered her weapon, but kept it close to her side. She crept forward, near to the kid, and then gave the door a push. She also ducked down—but there was no one waiting to attack.

The girl watched with curious eyes. "My mommy is in the bedroom."

"Thanks," Suzy said. She strode past her into a kitchen. Ricardo smiled at the girl but kept an eye on her as he followed close behind.

Suzy's eyes darted around to a small bamboo table, a few matching chairs, and some dishes in the sink. There were a couple of holes in the wall about the size of someone's fist, and a random pattern of cracks across the white tiles on the floor. Was being a member of the Snake Eyes lucrative? If so, it was well hidden.

The girl tugged at Suzy's scarlet skirt. "Can you help my mommy?" she said, and swiped some hair from her eyes. She was cute.

"Maybe," Suzy said. "Where is she?"

"In the bedroom," the girl said, pointing.

Suzy walked down a short, dim hallway. She paused at the bathroom and saw a shower dripping, but no one there. She poked her head into another room—okay, this one must belong to the kid. There was an unmade bed, an old dresser, and a few scattered piles of dirty clothes but not much else. Directly across was another bedroom with the door open. Suzy slipped inside.

The woven blinds were closed, and it was dark, and there was a young woman lying on the bed. She was on her back, propped on a pillow with her eyes closed; across her stomach was a wide bandage. She didn't look much older than Suzy. Suzy pointed the gun at her and walked forward, looking at her hands. They were both empty.

The woman's eyes fluttered open and she took a quick breath. Then she yelped and tried to get up.

"Vanya!" she said. "Vanya! Where are you?" Then she slumped a bit and groaned in pain.

"Don't move," Suzy said. "Your daughter is okay. She's right here."

The girl ran into the room. "These people want to help you, Mommy."

The woman froze and slid back down onto the bed. She seemed to be in agony. Finally, she gasped a few times and said, "Please don't hurt my little girl, Suzy. She's not involved in this."

Suzy cocked her head. "How do you know my name?"

The woman's half-closed eyes were staring at the ceiling. "You killed two brothers, and you wiped out a cartel assassination squad," she said. "Every brother and sister knows your name."

Suzy looked at Ricardo, who just grinned. "You're a legend, honey."

"Great, but I didn't come here to sign autographs. I guess you're Zehra."

"Yes. Don't hurt my daughter, please."

"We're not going to hurt anybody."

"Like you didn't hurt Farouk?"

"Farouk was an asshole."

Zehra gave a soft laugh. "True, but he was one of us, so now you're my enemy."

"Who stabbed you? Another enemy?"

"Another asshole."

"Jack?"

She gave Suzy a sharp look. "I guess you know him," she said.

"He's the reason I'm here. Where is he?"

"I don't know," she said with a sigh. "He stabbed me and ran off, after I tried to help him."

"How did you help him? Were you part of the attack on the rally?"

Zehra closed her eyes and rolled her head back. "I've made some mistakes, but my daughter hasn't done anything, and she's all I've got. So leave us alone, please. She needs me. That's why I left the hospital. I've got no one else here."

"What about your Snake friends?"

She just grunted and said nothing.

"Where's the girl's father?" Ricardo said.

Now Zehra's eyes snapped open. "Dead!" she said. "Killed by the cartel! Killed in the stupid war over veluva—the same war that brought you here."

Ricardo winced and didn't respond, but Suzy said, "You hurt a lot of people who were trying to end your war. Some of them were young, too—your daughter's age."

"I didn't hurt anyone."

"I saw a little girl get her head blown off. The Snakes did that."

"No!"

"I saw her brains on the street."

"No!"

"Who can tell me where Jack is?"

"Will that stop the war?"

"No," Suzy said. Then she shrugged. "This isn't about *your* war—it's about my war."

They locked eyes.

Zehra rubbed her temple and spoke in a low voice, almost to herself. "I had no home, no family, and I could've ended up on the street because that's what happens here. Then I met someone, a Brother of the Snake, and they protected me from all that. But I got involved with other things, and that was a mistake. And now I'm here again with no one."

Ricardo's allcom was beeping. He read a message and then stepped out of the room.

"I'm looking for a guy, a predator who rapes and kills young girls," Suzy said. "Jack isn't the guy but I think he can lead me to him. That's why I'm here." Then she waved her hands. "All this other stuff is just something I got involved in."

Zehra sighed. "Yeah, that's what happens," she said, and then scowled toward the doorway where Ricardo had exited. Then she lowered her voice to a whisper. "They pull you in, and then you're stuck forever. But I really don't know where Jack is, and if anyone thought I gave you information they'd kill me."

Suzy was about to ask a few more questions when Ricardo came bolting into the room.

"The cops just arrested Anika and Nuru," he said. "Also a bunch of other people downtown. They're rounding people up." Then he took a deep breath and said, "They got Kiara, too."

"What?" A stab of alarm shot through Suzy's head.

Ricardo ran to a blind and peered outside. "Crap! They're down there now. I think they're coming up here."

Suzy swore and looked at Zehra. "What's the best way out of this place?"

Zehra didn't answer. Vanya came back into the room and laughed, and then pulled on Suzy's skirt.

"Vanya, come here," Zehra said. Vanya smiled and went to her mother, who sat up and wrapped her arms around the girl. Then Zehra gave Suzy a sober look and said, "Are you really chasing a child killer?"

"Yes, if the cops don't get me first."

"All right," Zehra said. "There's a back door that goes to the street, but they'll be down there. Take the stairs in the hall up to the roof. There's cover there—you'll see—and the buildings are close together. If you hurry, you can leap between them. And tell Jack I said 'hello.' Tell him in your own special way."

"You can count on it," Suzy said. Then she added, "I hope you feel better."

"I'll be fine. Good luck, Suzy Spitfire. I hope you get your man."

"Good luck to you, Zehra. And thanks."

Suzy and Ricardo raced back into the hall and ran up the stairs. Down below they heard the commotion of law enforcement, lots of bellowing and banging on doors. But was Zehra telling the truth? Did this stairway even lead to the roof?

It did. After running up four flights they reached a door and entered a garden. Almost all the buildings on Baadal Shahar had roof gardens that produced food, oxygen, and not a bad amount of camouflage. This one was nice, with patches of broccoli, kale, and cabbage, and then a section of trees—peaches, apples, cherries, and more. There was also an epic view of the city, a collection of leafy rooftops and towers stretching out to the edges of the great dome.

Suzy ran to the edge of the building, right under a cherry tree, and checked the distance to the next building. It was about two meters, so she leaped and landed in a patch of lettuce. She swore and brushed some dirt from her bare legs. She liked cities, beaches, and outer space—but the lettuce patch, not so much. Still, it was soft, and Ricardo was right behind her.

"Oof!" he said. "Careful, honey. Don't crush anybody's carrots."

"It might be a little late for that. But tell me if you see any avocados."

There were no avocados, but there were peppers, squash, and celery plants all around the perimeter, and a forest of fig and plum trees everywhere else. They bolted through the fruity woods to the next ledge and jumped again.

"Where are we going, Suzy?"

"A couple of buildings over, and then we go down to the street. We have to rescue Kiara."

Ricardo hesitated. "She's in a police car, Suzy. We're not going to be able to blast them in the middle of a street, not without putting her at risk."

Suzy didn't answer. She was too busy staring at her allcom and studying the tracking information coming from Kiara's bracelet.

"She's close," Suzy said. "A couple of streets over—heading in that direction. It doesn't look like she's moving too fast."

"She's probably in traffic, heading toward the police station."

"We're going to get there first."

"And do what? The cops all have guns. And the police station is full of cops."

She didn't answer. There had to be something they could do— there was always something. *I can't let her be taken away!*

She was running fast now, looking at the allcom, racing across the roof and leaping and then running some more. The cops no longer existed, the trees and vegetables were nothing, and everything else faded into a blur. Finally, she stood on the roof of a building at the corner of an intersection, under a forest of almond trees, and looked down. She was breathing hard—but the sight below still caused her to catch her breath.

The main street was filling with people, a rolling ocean of heads and waving arms, and they were all chanting and screaming. Several police vehicles were trying to move forward, but they couldn't because they were surrounding by a human wave.

"We have to get down there," Suzy said, and she looked around quick, searching for a door—there it was, over by some tomato plants. Then she was rushing down the steps with Ricardo close behind, and he was yelling something but she didn't hear him because it didn't matter, and then she was running out of the building onto the sidewalk, just ahead of the police cars.

The sound on the street was deafening. "Let them go!" the crowd shouted. "Let them go!"

A cop started talking on a loudspeaker. "Clear away from the car. Clear away from the car!"

Suzy pushed her way through the crowd. There were two cars and a larger vehicle, an armored van that probably held the prisoners. Suzy was so close now that she could see the eyes of the cops inside the cars, and they looked nervous. Sure, they could fire stun shots, they could fire gas, they could shoot to kill—but they might be overwhelmed. There were too many people.

Just up ahead was the police station, behind a high wall and looming like a faceless grey fortress. As Suzy stared at the building, a gate opened and a hundred cops in riot gear came rushing out.

The crowd roared and attacked—but the cops were ready and started shooting. Flashes of light and the sound of gunfire filled the air. They were stun shots, but it was a barrage, and the crowd gave a collective wail as the bodies fell.

People around Suzy screamed and hit the ground, some of them stunned and some of them just trying to escape the hail of fire. Suzy dove for the ground and started crawling, trying to shove her way through the tangled mass of bodies. She was 20 meters behind the armored vehicle when a robot-controlled gun on top of the van started firing. All around her people were hit.

What could she do? If she fired fully-maxed shots she'd damage the van and maybe stop it—but would she hurt someone inside? Could she reach the doors and open them before being shot? Would the cops annihilate her and then start shooting others with similar blasts of their own? There was no cover out here on the street and the cops were still firing at anyone who got too close. It was impossible to get close enough.

Suzy felt dizzy and struggled to breathe—the van was moving away, and there was nothing she could do. She lay on the ground, feeling sick to her stomach, and watched Kiara being moved into a prison. The cops had won. A tear of rage ran down her cheek, and she knew it was also a tear of sorrow. She had failed. While she'd been away Kiara had been in trouble, and now she might never see her again.

Someone was talking to her; it was Ricardo. He was helping her to her feet.

He held her close. "Don't worry, Suzy. We'll get her out."

Suzy couldn't speak. She just shook her head and wiped her eyes. Finally, she said, "She's gone. It's all my fault."

"No!" Ricardo hissed. "You were trying to help! She'll be fine, Suzy, don't worry. She's a tough kid, and she's smart, too."

Suzy shook her head and spoke in a low voice. "She's not that tough, Ricardo. She just fakes it. We all do."

Ricardo hugged her and spoke into her ear. "She's a survivor—like you. We'll get her out but not right now. Come on, let's go."

Suzy felt Ricardo's arm around her shoulder as they walked away.

Chapter 42

Jack Ray cursed as the cops fired a storm of shots into the crowd. Then he cheered when the crowd erupted like a mushroom cloud, only to be cut down by a brand of brutality as old as human history.

He swore again and shook his head. That's how it goes, he thought. He'd given up on humans long ago, back when he'd been six years old and his dad had beaten him senseless for accidentally breaking a window with a football. He still had a scar on the back of his shoulder, the first of many. He still had all those other scars, the ones inside.

I wonder where that motherfucker is now? He'd disappeared one night after nearly killing Jack's mom, who'd responded by getting high for the next ten years and then giving up on life.

Too bad, she'd never really had a chance. Maybe he shouldn't have left her, but there'd been nothing there for him anymore. He was glad he'd ditched that world. And while the Snakes had been good to him, now they had to be left behind, too. He'd be moving on again but first he had to get a few things, and luckily there was a riot in progress. He didn't know a whole lot about politics but he knew it was a good time to go shopping.

He didn't need much for himself. He just wanted to get a few things for Kiara.

He grimaced at the thought of her being arrested. Why the hell didn't I save her? he thought. *I was too late.* He clenched his fists and tried to clear his head. Then he swore and told himself she'd be okay. After all, she'd been arrested before, and if someone messed with her and got her crazy, they'd be in trouble. He shoved his hands into his pockets and headed down the street.

I should've fucking saved her! Like she saved me!

The street was a mess, a conglomeration of bodies and broken glass. Stay calm, he thought. He could feel his heart pounding—all this violence had him on edge. The cops had fired a lot of stun shots that had missed the crowd but had broken a bunch of windows. He slipped into a store that sold women's clothing.

A bell rang when he entered but no one appeared. He surveyed the lonely racks of clothes and the vacant front counter—perfect. The owners had probably joined in the protest and were now face down somewhere outside. But that was fine because this pink shirt was just Kiara's size, and this purse was exactly something she'd like, and wow—they even had a jewelry case. He was trying to pry it open with the switchblade he'd taken from Zehra when a big guy came charging out of a back room.

His eyes were wide with rage. He was also holding a bat in his hand, and he raised the weapon over his head and shouted something furious in Chinese. Jack didn't speak much Mandarin, but he guessed what the guy was saying.

"Wait!" Jack said, jumping back. "Hang on! I was gonna pay for it."

The guy swung his weapon at Jack's head—but Jack stepped aside and the bat slammed down on the jewelry case, smashing a hole in it. The guy swore, and then Jack lunged forward and stabbed him in the stomach. The guy yelped like a wounded dog.

Jack snarled with satisfaction. It was a deep wound, and now the man moaned and dropped the bat. Jack kicked him hard, toppling him to the ground. Then he put the knife down and grabbed the bat and swung it at the guy's head. The guy let out a scream and tried to shield himself. The bat made a splattering sound as it struck him in the cheek, and the guy shrieked—and that just made it better.

"You motherfucker!" Jack shouted, and he swung the bat again and again. The guy yelled a few more times, and Jack yelled right along with him. It felt great; there was something about beating another person that felt so great every time. *Thwack! Thwack! Thwack!* Blood splashed against the wall as the guy's head split open. Jack grimaced and still hit him a few more times. Then he stopped.

His chest was heaving as he stared at the bloody pulp. Finally he winced and looked away. "Asshole," he said. Then he shook his head and muttered, "You and me both." He picked up the knife again and wiped it on the guy's hair before snapping it closed.

He glanced around quick—good, still no one else in here. But hell, there was probably a surveillance camera somewhere. He turned and examined the destroyed jewelry case. He gritted his teeth and reached inside, grabbing a shiny necklace. Then he bolted from the store.

Outside, sirens were wailing and the street was filled with people. There were lots of bodies on the ground, and lots of people standing over the bodies, crying and shouting and waving their arms for help.

Jack shoved the pink shirt into the purse and examined the necklace again. Yeah, it was pretty. Kiara would love it.

Chapter 43

Kiara took a deep breath and tried to stay calm. It was dark and stuffy in the back of the van. It was like she was already in a cell. There were no windows, only two stiff benches along either side that were packed with people fidgeting and glancing around. But she could hear the crowd outside the van chanting. She could feel the vibrations of a revolution building, and she could feel Anika's leg pressing against her own.

"I've been arrested before," Kiara said in a soft voice.

"It'll be fine, Kiara. Don't worry."

Kiara thought back to that first time. She'd been twelve years old and she'd been scared. She'd taken a payment from an undercover cop who'd arrested her like she was public enemy number one. He'd cuffed her and thrown her into a car and tried to get her to talk about Daniel, but she'd said nothing. Then he'd given her a lecture about her age and her future and she hadn't listened. The cop didn't care about a girl like her—it was just like Daniel and the other girls said it would be, and as time went by it became even more obvious. Why did the cop let the sleazy customer go? Because he had a family, a wife, a job, and it could all be ruined by this little mistake. Apparently, she was the mistake. She was the problem. And if one of the girls turned up strangled or beaten to death? Just another dead whore to be swept up and forgotten. No wonder she'd thought Daniel was the good guy for so long.

"This is different," Kiara said. "I feel like I'm doing something better with myself."

Anika smiled. "That's good. It's why I do what I do." Then she sighed. "It's always the same story, Kiara—all the girls I've worked with. And it's not anything that really interests the public."

"I know. That's why I want to stay here and help. I love Suzy, but I need to stay. I didn't tell her I let you give me the veluva inoculation. I plan to stay here and be part of this."

"We're happy to have you, Kiara. Most victims don't trust anyone outside the world they're trapped in. But you've been in that world, so you understand."

"Yeah, I do," Kiara said. She understood how she'd been manipulated and isolated until there was nowhere to go and nothing to return to, and it never would've worked, anyway. Old friends from school wouldn't have understood. She would've been treated like an outcast, someone from a freak show, someone to whisper about while they were talking about boyfriends and girlfriends and maybe having sex for the first time. And it would've all seemed silly to her after the things she'd done.

The van shook and they heard the sounds of a gun firing on the roof. They heard shots and screams outside. "Those bastards," someone said to no one in particular. "We'll make them pay, won't we, Anika?"

Everyone was looking at Anika now and she nodded her head. "Yes, we will." Then she lowered her voice and spoke almost to herself. "They're in for a big surprise."

Kiara felt her heart pounding. Was she scared? A little. But she'd faced lots of scary situations. Her mind filled with desperate flashbacks—beatings, humiliation, pain, and every perversion imaginable. This was none of those things. This was almost exciting. It was a thrill to be doing something better, and to be surrounded by people who cared, and they didn't just care about what they were doing—they cared about her. Just like Suzy did. *But what if I die?* Their last conversation had been so angry. *Suzy will blame herself for my death, and that'll be so sad.*

Her eyes wandered down to the bracelet around her wrist. It was primitive compared to modern injection methods used to track people, but it worked. *She's going to know where I am,* Kiara thought. *She's going to try and rescue me. I hope she doesn't get hurt.*

Now it was quiet outside, and the van stopped moving. The double doors on the back swung open, and there were a bunch of police officers waiting. They were in some kind of tunnel in the back of the police station. It was dark and Kiara stayed close to Anika as they were herded out of the vehicle. But then she saw someone pointing, and she was pulled aside by a big cop. He yanked on her wrist.

"You come this way."

"What?"

"Are you deaf? Come this way."

He spoke English with a strange accent and gave her a menacing glare. Kiara looked toward Anika, but Anika was being surrounded by a wall of police. Anika and the others were being shoved in a different direction while Kiara was being stripped away from them. And now Kiara felt a flash of fear.

"No," Kiara said, catching her breath. "I don't want to go!"

She heard Anika protest, but then Anika and the others were pushed through a doorway and forced out of sight.

Now Kiara screamed as the memories came flooding back to her—all the bad moments, all the close calls.

"No! I don't want to go!"

She shrieked and tried to fight but the guy had his hand clamped over her mouth. He was holding her tight, and she was flailing and struggling, trying to get free. He was cursing, saying something to her, telling her to calm down. Then he was jamming something into her ribs, and she saw a flash of white before her eyes and an explosion of stars.

She stopped struggling and sank to her knees. She took a deep breath. The last thing she saw was the bracelet on her wrist. Then everything faded away.

Chapter 44

Suzy didn't tend to wallow in despair for long. Most of the time she just turned her sadness into rage and shot something—or someone. But she was having a hard time with her sadness today.

As she walked with Ricardo away from the police station, her legs felt wobbly and she barely noticed the broken city around her, despite the smashed windows, police sirens, and people running amok. Close by, a bottle hit the ground near a group of cops and burst into flames. The cops returned fire but Suzy hardly glanced at them. She heard Ricardo's words but they seemed far away. He was trying to hurry her along, saying something about going to Mert's house. Apparently, the government believed Anika was the real threat and they thought they could work with Mert and Marcos, so now those two were holed up, plotting their next move. Whatever.

Suzy felt numb, like she was frozen. Sure, there were probably cops and assorted cartel assassins all over the place but right now it didn't matter. Let Ricardo look out for them, she thought. And he would, because he was good that way.

He really is a sweet guy. He was obviously concerned about her mental state. He didn't even try to cheer her up with a poetic atrocity. He knew she needed some time alone with this—some time and maybe a stiff drink or two.

She kept telling herself to hang on. *It's not like anything horrible has to happen to Kiara.* After all, the arrests had been made in public, and while the cops were aggressive in this city, Suzy had seen a lot worse. But it wasn't the cops that bothered her so much as the separation—the yearning sense of loss, and the feeling that she'd let Kiara down.

As they maneuvered their way through a throng of people outside Mert's house, images of Trish flashed through Suzy's mind. Such a sweet, happy kid—and then a depressed girl consumed by sadness. *It's not the same thing... It's not the same thing... It's not the same thing... But I should've looked out for her more. I should have and I could have but I didn't.*

Ricardo shook a few hands as they entered the house. Then they walked into Mert's living room—and lying on the sofa was Kiara.

Suzy stopped and stared, and then she raced toward the couch. Kiara's eyes were closed.

"Kiara! Kiara, are you okay?" Suzy leaned over her and shook her hard.

Kiara's eyes fluttered open. "Suzy? Suzy, I was going to call you." Then she closed her eyes and seemed to nod off.

Suzy kept staring at her, and then she whirled toward Mert.

"What's going on?" she said. "How did Kiara get here? Is she all right?"

Mert smiled. "She's fine, Suzy. She's just asleep. She got into a scuffle with one of the cops and they used a stun stick, but she's not hurt. I had them bring her here."

"You? How?"

He smiled again. "Suzy, I have friends at the police station; I have friends everywhere. Of course, I don't control the government, and I can't get Anika released—but Kiara isn't important to them. She was never scanned into the system, so I made a call and they let her go." He paused and added, "I know she's important to you."

Suzy hesitated. It was wonderful that Kiara was here and seemed to be okay, but why did Suzy feel uneasy? She glanced at Ricardo, who'd been watching the scene.

Ricardo said, "Thanks for helping her, Mert."

"Yeah, thanks," Suzy blurted. "I appreciate it."

"Don't mention it. By the way, where are her parents?"

The question caught Suzy off guard. Come to think of it, no one else had asked why this fourteen-year-old girl was travelling with her.

"I don't know," Suzy said. "Let's just say she didn't have the best home life."

Mert hesitated, and then nodded his head. "I understand," he said, and he did seem sincere. Then he added, "There are lots of people who shouldn't be parents. But it's good that she met you. I only hope it goes better for Anika. Anika is important to Kiara, and to all of us."

"True," Ricardo said. "So, what's happening with that?"

Marcos swaggered over and joined them. He had a drink in his hand and a gleam in his eye, like he was about to try and sell a used hover-car, or maybe a revolution.

"Now's the time," Marcos said with much bravado. "We have to take the city. Mert, you know that sooner or later Buso will send his people storming in here on some false charge. We have to attack! Ricardo can help—he has some people coming in soon, at the space-port. If we're going to change things, we'll need all the help we can get." Then he waved his glass in Suzy's direction and leaned toward her. "How about it, Suzy? Are you ready to help us change the world?"

"Why isn't Kiara at a hospital?" she said.

Mert shrugged. "We didn't want to take a chance on her being arrested again. I had someone look at her, a nurse I know, and she'll be fine. But we could use your help." Now he stopped smiling and flashed a sober look. "We need Ricardo's guns. Then we can rescue Anika, and she can help us put an end to all the horror in this city. We can get rid of the cartel and the corrupt casinos. And we can help people like Kiara."

With some effort, Suzy kept her face blank. "I don't have the guns, and even if I did, who would use them?"

"Ricardo's people," Marcos said. "And Mert's people, and my people—and some people from the Citizen Collective. We'll put everyone together and form an army. We'll storm the prison and start a revolution. It'll be over in a day."

"We?" Suzy said. "Are you going to be scaling the walls, Marcos?"

Marcos puffed out his chest. "I stand behind my people, Suzy."

"Yeah, I'll bet you do—way behind them. So far back they need a telescope to see you."

Marcos laughed, but his eyes flashed with anger. Ricardo quickly said, "Suzy, Marcos is on our side. He's just saying we need to make a move."

"Sure, a move," Suzy said. "Right into a graveyard. You've got an untrained army of how many? And they're up against thousands of cops, and those heavily armed cartel people. Your people wouldn't stand a chance. Besides, what makes you think I can get the guns? The cartel took them, right?"

Mert said, "Yes, but Ricardo says you might be able to find them."

She shot Ricardo a look. Then Ricardo smiled and said, "Excuse us, we need to talk."

Suzy followed him into the kitchen where she decided not to kill him. Not yet, anyway.

"Ricardo, what's going on?"

"This!" he said. He held up his allcom and she looked at it. It was now showing the guns, or at least the one she'd decorated with a tracking device. And it was moving.

He leaned toward her and spoke in a low voice. "I didn't tell them we had a tracking device," he said. "I just *insinuated* you might be able to help me find the guns. I let them read between the lines, that's all." He sighed. "Suzy, I came to this city to find you, but I also came to help Maria, remember? And so did you. So why not do it? Didn't you tell Kiara you'd help Anika? Well, this would be a big help to her because she's in prison."

"Yeah, I did say I'd help Anika, and I want to. But these people aren't really on her side, Ricardo."

"Maybe, maybe not. But they're better than the people who arrested her. And she knows Mert and Marcos, and we can work with them. We can make this city a great place."

Suzy didn't think so. But she thought of Kiara, lying on the sofa, and knew it meant a lot to her. And then there was Maria—a good friend who she'd promised to help.

"All right," Suzy said. "But we go alone."

Ricardo's eyebrows shot upward. "Alone? Against the cartel?"

"Yeah. We'll find the guns and then you can call your friends—if we need them."

He grinned. Then he followed her back into the living room.

"We'll find the guns," Suzy said.

Marcos and Mert nodded their heads, looking happy. "Good. We'll send some people with you and—"

"No," Suzy said. "I'll call you when it's time."

Mert and Marcos both frowned. "But we can help," Mert said.

"You can help by keeping Kiara safe. I'll call you when we have them."

They didn't like it. But when they looked at Ricardo for support, he just gave a slight shake of his head.

"All right," Mert said. "Marcos and I are going to split up. We don't both want to be in the same place. Call either of us and we'll be ready to move."

Suzy went to where Kiara was sleeping and sat beside her. She held her hand for an instant, noticing that she was still wearing the silver tracking bracelet. Then she leaned close to her ear and whispered, "I'm sorry I left you behind, Kiara. And I'm sorry I have to do it again."

For an instant, Kiara opened her eyes and smiled. "It's all right, Suzy," she murmured. "It's fine." Then she closed her eyes and went back to sleep.

Suzy did feel better. She said, "I'll be back, honey. I'll be back."

Chapter 45

Maria was tired of tossing around in bed, staring into the dark while the ceiling fan whooshed above her and Pablo snored like a chainsaw. He was angry with her for brushing off his amorous advances, something she rarely did—but she was angry with him for not listening to her, and she was angry with herself for making so many mistakes.

She slid from the bed and slipped out of the room. With light steps she crept downstairs to a small office and sat in front of a monitor screen. In a shaky voice she said, "Take a message" and the screen flashed to life, showing a welcome message along with a picture of the ocean near her hometown of Diego Tijuana. She'd taken the picture herself, and now more than anything she wished she was there rather than sitting in a villa—a gorgeous prison, really—perched on the coast of Africa.

She heard a noise and her heart leaped. *Pablo is in the hall!* She sprang from her chair and stared into the darkness—and saw no one.

She took a deep breath and sat down again. This was ridiculous. She shouldn't be afraid of her husband; she'd never been afraid of anyone. But then she realized he wasn't the real fear. No, what she feared was how she'd feel tomorrow. Would she feel dirty? Would she feel like she'd stained something in a horrible way? Well, their lives had never really been clean. Still, she started to tell the screen to shut off, but then didn't.

What Pablo was doing was a bad idea. In a way, she was saving him from himself. Besides, Suzy had a right to know about this situation. Suzy was a close friend and confidant, partly because she was so trustworthy. There was no guarantee Suzy would even do anything with this information, but she deserved to know about it. *And I deserve a new start.*

All I need is a small bag, a few clothes, and a ticket.

Maria swore and looked out into the hallway again. It was all quiet. Time to make a move.

She once again said, "Take a message…"

Chapter 46

Burt's eyes snapped open. Who was there?

He squinted at the doctor in front of him and noticed she was pretty, dressed in bluish green scrubs with dark eyes and an urgent kind of smile. She also had a cap on her head.

"Burt," she whispered. "It's me. Tala."

"Tala!" He tried to sit up and gave a grunt, realizing he was strapped around his waist. Then he glanced around and spoke in a voice that was low and fierce. "What are you doing here? You shouldn't be here. You'll get caught. You've got to take the ship back to Earth."

"I can't," she said. "The ship is impounded. But I came to get you out."

"No! Forget about me and save yourself."

She just shrugged and produced a small laser cutter. "This will go right through your ankle bracelet. But it'll also set off an alarm, so get ready to move quick."

"Tala—no." He grabbed her hand and whispered in a harsh tone. "I don't want you getting caught, you hear me? I don't want you to be arrested—please. I've messed up your life enough. Get out of here." Then he narrowed his eyes and said, "That's an order."

She smiled. "I don't think so—sir. I've got a hover-chair right here, and a car outside near the drop-off entrance. Can you walk? I'll cut this and we can go. Do you really want to go to prison?"

Burt hesitated. No, he didn't. Cops don't do well in prison. And every second she was standing here she was at risk. *Damn it!*

"What about the guard outside the door?"

"There's no guard."

"What?"

"The city is a disaster. I guess they pulled the guard to do other things. There are riots going on—they arrested Anika Anand. They also picked up that girl Suzy was with; I have a positive ID on her. But let's go!"

He swore and gritted his teeth. Yeah, he'd heard a few nurses talking about the state of the city. "All right," he said. "But I'll do the cutting and I don't need a hover-chair. You go to the car. If I'm not there in two minutes, you go."

"But you might need help," she protested. "And I want to push you out, so you look inconspicuous. It's part of the plan."

"I'm changing the plan." He looked into her eyes. "I'll be fine. It's the only way I'm going to go, Tala. We're wasting time."

He could see she was thinking it over. Then she frowned and moved fast, running to a nearby burlap bag where his clothes were stored.

"Put on everything you can before you cut," she said. "Just leave your pants and one boot until after the bracelet comes off."

"Right. Good idea."

It was easier said than done. First, he had to yank off the hospital gown using mostly one arm; the other one was in a bandage and a sling. He felt silly and helpless, and even a little embarrassed as she helped him while he was lying there in his underwear. Meanwhile, Tala kept glancing around as she handed him his shirt and then helped him put it on. Did she notice what good physical shape he was in? Except for all the burns and injuries, of course.

"How much pain are you in?" she said.

He was in a lot. "My legs are fine," he said. "I only need to run."

"You're not fine. You need help."

"I won't let you help me. I'll make it." He put out his hand, asking for the cutter. "I'm not doing it until you're gone."

She took a deep breath and handed him the tool. Then she hesitated and leaned close to him.

She gave him a kiss on the cheek. "Good luck," she said.

He looked at her, and he felt his heart pounding. "Thanks," he said. Then he added, "Tala, I mean it—if I'm not there, don't wait." He pointed at the door. "Go. I'll see you soon."

Her eyes lingered on him for an instant, and then she smiled. "My parents were disappointed when I became a cop. But now I'm a doctor." She turned and slipped through the door without looking back.

He counted a few seconds, giving her time to get a head start. Then he fired up the cutter and sliced through the bracelet. It went through easily. There's nothing like a woman who can pick the right tool.

His pulse was racing as he fumbled with his pants. For some reason, he'd expected a siren to go off but it didn't. Not in here, anyway. He winced in pain as he pulled on his boots and lunged toward the door.

Out in the hall, there was no one—except that cop. So there was a guard after all! Maybe he'd just been taking a break, or doing double duty somewhere else.

"Stop!" the guy said. He was running down the hall and reaching for his gun. Then a blurry figure came zooming out of a perpendicular hallway, running and pushing a hover-table. It was Tala! The cop didn't see her, not until the table smashed into his hip.

Burt gasped. The cop cursed and hit the floor hard. Then he looked up at her and cursed again.

"Oh, I'm so sorry!" she said. She ran to him while he was down, reaching out a hand to help him up—but then she grabbed his gun instead.

The cop stared at her with wide eyes as she leaped backwards. He held up one hand, in front of his face, and she shot him.

"No!" Burt said. "Tala!"

"He'll be all right," she said. "This way!"

He gritted his teeth and felt the burning pain shoot through his left side. But he ran to her, and they darted into a stairwell and raced to the ground floor.

"Give me the gun," he said.

She handed it to him. The door opened and he stepped back, pushing her behind him just as a salvo of energy blasts exploded against the stairwell wall. He ducked down quick and fired a barrage of his own into the area beyond, right near the back door. But he fired stun shots—and then he peeked out and saw he'd hit his target.

"Come on," he said. They bolted through the main doors and into the drop-off area outside. Tala was running for the car. Burt ran with her part of the way, then turned to see if they were being followed. Yeah, a couple of cops were coming, so he fired a volley of shots at the glass doors and they shattered. The cops hit the ground.

Tala was fast. In a flash, the car was sliding behind him, and he tumbled backwards into the open door. Tala gritted her teeth and gunned the hover-car onto the street and then around a corner. She was gripping the steering wheel so hard her knuckles were white.

"Hang on, they're following us!" she shouted.

Burt winced as his left arm banged against the seat. "Tala, slow down. You're driving like a maniac."

"They're coming!"

"Tala, no one's back there."

"They're gaining! I know it!"

"Tala! Slow down. *There's no one following us!*"

He reached across his body with his right hand and gripped her arm. Then he lowered his voice and said, "Tala, there's no one there. We got away."

He smiled as he felt her muscles relax.

"Oh, right," she said. She was taking deep breaths now. "Okay, we got away. That's good. Very good, right?" She took a few more breaths and eased up on the accelerator.

He grinned. "Right," he said. *Because I'd rather die in a car accident than in prison.*

But she was frowning. "Burt, I have to make a confession. I don't have a plan to get out of the city. I thought I'd help you escape from the hospital and then we'd figure it out." She gave him a sober look. "It's not my normal way of doing things, but I just didn't have time."

Burt laughed. "Don't worry about it," he said. "Because it's totally my way." He watched her face and found it amusing that she actually looked relieved. "So, you said the ship is locked up?"

"Yeah. No way we're getting back on the ship."

"How about a commercial flight? Can we get some fake lenses for the eye scans?"

"I'm not sure where to get those. I suppose there are places, but the city is a mess and I'm sure they'll be looking for us at the spaceport. Maybe our best bet is to call Earth. Maybe we can get some kind of diplomatic immunity."

"No way," he said. "No calls to Earth. They aren't going to help us, and I don't want to ask." He sighed. "I got a message from Banks. If we make it out of here, they want us to abandon the mission and report to Tycho City for reassignment. But until then we're on our own."

Tala didn't seem sure how to react to this news, but Burt pictured his uncle and his father and all their disappointment, and his heart sank into a deep hole. There was no escape from this mess. It was over. *Over!*

"I don't know what to do," Tala said in a shaky voice.

Burt grimaced. I've got to keep her feeling confident, he thought. But how long could the grim truth be kept from her? Damn that Suzy Spitfire—

"Suzy has a ship!" he blurted. "Maybe that's our ticket."

Tala broke into a gaping smile. "Yeah! Great idea! She has a fast ship. But won't the government impound it?"

"Probably not. They won't know where it is, Tala. She probably flew in here with some hi-tech, phony credentials, and there are thousands of docking bays in this city. So we'll need to find her—again."

"Right! She could give us a ride."

Burt rolled his eyes. "Tala, she's not going to give us a ride. We're going to lock her up and then fly her ship to Tycho."

"What? We're going to try that again? I thought you just said they wanted us to abandon the plan."

"That's true," Burt said. "But we're not going to do it." He was suddenly feeling better. "We came here to do a job, and we're not quitters. I told you on the first day, we don't need the local cops, and now we definitely don't want them around, right? This whole place is lawless. So we capture Suzy and then use her ship to escape. We'll redeem ourselves, and Banks will be thrilled."

Why didn't Tala look enthused?

"I don't need redeeming," she said. "Suzy saved our lives."

"Are you kidding me? So I'll thank her and then throw her in the brig. She's a killer, Tala."

"You were unconscious, Burt. She saved us both, and I don't want to be responsible for sending her to the reprogrammer. But I like the idea of finding her. If she can't fly us out of here, she might know someone who can."

"And why would she help us?"

"Because she's not that bad. I can tell."

"Are you best friends with her now? I think you're being naïve."

"I told you, you were unconscious at the time. So how do we find her?"

Burt hesitated. Tala is totally wrong about Suzy, he thought, but that didn't mean the plan was entirely bad—at least not the first part, where they hunted her down. He started thinking out loud.

"The city is big, but the areas she's most likely to be are small. We know she's mixed up with Anika, right? And I hear Anika's in prison, and the place is surrounded by a mob. She's also mixed up with Mert Kaya and his friend, Marcos—so there's a chance she'll turn up at either the prison or at Mert's house, where we found her before. Also, there's Ricardo and that girl. If we see either of them, Suzy is probably close by."

"Right," Tala said. "And I have an ID on the girl. I sent for it before we got arrested." She took out her allcom and tapped the screen a few times. "Kiara Silvia Garcia… Fourteen years old, arrested multiple times in Atlanta for solicitation. First picked up at age twelve. Released into the custody of a cousin more than once, but then went back on the street." Then Tala looked up and said, "Wanted for questioning in the murder of a pimp named Daniel Levon."

"Really? That's interesting. Did she do it?"

"She's not a suspect, but she might know something. He was killed by multiple stab wounds in the back, apparently during a struggle. No witnesses, except maybe the girl, and no real evidence—but it doesn't sound like the local cops were sorry to see him gone. She's just a kid."

"Don't turn your back on a kid like that, Tala. Trust me."

"I'm thinking about her life, that's all. It's probably a bad story."

"Yeah, I'm sure. But don't let your sympathy get you killed, okay?"

She nodded. "Okay. So now what?"

"Now we do a stake-out at those two places and see what happens."

"I've never done a stake-out."

Burt gave a soft laugh. "It's tedious, until you get lucky—and then it gets dangerous. But that's what cops do. Unfortunately, our resources are limited. It's just you and me."

"Okay," she said in a shaky voice.

"Don't worry," he said with a smile. "You'll do great. I'll drop you off near the prison and then head to Mert's house. Call me if you see anyone."

***

Tala felt her stomach quaking. Can I do this? she thought. *I can, I can—I hope I can.*

The hover-car couldn't go down the main drag because it was filled with protesters, so they ended up on a side street close to the prison. Tala navigated around the burned-out shell of a police car and parked. She opened the door, preparing to exit, and then she leaned over and kissed Burt goodbye.

"Be careful," she said.

He smiled at her. "I've never been careful."

"Start today."

He held her hand. "I'll be fine. *You* be careful—and call me if you see anything. You hear me? Anything! There's a definite chance she'll turn up around here. Be ready."

He drove off, heading to Mert's house. She was filled with longing as she watched him go. She was worried about his injuries, and she wanted him to stay. But now she had a job to do. She had to help them get home.

Stay calm, she thought. The plan was to get over to the main street and then sit on the rooftop of a nearby building. She had binoculars, and she had a gun; Burt had insisted she keep the weapon. Why did the gun make her nervous? *I'm a cop, dammit!* But she shuddered at the thought of encountering Suzy Spitfire. Sure, she liked Suzy, but Burt was right—the girl was a murderer. Then she saw a message on her phone and her heart skipped a beat. It was from Commander Banks.

Have not heard from Lt. Stone. I understand he was arrested. Please report immediately for reassignment to Tycho City where new plan is in place to capture the target. Banks.

This was news! For an instant she felt a wave of relief. But then she realized Banks didn't know their situation. He didn't know they were both wanted fugitives, and that they were counting on Suzy's ship to get them home—and if they were going to get her ship, they might as well get her, too.

So she might have to arrest Suzy after all. She shuddered again. And then a lime green car drove past, moving slowly through the wreckage—and she'd seen that car before. In fact, she'd ridden in it. Her eyes popped open and her heart pounded. Was that Ricardo and Suzy inside?

She took a quick step forward, and then stopped. She moved to her left, toward a doorway—and stopped again. Then she grimaced and swore to herself and saw a hover-scooter right there, parked beside an overturned trash can. She took a deep breath and jumped on the machine.

Chapter 47

Jack knew the cops were busy, so of course Elijah was busy. But hey, Jack was busy, too. He was trying to prevent himself from being killed while finding the girl he loved. He listened to the sirens howling downtown, and he shrugged.

Right now he was hiding outside Elijah's apartment. Elijah lived on the ground floor of a gated apartment development, and Jack had climbed one of the bamboo gates and dropped behind a bushy plant. He had no idea what kind of plant it was, but it looked like something that should be covered with bananas. As he peered between the thick leaves, he saw Elijah coming to the door, dressed in his police uniform and probably coming home for a quick break.

Jack smiled and stepped out of the foliage. "Hi, Elijah. Busy night?"

Elijah stopped walking. "What the hell?" he said. Then he looked around and lowered his voice. "What are you doing here, Jack?"

"I need your help."

Elijah reached for his gun. "Are you kidding me? There's all kinds of shit going on. I just came home for a few minutes. Why should I help you?"

"Because we've been friends a long time. All those times back in Atlanta—didn't I have your back? And I still do. You know what I mean."

Elijah hesitated. Then he looked up and down the street again. "Come on in," he said, opening the door. "But you're not staying. I've got stuff to do."

Jack smiled and slipped inside.

The place was clean and uncluttered, with turquoise walls, soft lighting, and a collection of plants in clay pots. Jack knew it had been decorated by Elijah's girlfriend who was also a cop.

"Where's Jen?" Jack said, noting a picture on a table of a pretty girl with long, black hair.

"Working, like I should be. Now what the hell do you want?"

Elijah walked into the kitchen, which was open to the living room, and pulled a purplish bottle from the refrigerator. He glanced at a few messages on his allcom and then poured himself a drink. "Want some grape juice?" he said. "It'll taste good before I blow your head off."

Jack swore. "What did I do?" he said. "I just warned Kiara to get away from the shooting. I also warned Suzy—and didn't Mert want to keep her alive? At least for now."

"You stabbed Zehra."

"I had no choice."

"Is that so? You're lucky she's alive. Otherwise, I would've killed you already."

Jack shrugged. "I didn't want to hurt her but they came to kill me."

"They were taking you to Mert."

"Same thing. And Mert's the wrong guy to be the Head. That was all bullshit."

Elijah grunted. "Maybe. But a lot of people supported him."

"How can you say that?" Jack said, waving his hands. "Most of the brothers and sisters don't even know him. Only the people in his band know him, like us. The system is fucked up."

"It is what it is, and the people that mattered supported him."

"I supported *you.*"

Elijah put his glass down on the counter. "I know that, and I appreciate it. But things have changed."

"They can keep changing, brother," Jack said with a smirk. Then he walked into the kitchen. "You can get that top spot before this is all done."

Elijah sighed and once again looked at his allcom messages. "Jack, get out of the city."

"Not without Kiara," Jack said with a scowl. "I know your people arrested her. All I want is to give her a message."

"What makes you think she wants a message from you? Has she been calling?"

Jack frowned. "She's been poisoned by that lying bitch, Suzy Spitfire. But she'll come around. I just need to talk to her."

"We don't have her, Jack. She was released. She's gone."

"What?" Jack felt his heart pounding. "How?"

"Mert asked if we could do it so I said, 'Sure.' I didn't do it, but it was done. In fact, Jen arranged it; you know she's got a soft spot for girls like Kiara. But the only guy she had available was Eduardo, who ended up jabbing her with a stun stick."

"What? That motherfucker!"

"Jack, she's fine. She was acting crazy."

"God dammit! Yeah—sometimes she gets that way. Where is she now?"

"I don't know. I guess she's at Mert's place, but I wouldn't go there. The place is surrounded by cops and reporters. Things are going to blow up."

"Mert's place," Jack clenched his fist. "Shit. I've got to get over there."

"Did you hear what I just said?"

"I heard. But I also heard some serious shit about Mert. Things you might want to look into."

"Oh, yeah? Like what?"

"Mert might be into some stuff we don't know about, stuff that a brother shouldn't be doing."

"Oh, yeah? Where'd you hear this?"

Jack hesitated. "From Suzy."

Elijah rolled his eyes. "Didn't you just call her a lying bitch?"

"Yeah, but listen. Mert asked me to get rid of this surgeon, and it was a secret job, okay? And Suzy came to Venus to find this other guy, a rapist serial killer—and she was in the surgeon's place, right after I did the guy, following up on some info, I guess. She said whoever put me up to killing the surgeon knows who this serial killer is, and is probably protecting him. Now she doesn't know the person who put me up to it is Mert—but I know. And now you know."

Elijah snorted. "Sounds ridiculous." Then he paused. "Who was she looking for? And who was the surgeon?"

"The surgeon was Artemis Hatzi. The guy she's looking for is Shogun Hunter."

Elijah slowly nodded his head. "I'll look into it."

"Do that. Might be a good move for you. Suzy's a bitch but she's not dumb." Then Jack shook his head and gave a little laugh. "I might even regret it when I cut her throat."

Now Elijah snorted. "You're going to cut her throat? I've seen her profile. Dangerous girl, with dangerous friends. Probably best to leave her alone."

"I'm dangerous, too!" Jack snapped. "And I'm done wasting time. I got to go." He glanced around the room. "You got another gun?"

"I have one gun, Jack, and it's mine. Sorry."

Jack shot him a fierce stare, but then relaxed. "Fair enough," he said. "I'll use a knife like a real man." Then he smiled. "You got anything to eat?"

"Maybe," Elijah said. He paused and then opened the refrigerator. In a flash, Jack snatched a vase filled with roses from the kitchen table and smashed it on the back of Elijah's head.

Elijah swore and hit the floor. He was only groggy for a second, but it was long enough for Jack to wrestle the gun from his belt. He slid the setting into a low-power range and leaped backwards.

"I'm sorry, too, Elijah. But like I said, I've got to go."

"No!"

Jack just grunted and pulled the trigger.

Chapter 48

Ricardo insisted on driving the car, and Suzy agreed. What the hell, it kept her hands free to shoot things.

"What a mess," Ricardo said as they passed by smashed windows and buildings burned by gunfire. There was rage, there was frustration—and there were still people wandering through the broken glass, looking dazed and happy. They were smiling in the bushes and sleeping in the gutters. Ricardo grimaced at the addiction and devastation. "The cops think they're getting things under control," he said, "but it won't last. And I hear the spaceport is jammed with tourists trying to get out." He gave Suzy a sideways glance. "We better clean it up. Maria won't like a messy city."

Suzy looked at her allcom and raised her eyebrows. "Funny you should say that. She just left me a message." Suzy patched it in from the ship. As it played, Suzy felt a chill go down her spine. She'd never heard Maria's voice sound so shaky.

"Suzy, how are you? I hope you're okay. Big things are happening here—crazy things. I'm sorry for any trouble I've caused you, and I'm sorry for other things, too. I'm leaving Earth, and I'm leaving alone. I've made some mistakes." She paused and then said, "Listen, your friend Captain Banks is planning to attend the Global Law Enforcement Conference in a few days and it's a bad idea, do you understand? Bad idea, bad plan. Maybe I'll see you soon. Tell Ricardo I'll be calling. And tell him to stay alive."

The message ended, leaving Suzy and Ricardo speechless.

Ricardo shook his head. "What the hell?"

"It sounds like she's had enough of Pablo," Suzy said, and she felt a pang of sadness. Maria was tough, but underneath her armored exterior, Suzy knew she was sweet—and romantic. So this had to be hurting her badly.

"Yeah, but how does that affect all this?" Ricardo said, waving his arms at the chaos outside. "How does that affect everything else? This is a disaster."

"No, it's not, Ricardo. It just makes a big mess a little bigger. But is she saying Pablo wants to kill Banks? That's not good. I should call Danielle and tell her to warn him."

"What? You can't do that. You'd be a traitor to the organization."

"I'm not in the organization."

"Suzy, I know you're not, but please do not call Danielle."

"Danielle has helped me, and so has her husband."

"Her husband put those cops on your ass. And think about Danielle's messages since you got here—aren't they strange? Don't call her! Besides, Pablo has helped you, too. If you stab him in the back, think about what happens."

"I'm not scared of Pablo. He'll just be one more guy trying to kill me."

"But it's not just about you. It's about me—and Maria, even though right now she's having some problems."

Damn, he was right. How would all this affect Ricardo? And Pablo had been helpful. After all, she was shooting around the solar system in his former spaceship. But there was no way she was going to let him kill Banks. And really, Ricardo would be better off leaving Los Pocos—as she'd told him many times.

She wanted to think more about the situation but then a police car came surging down the street and a flaming bottle came hurtling from a rooftop. The bottle exploded on the ground right behind the car, and Suzy returned her attention to the anarchy all around. Back to the riot, she thought. *At least for now.*

Suzy had Ricardo's allcom on her lap. "Turn up here," she said. She was hoping they wouldn't end up on the main drag because that's where most of the cops were, protecting the sleazy casinos. Of course the cops were also protecting the prison where Anika had been taken, as well as certain wealthy, pro-government neighborhoods, so the police force was stretched thin. All in all, people were ignoring the law pretty successfully—and the signal on the allcom was no longer moving. They were on a side street now, and apparently the tracking device was inside a local pub called The Blue Whale.

Pretty funny, Suzy thought. Was there a less likely place to find a blue whale than a city floating above Venus? Ricardo drove the car around a corner and parked.

He shifted around a bit. "Suzy, listen—I think I should go alone." Then he held up his hand and said, "Just think about it, okay? Lots of people know you, and they all want you dead. I can go in quick and check it out. You can stay here and leave the car running, ready to go. I'll bring you a beer."

"No way, Ricardo."

"Okay, two beers." He could see she wasn't laughing. "Suzy, try and understand." He reached out and took her hand. "There's no one I'd rather have next to me in a gunfight—no one. But I don't want you getting killed over these guns that I put on your ship. I'd never forgive myself if you got hurt. Do you see?"

She was quiet, but she felt better.

"Yeah, I see," she said. "And I appreciate your concern. But I'm still going in there."

He sighed. "Yeah, that's what I figured. Hey, you should be wearing body armor."

"Are you wearing it?"

"No."

"Let's go."

As they reached the door she cut in front of him, and before he could object she was inside. It was dark, and there were five or six people sitting at the bar, and Suzy had one hand close to her thigh, ready to reach for her weapon—but the only person who looked their way was the bartender. She was a willowy young girl with hair and eyes that matched the darkness. Wait a second—Suzy knew her! She was one of Anika's people.

Well, well, isn't this interesting.

The girl smiled. "Hello, Suzy," she said. "Anika said you would come."

Now the people at the bar turned to watch, and Suzy could see who they were—four young girls and a boy. None of them looked older than sixteen, and they were all giving her looks of admiration.

"Sara, right?" Suzy said. "I don't think we were ever introduced. Do you know why we're here?"

"I know you might want a drink."

"That doesn't make you psychic. But maybe I'll wait until after your revolution."

Now Sara's eyes got wide. "I heard Kiara was arrested and released. Is she all right?"

"Yeah, she's fine."

"Good," Sara said, breathing a sigh of relief.

"How's Anika?"

"Okay, except for the prison cell. But we're going to change that." Then she spoke in a steely voice. "We're going to change everything. Here, come this way."

She turned and sashayed down a short hallway. Suzy looked at Ricardo, and they followed. Suzy had to admit, Sara seemed confident. She passed an eye in front of a scanning lens and a door slid open. Ricardo peered inside a cluttered back room and grinned.

"My guns," he said. "Well, some of them. Where are the rest? And how did they get here?"

"There are only ten guns here," Sara said. "Also some grenades. The rest of the weapons are being distributed." Then she reached into her pocket, pulling out a small object and offering it to Suzy. "Here's your tracking device."

"Thanks," Suzy said. "When did you find it?"

"An hour ago. So I thought you'd be coming, and that was good."

Ricardo seemed a little lost. "What's going on?"

"I'm guessing Anika stole the guns," Suzy said. "Anika and Nuru. Now I understand why they weren't too concerned about finding a traitor; there was no traitor. She didn't want the guns to get stolen for real—by one of her enemies, or maybe one of her so-called friends. So they faked an attack."

"But there were dead people there," Ricardo said.

Sara shook her head. "It wasn't real. No one was hurt."

"But Nuru and Anika seemed upset."

"They were pretending. They're good at it."

Ricardo grinned. "Okay, I guess that saves us one fight." Then he looked at Suzy. "When push comes to shove you'll still see my love—like a fat cloud hanging above."

Sara gave him a curious look. "Don't worry," Suzy said. "His fighting is better than his poems. So I guess you're part of the underground warriors I've heard about. How are you organized?"

"In *nodes,* strategically placed throughout the city. Each node has a captain and nine others."

"So how many nodes are there?"

"Five hundred."

"What?" Suzy said. And she stared at Ricardo, who also seemed shocked. "So you have five thousand people? And do they all have guns?"

"They do now. They've been practicing for months, with simulators—waiting, thinking that one day we'd be able to fight for real. And now it's time… But we're having some issues. Anika was in charge, with help from Nuru and the Council. She gave the order to distribute the guns and then everyone in the Council was arrested. Anika said if anything happened to her we should reach out to you. She thought you could lead us. Everyone will follow you."

"Me? Why would anyone follow me? I'm not from this place. No one here knows me."

"Most of us aren't from this place. It's a city of immigrants, and people who were brought here. We know it's destiny for this to happen because Kiara is one of us, and you came here with her."

"I think she came with me."

"Anika says destiny works in strange ways. She said you were here to help, and you could be trusted. And here you are, and we need help." Now Sara leaned toward Suzy and spoke faster. "Most of the warriors are young girls, age thirteen to sixteen. But we know where to find the leaders of the cartel, and the Snake Eyes. We know where the police are vulnerable. No one knows the city better than we do—no one."

While Suzy was absorbing this information, Sara pressed a button and a glowing three-dimensional map of Baadal Shahar appeared above a table. She pointed at different colored orbs scattered across the panorama. "Green represents our nodes," she said. "The yellow orbs are the Snake Eyes, and where they like to meet. Blue is the police and security forces, and red is the Casino Cartel. So what do you think?"

"I'm not a military tactician," Suzy said. "I'm just an angry girl with a gun."

Ricardo laughed. "You're a girl with a gun who's been in lots of fights, and won them all."

"I didn't win them all," Suzy said, looking away. And for a second, her mind flashed with painful memories. Then she turned back to Sara. "These are serious guns, and you won't need to do much, just watch things burn and count the bodies. But are you ready for that? Because real death is the part that's different from your simulations. It's the part that's going to stay with you—forever."

A spark of fear jumped in Sara's eyes, but then she narrowed her stare and looked determined. "We're ready," she said. "We want to attack the prison."

Suzy felt a pang of sadness. *Five thousand Kiara's entering a world of violence and death.*

"So, can you help us?" Sara said.

Suzy hesitated. She tried to focus on the three-dimensional map as her eyes roved across the key locations. It was a blur. The prison, the capitol compound, the spaceport, the casinos, the industrial complex—and the air treatment facility. Then inside her head, something clicked into place, like an equation being solved.

Suzy pointed at the air factory. "How familiar are you with this place?"

Sara cocked her head. "I've been inside. I've gone there, along with some others, to 'entertain' the director. He's a pervert, a real piece of shit. He gets entertained there all the time. I guess his wife never visits him at work."

"Can you get us in?"

Sara hesitated. Then she said, "There's a back entrance that's used for special deliveries. That's how I got in, ha. But it's still heavily guarded, and with so much going on in the city I don't think they'll be looking for any girls to come over."

"But do they know you?" Suzy persisted. "Can you get us close enough to be…persuasive?"

"Maybe. But why?"

"Are all your fighters inoculated against veluva?"

"Yes, definitely."

"Great. And can you give us that inoculation right now?"

"I suppose. But what's going on?"

"Sara, we're going to put this city to sleep."

Sara raised her eyebrows and Ricardo grinned. "Hey, great idea!" he said. "Plus we have others who can help. I can call Marcos and Mert, and I have people at the spaceport." He took out his allcom and started to touch the screen. But Suzy reached out and stopped him.

"No," she said. "Bad idea."

Suddenly there was a commotion in the hall. *What now?* Suzy pulled out her pistol and peered around the doorframe—what the hell?

It was Tala, and she had her hands in the air. She also had a girl standing behind her, pointing a gun.

"We found her outside," the girl said. "She came on a scooter and was snooping around. Isn't she one of the cops from Earth?"

"Yeah," Suzy said. "Tala, I told you to go home, and I'm pretty sure you don't live here."

Tala looked scared. "Hi, Suzy," she said in a quivering voice. "We can't go. We're in too much trouble, and so I was looking for you. I thought maybe you could give us a ride when you leave."

"Do I look like a taxi service? Where's your friend?"

"Over at Mert Kaya's house."

Suzy sighed. Her instincts told her that Tala was harmless, but then again, Tala was also a cop, and they should probably lock her up for now. Suzy started to give Tala the bad news—but then stopped, because she usually followed her instincts.

"Hey, Tala, didn't you tell me you were a chemical engineer?"

"Yeah, for one year."

"You know, that might be helpful. Do you want to go for a ride?"

"What?"

Suzy leaned toward her. "Back at the hospital you told me you wanted adventure. Do you want to help save thousands of lives?"

Tala glanced around the room with jumpy eyes. Then she said, "Yeah, of course."

"Good," Suzy said. "Sara, we've got one more to get the inoculation. Then we go."

Chapter 49

Kiara rubbed her eyes. Everything was fuzzy, and there was a dull pain throbbing between two ribs. But then things came into focus. She was lying on a sofa, and there was Mert Kaya.

He was standing near her, just staring. She moved a bit, and he narrowed his eyes, and her mind flooded with dark memories. For an instant, she couldn't breathe. "Calm down," she thought. *This isn't like that.* Then she gasped a few times.

He leaned over her face. "Kiara, are you all right?"

"Yeah," she said. Then she blurted, "What's going on? Where's Suzy?"

He shrugged. "You're in my house and we're surrounded. There are people outside who support us, and people who don't. We seem to be in a standoff."

For some reason, the news that there were other people around made her feel better. Another man came into the room and said, "Mert, more cops are coming. I think they're going to storm the place."

The man had a gun, the same kind Suzy carried. So did the other two guys who followed him. On the wall was a screen that showed Buso, shouting about law and order.

Mert seemed calm, as usual. "We won't be here," he said. "We're getting out. Let's go."

It sounded like a good plan, but it was a few seconds late.

"They're coming!" someone yelled. "Get down!"

Kiara shrieked as a deafening explosion shook the building. She dove to the floor as windows shattered and the crowd outside roared.

Energy blasts ricocheted around the room, furniture splintered, and pictures crashed from the walls. Kaya was quick—in an instant he was on the ground, pulling at Kiara's shirt. "This way!" he said.

She was crawling fast now as people inside the house returned fire. Outside, Kiara could hear the cops firing at the unarmed mob. There were screams and more explosions. She was gasping as they reached the kitchen, with dishes crashing down and broken glass flying.

But the door in the floor was open. "Get in!" Mert shouted.

Kiara slid fast down the ladder and into the dim passageway. With her heart pounding, she ran toward the other end, toward the other ladder, and climbed up fast.

Kaya was right behind her. He even bumped into her a few times. She was about to open the door to the outside when he yanked hard on the collar of her shirt.

"Wait!" he said. She felt a moment of panic, but then he put a gentle hand on her shoulder and motioned for her to be quiet, and she forced herself to be calm. He slid the door open a crack and peered out. "We're clear. Come on."

She didn't want to go with him. She wanted to run and take her chances on the street, like she always had. But then she saw a woman in the alley, smiling and motioning toward them.

Kaya ran toward her. "Do you have a car?" he said.

"Yes. We can get you to the Cave."

He turned to Kiara and said, "I told Suzy I'd keep you safe. We have a place."

Kiara hesitated and then said, "All right. Let's go."

They raced down the alley, stumbled through a backyard, and burst onto a familiar street. Then they got into a car and drove away.

***

High on a rooftop, Burt Stone watched through a pair of binoculars. He shook his head as the surging crowd hurled bottles at the cops, and he gave a grunt as the cops responded with heavy stun shots. He could've been down there with the crowd but he wasn't that stupid, at least not today. He was on a rooftop garden across the street, lying on his stomach in a pumpkin patch, on the opposite side of the road from where a tactical expert might suggest—but he'd picked this location for good reason. While this spot didn't provide the best view of the house, it provided an excellent view of the streets around it, and Suzy had appeared on these streets after escaping from the house without being seen.

Burt had read the profile on Mert Kaya. He was a political figure, and that's all Burt needed to know. Political guys don't go down with the ship; they jump off like rats. So Burt smirked when Mert appeared on the street. Then a car came gliding along and stopped. Damn, no sign of Suzy—but wait! There was the girl, Kiara.

He focused on Kiara as she got into the car. Pretty girl, he thought, petite with a shambles of long dark hair. But then he zeroed in on her face, on her eyes, and for a second he saw it all—the fear, the angst, and the barely restrained panic. Well, Tala was right. *Poor kid. Got away from one pimp but found another one.*

Burt scrambled up from his position, ignoring the pain in his left arm and body. Tala had insisted he keep the car, but he had to get down there in time to use it. He gritted his teeth and ran toward the stairs.

Chapter 50

Suzy was ready for a gunfight but Sara had a different plan. Apparently, Sara's plan involved a few fast calls and a couple of girls in skimpy outfits. Sara trained her eyes on Suzy, who was wearing a black skirt, a crimson shirt, and a black jacket. Her hair was its natural shade of coppery red.

Sara shook her head. "You look more dangerous than slutty."

"You say that like it's a bad thing."

"Right now it is… You need to look less like Suzy Spitfire. You need to look like one of us, with a shorter skirt, heels, some cheap jewelry—definitely more makeup."

Suzy laughed. "Sara, I have a gun. That's usually the thing that works best."

Sara was unconvinced, so Suzy grudgingly changed her hair to black and smeared on some blazing red lipstick. She made the shirt orange and switched the skirt to an animal print. At least there was no argument with Ricardo concerning body armor. It just wouldn't work with her ensemble.

"What about Ricardo?" Suzy said. "Do you have some lipstick for him, too?"

"No. But we'll say he's for security, or maybe he just wants to party."

"I'm ready for both," Ricardo said. Then he grinned and showed off the Series 10 pulse rifle he was placing in a bag. It was one of the 5,000 guns Suzy had brought from Earth, and it was a formidable weapon. It had a collapsible barrel and stock that made it easy to conceal, and it could stun, kill, or be cranked up to destroy robot fighters and pieces of buildings. Luckily, Baadal Shahar didn't have too many armed robots. But there were still some in the casinos, and at the prison, and probably in the air treatment facility, and they'd need to be dealt with.

They crammed themselves into Ricardo's car and got underway: Suzy, Sara, Ricardo, Tala, and two other girls. All the girls were armed with Ricardo's rifles, stuffed into their large purses. Suzy had her usual pulse pistol, along with a couple of grenades. Outside, the streets were still filled with broken glass and burning bits of garbage. The police sirens had quieted but the air was thick with tension and drifting clouds of smoke. Ricardo was in a good mood.

"I need a pimp name," he said. "Maybe I'll be Big Banana."

"Subtle," Suzy said. "A true fruit lover."

"When the world is on fire your only desire will be to run through my orchard of love."

The two girls, Sharonda and Melissa, both laughed. Suzy almost laughed, but she was too busy thinking about the potential battle. Then they turned a corner and saw their destination emerging through the haze.

It was a fat green building that reminded Suzy of a beached sea monster, and for an instant she thought about her childhood home near the Pacific Ocean. She studied the shimmering energy fence and wondered what her mother and grandmother were doing right now. *Hopefully, nothing that involves violent revolution.*

They drove down a ramp and into a grungy area where there was a guard booth, a high gate, and a loading dock. Suzy held her pistol down low as her eyes darted around. Above the guard booth was the flickering hologram of a guy's head, and he looked grim. Damn, this meant the real guard was inside the main building and out of reach. Also, the gate was actually an energy barrier, and there were guns on the roof, and the main door beyond the loading dock looked heavy and blast proof. Why hadn't she scouted this better? They could never fight their way into this place. They needed a new plan, and they needed it fast.

But maybe not. The holo-head was smiling.

"Really?" he said. "Tonight? That's crazy. I didn't hear anything."

Sara smiled back. "I think it's supposed to be a surprise for Tanet."

The guard grinned. "From Arjun?"

"I don't know who called it in. I just come when they send me."

The guard grinned again. No search, no scan, no words—they just drove through.

Suzy had to laugh. "Sara, I thought you said this was a government installation with all kinds of security."

"It is," Sara said. "But that never applies to a bunch of whores." Then she added, "I haven't been here for almost two years. I'm out of that game. But I guess nothing's changed."

Suzy glanced over at Tala. She was wearing a flowery dress supplied by Sara that looked pretty without being overtly sexy. Sara had said, "Smile a lot and you'll be fine." But Tala wasn't smiling. It was hard to tell if she was confused or just nervous. She was definitely squirming a lot. I better keep my eye on her, Suzy thought.

They slipped into the building quick and followed Sara down a short hallway. And then they were in the director's office.

The Director General was sitting behind a wide acrylic desk. He was a big guy with a bushy black mustache, sagging jowls, and a gut flopping over his belt. He wore a drab green uniform and shiny black boots. Nearby, there was an oversized couch and a fish tank. Suzy wondered about the things those fish had seen. She wondered about a government that left the city's atmosphere in the care of a guy who held orgies inside his air factory.

The sign on the desk said "Tanet Anuwat." Tanet's teeth were bright but his grin was crooked. "What's going on?" he said as he stood up and walked toward them. "I didn't send for anyone. What is Arjun thinking? We're busy here tonight." Then he looked at Sara and leered. "Although I suppose I could take a quick break."

He also glanced at Suzy, and his eyes narrowed. "Wait," he said. "I know you."

"I don't think so. I'd remember being this disgusted."

His mouth dropped open. "You're the girl on TV! You killed those cartel people."

"Does everybody watch that channel?"

Anuwat turned and lunged toward his desk, probably to trigger an alarm. But Suzy shot him in the ass.

He screamed with pain. It wasn't quite a stun shot; it burned a hole through his pants and fried his skin. He gasped but still groped toward the button. Ricardo grabbed his arm, twisted it behind his back, and shoved him down onto the desk. Suzy jabbed her pistol into his ear and smiled.

"Tanet, I have some bad news," she said. "These girls are nice—but me, not so much. Now take us to the control room or I'll blow your fucking brains out."

Sharonda and Melissa pulled out their rifles while Tala watched with wide eyes. Two more guys walked into the room and stopped short, looking confused. Obviously, they'd been expecting the girls to be friendlier. Sara shot them both.

"They're not dead," Sara said to Tala. Then Ricardo shoved Anuwat toward the door. They got halfway down the hall before a siren sounded.

"What do you want?" Tanet said. "I'll never let you into the control room."

Suzy smirked. " 'Never' is a tough word."

They reached the metal door to the control center and Ricardo pushed Tanet's face against the eye sensor. Meanwhile, two people with guns appeared at the end of the hallway. Suzy and her crew opened fire and shots echoed through the building.

Tanet's eyes were closed tight. "No," he said. "I can't let you in."

Ricardo slammed Anuwat's face against the wall but he still kept his eyes closed. Then Suzy pulled out her knife. "I admire your dedication," she said. "So I'll just cut out your eyeball and use it that way. I'm sure it'll work fine."

She jammed the blade under his eye. Then his eyes popped open and so did the door.

A salvo of shots blasted though the opening. Unfortunately, they all hit Tanet in the chest and he exploded like a bag of blood. Two more people came running around the corner at the end of the hall but Sara and her girls laid down a barrage of fire that sent them back.

Suzy pulled out a grenade and set it to deliver a heavy stun blast; after all, they needed to preserve the machinery. Then she tossed it into the control room. She heard someone swear, and then there was an explosion—an energy blast that produced no fire or smoke. Suzy waited a few seconds and peered inside.

Two people were on the floor but the consoles looked intact. Perfect.

"Come on!" she said. She ran into the room with Ricardo, Tala, and Sara close behind.

They left the door open. Sara instructed Sharonda and Melissa to point their guns down opposite ends of the hall. We don't have much time, Suzy thought. Unfortunately, the people who knew how to work this stuff were either dead or unconscious.

Suzy scanned the consoles fast. She was tech savvy, but there were lots of unknown controls. Then Tala said, "Here! This one is controlling the release of a drug. It's at a very low level... I've seen this kind of console before."

Up on the wall, there were screens showing the city outside. One of them showed the prison, and the cops were firing at the crowd—and they were firing kill shots. There was a lot of wailing and screaming. Some people were shooting back, probably some of Anika's fighters. The battle was on.

Out in the hall, a deluge of fire was coming down the hallway. A pair of robot fighters had arrived, each over two meters tall, sitting on treads, and bristling with silvery armaments. Sharonda shouted and fell backwards to the floor. Melissa and Sara cranked up the power on their weapons, destroying the machines—as well as a good bit of the hall.

"All right, Tala," Suzy said. "Can you increase the amount of veluva?"

Tala hesitated. "Yeah, but how much? That's a difficult calculation."

Ricardo was shooting alongside of Sara. A shot pinged off the doorframe by his head and ricocheted around the room. "Do the easy version," he said.

"Crank it up," Suzy said. "Dump it all."

"That's crazy," Tala said.

"Do it!"

Tala froze for a second but then selected a few options. Her hands were shaking as she pressed a button.

"Is that all of it?" Suzy said.

"Yeah," Tala said.

"Great. Now can you speed up the air system in here?"

Tala once again paused. She looked like she was in shock but she touched a few controls and the air vents started to hum.

"I hope this stuff works fast," Suzy said.

Sara fired a few more shots. "Don't worry," she said. "It does."

Chapter 51

Kiara stumbled down the stairs and into a dark room that looked like a pub. It was stuffy and musty. They were below the main level of the city, and what was that picture hanging above the bar? She caught her breath as a chill went down her spine. It was an image of a snake with bright gold eyes—an image she'd seen before.

Her pulse started racing. *These people are Snake Eyes!* But what was Mert doing with them? From the way Mert and the others had been talking in the car, they were obviously together. So Mert was involved with the Snakes!

Mert smiled and led Kiara to an office. He said, "Kiara, we're going to have a meeting in the other room, but you'll be safe here."

"Where's Suzy?" she said.

"We don't know. We're trying to figure out what's going on and coordinate things."

"I don't want to stay here. I can help."

He smiled again, but this time his eyes did not smile. "You need to stay here for now."

She started to protest again, but stopped. It was better to pretend. Maybe I can find out something, she thought. *Something I can tell Suzy and Ricardo.*

"Okay," she said with a smile. He gave her a friendly nod and closed the door.

She stopped smiling. Maybe I should call Suzy, she thought. No—bad idea. Suzy was probably in the middle of a shit storm, and it would be stupid to act like a kid in need of attention. *I've got to stay calm.* She'd been in tight spots before, lots of them, and she'd survived—although there had been some close calls. She closed her eyes and blocked out a few horrific memories, like she always did; she touched the scar on her jaw line, and thought about other scars no one ever saw.

She yanked open a desk drawer and started rummaging around, but then froze. Shouts and gunfire were coming from the other room. *What the fuck?* Then there was a loud scream, and more shots. Then silence.

Her heart was pounding. She ran to the door and pressed her ear against it—nothing. She opened it a crack and peered out.

There was Jack.

He was standing by a table in the middle of the room, with a smirk on his face and a gun in his hand. On the floor were the bodies of the two people who'd been in the car with Mert.

She gasped and opened the door. Then she whispered, "Jack."

His eyes lit up. "Kiara," he said, and he ran to her. He put down the gun and hugged her hard, and she hugged him back, squeezing him with all her might. She felt warm and lost in his arms.

"How did you find me?"

"I saw the cops bust Mert's place but then he wasn't there, and neither were you. So I guessed he'd come here. I didn't know you'd still be with him, but I was hoping. I was planning to find him and ask him some questions."

"Mert's here," Kiara said.

Jack whipped his head around fast. "Not when I came in," he said. "I shot those two over there and he probably ran 'cause that's his style." He nodded toward an open doorway next to the bar. "There's another way out, through that kitchen."

He narrowed his eyes. Then he picked up the gun and walked toward the doorway.

"You in there, Mert?" he said. "Come on out. Let's talk, motherfucker."

He poked his head into the kitchen. "Jack, wait," Kiara said. She hurried past the bodies and ran toward him as he entered the room.

There was a stainless-steel sink, a counter, and a heavy metal table, but no sign of Mert. There was another door. Jack opened it and looked up a flight of stairs.

"Like I thought," he said. "He ran for it. I'd chase after him, but now that you're here I got better things to do." He put the gun down on the table and once again took her in his arms. "Kiara, I missed you."

Kiara sighed. "I missed you, too. But I'm really nervous."

His face got serious. "Don't worry, Kiara, it'll be fine. But I need to tell you something. I know you and Suzy came here looking for a guy, right? And you think the surgeon was killed by that guy, or someone who knew him. Well, I killed the surgeon—because Mert told me to."

Kiara hesitated. "So Mert might know Shogun Hunter?"

"Yeah, I think so."

Then they heard a sound, a low grunt, and they looked at the doorway. Mert was standing there with a gun. Kiara felt her blood run cold.

Mert was not smiling. "I might know Hunter," he said. "I might know him well. Don't go for the gun, Jack. I'll kill you both."

Jack stared at him—and then lunged for the gun like a guy with nothing to lose.

Kiara shrieked. Mert fired, and Jack gasped and crashed to the floor.

Kiara screamed again and dropped down beside him. He wasn't dead! Not yet. Meanwhile, Mert picked up Jack's gun and put his own gun on the table. Then he frowned and looked down at Jack.

"Get away from him, Kiara. I hit him with a low-powered shot and he might still be dangerous."

Jack was trying to get up. Mert was adjusting the settings on Jack's gun.

"No!" Kiara screamed. "What are you going to do?"

He shot her in the chest and she tumbled to the floor, hitting her head on a table leg.

Everything was blurry, but she was still conscious. Apparently, he'd used a very low power stun shot. She tried to shout and move her arms, but no words came out. It felt like she was swimming in sand.

Mert smiled down at Jack. "I went outside, through that door," he said, motioning toward the door that led to the stairs. "But then I came back around through the front door… I didn't have one of these military grade weapons, so thanks. I had a civilian pistol that could only fire stun shots. It was a good tool for me. I have better ways to kill."

Jack once again tried to get up but he could barely thrash around.

Mert reached down and rummaged through Jack's clothing a bit. He pulled out a knife. "You said I couldn't use a knife, right?"

"Fuck you," Jack spat.

Mert just smiled again. "So clever with words," he said. Then he snarled and plunged the knife into Jack's lower spine.

Jack sucked in his breath. Kiara tried to shriek again but couldn't. Mert looked over at her, and now his eyes blazed. "I came here to start over," he said. "And you're going to be a great place to start. Do you hear me, Jack? I'm going to hurt your girlfriend *so much,* and I'm going to fuck her *so hard,* and I'm going to do it over and over again, until she's sobbing like a baby. Then I'll hang her from a pipe and watch her die. Can you picture that, Jack? Can you see her gagging and kicking and trying to scream? Are you scared, Kiara? You should be. You haven't seen anything yet."

Jack was staring at Kiara. He was trying to speak, but he didn't need to. She knew what he was saying. Then Mert grabbed him by the hair and pulled his head upward. Mert forced him to look at Kiara as he yanked the knife out of his lower back and shoved it hard between his shoulder blades.

Jack gasped as his eyes rolled upward.

Kiara thought her heart would explode. Then Mert came toward her. He wiped the bloody knife in her hair and watched her face. Did he like what he saw? He was smiling again.

"Not yet, Kiara," he said. "I'm saving you until I've got more time. But remember what I said—I'll be coming."

He dropped the knife and grabbed her feet. He snarled once again as he dragged her out of the kitchen. She looked at Jack one last time, reaching out a hand toward his body.

Then she was back in the office, in a closet. Her wrists were tied behind her back, and a piece of heavy tape was across her mouth. The door closed and it was dark.

Chapter 52

Andre Banks didn't care much for conferences, even when he was the star speaker. In fact, those were the conferences he liked the least.

He was sitting at the elegant bar in the Windy Sea Hotel, located on the beach in Melbourne, Australia. It would probably be better to go outside and get some sun, but he wasn't in a sunny mood. He stared into his glass of Bass ale and pondered getting something stronger for the next round.

I never really wanted to play the game, he thought. Then he gave a sardonic laugh. *But here I am, a big winner. And what do I get?* Well, there was a pretty woman staring at him from across the room. But that was about it for now.

He'd gone into law enforcement with the idea that one person could make a difference, and he'd reached the conclusion it was possible—but just barely. It was like scaling a skyscraper with a boulder chained to each ankle. It was damn tiring. At least he'd had Danielle by his side. But was she still there? He'd gone over it a million times in his head, until every cell in his brain felt dead and deflated.

I've got to let it go, he thought.

She'd always been a results-oriented person. She liked to get things done, and if she had to bend a few rules, she still got them done—because "no rule was more important than justice." It was something he'd always admired about her, even while he was often obsessing over every ridiculous regulation. But how could she have possibly thought meeting—and *hiring*—Suzy Castillo was a good idea? Of course, Danielle was the only reason he'd allowed Suzy to go free in the first place, after she'd killed that bastard Blurr and shot up the city of

Choccoban. He'd known it would make Danielle happy. And now?

The pretty woman was sashaying toward him. She had creamy brown skin, shiny lips, curvy hips, and long legs.

He vaguely wondered how his task force in Baadal Shahar was doing. They weren't answering his calls and the fiery images on the nightly news were not encouraging. The city was a shambles, and he didn't care. He really should try calling them again, but he wasn't going to bother. Not right now.

Right now a woman was standing in front of him, smiling. "You're Commander Banks, right?"

"Yes," he said. "That's me."

"I'm Lorraine. I was hoping to meet you. I'm a writer, and a big fan."

She was wearing a low-cut red dress, and smiling like a sweet slice of melon, and puffing out her chest to show off her sizable assets.

He smiled back at her. "I have fans? I didn't know. Nice to meet you, Lorraine." Then he paused and said, "But I have to go."

"No, wait!" she said in a rush. "I'm writing a book about law enforcement, and I was hoping I could interview you. I think people would love to hear what you have to say. If they aren't your fans now, they will be."

She smoothed her dress a bit and smiled again.

"I'm sorry, Lorraine, but it's not a good time."

Her smile drooped a bit. "Okay," she said. "Maybe later?"

"Maybe." He gave her a quick smile of his own—no point in being rude. But then he turned without another word and left the bar. He had to give his wife a call.

Chapter 53

From the control room of the Baadal Shahar Air Handling Facility, Suzy and her crew watched as five million people went to sleep.

It didn't happen right away. First, everyone was filled with euphoria. They smiled, they laughed, and then they started dropping things. They dropped their sandwiches, their digital devises, and their guns. And then they slumped to the ground.

The people on the news networks were only semi-aware of what was happening. They tried to report, but it was difficult because they were affected themselves. It made for a comical broadcast. On the screen was a news anchor, speaking from the studio to a reporter standing near the prison. "So what's happening on the street?" he said.

"Everyone is feeling good," she replied. Then she smiled. "I'm feeling good, too. How about you?"

"Yes, I feel wonderful. I think we're all being poisoned. How nice."

The street reporter gave a dreamy look and fell to the ground, along with whoever was holding the camera. An interesting picture of the city filled the screen. It was from the viewpoint of an ankle.

Suzy laughed. "I know this is serious," she said. "But it is kind of funny. So, are we sure they'll be okay?"

"They'll be fine," Sara said. "It's impossible to die from an overdose of veluva."

Tala looked horrified. "Too much of anything can kill," she muttered.

"They will *not* die," Sara said. "In fact, they'll probably wake up too soon—maybe a couple of hours. So we need to move fast."

Sharonda said, "Right." She was burned a bit but seemed okay. She walked into the hall and found their attackers on the ground, along with two destroyed robots. Apparently, there were no more robots in the building. "We should go through this place and find all the weapons," she said. Melissa nodded and both girls ran from the room.

Sara was on her radio, talking with the captains of the 500 nodes. She was giving orders like a pro. She seemed quite familiar with Anika's original plan; she'd just needed some help getting things started. Now she was doing a great job of integrating Suzy's "sleep strategy" with the old strategy. The captains had key areas targeted, and they had many people on their side from the general population—supporters of the Citizens Collective—ready to step in and take over. Some were asleep but many had been inoculated. So it was the same plan, only without the slaughter. They were moving fast.

"Pick up all the guns," Sara was saying. "Collect every weapon you see. Arrest the cartel people and cuff them for now; we'll deal with them when they wake up... The robots can be destroyed with the rifles, but be careful. There aren't many, but they'll all have to go."

They were taking over the capitol building, they were securing the spaceport, they were disarming the entire security force of the city—and of course they were freeing Anika from the prison.

Ricardo was impressed. Then he said, "What about Marcos and Kaya?"

"I don't know about them," Sara said in a cool tone. "Anika never gave me her plans for those two."

Ricardo looked a bit uncomfortable with that answer. Suzy felt fine but decided not to comment. Ricardo was now listening to the chatter on Sara's radio.

"Hey, it sounds like Kaya's house was raided by the cops."

Suzy felt a jolt. "Kiara's with Kaya."

Sara listened to the radio reports and asked the captains a few questions. Then she said, "Kaya's place was raided while we were busy here, but Kiara was inoculated, so she should be awake. I don't think the others were inoculated."

"She was inoculated? When?"

"When you left to go find the guns."

"Okay," Suzy said. "That's good."

She pulled out her allcom and made a call. No answer. *Damn!*

Ricardo was looking at his own allcom. "The tracking device in her bracelet shows her at a different location. That's not where we left her."

Sara glanced at Ricardo's device. "That's in the industrial district. Maybe she's hiding there with Kaya. He probably had to hide, and it might have been a safe place at the time."

"Sara, do you have anyone near there who can check it out?"

"Let me see." Suzy knew Sara liked Kiara, but Sara only had a limited number of people, and they were busy right now trying to take over the city.

Suzy kept looking at the signal from Kiara's bracelet, and then it went off.

Her heart skipped a beat. But then it came back on, only for an instant. Then it went off again, and on again. Then it was on for a longer period. Then it was off. Then it was on…for a longer few seconds. Then off, and then on…and then off and on and off and on and off and on.

"What the hell?" Ricardo said. "I don't think that thing is working. Cheap piece of crap."

"She's turning it on and off," Suzy said. "It's an SOS! We have to get over there!"

She bolted out the door with Ricardo close behind. Tala followed.

Chapter 54

Mert Kaya was not asleep, but apparently lots of other people were. What was going on?

He was viewing the news as people started dropping off. He waved his hand at the screen and watched the stations scroll by. Nothing… Nothing… Nothing… The news was usually a bunch of half-baked bullshit—but *no* information? Nobody awake?

He frowned. Certainly, the government was known to infect the air with low levels of veluva, but was that the cause of the problem? Well, he was inoculated against veluva, and he was awake—and yeah, the drug would put people to sleep if the dose was high enough. Clever, he thought. *Downright insidious.*

He called Marcos and got no answer. He called more of his own people and got no response. Of course, few of the Snakes were inoculated because it would interfere with their addiction.

The government wants to make our capture easy. Scum!

But wait—his eyes caught some movement on a surveillance screen. Three people with rifles were right outside the warehouse, but they didn't look like cops. They looked like young girls.

He crinkled his forehead and zoomed in on the image. Who the hell were these kids? Obviously, they must be inoculated. He scowled; there was only one group of people in Baadal Shahar who actually bothered with the veluva inoculation: Anika's gang of ex-whores, many of whom were also ex-addicts. Maybe they were seizing the moment to loot the city. But they didn't seem to be looting. No, they were talking on link chips and looking coordinated, and they were coming this way.

He cursed as his eyes swept over the bodies on the floor. Jack looked dead enough, but the two Snakes Jack had shot were only stunned. Mert thought about the girl in the closet.

I should kill her now, he thought. Telling her that he was Hunter had been fun because it was so beautiful to see them terrified—it was the best thing. But now she has to die. *I'll claim Jack did it.*

But wait, that won't solve the problem. Jack had pretty much zeroed in on him being Hunter—certainly, he'd known enough to start asking questions. So how many other people knew? Had Jack talked to anyone else? What about Suzy Spitfire? He scowled, and then he laughed. *She's no match for me!* She was a loudmouthed bitch who needed to be taught a lesson. But dammit, her ability to cause trouble could not be denied. *Did she know?*

I've got to get out of this city!

But first he had to kill Kiara. He felt a pang of sadness; he wasn't going to get to enjoy it.

He looked around fast and then grabbed the gun he'd gotten from Jack. He also eyed the surveillance screen, and now those stupid whores were inside the warehouse. They'd broken in through a door, obviously with a purpose. Were they looking for him? Or for Kiara?

He ran to a drawer, pulled out an egg-sized bomb, and slipped it into his jacket. He also grabbed a knapsack, the one that held a few other useful toys. Then he went to the closet. Maybe he'd scare her one last time before he shot her. She seemed like a scared little girl and those were always the best kind. He paused, fantasizing about how delicious it could've been, imagining her wails and screams. He shuddered and forced himself to stop getting so aroused, and he swore again about his lack of time. *But I can still yank her hair, shove the gun into her mouth, and make her stare into my eyes as I pull the trigger.*

He took a deep breath and opened the door—and there she was, standing in the corner, scrunched up and shaking with fear. He grinned as he reached for her. He gasped as she kicked him in the balls.

The bitch! He swore and doubled over. He dropped the gun as she pushed past him and ran into the room.

Her mouth was still taped but she was making a high-pitched, muffled kind of shriek that sounded like a crazed animal.

"MMMM!"

He felt nauseous but still dove for the gun. He tried to grab it, but she stomped on his hand. It was a good hard stomp, deliberate and forceful. He grunted as she swept the weapon away with her foot. Then the same foot smashed him in the face.

He rolled across the floor and crashed into a small table. She was coming after him. His mind flashed to a past encounter with a young girl, the one who'd escaped his "killing room." The one who'd gotten him arrested and ruined his life. Not again!

He jumped to his feet and seized a bottle of beer. He threw it at her head but she ducked under it and it shattered against the wall. She tried to kick him again, but he blocked her foot with his thigh and then punched her in the face. She staggered backwards and ran for the door.

He smirked. "It's locked, honey. Game over."

The door was located at the end of a short hall. She reached it and turned around, fumbling with her bound hands, trying to open it.

She shrieked again and kicked at the door.

"MMMM! MMMM!"

Someone was outside. A girl's voice said, "Kiara, is that you?"

"MMMMM! MMMM!"

"We're coming! Stand back!"

Mert grimaced. "Damn you!" he said and charged at her. She kicked at him but didn't do any damage. But then someone was blasting the lock on the door. It was opening! They were coming through!

Crap! Where the hell is my gun?

His heart was pounding as he bolted into the kitchen toward the other exit. But then he saw his gun lying on the table, right where he'd left it before picking up Jack's weapon. He snatched it and turned back around. Okay, it could only stun—but if he stunned them all he could kill them easily enough. He leaped back into the main room and started shooting.

He hit one girl in the chest, but another girl ducked back into the hallway with Kiara. Then a rifle poked around the corner and fired.

Mert leaped backwards as the shot destroyed half the doorframe. *Damn!* These were not stun guns! He stumbled over Jack's body. Then he opened the door in the kitchen and ran up the steps. He pushed open a door and leaped out onto the street—and there was another girl standing in front of him. Her eyes were wide as he shot her in the face; she hit the ground hard. He swore and snatched her rifle from the pavement. Then he glanced back down the stairs and paused to listen. He heard Kiara shouting. He pulled out the bomb.

It wasn't a big one, but it should do the trick. He sneered as he clicked a button on top of the device and tossed it down the steps.

Meanwhile, downstairs, Kiara was free. The girl with the rifle had cut the binders around her wrists and removed the gag. They both ran into the kitchen. Kiara screamed as the bomb bounced into the room—but it stopped as it banged into Jack's body. Then Jack opened his eyes.

He was still alive! He saw the bomb. He looked at Kiara.

She screamed, "Jack!"

He grunted and then reached out and shoved it under his stomach. "Run, Kiara!" he said. Then with a shout he pulled himself forward, right underneath the heavy metal table.

Kiara screeched as the other girl yanked her out of the kitchen and pushed her to the floor. The bomb blew up.

Up on the street, Mert heard the shouts and smiled. He listened and heard nothing more as smoke wafted up the stairs. He hesitated. Should he go down and check it out? It didn't matter. More people were on the way, and he had to believe his identity was compromised. He had to get out of this city now.

But damn, he was very conspicuous, being one of the few people who was upright. Then he heard a cough, and he looked across the street and saw a security guard on the sidewalk in front of the warehouse. He was waking up. Mert looked around the industrial area and saw people in vehicles starting to wake up as well. Okay, that had been quick.

He ran to a car that was in the middle of the street. There was a guy inside, looking groggy but definitely awake. Mert aimed his rifle at the guy's face.

"Get out," Mert said. "I need a ride."

Chapter 55

Suzy was driving like a maniac. Luckily, there weren't a lot of vehicles on the street. But now there were some cars moving, and there were people scraping themselves off the sidewalk.

"Crap," Suzy said as she swerved the car around a corner. "Why are all these people waking up?"

Ricardo was sitting beside her and he shrugged. In the rearview mirror, Suzy could see Tala in the backseat, looking relieved.

"Tala, you did dump all the veluva, right?"

Now Tala squirmed a bit. "I used a fair amount," she stammered.

"You what?" Suzy swerved the car again, this time to avoid a couple of people staggering around in the middle of the road.

"I gave them enough," Tala said. Then she blurted, "I had to be careful, Suzy! I didn't have time to do a calculation, and I didn't want to kill five million people."

"We weren't going to kill anyone!"

"You don't know that, and it's reckless to dump a dangerous narcotic into the atmosphere of a city without being sure."

Suzy wanted to bang her head against the windshield, or maybe Tala's head. Ricardo frowned, and then he was on his allcom.

"People are waking up," he said. "But the girls got a lot done. Still, it's going to be tougher now. There's going to be more fighting."

Suzy could hear the chatter on Ricardo's device—Sara's voice, and a lot of others talking fast. And then she heard Anika, who was free! But it wouldn't matter if the bad guys still had too many guns.

Suzy slammed the car to a stop in front of a warehouse. She leaped from the vehicle and scanned the scene—and there was Kiara.

She looked dazed. But then she saw Suzy, and she gave a shout. "Suzy!"

Suzy ran to her and hugged her. "Are you all right? What happened?"

Kiara was covered with dust, and her face was bruised. She was shaking in Suzy's arms.

"It's okay," Suzy said. "It's okay… You're going to be all right."

With a visible effort, Kiara seemed to pull herself together. But her voice trembled as she spoke. "I was trying to call you," she said. "Mert Kaya is Shogun Hunter! He must have had some surgery."

"What? No. Kaya has been here for fifteen years. He—"

Suzy stopped talking. A DNA test would tell the story. The main thing now was to make sure the bastard didn't escape.

"Kiara, did he hurt you?"

"No," Kiara said, shaking her head. "He wanted to, but I was fighting with him. Then the girls came, and he ran."

Suzy felt like a bomb had gone off inside her head. "That motherfucker," she said. Then she turned to Ricardo. "He's probably trying to leave the city. Tell Sara. Tell everyone to stop Mert Kaya!"

"Someone's hurt," Kiara said. "Her name is Sira, and she's down there—with Jack." Kiara started sobbing now. "He's gone, Suzy. He's gone." Then she pointed down the street and tried to stop crying. "Mert just took off. I saw him hijack a car."

Suzy grabbed Kiara by the shoulders and stared into her teary eyes. "We need to get you out of here. We'll go back to the ship."

Kiara just sobbed again. "No, I'll be okay," she managed to say. Then she stopped crying and wiped her eyes. She stood up straight. "I want to stay here with Sira. There are people coming, and I can help. Really, Suzy, I'll be fine… Go get Hunter."

"What? That's crazy."

"No, it isn't. I don't want him to get away. Go!"

Suzy hesitated. She didn't want to leave Kiara—but she couldn't bring her along, either. And she really wanted to get this guy now. She wanted to kill him, and she wanted it to hurt.

"All right," Suzy said. "But call if you need me, okay? I mean it."

"I'll call," she said. "I'll be fine."

Suzy tore herself away from Kiara and raced back toward the car. Ricardo was right behind her. They left Tala on the sidewalk with the others. As she hit the accelerator, she heard the sound of gunfire in the distance.

Chapter 56

In a dirty alley between two warehouses, Burt Stone rubbed his eyes. What was that ringing sound? Someone was calling him.

Damn, I must've fallen asleep! He swore and fumbled for his allcom. What kind of donut-sucking sack of shit cop falls asleep on a stake-out? *I'm such a loser!* Then he saw it was Tala calling and his heart leaped.

"Tala, what's happening?" he shouted. "Are you all right?"

"You're awake!" she said, sounding frantic. "I'm fine. We put veluva in the air to knock everyone out. We're chasing a serial killer who might be Shogun Hunter!"

Burt paused. This was not the report he was expecting. "What?"

"Me and Suzy and the girls! We've got to get Mert Kaya!"

"You and Suzy? You mean Suzy Castillo, the person we're supposed to be arresting? And who are 'the girls'?" *And god damn, how long was I asleep?*

"Burt, you need to get over here. We need a car. Where are you?"

He was close. In fact, he was looking right at her because he'd followed Mert and Kiara to this location and found an alley to use as an observation post, and now Tala was just down the street.

"Tala, I can see you from where I'm standing. Wait right there, okay?"

His arm and left side still felt like they were on fire, but he staggered out into the street. Tala spotted him right away and started jumping up and down and pointing him out to her new friends. No doubt she was screaming how an undercover cop on a secret stakeout was on his way. On a bright note, it looked like she still had the gun he'd given her. In fact, all her friends had guns, too—big ones.

He frowned, wondering if this was good or bad. She ran toward him and wrapped him in her arms; he winced in pain.

She saw his reaction and pulled away. "I'm sorry!" she shrieked. "Are you okay? I'm just happy to see you. Are you all right?"

She did look happy, and he grinned. It was good to see her, too—very good. But he had some questions.

"Tala, what the hell is going on? Where's Suzy?"

"She was here but she left! I followed her to a pub, and then we went to the air factory, and then we came here. We're taking over the city."

Burt cocked his head. "Tala, we're not here to take over the city. And who are these girls?"

She leaned close to him, lowering her voice. "They're an army of teenage prostitutes—actually, ex-prostitutes. There are five thousand of them! They all have guns."

Okay, he thought. *I did ask.*

She pointed at the car he'd come in that was parked nearby. "Let's go!" she said. "I have a gun for you, too. We have to find Suzy."

"That's right," Burt said, excited now. "And maybe Hunter, too. We'll get them both." Then he noticed Kiara standing outside the warehouse, being comforted by another girl. He spoke softly. "Wait a second. Suzy might be hard to find, Tala. Maybe we should stay close to the girl. They'll end up together eventually."

Tala hesitated. "I told you, I don't want to arrest Suzy."

"Tala, it's our mission. We could be heroes. Me and you."

"Me and you?"

"Yeah." Burt shuffled his feet a bit and contemplated the feeling in his stomach, a feeling like he was standing on the edge of a cliff and maybe it was time to jump. Then he looked right at her and said, "I like you, Tala. I like you a lot. I think we make a good team."

She looked away from his gaze. "I like you, too, Burt. But I've been thinking about it—and I don't want to be a cop anymore. My parents were right. It was a bad move for me."

"What?" He felt his face getting red. "No, your parents were not right! What do they know? And besides, I can't go back to Earth empty-handed, do you understand? *I just can't!*"

His chest was heaving and his head was pounding.

"I'm sorry, Burt. But it's not for me. I know it. And I don't want to be part of a team that arrests Suzy Spitfire."

He said nothing.

Now he felt his head spin. He stood still for a long second, like a statue made of stone. His mind was suddenly filled with images of his family and his failures—and how maybe none of it mattered. Or did it?

He leaned toward her, intending to give her a kiss.

She turned her head and didn't look at him.

Chapter 57

Mert grimaced from behind the wheel of his hi-jacked hover-car. He was moving fast through a smoky war zone, swerving around debris and making calls using a link chip on his collar. People were waking up and that was good because he needed a few friends. But did that include Marcos? Probably not, but the sleazy bastard might have some news.

"They're after you," Marcos said. "But don't worry, I'm sure you can fight it."

"Fight what?"

"The rumors that you're a serial killer," Marcos said with a hollow laugh. "A guy from Earth who changed his identity. Crazy…right?"

Mert swore softly to himself. He could tell Marcos wasn't going to be much help.

"What's going on with Anika?" Mert said.

"She's taking over the city, her and those fucking whores. Can you believe it? She actually armed those girls—thousands of them! A lot of my people are joining her, too, and a lot more aren't answering. Things are very messed up."

"I need to get out of here."

Marcos hesitated. Then he said, "Mert, you know I'd like to help but I've got a lot going on here. It's nothing personal, so try and understand. You need to lay low and get a lawyer. Call a few friends."

"Right. That's about what I expected."

"Mert, it's nothing personal—"

Mert hung up. The asshole had obviously written him off and it was useless at this point. *I'm either going to get out of the city or it's over.* Then he swerved around a burning truck in front of a Chinese grocery store and called Elijah.

"Mert!" Elijah said. "Where are you? Are you in trouble?"

Mert's heart leaped.

"I need some help, brother," Mert said. "I need to get out of the city."

"Listen, things are not good. A lot of our people have been captured. They knew where we were, where to find us. It's a disaster, and I was lucky. There's lots of fighting at the spaceport, and you'll never get out of there now. You need to hide out for a bit. I've got a place they don't know, and I can send you the address."

"Good. I knew I could count on you, brother. I'll be right there."

As he disconnected the call, he thought about where he could go—and the places he'd been. It wasn't anything he pondered much anymore. He'd been made this way. Sure, his father had been a mean bastard, and his mother had been weak, but his brother and his sister were normal enough. The psychologists might think differently, but they were wrong. It wasn't his fault! *They can all kiss my ass.*

He had a rifle, a pistol, some bombs, and a few other surprises. Maybe I can go to Mars, he thought. There were big cities on Mars, teeming with people. There were lots of opportunities.

Chapter 58

Suzy knew she was driving too fast. But she kept doing it.

Ricardo grimaced. "Slow down, Suzy. You're going to send us right through the dome."

"He's heading for the spaceport," she said. "He's probably got some kind of sneaky escape plan."

Ricardo gripped the armrest and listened to the radio chatter. In the distance, they heard more gunfire.

"Anika's in charge now," Ricardo said. "It sounds like things are going well, not too much violence. But hey, it sounds like Marcos is trying to get in on the action. He's downtown with some friends, trying to rally people."

Suzy gave a grunt and turned the car onto a wide street lined with restaurants and orange-flowered date palms. How far ahead was Kaya? Was this the fastest way to the spaceport? She kept imagining what he'd almost done to Kiara. She tried to block the horror out of her mind. Meanwhile, Ricardo was still talking politics.

He was smiling. "Marcos is trying to figure out how to get in on Anika's big move. But his people don't have the guns, so just watch, he'll try and schmooze her. And at the same time, behind her back, he's probably calling every thug who he thinks can give him some muscle."

Just then Ricardo's allcom rang. "Crap," he said, raising his eyebrows. "It's Marcos."

Suzy laughed. Ricardo looked out the window with a sheepish expression but then picked up the call. The voice of Marcos boomed through the cabin.

"Ricardo, how are you?"

"I'm fine, Marcos. I just—"

"I need your help! They're trying to cut me out, and that means they're cutting you out, too—and your organization. But they like you, and they like your girl, right? I just want a meeting, that's all. Just me, you, Nuru, and Anika. That's all I'm asking for, okay?"

"I hear what you're saying, but—"

"Pablo wants this to happen, right? We don't need to take over, but we need to stay involved, and he won't be happy with anyone who hurts his chances. Do you see what I'm saying?"

"Sure," Ricardo said. "I know Pablo."

"I know you do. So you won't underestimate him."

Ricardo glanced at Suzy. "I'll see what I can do."

"You're a good man," Marcus said. "We'll do great business together. I know it."

Ricardo hung up and Suzy laughed again.

"I think Marcos is feeling lonely," she said.

"Yeah, maybe."

"Don't worry, Ricardo. Pablo will get over his man losing. And if he doesn't, he doesn't."

Ricardo was quiet. Then Suzy swerved into an intersection and ended up in the middle of a car accident.

"Whoah!"

A long black car came careening out of a cross street, and for an instant she saw the startled looks inside the vehicle. There was a loud crash and a heavy thud as the big car slammed into them. In a flash, an energy cushion switched on and kept Suzy and Ricardo from smashing against anything inside the cabin. But the hover-car spun sideways and slammed into a coffee shop, shattering a huge window.

Broken glass rained down around them. Suzy cursed, trying to wrestle the car back onto the street, but it wouldn't move. She watched as the other vehicle skidded a bit farther down the sidewalk and twisted around to face them. It wasn't moving but people were leaping out of it—people with guns.

"Look out!" Ricardo said. Suzy saw them, too. They both jumped out of the car, crouching behind the open doors.

Who were these people? They were dressed in military gear, and they looked like they were about to start shooting—and then they did.

Two shots smashed into the open car door while two more sailed high above Suzy's head. These guys are panicky, Suzy thought. They were also firing kill shots. She gritted her teeth and returned fire, cool and deliberate, and hit the shooter in the face. Ricardo shot the other one, who was still fumbling with his gun. Then a third guy jumped out of the vehicle. He was screaming, and he might have been putting his hands up—or he might have been raising a weapon. Either way, his timing was bad because Suzy shot him in the chest.

He screamed again and fell backwards.

Suzy and Ricardo glanced around quick and then glided forward with their guns ready. But that was it—three people, all dead.

"These two look like bodyguards," Ricardo said.

"For who?"

"That guy over there," Ricardo said, pointing to the person Suzy had just killed.

Why did he look familiar? Well, after a while, every bad guy looks the same. He was lying there like a cardboard cutout.

"Our car is totaled," Suzy said. "Let's take theirs."

The other car was luxurious, heavily armored, and barely damaged.

"This guy must've been rich," Ricardo said as they leaped inside.

Suzy swung the car onto the street. "Yeah. I guess he should've bought better bodyguards."

"Why did they start shooting?"

"I don't know. Maybe they're cartel people who recognized us, or maybe they're cartel people Anika's girls are looking for and they just got scared. I'm sure lots of people are going to be on the run today—like Mert Kaya. He can't be that far ahead of us. Did you tell everyone to stop him?"

"I sounded the alarm, but let's face it, Anika's people have other priorities, like capturing the security forces and the cartel." Then Ricardo turned up the volume on the special radio frequency used by Anika's group. Most of what they heard was good.

"Prison is secure…. We have the Capitol Building… Heavy fighting at the spaceport… We need more people there… We have a report that Buso is trying to flee the city… Last seen in a black armored limo, heading east on Sunrise Avenue."

At this moment, Suzy noticed a street sign—well, damn, if this wasn't "Sunrise Avenue." Then she looked at Ricardo, who was looking at her.

"Damn!" they said together. Then Ricardo said, "So that was Buso back there."

"I guess. He looked taller on the screen."

"The bad guys always look bigger on TV. Look, here's the Capitol."

Suzy slowed down as they tried to drive past, but the building was surrounded by a rowdy crowd. There were people holding rifles, shouting from the roof and cheering from the balconies with their guns held high. Most of the fighters were young girls, but there were women, men, and boys, too—quite a few looked like they were from the Citizen Collective. For an instant, Suzy felt good about it. But then the same people started shooting at them.

"Look out!" Suzy said.

A deluge of fire came blasting from above, pummeling the car. Luckily, the car was heavily armored. Suzy swerved the vehicle off the road and rumbled onto a sidewalk. She crashed into a palm tree and then slammed to a stop as more energy blasts rained down. Ricardo was screaming into the link chip.

"Hold your fire! Buso is not in this car! This is Suzy and Ricardo! Hold your fire!"

The gunfire ceased but there was a lot of commotion. Then people were pointing and shouting, and several girls with guns were coming through the crowd. Suzy saw no one she recognized, but they obviously recognized her. "Come this way," one of them said with a smile. So Suzy and Ricardo walked through the pulsating throng and entered the stately building. They walked down an arched hallway, all white with a high ceiling and filled with statues and stiff-looking portraits with empty eyes. They reached a sprawling office where there were about ten people. There was a radio on, and the air was buzzing with chatter and reports of the fighting. Anika and Nuru were fielding calls.

Anika saw Suzy and ran to embrace her. Suzy hugged her back, but really, she just wanted to get on her way. She was busy thinking about Kiara—and Kaya. Then Anika said, "Suzy, we've taken over most of the city! Putting people to sleep was a brilliant idea. How can we ever thank you?"

"That's easy," Suzy said. "You can help me find Mert Kaya. He tried to hurt Kiara, and I think he might be Shogun Hunter."

Anika's face crinkled up, while Nuru looked equally surprised. "Mert Kaya?" Anika said. "No, I don't think so. He's been here a long time. But we do need to find him, because Mert Kaya is the Head of the Snake Eyes."

Now Suzy froze. "What?"

"Yes, he's in charge. But we've captured most of them, and he's probably trying to get out of the city." Anika hesitated, studying the fiery look in Suzy's eyes. "Suzy, please don't be mad. I had good reasons for not telling you. We can talk later, after the city is totally secure."

With some effort, Suzy kept her temper in check. "We can talk now," she said. "I'm tired of all the plotting and secrets. Where is he?"

"If I knew, I'd tell you—believe me."

"I don't."

Anika sighed. "I didn't tell you about Mert and the Snake Eyes because I thought you'd react badly, and the Snakes were useful."

"Useful? They're about as useful as brain cancer."

"Yes, and they're through operating in this city. But Mert helped us fight the government. His group fought the worst elements in the cartel. His group wiped out hundreds of surveillance cameras throughout the city… He didn't know that we knew, and we used him for his political contacts. It was all part of the plan."

"Really?" Suzy snapped. "Was it part of the plan for me to leave Kiara at his house? Was it part of the plan for Kiara to be around a guy connected to her asshole ex-boyfriend?"

"No! Suzy, those things just happened…" Then her voice trailed off.

"What about Marcos?" Suzy said. "What did he know?"

Anika shrugged. "I never discussed any of this with Marcos. He might have known Kaya was with the Snakes, but I doubt he knew about any possible connection to Hunter—just like we didn't know. I'm sure he'd be surprised by that."

Suzy stared at Anika while Anika looked uncomfortable. Meanwhile, Nuru was on his allcom while the radio in the background crackled with updates. Suddenly, Buso's death was announced, and there was a brief moment of excitement in the room—but then everyone returned to what they'd been doing. Nuru ended his call and spoke to Ricardo, and they both grinned.

"Anika, some good news," Nuru said. He motioned for her to come over, and when she did he spoke to her in a low voice.

When Anika walked back toward Suzy, she looked happy. "We can get Mert Kaya," Anika said. "But we have to wait until tomorrow."

Suzy scowled and felt herself filling with suspicion. "Why?" she said. "What's going on?"

"Suzy, please. Trust me, okay? We're setting something up. I'm on your side—yes, really! And you can do what you like with him. In fact, it might be better that way."

Suzy gave a sarcastic laugh. Then Ricardo stepped between Suzy and Anika, and he smiled.

"So, Anika, what's the plan?" he said.

Anika started to speak but then Suzy held up her hand. "Wait," she said. "I need a minute."

She turned and walked out of the office. She moved fast down the hall, past groups of people rushing around, and ducked into the doorway of another office that was dark and empty.

She had to cool down. Am I being immature? she thought. Maybe, but it was better than screaming things she'd regret later. Besides, she had something important to do. She pulled out her allcom and called Kiara.

"Suzy, I'm okay," Kiara blurted. "I'm with Sara. Are you all right?"

Sara? Suzy felt her pulse pounding; Sara was in the middle of everything. Stay calm, she thought. Sara's a smart girl.

"I'm okay," Suzy said. "What are you doing? Is there fighting going on?"

Suzy was straining her ears, trying to hear the sounds around Kiara.

"I'm not fighting," Kiara said in a shaky voice. "I could be. But I'm not." Then she took a deep breath. "But I'm not fighting," she said again. "I'm just helping Sara with other stuff. Don't worry about me. I'll be okay. Did you find Hunter? I'm fine."

"No," Suzy said. She started to tell her they might find him tomorrow—but she didn't. "We don't know where he is," Suzy said. "Not yet."

There was a long pause. Then Kiara said, "Jack saved my life, Suzy. I want to be there when you find him. You'll call me when you know where he is, right? I need to be there. You'll let me know when you're going to get him, right?"

"Yeah. I'll call you."

"Okay. I'll be fine. Don't worry about me. I'm fine."

Kiara hung up just as Ricardo appeared. "So, was that Kiara? Is she okay?"

Suzy shook her head. "I should go to her." *Because she sounds like a wreck.* "I hate lying to her—again. But I don't want her with us when we find Hunter. I think it would only make things worse for her."

Ricardo shrugged. "Why don't we go hear Anika's plan? You can decide then."

"Yeah, okay," Suzy said. *But I'll feel bad either way.*

Chapter 59

The plan was fine—maybe.

"But it could be a set-up," Suzy said. It was early evening, and she was walking with Ricardo toward a small café. "We get rid of Hunter, and then they get rid of us, and Anika doesn't have to worry about us interfering in the city. She uses us just like she used Kaya and the Snakes."

Ricardo shook his head. "No, I don't think so. You're being paranoid because Anika didn't tell you about Kaya and the Snakes, but try and see her point of view. She figured you might do something crazy—well, let's be honest, you've done some crazy shit. But she also knows you don't want to run this city."

"Yeah, I get that. And I know she's been fighting for good things, and Kiara likes her a lot. But I'm also here with you, Ricardo. And you came here to make a deal with Marcos."

Ricardo laughed. "Are you with me? I think I'm with you—and she knows that, too. And that's fine."

Suzy was quiet. In the end, she knew she'd go with her instincts.

"All right," she said. "We'll do it. Now let's get something to eat."

The city was brimming with wild food and people who knew how to cook it, like the spicy stuff they ate at a place called Mahal Tacos. It was the first casual dinner she'd had with Ricardo since she'd left Earth, and it felt good. Suzy wore her silver dragonfly earrings; she thought they brought her luck.

When they were done eating, they headed up the street, a major thoroughfare where the buildings were hardly damaged and the air was calm, yet there were few cars or people out tonight. As Suzy looked at the leafy trees blooming all around, she noticed none of the branches were moving. There was very little breeze on this artificial world. Everything looks stiff, she thought. *Stiff and tense.*

Suddenly, Ricardo was fumbling to answer a call. He motioned toward Suzy as she listened to the conversation.

"Maria!" he said. "Hey, how are you? What's happening?"

"Hi, Ricardo. My life is happening, I suppose. But don't worry about it. How are you?"

"Fine! Are you all right? Where are you?"

"I'm on a commercial flight. We're waiting to dock, but there are problems at the spaceport. I guess we'll have to wait for the war to end."

"The war's over, Maria. What about Pablo? You left him?"

"I'll tell you about it when I get there. But yes—I'm alone."

"No! You're not alone, Maria. But are you in danger?"

There was a moment of silence. "I don't know."

Ricardo swore softly. "Don't worry about it. It'll be okay."

"Maybe, maybe not. But he was the wrong man for me," she said, and now her voice cracked with emotion. "I've known him my whole life. How could I have been so wrong?"

"It's easy to be wrong, Maria. Don't blame yourself."

"I hope you do better, Ricardo. I hope you make the right move. Either way, I'm not going back—to any of it. I need to think about what's really important. Does that make sense?"

Ricardo was silent, and Suzy noticed he was staring at her.

"Ricardo, are you there?" Maria said.

"Yeah, I'm here. And yeah, it makes sense."

"Good. So, how's the revolution? Are we winning?"

"It depends on how you look at it. But I think we're winning big."

She gave a soft laugh. "It'll be good to see you, Ricardo."

The connection ended. "Wow," Suzy said. "Pablo lost this city, and he lost the best woman he'll ever find. A tough week."

"Yeah."

"And she's out of that life. Good move."

"Yeah," Ricardo said again, looking away from her gaze. "But it's not always so easy. Our kind of life has a way of following you."

Suzy wandered ahead of him, checking her allcom to see if Kiara had left a message. From the corner of her eye, she noticed a long blue car moving slowly down the street. She started to turn—and then Ricardo was shouting.

"Suzy, get down!"

He tackled her as a shot rang out. "Oof!" she said and hit the ground hard. The café window behind her burst into a cloud of shattered glass, and the vehicle started pulling away fast.

Suzy swore and jumped to her feet. Ricardo was still on the ground. He tried to grab her leg but he was too late.

"Suzy, stay down!" he said.

The car was already a hundred meters away and turning a corner fast when Suzy aimed her pistol and fired. It was a longshot, but those were her favorite kind. She hit the driver-side window with a fully-maxed bullet and the car swerved, smashing into a storefront. Then she was running toward the car and Ricardo was leaping to his feet, chasing after her.

"Suzy, stop! Wait!"

She didn't stop; she wanted to know who wanted her dead. She fired a salvo of higher energy shots. She was closer now, and there was less danger of hitting anything but her target. Someone was staggering from the vehicle, trying to run. Then the figure collapsed.

The car was in flames. Whoever was in the driver seat was dead but the guy on the ground was still alive. As she got nearer, she expected to see someone from the Casino Cartel, or maybe one of the Snake Eyes. But why only one shot? They could have easily fired a deluge. She stopped running just as Ricardo caught up to her. Then they both stared.

"Raphael," Ricardo whispered.

Raphael was on the ground, breathing hard. "Not for you, Ricardo," he said. "It wasn't for you."

His face was badly burned, but it looked like he'd be okay.

"Right," Suzy said. "It was meant for me. Who's the driver? David? I guess Pablo's a little upset about the way things have been going."

Raphael glared at her. "He never liked you—and I never liked you either, you bitch. You ruined everything here."

Ricardo kept staring at him in silence, but Suzy could see the fury swelling up inside, a white-hot anger like she'd never seen from him before. He grimaced and pointed his weapon at Raphael's head. "I like her a lot," he said. "And I have a message for Pablo. You tell him I quit. Hey, maybe I'll tell him myself."

He pulled the trigger and Raphael's head exploded. Then he lowered the weapon and didn't move. After a few long seconds, Suzy grabbed his arm.

"Come on, let's go," she said.

He glanced at her but said nothing. They walked fast to where they'd parked the car. The whole way back to the ship, he didn't say a word. She only tried to talk to him once, in a soft voice. She said, "Ricardo—"

"Not now."

She decided to be quiet. He needs some time, she thought. *I understand that kind of thing.* When they got to the *Correcaminos Rojo,* he headed for his cabin and started to shut the door, but she followed him.

"Ricardo, are you all right?"

"No, not really." Then he hesitated and said, "But I'm glad you're here."

She kissed him, and he kissed her back.

"Suzy, I don't think—"

"You don't need to think. I love you, Ricardo. That's all."

She kissed him again. She started taking off his shirt, and they went into the room.

Chapter 60

The next morning Suzy's eyes snapped open.

Her heart was pounding. I need to have better dreams, she thought. Then she gazed at Ricardo, who was stretched out on the sky-blue sheets. He was wearing a pair of blue boxer shorts and staring at the ceiling. She was wearing only a loose gray T-shirt.

"Good morning, Suzy. Did you have a nightmare?"

Suzy took a second to gather her thoughts. "Yeah, but nothing too serious. You were reading me a poem."

He didn't laugh. Instead, he gave a little smile and said nothing.

"Ricardo, I'm sorry about Raphael."

"I'll be fine," he said. Then he scowled. "It's not just Raphael, Suzy—it's Pablo. I can't believe he wanted you dead."

"Raphael was right. Pablo never liked me."

"Oh, yeah? Well, I'm going to kill him."

Suzy gathered her clothes from the floor. Then she said, "Ricardo, we've got other stuff to worry about."

"Yeah, I know. But when we're done with that stuff, he's dead."

She sat back down on the bed. She hesitated, and then said, "I know I'm the last person who should be giving this kind of advice, but I think that's a bad idea. It's tough when a friend stabs you in the back, but if you really want to quit that life, that's not the way to do it. Pablo is hardly the first guy to want me dead. It's pretty common."

"I'll kill anyone who tries to hurt you, Suzy."

She gave a soft laugh. "That's very romantic. But it's complicated, because the guy is still married to your sister, even if they're having some problems. And you might also end up getting yourself killed, and I wouldn't want that."

She leaned over and gave him a kiss on the cheek. He was silent again. Finally, he smiled and said, "No one's going to hurt me. I'll be fine."

"Anyone can get hurt, Ricardo. A couple of guys almost killed me last night. But you were there—and you saved me, like the tough guy that you are. And by the way, thanks."

He looked at her for a long second. "No problem," he said, and then he grinned. "When the sun is white fire and the desert is drier, I will have my revenge."

Suzy laughed again. Somehow, she knew his bad poetry was a good sign.

"Hey, you know what?" he said. "I'm hungry. I could go for some blueberry pancakes."

"Sounds good," she said. "Make me a couple, too." Then she heard a beeping sound, signaling that someone was outside the doors of the docking bay. She reached for her Series 7 pulse pistol and glanced at the image on the wall—and felt a jolt of alarm. Standing there was Kiara.

Damn! She hadn't forgotten about Kiara. But she hadn't called her, either.

Kiara had stayed with Sara last night. It had been fine, Suzy had liked being alone with Ricardo—but that wasn't why she was glad Kiara had stayed elsewhere. And now she still didn't want Kiara around.

It looked like she was alone. Behind her was a hover bike. *What's she doing with that?* Suzy thought. *Those things are dangerous.*

Suzy pulled on her clothes, went into the lounge, and opened the doors to the docking bay. Kiara bounded up the gangway, dressed in a black skirt with a loose gray top. Her long hair was flying as she charged onto the ship. She stomped into the lounge and glared at Suzy.

"You didn't call me," Kiara said. "But I know what you're doing today—and I'm coming with you."

"No, you're not. It's too dangerous."

"What are you talking about? You said you'd call me, and you didn't. You lied to me!"

Suzy shook her head. "I'm sorry I had to lie. But I don't want you to come."

"Suzy, how many times do I have to tell you? I'm not a little girl."

"I know that, Kiara. But if you got hurt, I'd never forgive myself."

Kiara gazed across the lounge and blinked back a tear. "Suzy, he murdered Jack," she said, and her voice trembled. "I know you don't care about that—but Jack was important to me." Then she wiped her eyes and scowled again, and Suzy noticed the shape of a gun briefly outlined on her skirt. She had a weapon strapped to her thigh. *Damn!*

"Kiara, what are you doing with the gun?"

"The same thing you're always doing!" Kiara snapped. "I want to protect myself, okay? I'm tired of being pushed around." Then she paused and took a deep breath. "I just want to be there, that's all. I need to be there... Why can't I be there? Why?"

Suzy sighed. "Kiara, I understand. But I've *been there* myself, and it's not a good place for you."

"You're going to kill him, right?"

Suzy was quiet. *You bet your ass I am.* "It depends," she said.

"I want to go."

"I know you do. But it's a bad idea."

"I'm not staying here."

"You're not coming," Suzy said. "No way, no chance."

"Fine!" Kiara shouted. Then she whirled like a tornado and stormed past Ricardo who was just walking into the lounge.

He had a quizzical look on his face. "Hey, what's happening? Does this mean no pancakes?"

Kiara raced down the gangway with Suzy close behind—but Kiara was quick and jumped on the hover bike. She ignored Suzy's yelling as she revved the engine and roared off.

Suzy swore as she watched Kiara disappear. She yanked out her allcom and made a call.

"Anika—hi. Hey, does Kiara know where we're going?"

"Hello, Suzy. What's happening? Is there a problem? No, not as far as I know."

"What about Sara?" Suzy said. "Does she know?"

"She doesn't know. Everything is the way you wanted it—although we could still change the plan. We have lots of people who can help."

"No, that's fine, Anika. We don't want help. I'll talk to you soon. Thanks."

Ricardo came down the gangway and stood beside her. "Suzy, stop worrying," he said. "She's a tough kid."

"Yeah, I know. But she's not like me, Ricardo, and she has a chance to stay that way. Do you understand?"

"You're not so bad, honey. I'm making you pancakes."

Suzy hardly touched the pancakes, but Ricardo ate them all.

As they were heading out of the ship, Ricardo said, "Hey, what about these?" He pointed to a package on the table in the lounge. It held two vests made from a thin body armor called Coblar. These could be concealed underneath a loose shirt, and they were gifts from Nuru.

"I'll wear it," Suzy said. "But how about you?"

Ricardo cocked his head and then grinned. "One of them looks like my size."

They put on the vests and got into a hover-car borrowed from Anika. As they headed into the city, Suzy was thinking about Kiara, and Ricardo was gazing through the side window. Suzy fingered her pistol and tried to concentrate.

They were on the fringe of the downtown, where broken glass and assorted trash were still strewn across the streets, and the buildings and palm trees were burned and smoky. Despite the signs of destruction, many businesses were now open, and the few people they passed were smiling. There were still pockets of unrest and occasional gunfire but not much. Anika's army had done the hard part and then the Citizen Collective had stepped in to help, and they had the support of the local population. With Buso dead and the Casino Cartel and Snake Eyes incapacitated, a large chunk of the security forces had switched sides. In fact, it now seemed that a lot of them had always been sympathetic. They'd been *waiting* to switch sides.

Ricardo adjusted a local radio station where a voice was talking about their target.

"Where is Mert Kaya? It's now been confirmed he was the Head of the Snake Eyes, but he seems to have vanished. There are rumors he's left the city."

Ricardo gave a grunt. "Who's behind those rumors?"

"Who knows?" Suzy said. "Maybe tomorrow there'll be a rumor about us. Nothing too good, I'm sure."

Ricardo laughed. "Suzy, we gave five million people a drug overdose and then killed the President of Venus."

"True. A banner day."

"It'll be hard to top, that's for sure. Although we *are* searching for a serial killer who's the head of a snake cult."

"How fucked up is our life, Ricardo?"

He laughed again—but then he got serious. "Hey, here's the place."

It was a restaurant called The Sweet Orange, part of a one-story building with tinted glass doors and a window decorated with the image of a blooming tree. But Suzy wasn't interested in the décor. She was only interested in the two men standing outside. They were both well-dressed, and one of them was a dark-skinned guy with a shaved head.

Ricardo drove past the place at normal speed, then made two right turns and parked the car on a street behind the restaurant.

"What do you think?" Ricardo said.

"Hard to say," Suzy said. "Plenty of bad guys know how to dress. But the bald one looks like the guy Anika described."

There was no sign of Kaya.

Ricardo took a deep breath. "Do we stick with the plan?"

Suzy just nodded and fingered her pistol again. That bastard was going to die today.

They'd studied an aerial view of the neighborhood, and now they slipped out of the car and headed into a tight alley between two tall buildings made of reddish stone. Suzy kept her eyes on some narrow windows up high, but saw no sign of trouble. The alley quickly opened up on the right, leading into a courtyard between the back of the restaurant and one of the red buildings. Standing by a doorway was the black guy they'd just seen out front.

Suzy had her gun up and ready. The guy spotted them and waved.

Suzy's eyes swept the area, studying the windows and the walls all around. She moved forward.

"Are you Elijah?" she said.

He grinned. "That's me—and you're Suzy. Let's go. It's this way."

They walked into the restaurant, moving fast through a deserted kitchen filled with hanging pots and pans. The kitchen opened into a cushy dining room, orange and brown with dark wood floors and small chandeliers that looked like burning pieces of fruit. Elijah put up his hand to stop them. "Let me introduce you," he said. He walked into the dining room while Suzy and Ricardo waited and listened.

"Mert, the pilot is here."

"That's good, Elijah. Send him in."

"The pilot is a woman, Mert. I think you know her."

Suzy walked into the room—and there was Mert Kaya.

He was sitting at a round table with a white tablecloth, along with two other guys. The two guys stared at Suzy as they raised their hands and stood up. Mert had a crust of bread in his mouth, but his jaw still dropped. He also stared at Suzy and then at Elijah.

"Elijah," he said. "You fucking snake."

Elijah smirked. "That's right, Mert," he said. "I'm a Snake, and Jack was a Snake—and you were always something else. So I made a deal with Anika, and now you're going back to Earth to answer for a few things."

Not quite, Suzy thought. She aimed her gun at Mert—and then there was an explosion.

Damn!

Something struck her hard in the chest. She flew backwards, crashed into a wall, and fell to the floor.

Elijah swore and somebody shouted. Suzy gasped and looked for her gun—and for Ricardo. Meanwhile, Mert ran past her, heading for the front door.

Ricardo was on the floor nearby but he was staggering to his feet.

Now he was hugging Suzy. "Are you okay?" he said. *"Suzy, are you all right?"*

"Yeah, I think so. Are you? What happened?"

"I think it was a dart vest," he said. He was fumbling around, checking Suzy for signs of injury. He sighed with relief. "I think you're fine," he said. "It just sprayed the Coblar—same as me."

Suzy knew the basics; hundreds of miniscule poison darts fired from a special vest would instantly burn through the wearer's outer clothing and blast across the room, zeroing in on the largest areas of body heat they could find—usually the chest of anyone nearby. It was an effective weapon, but limited because it didn't discriminate against who it killed. Of course, this wasn't a problem for the average sociopath.

The poison worked fast. The body armor had saved Suzy and Ricardo, but Elijah and his two friends hadn't been so lucky. They were flat on their backs, staring at the ceiling through dead eyes.

Shots echoed outside. Suzy bolted to the front door, and there was Mert Kaya—but he wasn't running. He was pinned behind a car as a deluge of energy shots blasted from across the street. He was grimacing as they pummeled the vehicle. Who the hell was shooting at him? Suzy scanned the area but no one was visible. Then Mert pulled a weapon from a knapsack, one of Ricardo's collapsible assault rifles—but he didn't fire across the street. He whirled and fired at Suzy.

"Get back!" Ricardo yelled, and he yanked her into the restaurant just as an explosion obliterated the front door and all the windows. Suzy swore as pieces of the ceiling crashed down. The two of them crawled fast away from the fusillade, into a corner of the room.

That's a serious gun, Suzy thought. But she still crawled back toward the front of the room and poked her head up through the shattered front window and saw Kaya now raining destruction upon the buildings across from him.

"Come on!" she said, pointing to the back of the room. They raced through the restaurant and into the kitchen. They headed out the back door, through the courtyard, and back into the alley, now heading toward the street in front of the restaurant—but they stopped, because someone was already there by the street, pressed against the corner of the building.

Suzy felt like her heart stopped. She wanted to yell, but she didn't—it was Kiara, and Suzy knew she was hiding. And then she was firing a gun.

"Kiara!" Suzy shouted. "No!"

Kiara ran onto the street as Suzy raced toward her. And there was Mert Kaya, sprawled on the sidewalk.

He was burned and bloody, but still alive. His gun was lying on the sidewalk out of reach. Standing two meters away from him was Kiara. She was pointing her gun with two shaky hands. She had tears of rage in her eyes, and she was moving toward him with the weapon aimed at his head.

"Kiara!" Suzy said. "What are you doing here? How did you find us?"

"The bracelet, Suzy. You never took it off."

Damn, that's true.

Kiara turned her attention back to Kaya. "You killed Jack!" she shouted.

"Kiara, stop," Suzy said. "Don't do it."

"He killed Jack," she said again, and now a tear streamed down her cheek. "You weren't there, Suzy. You didn't see."

Kaya said, "Do it, Kiara. Go ahead."

"Don't worry, I will."

"Good," he said, and he smirked. "I would've killed you—and I would've enjoyed it. I was born this way, and I'll always be this way." Then he looked at Suzy and said, "If you can't do it, let her do it. She understands."

Kiara moved forward, still pointing her gun at Mert's skull. "Oh, I can do it," she said, and then she choked back a sob. "You have no idea."

"Kiara, don't," Suzy said.

Kaya said nothing now, but his face was defiant.

"Why not?" Kiara shouted as more tears fell. "He killed Jack. He wanted to murder me, too. And he killed a lot of girls—girls like me."

"Yeah, that's true," Suzy said. "But I'm telling you, killing him won't help. You'll still feel empty inside—and angry. The anger won't go away. It never goes away."

"I don't care, Suzy. I'll live with it. Just like you do."

She would've done it—there was no doubt in Suzy's mind. But she didn't because Suzy shot her in the chest.

Kiara gasped. She stared at Suzy, and her face was a twisted picture of shock, grief, and rage. Suzy stared back at her, feeling like her heart would burst. The sadness overwhelmed her like a wave. Then Kiara moaned and collapsed onto the sidewalk.

Kaya looked surprised—but only for an instant, since Suzy shot him, too. But it was with the same stun setting.

Ricardo hugged Suzy. "You did the right thing, honey."

Suzy felt dead, like a statue.

"She'll hate me forever, Ricardo."

"No, she won't."

"She will."

"No, she won't. She'll be fine."

Suzy knelt down near Kiara's sleeping body and touched her face. Then she stood up and saw Burt and Tala. The two cops were running toward them from across the street. So they'd been the ones shooting at Kaya—and watching. They weren't showing any weapons now.

From the corner of her eye, Suzy saw Ricardo point a gun at them. Suzy did nothing.

Burt raised his hands a bit, while Tala was breathless and shouting.

"Suzy, we're here to help!" she said. "We've been following Kiara... Burt's good at following. He's a good cop." Then she showed a small device in her hand. "A DNA tester," she said. She knelt down and pressed the device against Kaya's unconscious head and stared at the results. Her eyebrows went up, and she said, "This guy is Shogun Hunter."

Suzy didn't care. But she muttered, "Okay, good. I guess Danielle will be happy."

Tala looked at Burt, who shrugged and said nothing. Then Tala said, "Suzy, there's something else." Then she glanced at Burt again, who remained silent as she continued. "Don't take him to Tycho City—it's a trap. Commander Banks is waiting for you there."

Now Suzy felt a jolt of surprise, but she showed no expression. Ricardo frowned and swore.

"Danielle," he said. "I knew she couldn't be trusted."

Suzy glanced at the two cops. Were they telling the truth? Then she was staring at Kiara again and hardly paying attention. Finally, she blinked a few times and said, "You two can take him to Tycho. I'll give Danielle a call."

Chapter 61

Danielle almost dropped her allcom as she listened to the message.

Hi, Danielle. It's Suzy. I hope you're doing okay. Los Pocos is planning to kill your husband at the Global Law Enforcement Conference, so please let him know. Also, I have Hunter. You'll be seeing him soon.

Short, concise—and terrifying. She took a few deep breaths and fumbled with the screen.

Her pulse was racing. "Andre!" she shouted. "Are you all right? They want to kill you."

"What?"

He sounded calm, as usual.

"They're planning to kill you at the conference! You've got to get out of there."

"Danielle, calm down. What are you talking about? How do you know about this?"

"I got a message from Suzy. She said they're planning to assassinate you."

"And you believe her?"

"Yes, I do!"

"Why?"

"Because she's not a lying snake like me, that's why! So get out of there."

There was a moment of silence, and she could tell he was thinking it over. Then he said, "You're not 'a lying snake.' What else did she say?"

"She said—nothing. It was just a warning, okay? So please come home."

He hesitated once again. "All right. I'll take precautions—don't worry. I'll be fine."

"You need to come home *now.*"

"I can't do that, Danielle, but I'll be home soon. I'll be careful."

"I love you!"

"I love you, too."

Then he was gone and Danielle was alone with her racing mind. She swore to herself and shook her head. Why had she ever betrayed that girl? And did Suzy know about her betrayal? Her tone had been so quick, so matter-of-fact. Maybe that was just her style. Or maybe, just maybe, she was annoyed.

A wave of regret washed over her as she grabbed her allcom and called Venus. Her voice was shaking as she left a message.

"Suzy, this is Danielle. Thank you for the warning. I really appreciate it and I've passed it along. It's great that you have Hunter— but do not bring him to Tycho City! Do you hear me? Do not go to Tycho. It's a trap... It's a long story... Suzy, I'm so sorry. Please stay safe."

Chapter 62

Far away in his Melbourne hotel room, Andre Banks considered his wife's serious phone call and laughed a bit. She didn't realize the kind of danger he'd often been in over the years, because he'd never told her. So this was nothing new, assuming it was true. But was it? And what was Suzy's game?

He frowned because she might not have one. Once upon a time, he'd chased Suzy Spitfire across the solar system, and he'd even captured her—and then he'd let her go. So he knew a few things about her. She was a violent criminal who was sometimes reckless and impulsive. She was also brave, intelligent, and loyal to her friends—and she usually told the truth. She was a standup girl who just happened to stand up a little too often with a gun in her hand.

Still, Suzy was in bed with Los Pocos—literally. So how would a phony warning to him benefit that gang of cutthroats? Well, if he left the conference early, he wouldn't give his speech. Would Los Pocos care? It was doubtful. The only thing that mattered to them was sending a message. They'd want to slaughter him in an appropriately horrible way.

A chime sounded, indicating someone was at the door.

His heart leaped as he grabbed his gun from a nearby nightstand and then brought up the image of the person outside. It flashed on the back of the door.

He sucked in his breath. Who was this woman? She was attractive, and he'd spoken to her the other day down in the bar. She'd seemed harmless at the time, but he didn't recall giving her his room number. In fact, he didn't recall being overly encouraging, but had he been totally discouraging? Apparently not.

She rang the bell again, and he realized he wanted to answer. *If she's working with the bad guys, she might have some good info.* Of course, he'd need to be on guard. He also knew he should be more afraid, but he wasn't. He couldn't deny that a woman never seemed as dangerous to him as a man. This wasn't pure macho cockiness on his part, at least he didn't think so. He'd been a cop long enough to know that the vast majority of killers were men, with notable exceptions (like Suzy). But this was nothing he couldn't handle.

"Can I help you?" he said as the door slid open. She was wearing a low-cut red dress. Over her shoulder was a small, sequined purse. "Lorraine, right?"

"Right," she said with a smile. "And I'm still looking to get an interview, if you have time."

"How did you get my room number?"

"I have a friend who works here."

"It's good to have a few friends."

"I'd really love to ask you a few questions about law enforcement and where it's going in the modern world."

They just looked at each other. This girl didn't seem like an assassin. But the best ones never do.

"Sure, come on in," he said.

He kept his eyes on her. It wasn't difficult. She smoothed her dress again, and he recalled that she'd done that before, down in the bar.

"Nice view," she said, looking toward the balcony. She walked toward it.

"It came with the place," he said.

Was she carrying a weapon? It was always best to assume the worst. Sometimes they'll give themselves away. Sometimes they'll try to appear casual while adjusting their sexy dress to make sure the weapon stays hidden.

Damn! He moved closer to her—and he lunged as she moved her hand under the hem. She shrieked as he grabbed her wrist and then pushed the gun away.

The gun fired, and the energy blast struck a lamp, knocking it over. He stripped the weapon away and it fell to the floor. Then he slammed his elbow into her face and she tumbled backwards onto the bed.

He pulled his own gun out and pointed it at her.

"Fuck you!" she said.

Stupid, he thought. *I should've just shot her with a stun blast as she turned.* Would he have shot a man? Definitely. He made a mental note to stop being so damn cocky.

"Don't move, Lorraine," he said. "That was a stun shot you fired at me, right?"

Her smile was gone, replaced by a scowl. "Yeah," she said.

"So where are the killers?"

"They're coming."

He doubted it. They were probably waiting for her to call, so they could come up here and do it in some special way—and it wouldn't be pretty.

He smiled. "This building is full of cops, Lorraine." He pulled out his allcom. "I'm going to call a few of them, and then you're going to tell us about your friends."

He was guessing their numbers were on her allcom. They wouldn't get far. Then he'd go home to Danielle, who'd sounded so scared and regretful. He wondered if she'd called Suzy and thanked her for the warning. He wondered if she'd told Suzy not to go to Tycho City.

It doesn't matter, he thought. *If she did, that's fine, and I can't wait to get home.*

Chapter 63

Suzy stared at the console in the cockpit of the *Correcaminos Rojo*. She was sitting in the pilot chair and everything looked ready to go. That was good because she was more than ready to leave Baadal Shahar.

"There's still a lot to do," Ricardo said. He'd come in quietly.

"Yeah," Suzy said. "But I don't want to do any of it."

"Why don't you talk to Kiara? You'll feel better."

"She doesn't want to talk to me, Ricardo."

"Yeah, she does. She's right outside."

"What?"

Suzy caught her breath as Kiara walked into the cockpit.

She was still wearing the black skirt and gray top. Her long hair was even more frazzled than usual, but she still looked pretty—pretty, yet tired.

"I'll leave you two alone," Ricardo said. Then he smiled at Suzy and headed into the lounge.

Kiara stared at Suzy for a few seconds and then sat down in the co-pilot chair. She fixed her gaze on the gray docking bay outside.

There was a long silence. Finally, Kiara said, "You never showed me how to fly a spaceship."

"That's true," Suzy said. "But it's easy. Just press the big red button."

"Really?"

"No, not really. Are you okay?"

"I'm all right." She leaned toward Suzy a bit, staring right at her now. "Wouldn't you have killed him if you were me?"

Suzy hesitated. "Yeah," she said. "It's the way I am, Kiara, for better or worse." Then she sighed. "But you're different, and that's a good thing. I think you need a different path, and you would've regretted pulling the trigger."

Kiara's eyes flashed with anger. "Suzy, how many times do I have to tell you? I'm not that innocent." Then she lowered her voice and spoke fast. "I'm not talking about Farouk—yeah, I know I killed him… I'm not talking about my time on the street. I'm talking about what I did with Jack, because Daniel was going to murder him, and they were fighting, and Daniel hurt me so many times, and it was so crazy, and—"

"Stop," Suzy said. She reached out and put a hand on Kiara's shoulder. "I know you've done some extreme things, Kiara. But you were thrown into an extreme world, and that wasn't your fault, right?"

Kiara hesitated, and then said, "I don't know."

"You were a victim," Suzy said. "It was *not* your fault. But you can start over. You can be the person you were meant to be, before the world got in the way and tried to turn you into something else—and maybe you can make peace with it all. That's what I wanted, okay? I wanted you to have that chance."

Kiara's eyes started to get watery, and she turned her head. For almost a minute, she said nothing. Then she wiped away a tear and looked back. "I'm going to a doctor, Suzy—a therapist. Anika and Sara set it up. They said it's part of a program to help me. And you're right, it's good I didn't kill Hunter. I've got enough bad things in my head—crazy, horrible things. So thanks…Thanks for stopping me."

Just like that, a huge weight lifted from Suzy's heart. "You're welcome," she said. "And that's great, about getting some help. I'm glad to hear it. I'm sure you're going to do real well."

Kiara seemed to relax a bit. She sat back in the chair.

"Do you ever have nightmares, Suzy?"

"All the time. But they're not about the things I've done. They're about the things I didn't do, like protect my sister better, and be nicer to my parents, and stuff like that. Those are the worst parts of my nightmares, and those are my regrets. Those are the things I'll never forgive myself for screwing up." She shook her head. "I don't know what makes me more violent than other people. I guess I have a bad spot in my brain."

"But you didn't kill Hunter."

"Yeah, because I had this silly thought, like maybe I could set an example for you—and it was ridiculous because I'm the worst role model ever. But I don't want you to be like me."

Kiara stared at Suzy. "You're not a bad role model," she said. "You're a great friend. You're the best friend I've ever had. And you helped Anika and her girls—girls like me. You've made a huge difference in my life, and for others, too, and I'll never forget you. *Never.*"

Now Suzy was quiet. But once again, she felt like a weight was lifted from her heart.

She smiled. "Maybe coming to this city was a good idea. I did something better with myself here."

Kiara smiled back at her, and she spoke slowly. "I never had a sister," she said. "But you're my sister now." Then she sputtered, "I mean, if you want to be."

Suzy felt her own eyes tearing up. "I'd like that a lot," she said. Then she stood up, and Kiara did the same, and they embraced.

Chapter 64

Burt stood in the tiny galley of the police cruiser, staring through a porthole at the stars. It was hard to judge distances in space—but for sure, everything was far away. Meanwhile, Tala was in the cockpit, just down a short passageway, and the ship was finally heading back to Earth. Of course, they'd be stopping first in Tycho City to deposit Shogun Hunter, who was safely locked in the ship's single holding cell.

Should I be happy? he thought. He wasn't sure. He knew he was sweating, and his stomach was jumpy. He felt happy, he felt anxious—he felt unsure about how he felt. The future was a wave that seemed overwhelming. Then Tala came walking into the cramped space, and his heart jumped.

She was smiling. They hadn't talked much since hauling the prisoner to the spaceport. They hadn't spoken much since they'd gone downtown looking to aid in the capture of Shogun Hunter—and then when that was over, he'd put away his weapon and walked across the street to meet with Suzy 'Spitfire' Castillo, the killer he'd sworn to bring to justice. And he'd been perfectly nice to her.

Had it been worth it?

"We're all set," she said. "We'll be in Tycho City in about four days."

"Good. That's good."

She smiled again, but didn't say anything. She was just looking at him with those big brown eyes.

Why isn't she talking? What should I say? What's wrong?

"Are you all right?" she said. "You haven't said much."

"I'm good!" he blurted. "I'm fine. I'm just…wondering how we're going to explain that we let Suzy get away."

This was not what he'd been wondering. But come to think of it, it was probably something he should be thinking about.

"I have an idea," she said. "We'll say there was a revolution, and Suzy was part of it—and the new government refused to allow her arrest, but they were nice enough to recognize our valiant capture of Shogun Hunter and then allow his extradition."

"Oh. Hey, that's good. How did you come up with that?"

She's so smart.

She smiled again. "Well, it's more or less true." Then she sighed. "I know you're unhappy we didn't arrest Suzy, right?"

"No!" he said, surprised by his passion. But then he continued in the same tone. "I don't care about Suzy. I don't care about my dad, or my uncle—or redeeming myself. I don't care about any of that stuff anymore. I just care that you're happy. If you're happy, I'm happy."

"I'm happy, Burt," she said, and then looked down for a second. "I still don't want to be a cop. I think I'd be better at something else." Then she looked into his eyes. "But I do want to be on your team."

"Oh. Really?"

"Yeah, really."

"You mean—what team? The two of us?"

"Yeah," she said with a laugh. "The two of us. Together."

He stepped toward her, and then she was in his arms.

Chapter 65

Suzy and Ricardo made one last trip into the city. On their way into the Capitol building, they saw Marcos storming out. He was alone, and he stopped on the landing at the top of the wide stairs.

"She gave me six hours," he said. "Six hours to get out of the city! Can you believe that?"

Ricardo shrugged. "I guess you better get going."

"What?" Marcos came closer. "Ricardo, what about our meeting? Can't you do something? That ungrateful bitch."

Ricardo stood up tall. "Marcos, I'm not on your side. I'm done with your side. So get out."

Marcos's jaw dropped. "Are you serious? What about the plan? What about Pablo?"

"There's a new plan now, and Pablo will have to find another city."

"That's crazy! Do you know what you're doing?"

"Yeah, I know. So long, Marcos."

Marcos stared at Ricardo and then looked at Suzy, who said nothing. Then he threw up his hands and headed down the steps.

Ricardo watched him go. "I should've shot him."

Suzy put her arm around him and kissed his neck. "You did fine. Good job. Now let's say our goodbyes and get the hell out of here."

They met Anika and Nuru in the big office that was in the process of being transformed. Mainly people were trashing all the pictures and statues of Buso. It would take a while but they were moving fast.

Anika hugged Suzy. "Do you have to go? We'd love for you to stay. You've been a huge help."

"Yeah, but staying isn't something I do well, Anika."

"If you ever need anything, just call—or come back."

"Thanks. And good luck."

They returned to the ship, where Kiara and Sara were waiting for them. And then Maria showed up. Her ship had finally landed. She'd called Ricardo and he'd given her the number of their docking bay.

She looked tired, but she looked good. She still had a spark in her eye, like someone starting a new adventure. Suzy embraced her. Then she said, "We changed the plan, Maria. No city for Los Pocos."

"I know. Thank you."

Suzy laughed. "Are you coming with us?"

"If you want me," she said with a shrug. "I have nowhere else to go."

"We want you, and you'll probably regret it."

Suzy turned to Sara and Kiara. Kiara said, "I'll miss you, Suzy—a lot. I wish you'd stay."

"I'll be back."

"Will you really?"

"Yeah, I promise. And we'll stay in touch—call if you need me. I mean it."

"I'll call you anyway."

Suzy gave her one final hug and then walked into the ship. She settled into the cockpit with Ricardo in the co-pilot chair.

"So, where are we going?" Ricardo said.

"I'm not sure," Suzy said. "We'll think of something."

The End

About The Author

Joe Canzano is a writer and musician from New Jersey, U.S.A. For more information please visit happyjoe.net.

He invites you to email him at happyjoe800@gmail.com

Novels by Joe Canzano

MAGNO GIRL
SEX HELL
SUZY SPITFIRE KILLS EVERYBODY
SUZY SPITFIRE AND THE SNAKE EYES OF VENUS
RUNE AND FLASH: INSIDE THE DREAM PRISON
ESCAPE: RUNE AND FLASH BOOK 2

For more information check happyjoe.net.

www.ingramcontent.com/pod-product-compliance
Lightning Source LLC
Chambersburg PA
CBHW060937120726
47910CB00002B/370